***

'Part thriller, part love story ... it's hard to resist turning the pages.'

'Ghosts in Sunlight succeeds in combining a fast-paced tale involving vast sums of money, immense power, women both wounded and wounding, and a variety of credible male characters from the traumatised Vietnam veteran Jimmy Overman to the seedy publisher, James Duncan ... an excellent book.'

'Books are often described as "page-turners" but this is very true of 'Ghosts in Sunlight' ... Once started the reader will find it very hard to put down.'

'Plenty of suspense and drama ... Very enjoyable.'

'Browne has a talent for drawing us into her characters and situations ... this is a real page turner.'

'Add another name to the growing list of successful Dublin authors – Gretta Curran Browne ... The story is a modern thriller, a "page turner" and the author has two more books in the pipeline...'

Ghosts in Sunlight

Ghosts in Sunlight

***

Ghosts in Sunlight

*GRETTA CURRAN
BROWNE*

Payges Publishing

PP

***

Published by Payges Publishing Ltd
2 Spencer Avenue
London N13 4TR
Tel: 020 8343 3742
Email: mail@paygespublishing.com
www.paygespublishing.com

A CIP catalogue record for this book is available from the British Library

ISBN 978-0-9558208-0-9

10 9 8 7 6 5 4 3 2 1

Author photograph: Chris Baker

Lines from `Strangers in the Night' (words and music by Bert Kaempfert, Charles Singleton, Eddie Snyder) reproduced by kind permission of MCA Music Ltd

Cover photograph © Sean-Paul Browne
Cover design: Ellena Browne

Printed in the UK by CPI Bookmarque, Croydon, CR0 4TD

***

Gretta Curran Browne was born and grew up in Dublin City. She left Dublin as a teenager and went to London to study drama. In January 1984, after the births of her two children and becoming a full-time mother, she started writing. She had a number of articles and two prize-winning short stories published, which encouraged her to start writing her first novel, *Tread Softly On My Dreams,* which was published to critical acclaim and became a best-seller in Ireland, as did her second novel *Fire On The Hill.*

In 2000 she wrote the novelisation of the Miramax/Little Bird film *Ordinary Decent Criminal* starring Kevin Spacey, and later the book of the major TV drama *Relative Strangers* starring Brenda Fricker. Gretta is now a full-time writer and lives with her family in London.

Out now in paperback, *Ghosts in Sunlight* has already been translated into six languages.

***

Acknowledgements

To Officer Vincent Demma, US Army Headquarters, Washington, for his valuable advice about Vietnam.

To the office staff at Fort Devens Military base, Massachusetts; Linda Jelenewski, Karen Buckley, Philip Morris and also Sergeant Martha Chavez.

To a terrific police officer in the Vice squad in London, who shall, as promised, remain anonymous: my thanks for his unstinting help and technical guidance.

To Birgitta Sundström and Oscar Hellström at the SAS Strand Hotel for their delightful Swedish kindness and the help they gave to me during my research in Stockholm.

To the late and great Mr Truman Capote for posthumously supplying me with the title of this book.

To Richard and Maíre Browne, to Dominic and Joanne Browne, to Una and Peter Woollaston. To Lorna Byrne, Carol Bruce, and Irene Ash – my sincere thanks . (You all know why).

With double-thanks to my pal, Mike Keane, for all his good advice over the years.

And finally, my endless thanks to the two treasures of my life: my daughter Ellena, and my son Sean-Paul; without the unfailing love and support of you two and Paul, the bad times would have been completely unbearable, and the good times would have meant nothing at all.

***

Ghosts in Sunlight

TO

CATHERINE KEANE, MARY BARRY WYNN and BETTY KELLY
my best friends, and none better exists anywhere

And especially - to my darling Paul, for his constant support and love and patience, and without whom the production of this book would truly have been impossible. Thank you with all my heart.

Prologue

London
September 1980

Their footsteps were slow, but direct.

The two police officers walked each side of him down a long corridor that looked very white and felt very cold, but all else was a blur.

He wore blue jeans and a red sweatshirt and he was sixteen years old. His hair was as black as his eyes, and his eyes were staring straight ahead.

They stopped at a door on the left. The young policewoman caught his arm, holding him back while her male colleague went inside.

As they waited the policewoman spoke to him softly, but he did not reply, his stare fixed rigidly on the closed door. Still she regarded him with compassion. He was a very good-looking young lad, but his manner was as cold as ice.

He was frigid with terror.

The door opened. The policeman, silently and gravely, beckoned them both to come inside.

The policewoman gestured for him to go in first.

He stepped through the door, unprepared for the chilliness of the room. He shivered, suddenly and violently, and it broke his trance. A man dressed like a doctor was speaking to him, but he was not listening.

He was staring at the woman lying on a trolley-bed in the centre of the room, her slim body covered to the shoulders by a white sheet. He walked forward slowly and looked at her, and he felt his last faint hope drain away.

They had tried to clean her up, make her presentable, but the

11

blood was so thickly matted in her hair it was impossible to remove.

He slowly stretched out a trembling hand and let his fingertips touch her face in a helpless caress, and continued his silent gazing.

Her face looked so pale, and she looked so young, even younger than she had looked in life. Too young to be dead.

The policeman spoke gently to him, hesitantly, asking the vital question.

`Is it ...?'

`My mother,' he whispered.

He was still shivering violently. The policewoman attempted to put a blanket around his shoulders but he jerked away from her, taking a startled step back, staring at her as if she had struck him.

He did not want her comfort, did not want anyone's warm touch. The coldness inside him was like a protective shield, his only armour against the hatred building inside him, dense and dark and dangerous.

Her killer – nothing else stirred inside him now save thoughts of the man who had killed her.

The police had said his name – a name he had never heard before – a name he would never forget.

Find him, get him, destroy him.

He turned his head and looked at her face, her pale, lovely face; and in that moment he swore it.

Find him, get him, *annihilate* him. And he would – oh yes he would – somehow, some way, some day.

Throughout the return journey to the flat in Hampstead, he sat in the back of the police-car in silent coldness.

From the driver's seat – a distance that seemed miles away – the policeman kept speaking to him with grim gentleness, but he gave no answer, his face turned toward the window, staring out blindly at the dark lamp-lit streets.

He was thinking of how she had scrimped and saved and worked so hard to give him everything he needed, paying for his private art classes with Mr Hughes, his karate lessons in the church hall, even providing the fees when he wanted to move on at fifteen to a more sophisticated form of martial art.

'It's after midnight,' the policewoman said, but he was listening to the voice of his Wing Chun teacher, a master in the centuries-old system that prepared Chinese warriors for combat ... *Others may seek only to grasp the bird's tail, or play with the monkey, but you must face the tiger ...*

The policeman was asking him about his father, but he didn't want to think about his father, not tonight.

He was thinking of how she sometimes cried a lot, not regularly or openly; but secretly, alone in her room, locked away with her photographs and love-letters, and only in summer. Always in summer. The rest of the year she never cried at all.

The car finally stopped.

The private forecourt of the red-bricked block of apartments was brightly lit, the green lawn in the centre neatly trimmed.

Inside the flat, the policewoman spoke to him in a sad, almost chiding tone. 'Listen, Phil, you can't stay here. Not all on your own. Is there anyone else you can stay with tonight?'

He thought of Chef and Sofia, but he shook his head, 'No, I want to stay here,' he whispered, and gazed slowly around the living-room, so neat with her tidiness, 'I want to be ... with her.'

'Phil, can you give us the name and address of someone who knows you?' the policeman persisted. 'Someone who can pop in and keep an eye on you. Someone in the other flats, perhaps?'

'No,' he said quietly, 'I don't want to see anyone from the other flats. Not now, not yet ... not tonight.' But he knew from the glance they exchanged they were determined, and eventually he gave them Chef and Sofia's address.

The policeman nodded, putting his pen away, satisfied. 'This

13

Chef, is he a cook?'

`His real name is Albert.'

`And he knows you well, does he? Do you mind if we pop over there, on our way back to the station, just to let him know what's happened.'

Pop over there, on our way back to the station – it was a detour of at least six miles out of their way. But he didn't care where they went. He just wished with all his soul that they had never come into his life. And now all he wanted was for them to be gone.

A spring inside him was winding up, tighter and tighter, and if he didn't slow it down soon, his armour of coldness would shatter and break into a roaring agony, and he would start crying like a child at the horror of what he had seen – his mother, dead.

The policewoman gently touched his arm again, spoke to him in a hushed voice, words he didn't even try to hear.

They left the room, moving out to the hall, and he heard her voice again, more audibly this time.

`He's still in shock.'

`Not surprising. Only sixteen, poor lad.'

She suddenly turned back into the room. `Phil, are you *sure* you're going to be all right?'

He nodded his head with a desperate insistence.

Slowly, hesitantly, she turned away, then abruptly brisked forward with a command to her colleague. `Let's get over to this Albert and his wife. I don't feel right about this, leaving him here all on his own.'

The hall door closed.

The sudden silence was eerie. He stood alone in the empty desolateness of the flat, so strange now, without her.

He wanted her to come home ...

For a long time he stood unmoving in the vacuity of the silence, a tearful haze swimming over his eyes, pictures of her floating in his mind – just this morning, how *happy* she had been, excited, triumphant, like a perverse schoolgirl who had

14

boldly defied the rules and proved everyone wrong.

She had done it. The night before. She had finished her book. And there it was, on the desk by the window, a proudly stacked manuscript waiting for a padded envelope and a professional opinion.

He moved towards it ... her book, her gift to Marc, her promise from a long-ago morning. The story of Marian, the story of Marc, the title: *Some Kind of Wonderful.*

Part One

Marian and Marc

1963 – 1968

One

London
July 1963
_____/

It was Marian Barnard's eighteenth birthday, and a beautiful summer's day.

A day so perfect in temperature and sunlight, Marian did not want to go to work at the restaurant. It was three o'clock in the afternoon and the sun was at its highest, blazing on the rooftops of the houses opposite, slanting the grey tiles with a blistering sheen that made them look wet.

She stood by the window, gazing down on the quiet tree-lined avenue in Belsize Park. Her room was at the very top of the old Victorian House: a large attic, turned into a bedsitting room. One corner of it – the kitchenette –contained a small cooker and a sink, with white louvered doors built around it, so when not in use it could be closed off to give the appearance of an ordinary closet.

Marian turned away from the window and looked around her one–room world. It contained everything she owned, which was not much: but Miss Courtney, her former House–Mother at the Barnardo's Home in Barkingside would be so proud of it. Every piece of furniture, every surface, every corner – all of it, the whole room – kept as neat and clean as she had been trained to keep it.

Her most precious possession of all – and she still felt a thrill whenever she looked at it – was the new record– player on a stand by the fireplace. She had saved up for months to buy that record player, going into the shop every week with another payment, until the day finally came when she was allowed to carry it away.

It was very heavy. At the Underground Station she had

almost fallen down the moving escalator, trying to balance it, then hauled it aboard the underground train, hauled it off, struggled up the winding stairs at Belsize Park station (the lift was always out-of-order) then gasped and panted as she carried it up each flight of stairs to her fifth-floor attic.

But then—Heaven!—music in her room. It was a very special record–player because it had a continuous replay facility, which was a good thing because she only had two records: one by Elvis and the other by Roy Orbison.

Still, come the weekend, when she got paid, she intended to buy the latest Beatles record.

She sighed, wondering if it truly *was* her birthday today? It could have been yesterday. Or maybe it was really tomorrow. No one had ever been sure of the *exact* date of her birth.

At the time, in July 1945, when she had been left inside the main doorway of Barnardo's Reception Centre at Stepney Causeway in London, the person who had left her there had not been seen entering or leaving, so no questions could be asked, no information obtained.

All that the staff at Barnardo's knew for certain, and recorded, was the child was: *A girl. Five or six days old. Abandoned – probably illegitimate.*

Marian's eyes clouded, but her hesitation was brief. Well, birthday or not, it was time to go to work, time to do another four–to–eleven shift at the restaurant.

It was early evening. The centre of London was as busy as it always was – the usual tourists sitting in the small bistro off Tottenham Court Road.

Marian lifted her pen and pad and walked over to a small table by the window where two young men, aged in their early twenties, sat opposite each other. Both had their eyes fixed on the menu. Both wore summer shirts and jeans. More tourists.

One, she noticed, was black-haired and very good-looking. The other was thin and fair and as plain as a plate of French fries.

She knew they were Americans as soon as the fair-haired one looked up from his menu and spoke to her.

'How-de-do?'

'How-de-do,' she replied just as pleasantly.

Then the fool turned all macho and began to flirt, sitting back with an Elvis Presley leer misfiring all over his face as he drawled, 'Say, honey, did anyone ever tell yuh – you are one bee-yew-tiful chic!'

The black-haired one lifted his eyes from his menu and looked at her. He didn't speak, he just looked, absorbing every detail of her face with his eyes – eyes as dark as his hair. She looked back at him and for a moment felt slightly weak ... there was something so *gorgeous* about him.

'W-w-what would you like?' she stammered.

'Just coffee,' he murmured. 'I'm not hungry.'

She felt herself blushing and quickly turned back to the fair-haired one. He ordered almost everything on the menu, which surprised her, because he was thin.

'I know what you're thinking,' he said with a friendly grin.

'You're wondering how I can eat so much and not look like Chubby Checker? Right?'

'Right,' she agreed with a smile.

'Something to do with my metabolism,' he told her, then chatted on. 'When I was a kid the family used to call me trash-can, seeing as how I used to eat up anything and everything left over from supper. But, aiyyy, listen – I may be thin but I'm strong as a horse. Here, feel those biceps!'

He pumped up his arm. She didn't want to hurt his feelings, so she laid down her pen and felt the front muscle of his upper arm – rock hard.

'Rock hard,' she said in amazement.

'Now the triceps,' he said, pointing to the muscle at the back of his arm, which was also rock hard.

'Yep!' he said, grinning proudly. 'I'm what you call *deceptive*.

A lot tougher than I look. Right?'

`Right,' she agreed with a smile.

`I'm also called Jimmy, by the way, and this guy here is my buddy Marc.'

She looked at Marc. His dark eyes were still watching her, observing her reaction to Jimmy.

`Hi,' was all he said.

Her smile was nervous, and she suddenly became conscious of her appearance. She wore a spotless white apron over a blue cotton summer dress, and was glad she had not been forced her to wear a waitressing uniform – Chef simply *hated* waitressing uniforms, insisting they spoiled the relaxed atmosphere of his bistro.

When she eventually entered the kitchen with her order, Chef's expression widened into a smile. He was a huge man, endowed with natural good will and a pleasantly intelligent face.

`My dear girl!' he exclaimed. `You are blushing like a rose!'

Marian ignored him, because she didn't even hear him – it seemed so unbelievable. She had seen him for less than a minute, had exchanged hardly a word with him, but as soon as Marc had lifted his eyes and looked at her – oh, she just fell! Her teenage heart was still fluttering wildly.

Marian stood in a day-dream as she waited, and Chef watched her as he prepared the order, remembering the vulnerable young girl he had first met almost two years previously, sensitive and nervous and pathologically shy with strangers. He had known instantly that she was just too reserved, all wrong for the job of a waitress. But she was such a beautiful young girl, with such hope in her eyes, he had been unable to refuse her and had given her the job after only a slight hesitation.

It had taken months of constantly teasing her to bring her out of herself finally and turn her into a decent waitress. She was still shy, but no longer awkward and nervous, and her intelligence and capacity for hard work had surprised him.

He adored her!

Even his wife, Sofia, adored her.

Everyone who got to know Marian grew to love her, wanted to protect her, wondered at the mystery of her.

And now she was smiling at him, because the order was ready.

Jimmy smacked his hands with anticipation when Marian set the huge plate of hot food down before him. She heard her own small intake of breath as she placed the coffee before Marc, unable to look at him, but aware of his eyes on her.

Even when she moved on to present the bill to another table of customers she was still aware of Marc's eyes on her, and the excitement inside her made her heart thump even faster.

Then, to her utter dismay, she was called for her supper break, and didn't want to take it. But Chef's word was law, so she reluctantly left the restaurant and returned to the kitchen.

`My dear girl,' said Chef, handing her a plate of her favourite walnut-and-cheese salad. `You are *still* blushing like a rose. Has someone been trying to chat you up?'

He laughed at her with teasing affection, then turned to his new assistant. `Our Marian doesn't like it when the men chat her up. She has no idea what to do with men, you see? Don't you think there's something terrible and delightful about that kind of innocence?'

Chef's new assistant, a timid and serious-faced young man named Peter, seemed too embarrassed to lift his eyes and look at her, engrossed in trimming and shaping his carrots. Marian was not quite sure which of them Chef was baiting – his new assistant or her.

Chef grinned wickedly at Peter's bent head. `Lift thine eyes, young knave, and cast them upon the lovely wench who stands on yonder side of the table. Look at that beautiful long, dark hair, that slender and curvy body, those slender legs. From the

23

back, some dark and exotic flower! But then she turns, and those lovely dark-blue eyes stare back at you, like the sky at twilight.'

Marian restrained a giggle. Chef often spoke like an old Shakespearean actor. Yet he had surprised her one day by confessing that his *real* ambition, his most *passionate* dream as a young man, had been to become a professional dancer like Gene Kelly, until he took a trip to America and toured down to the Southern states where he saw a team of skilled black men tap-dancing in a club in New Orleans `and the rhythm they shuffled to was red-hot jazz.'

His dream had faded as his weight ballooned until he was as big a man as his own father had been, and he might have killed himself then, faced with the death of his dancing dream, if he had not met and fallen in love with his darling Sofia — an Italian girl who had given him back his glad–to–be–aliveness and who had finally persuaded him to devote his life to the second thing he loved doing – cooking food.

`... such delightful innocence, don't you think?' Chef was still teasing Peter, and Marian saw Peter's head was bent even lower, and his embarrassment concerned her.

`Chef, please stop teasing us!' Marian pleaded. `It's no longer funny.'

`My dear girl,' Chef confessed with a tragic sigh, `your anger breaks my heart! You have a face of such tender beauty it makes men sigh and other women despair. And when you blush like that—' he put a hand on his heart, `*bellissima!*'

Peter suddenly chuckled, and Marian grinned. It was impossible to stay angry with Chef. A man as big in heart as he was in size, and at the end of all his teasing, he was very caring and kind to his staff. The only people he couldn't abide were complaining customers. But his food was so good, the customers rarely complained.

When Marian returned to the restaurant, Jimmy and Marc were paying their bill, standing up to leave. She saw Marc shrug on a black leather jacket over his short-sleeved summer shirt.

Chef appeared at her shoulder, his eyes following the direction of hers. 'Which one?' he asked in a confidential whisper. 'Which one made you blush like a rose? Or shall I just make a guess?

The black-haired one?'

'He's American,' she whispered back.

'American?' Chef gave a swift sigh of nostalgia, and looked down at his feet, his shoes instantly wanting to dance. 'I met a very handsome lady in America once,' he confided. 'Beautiful red hair. Loved to dance. Broke my heart. Dangerous people those Americans. Make you fall in love with them, then break your heart – just like Italians.'

He sighed again and turned back towards his kitchen, his shoes making a tapping sound as he broke into song, '*I met a big fat Mama, down in Alabama....*'

The singing made the Americans look round, and see Marian.

'So long!' Jimmy called to her. 'Nice meeting ya!'

'Nice meeting you, too,' she called back.

Marc lifted his hand and gave her a brief little salute. She gave him a small smile of acknowledgment. The sort of small smile one gives to a stranger after sharing a train journey, or the same table in a crowded restaurant.

She noticed two young women at a table near the door were also looking at Marc, whispering together and smiling. Well, he had those kind of looks.

The door shut behind the Americans. And that was that.

She didn't hear the customer speak to her. Not until the voice was edged with impatience. Then she turned to take the order with a forlorn, tight smile.

He came back a few hours later. On his own. Just before closing time.

Marian was standing behind the counter, adding up the till receipts and writing down the total, when she looked up and saw him. She stood with pen poised, motionless.

`Hi,' he said again.

She looked slowly around the empty restaurant as she tried to slow the rapid beating of her pulse, finally meeting his eyes again.

`We're closed,' she croaked.

`I know. I just came back to see ... if maybe, you'd like to go out somewhere?'

`With you?'

Now it was he who looked slowly around the empty restaurant, finally meeting her eyes again.

`With me.'

Oh, he was *g-g-gorgeous* – her excitement was making her hands tremble; she quickly put them under the counter. `You don't even know my name.'

`No, I never got the chance to ask. That's why I got rid of the talking machine.'

For a moment she didn't understand, then it dawned. `Oh, you mean Jimmy?'

`Yeah, Jimmy. Nicest guy in the world, but never stops talking.' He smiled. `It's something to do with his metabolism, he reckons.'

It was the smile that finally did it – made her ready to fly anywhere with him. She looked at the clock on the wall. `But it's eleven o'clock. Where would we go?'

He had already decided where. `We could go to a nightclub. Do you like soul music?'

The nightclub, off Shaftesbury Avenue, was small and dark and throbbed with black soul music.

They sat in a dark corner, drinking wine, their bodies unconsciously moving with the beat of the music, moving with the same subtle rhythm.

By the time she had finished her second glass of wine, she had learned that he was a lieutenant in the US Army, stationed at Fort Devens in Massachusetts. He and Jimmy were first and second lieutenants with the same combat unit, and they had come to England for a very short holiday, just one short week, which was now over. They were flying back to America the following day.

It almost broke her heart. So this was just a one–night, last–night, holiday fling.

He asked her questions about herself. Up until now she had been reticent, answering vaguely, but now she realised she had nothing to lose, and told him her life story.

She was a student at Oxford University, studying Philosophy. The waitressing was just a holiday job. Just something to give her a bit more life experience. You know? Something to remember and keep her feet on the practical ground when she got back amongst her intellectual friends.

She drank another sip of wine, and smiled at him as her body continued to subtly move to the music.

`Philosophy?' he said thoughtfully. `The study of human perception and understanding. Is that why you were so nice to Jimmy?'

For an instant the question caught her off balance.

`I liked the patient way you reacted to him,' Marc said. `Jimmy can take some getting used to at first, but he really is a nice guy.'

She smiled in agreement. `As soon as he started talking, I liked him. I thought he was very sweet.'

`I thought you were very sweet.'

He was looking at her in that way again, that thoughtful way he had looked at her in the restaurant and made her feel weak. She quickly took a sip of wine.

`Do your parents live in Oxford or London?' he asked.

`My parents?'

She took another drink of wine, then explained that although her parents lived in Oxford, her father was a diplomat who spent most of his time travelling all over the world; hardly ever saw him. But her mother made up for him – *so loving* – a bit too much at times. A bit *too* possessive of her darling child. You know?

Yes, he knew.

Marian looked at him curiously, eager to know. 'Is your mother like that? Very loving?'

'Yes.'

'Did she look after you when you were small?'

'Of course she did.' He smiled with some perplexity at the question, then gave a shrug. 'Hey, come on, let's not talk about our mothers.' He took her hand and pulled her to her feet. 'Let's dance.'

The dance floor was dark and dimly lit, the music slow and soulful, Otis Redding sobbing it out. 'This is my kind of music,' Marc smiled. 'Black and blue.'

Naturally and easily he took her into his arms. Her own response was hesitant, not sure what to do with her hands. She quickly glanced at other couples on the floor and saw they were all hugging each other – swaying rather than dancing. She couldn't do that – hug a stranger.

Marc stopped, looked at her thoughtfully, and said, 'It's this, or some other place full of flashing lights and thumping rock 'n' roll. Do you want to leave? Go somewhere else?'

'Oh, no,' she said, embarrassed – terrified he might think her innocent and childish. She quickly moved her hands up to his shoulders, and seconds later she found herself hugging a completely strange man in a strange place full of strangers, dismissing prudence and convention and everything Miss Courtney had taught her.

The music was lovely, their bodies began to move together in a slow smooch, and the magic began.

The record ended, but another immediately started. Marian felt as if she was in some kind of romantic dream, smooching with this gorgeous guy to this fabulous music. She had never been in a nightclub before, never danced this close before.

They smooched into a dark world of their own, lost in the blackness of the music and the magic, moving to the beat, in the heat, eyes closed.

A number of small eternities passed them by. Smokey Robinson, The Drifters, Otis Redding ... the swooning agony of the Blues. The rich melodious voice of the lead singer of the Drifters again, crooning out the melting bliss of being young and in love, heightened moments ... `It's some kind of wonderful....'

His arms tightened around her. They were melting into each other. She felt oddly breathless. Something was burning and moving and lusting inside her. She felt a wild desire to kiss him. It was the only relief for the way he was making her feel.

`It's some kind of wonderful....'

Slowly he drew back, his dark eyes looked at her. A moment of silence as she looked back at him, a moment of quickening and silent longing. Then he bent and kissed her softly on her mouth.

A primal flame ignited between them. It was like no other feeling she had ever experienced. The room became as hot as a furnace, flames of fire hissing off the walls, faces moving against each other in a blind fever ... her mouth opening under his, trying to swallow his breath.

`It's some kind of wonderful....'

A church clock chimed out in the silence of the night as the taxi sped them through the dark streets towards Belsize Park – the dancers still clinging together in a moving embrace, mouth kissing mouth, face, throat, neck ... sweet music and hot emotion still flowing over them ... *It's some kind of wonderful.*

The taxi stopped. Reluctantly they broke apart and climbed out. The night air was still warm with the smell of summer. She looked up at the house, then at him. She didn't want to say goodbye. He didn't want to say goodbye.

Money changing hands. The sound of the taxi's engine receding into the distance. A dim light in the hallway and up the stairs. Then the small door leading up the last flight of stairs and her own private landing. Two rooms, a small bathroom and her bedsitting room. She took out her key and trembled the door open. As soon as they were inside the room they moved back into one another's arms, even before they had turned the light on, her body responding to him incoherently, her lips moving wildly against his. She could not think, did not want to think, could not bear the dream to end.

The curtains were open. He removed her clothes in the dim light from the street lamp, her white slip crackling as he raised it over her head, her hair falling darkly down her back.

The bed creaking under their weight. His body hard and strong, hers soft and yielding. A crimson star crashed into the moon and exploded as he entered that dark place which no man had ever touched – she cried out in pain, her senses slaughtered, tumbling into nowhere, the pain subsiding into a slight, tremulous ache.

In the quietness and the stillness he drew back and looked at her. `You were a virgin,' he whispered.

Her palms stroked him gently, as if it was he who had suffered the pain. He turned onto his back and lay in silence for long minutes.

`Where's the light?' he finally whispered.

She stretched out her hand and switched on the bedside lamp. After a few blinded blinks, he raised onto his elbow and lay looking at her face under its yellow glow.

`It's trite, but it's true,' he said. `I never meant this to happen.'

`Neither did I,' she whispered.

`When I walked back into the restaurant tonight, believe me, I was not looking to get you into bed.'

`What were you looking for?'

`Just a little romantic smooching with a beautiful girl.'

She believed him.

'Did it hurt?'

'Only at first.'

'I'm sorry.'

She gazed at him; at the way a sunset look of genuine contrition came into his eyes. 'Already I love him desperately,' she thought. *He's the dark and fabulous angel that I always dreamed would come. Let the dawn never come.*

Even in the nightclub, she had known that both love and loss awaited her. Tomorrow he would be gone. But for this one night, she thought, he is mine.

The curtains were still open. Marian awoke when the sun came glancing in.

Marc was still asleep. She lay very still, watching him dream-like, thinking, remembering, feeling. Her dark and fabulous angel. Her American dream. Soon to be gone. She touched his face gently, wanting more of him than a memory.

Her touch awakened him. His eyes flickered open, closed, then opened again. He lay gazing at her in a drowsy immutable silence.

'Last night,' he finally whispered. 'Something strange happened to me. Some kind of madness. I fell in love with a stranger, even before I touched her, even before I knew her name. And you know what ... it was some kind of wonderful.'

She smiled; her fingers tenderly stroked his face. 'I don't want you to go back to America.'

'I have to go back. I work for Uncle Sam.'

'Who's he?'

'A real sonofabitch.'

He stirred and looked round the small room, saw it for the first time, meticulously neat and clean, but very cheaply furnished.

'I thought you said your father was a wealthy diplomat?'

'I lied.'

'You *lied*?' His eyes widened in smiling disbelief. 'So you're not perfect after all. Oh, damn.'

He didn't go back to America.

He found a doctor in Harley Street who sympathised with their situation and gave him a note confirming that he was suffering from chickenpox.

'You too?' Marc asked Marian. He looked at the doctor and laid down another ten–pound note. 'She's got chicken- pox too.'

Marc lifted up the two sick-notes and read them ... 'Isolation, incapable of work for two weeks.' He grinned and shook the doctor's hand. 'Thanks a lot.'

Back out on the street, they held hands and laughed. They found a telephone box and the two calls were made – hers to Chef and his to Jimmy.

Holding the phone against his ear, Marc grinned at her as Jimmy's voice talked on and on and on through the receiver.

Finally Marc interrupted. 'Okay, old buddy, you tell them that, shaking with cold sweats and delirium and couldn't even bear to have the light on. Hey, wait a minute, that's *malaria*, you dumshit! ... I don't care! I got chickenpox! That's what the doctor says I got!'

When he finally put down the phone, they stepped out of the box into a sunny day. Marc looked around him, and smiled at her. 'So, we've got two week, babe. Two weeks to find out where this thing is going to take us.'

Two weeks of some kind of wonderful.

As soon as Marc was sure Jimmy had left, they went back to his hotel. The door of Jimmy's room was wide open, the chamber-maid preparing it for another guest.

'Even for a minute,' Marc said, 'if Jimmy had caught us even for a minute, he would've talked until he missed his plane – then guess who else would be suffering from chickenpox and spending two more weeks in London.'

In his own room, she waited while he had a quick shower

and changed his clothes. She wondered why he was not collecting his things together and checking out, but didn't like to question why.

In the lobby downstairs, he questioned her. 'Where now?'

London Zoo – because she liked the chimps. They caught a taxi to Regent's Park and when they reached the zoo and the chimps, Marian was smiling like a child.

She simply *adored* the chimpanzees, she told Marc again. Always had done. Told him she would love to adopt one, steal one, bring one home with her.

One particular young chimp took a fancy to her. She stood at the rail blowing kisses at him. The chimp pursed up his lips in the shape of a kiss and clicked back at her lovingly. Their love affair continued for about five minutes, until the chimp suddenly jumped onto the wall of the cage and began to rattle the wire excitedly, clicking kisses at her.

'I think he's in love with me,' Marian said.

'He's a she,' Marc murmured.

Marian's expression made Marc turn away in laughter.

Afterward they caught a bus back into the centre of London and just walked around, as all tourists do. Their love affair had begun the moment they met. Their friendship began the day after.

They quickly discovered they had the same sense of humour, laughed at the same things. She recounted a comical incident between an angry customer and Chef – which Miss Courtney had not thought a bit funny when Marian had told her about it – but when she told Marc, he just laughed and laughed until he had to stop walking and hold on to a lamppost.

'Some guy, that Chef. Is he married?'

'Oh yes. And his wife is just as nice and kind as him. She's Italian, big and fat and lovely. Chef likes his women big.'

'Is he Italian?'

'No, he's English and Jewish'

'English and Jewish – married to a Catholic Italian!'

`And blissfully happy, both of them.'

Marc grinned. `Goes to show, doesn't it?'

She asked him about his life in the Army, and what exactly they did?

`Well, right now,' he said, `we're all just watching and waiting to see how this thing between Khrushchev and Kennedy develops.'

`What thing?'

He looked at her. `You know – since Cuba – last October.'

She smiled apologetically and admitted that she really didn't pay much attention to politics. Rarely sat down to read the newspapers.'

`So what do you read?'

`At the moment, Dostoevsky.'

His smile seemed to be one of relief. `Which one?'

`*The Brothers Karamazov.*'

`Is it good?'

`Engrossing.' But she didn't want to talk about Dostoevsky. Not right now. She was more interested in his life in the US Army.

`So tell me about this thing between Khrushchev and President Kennedy?'

`Well, it all really started in sixty-one, after the Bay of Pigs fiasco when the CIA tried to depose Fidel Castro's regime in Cuba and failed abysmally. That gave the Russians the idea that they were dealing with a weak US President: the glamour boy from Boston. Then the summer before last – up goes the Berlin Wall. A hundred miles of barbed wire and brick and two hundred watchtowers. The Commies were going crazy because every month thousands of East Germans were defecting and flooding into West Berlin. The Wall stopped the flow. The East Germans were trapped. But there was nothing either Kennedy or Adenauer could do about it. It was a choice between a wall or a war.'

He stopped for a moment, peered at something in a shop

34

window. When they walked on she squeezed his hand and urged him to tell her more.

He turned a smile to her. `I thought you weren't interested in politics.'

`I am now. So go on.'

`Well, then Khrushchev became convinced that he was not only dealing with a weak American President, but an indecisive one. So last October he decided to threaten America itself, by installing long–range ballistic missiles in Cuba. All very secret, of course. But American reconnaissance planes got photographs of the Soviet military bases – with nuclear missiles aimed directly at New York, Chicago and Washington. Kennedy didn't panic – not publicly anyway. He just told Khrushchev to get those missiles out of Cuba or else.'

`Or else what?'

`Or else, high noon.'

Marian stared at him. `You mean ... war?'

`Khrushchev didn't believe it. He thought Kennedy was bluffing and gave the order for more nuclear missiles to be shipped to Cuba. That's when Kennedy made his move. The entire US military was put on red alert, a massive air attack on Cuba was at the ready, and when the Soviet missile ships approached Cuba, they found a full-scale US naval blockade waiting for them.'

Marc suddenly looked at her with some perplexity.

`I can't believe you know nothing about it, Marian ... Last October, for ten long days, the entire world held its breath while the two superpowers faced each other out. For ten days Khrushchev waited for Kennedy to crack, but Kennedy kept his nerve. No way was he going to allow the Soviet Union or anyone else to threaten America.'

`But...' Marian was appalled. `It could have led to a *nuclear* war.'

`Yeah, annihilation. But Kennedy knew it wasn't going to happen. He knew Khrushchev wasn't that stupid. He was just

35

employing the basic rules of the schoolyard and the battlefield – you've got to out-bully the bully, out-Nazi the Nazi. So Kennedy remained resolute, held firm, refused to back away, and in the   end it was the Soviets who backed down. Khrushchev took the escape route Kennedy offered him, and agreed to talks about concessions on both sides.'

`I think I remember now—' Marian said thoughtfully. `Last October, Chef had the radio on all day in the kitchen, listening attentively as he did his work, kept frowning and muttering to himself. Were you in the military when it was put on red alert?'

Marc smiled at the memory. `I'd just come out of OCS at the time. Just arrived at Fort Devens and found myself facing the prospect of a nuclear war. But nah! We all knew it wasn't going to happen. We all kept our trust in Kennedy's cool intelligence.'

`OCS? What's that?'

`Officer Candidate School.'

`Did you go there instead of college?'

`No. I went to Harvard for two years, then dropped out and signed up with Uncle Sam.'

`Why?'

Marc hesitated. They were strolling past a Travel Agent's window and a huge poster for *PARIS* had caught his gaze, depicting the magnificent Arc de Triomphe. It suddenly reminded him of Jacqueline.

Two

Paris
June 1940

_____/

Paris was like a ghost town.

Everywhere the streets were empty, windows shuttered, doors firmly closed. Even the Friday-morning markets had not opened for business. It was 10.45 a.m., the June sun was already very hot, yet not one Parisian was to be seen.

Except Jacqueline Castineau.

Slim and dark, only sixteen years old, her long, black hair was pushed up under a delivery boy's cap, her feminine young body hidden under rough baggy trousers and jacket as she rode her bicycle through the empty streets.

An hour earlier she had seen three French soldiers, their faces and uniforms dirty with mud; one wore an arm bandage, all of them limped. The French units fighting in the northern suburbs had been wiped out.

Her front wheel abruptly swerved onto the pavement as two motorcycles roared past her, followed by officers in two command cars, heading towards Place de la Concorde. They showed no interest in the lone delivery boy, too eager to reach their destination.

Jacqueline rode on at speed. At Place de la Concorde she saw them again, spread over the square, German trucks, tanks and armoured cars everywhere, with more coming from rue Royale.

She stared across at Paris's magnificent Hotel Crillon, built during the reign of Louis XVI, its doors wide open, its interior already occupied. On the hotel's flagstaff the swastika flew victoriously.

Jacqueline rode on.

At the Arc de Triomphe she watched columns of German troops in green and grey uniforms take up parade formation, raise their arms in the Nazi salute, then military music as the troops began the march past their victorious generals.

Jacqueline's dark eyes filled with tears as she stared at the most grotesque sight of all – a swastika flying on the Arc de Triomphe.

Paris had fallen.

By noon, German soldiers paraded everywhere, many taking up guard positions outside buildings. And now there were other Parisian civilians on bicycles speeding through the streets. One shouted to her that more Nazis were arriving via Boulevard Victor-Hugo in Clichy.

By late afternoon detachments of Nazi troops were busily plastering notices on walls and windows, written in French – *ORDRE* – warning all French citizens that the German High Command would tolerate no act of hostility. Aggression or sabotage would be punished by death. All arms must be turned in. All Jews must register their names at the local police station.

Cycling down a narrow street Jacqueline was stopped by four German soldiers, helmeted to the eyebrows and carrying submachine guns, barring her way.

Immediately their attention was drawn to the delivery basket on the front of the bicycle, still piled up with loaves of bread. They lifted out the loaves and searched the basket, found nothing, and threw the bread back in.

They spoke to her in German.

She stood clutching the handlebars of her bicycle, and stared back at them silently.

Realising she did not understand what they were saying, one spoke to her in French.

She had prepared for this.

She took a piece of paper from her pocket and handed it to the French-speaking soldier. On it were written the words – *Je ne peux pas parler. Je suis muet.* (I cannot speak. I am dumb).

The soldier looked at the paper, then at her; his helmeted gaze focused curiously on her eyes – the eyes that Monsieur Haffel had once described as the most beautiful black eyes he had ever seen.

She quickly looked down at the bread, sniffed, and rubbed her nose crudely like a boy.

The soldier shrugged at his comrades. `*Dieser Idiot von Junge. Er kann night sprechen.*' (This idiot of a boy! He can't speak.)

His comrades understood, and dismissively waved her on.

Where was Jacqueline?

Philippe Castineau, an extremely handsome Frenchman in his early forties, stood behind the thickly laced-curtained window of his apartment on rue de Berri and watched a German armoured car drive slowly beneath his window. A megaphone was attached to the roof, blaring out an order in French – all citizens were to remain in their homes for the next forty-eight hours. Any French citizen attempting to leave Paris would be shot.

Philippe grimaced contemptuously at the warning. The Parisian exodus had taken place almost two weeks ago, after the bombing of Paris on June 3rd. All children under fourteen years of age, all girls under eighteen, all mothers, and all pregnant women had been evacuated. The Prefect of Police, Roger Langeron, had insisted upon it. Free transportation was guaranteed on trains leaving the city, only the final destination could not be revealed.

Many of the young girls refused to go, refused to run, including his own defiant daughter.

Where was Jacqueline?

Jacqueline was laying on the ground, stunned, the wheels of her bicycle still spinning. Something very heavy had fallen from the sky and narrowly missed crushing her, sending her bike swerving sharply into a wall on which she had banged her head, causing her to lose consciousness momentarily.

She sat up and looked dazedly at the heavy object that had so narrowly missed her; her eyes slowly widening in horror. It was a man – the body of a man – his blue eyes staring up in death, blood pouring from his ears.

A woman screamed. Doors opened; soon the body was surrounded with people, all in a commotion as the screaming woman threw herself on the dead man's body and wailed incoherently.

Jacqueline pulled herself to her feet and tried to ascertain what had happened. A neighbour of the dead man eventually told her. He was a Jew. As soon as his housekeeper told him the Nazis had entered Paris, he had gone up to the roof of the house and jumped off.

It was the first of many suicides that were to take place that day, not only of Jews, but Frenchmen, mostly from the older generation, who preferred to die rather than witness the fall of their beloved Paris.

Jacqueline cycled on at speed, her breath harsh in her throat, anxious to reach the bakery of old Monsieur Haffel who had loaned her the delivery bicycle.

When she reached the bakery Monsieur Haffel was waiting for her, his face wildly alarmed.

`Is it true?' he cried. `Is it true – all Jews must register? All must wear the yellow star?'

`Yes,' she said, placing the bicycle against the wall. She turned her head and looked at him, her dark eyes cold and threatening. `But if you *dare* to attempt suicide, I shall kill you!'

`But Jacqueline—'

`No more talk. My father is waiting. I shall come back to you tomorrow. But remember—' she pointed a finger at him sternly, `there is no need for suicide, because from today *we* shall be your protectors.'

`We?' Monsieur Haffel shrugged up his shoulders. `Who is *we?*'

40

Jacqueline lifted her young chin haughtily. `We of the French Resistance.'

`*Mon Dieu!*'

Monsieur Haffel watched her running off, a young girl dressed in the scruffy clothes of a peasant boy – no one would ever guess that her father was a very rich jeweller – one of the most highly-esteemed gem experts in Paris.

Philippe Castineau watched a German jeep pull to a halt outside his jeweller's shop on the street below. Three officers stepped out; only their driver remained in his seat behind the wheel.

It was not his establishment they were interested in, but the one next door – the Hotel Lancaster, where most of the American journalists were lodged.

He heard the Germans bang loudly on the hotel's closed door. Minutes later it was opened to them.

Philippe Castineau stood thoughtful: the Hotel Lancaster would be empty; all the journalists out doing their job for the Associated Press or whoever else employed them. The difference now was that their reports would be subject to Nazi censorship.

Ten minutes later Philippe heard a knock on his apartment door. He opened it to a young American correspondent from the *New York Times*.

`Alexander!'

`Yeah, I saw the jeep and came round the back way.' Alexander Gaines looked furious and desperate. `Philippe, you've gotta help me. I've got to get my report in before the Germans take over all the telephone lines. Even more imperative – I must get the report in before Walter Kerr of the *Tribune* gets his in! Will you try for me?'

Philippe nodded, moved to the telephone and dialled the operator.

`*Ja?*' a male German voice answered. `*Kann ich Ihnen helfen?*'

Alexander watched Philippe as he stood silent, phone to his ear. After a few seconds he slowly replaced the receiver. As always, Philippe Castineau remained dignified.

`It is too late,' he said quietly. `They have control of the telephones.'

`Damn!' Alexander shook his head in defeat. `Just what I feared! I saw German soldiers climbing on to the roof of the American Embassy, stringing up telegraph and telephone lines for use in their headquarters across the way at the Crillon. The American Ambassador, Bill Bullitt, came out, screaming fury. He warned the soldiers that if they didn't remove the lines instantly he would consider it a violation of American soil and would personally shoot any German still on his roof three minutes from then.'

Philippe smiled slightly.

Alexander nodded. `And true to his name, Bullitt came back out three minutes later holding up a revolver, shouting that it was loaded with six bullets and four Germans were still on his roof!'

`Did he shoot?'

`Nah, but now half his staff are up on the roof, guarding it with guns in their hands.'

`So,' said Philippe, `why cannot you make your report from the phones at the American Embassy?'

`No way. Not now. Not even if Mr William C. Bullitt himself agreed. The Nazis have forbidden all foreign correspondents to visit their respective embassies until further notice.'

`Why is that?'

`Because they want to get their own propaganda out first.' Alexander sighed. `Listen, Philippe, so far as the Nazis are concerned, the fall of Paris is *showtime*. They must have brought a truckload of their own reporters with them. Photographers, newsreels, the whole shebang. Soldiers climbing the steps of the Eiffel Tower to hang the swastika – all captured on newsreel for the Führer in Berlin.'

Philippe Castineau did not react. He simply took a deep breath to ease the pain.

Alexander looked slowly around the beautiful apartment: marble fireplaces, exquisite tapestries, and genuine Louis XVI pieces of furniture everywhere ... He had always loved this apartment.

`One Nazi photographer,' Alexander continued, `even ordered two Parisian spectators to smile for his camera. Of course, he made sure the revolver pointed at their heads was not included in the shot.'

After a heavy silence, Philippe asked: `What about your report?'

Alexander shrugged. `Oh, I can still send it out – once it has been edited by the censor.'

`*No!*' Philippe responded angrily. `No, you cannot allow the dictators to use your newspaper to feed lies to the free world. You must tell the *truth* to the world. You must tell them how bravely, how selflessly, Frenchmen fought and died in the battle to save France. And that the people of Paris – vanguards of liberty – did *not* surrender with open arms to their conquerors.'

`Yes, well, I hate to say it, Philippe, but that *is* what the Nazis are saying.'

`But you will tell the *truth!* Without the smear of the censor's pen.'

`How?'

Philippe Castineau looked at him darkly. `There are still ways, Alexander, cables in code, secret telegraph, secret radio, many ways ... What is that?'

Philippe moved to the window and looked down, heard the sound of a German voice and quickly tried to translate what he heard into French. He turned his head and looked back at Alexander.

`A boy. They are questioning some boy.'

Jacqueline cowered mutely by the hotel door, eyes magnified with innocence as she held up her piece of paper – *Je ne peux pas parler. Je suis muet*.

Madame Poirey appeared at the door.

'Oh! this boy!' she declared to the officer in French, although she could speak fluent German. 'He is supposed to bring bread – but he is an *imbécile!*' She slapped Jacqueline angrily on the head and ordered her inside.

Jacqueline cowered past Madam Poirey into the hotel, then cowered past the three German officers sitting at a table drinking.

The three officers glanced at her: she scratched her crotch absently like a boy – something no female would ever do – sniffed noisily, and cowered on past the empty tables. Usually there were a few of the American journalists in here drinking and playing poker; it seemed very empty without them.

'*Imbécile!*' Madame Poirey shouted behind her.

Outside, in the pretty back garden of the Lancaster, as Jacqueline prepared to slip through the gate leading into her own building, Madame Poirey caught up with her.

'I heard them talking,' Madame whispered. 'They say it will not be long before all British subjects remaining in the city will be rounded up. They say now Paris is taken, Hitler intends to bring England to its knees. Tell your father.'

Jacqueline nodded, and swiftly disappeared.

Philippe Castineau breathed a sigh of relief when Jacqueline entered the apartment, took off her cap, threw it at Alexander, and disappeared again.

'*Jacqueline!*' her father called.

Alexander stared at the cap, then at Philippe. 'Where did she get those clothes?'

Philippe Castineau shook his head in despair. 'It is at times like this I yearn for my late beloved wife. She, I am sure, would have known better than I how to handle a girl like Jacqueline.'

Minutes later his daughter reappeared, looking beautifully feminine in an expensive red dress, her hair a tumbled mass of black curls. She smiled at the handsome young American.

'Hello, Alexander.'

Alexander Gaines stared at the beautiful vision before his eyes, and knew he was in love with her, really in *love* with her. He had been in Paris a year, and although he was now at the ripe old age of twenty-five, and Jacqueline Castineau was only sixteen, she was still the most stunningly beautiful girl he had ever seen. Her skin was smooth and olive, her dark eyes magnificent – and when she wore a dress she had a regal way of moving that was pure class.

Alexander realised he was staring, and tried to cover it up. 'So why were you dressed like some spunky kid?' he asked her.

'Alexander, please,' Philippe Castineau urged, 'please leave us now. I must speak in private with my daughter. Later tonight you and I will speak again, yes?'

'Yes.' Alexander handed the cap back to Jacqueline, and saluted them both with a smiling 'Au 'voir.'

As soon as he had gone, Philippe faced his daughter sternly.

'Jacqueline, I cannot allow you to stay in Paris. I have my work to do. My duty. I cannot have my mind always worried by my daughter living in a city filled with German soldiers. You must be as obedient as your brother and go without argument to where I send you – to the chateau. You will be safe there.'

'No! Jean-Michel was obedient because he is only ten years old. It was right that he should go. But I shall *not* go away to hide. Like you – I shall stay and serve.'

'You are too young for resistance, Jacqueline! You do not know what it involves!'

'I shall learn. And already I am a competent clandestine. All day I moved through the city and no one suspected I was not a boy.'

She smiled at him. 'You see, Papa, already I am two different

45

people. And I wish to use both in the service of France.'

Philippe Castineau heaved a long, weary sigh – knowing his strong-willed daughter too well – knowing he could not stop her. She was truly afraid of nothing. Even as a child she had always been different to other girls. At school, at lessons, at games, at running, she could beat them all.

Yet as she grew she remained essentially feminine: she loved wearing beautiful clothes and beautiful nightgowns, and always insisted on being beautifully fragranced with the most expensive delicate perfumes. But she was truly afraid of nothing.

Philippe took his daughter's slender hand in his own, holding it tightly as he looked into her young face. 'As a father,' he said softly, 'I think my biggest mistake with you, Jacqueline, was the day I brought you home a book about *Joan of Arc*, and introduced you to your heroine.'

Jacqueline smiled at him. 'And now Saint Joan will not find me unworthy of her.'

'Saint Joan ... ' Philippe sighed. 'From that day forward you cared for no saint but Joan.'

Jacqueline's dark eyes flashed passionately as she quoted her heroine: 'I will yield to no man, to no threat, no – not even before fire!'

Philippe turned away, a weight of worry on his shoulders. 'No wonder your brother wants to be a saint ... You have filled his head with too many stories, and too much religion.'

Jacqueline was unrepentant. 'Jean-Michel has promised me faithfully – *faithfully* – that he will spend every night in the chateau praying long prayers that we may be as courageous in Paris as Saint Joan was in Orléans and Rouen.'

Philippe lifted up a book lying on a side-table, gazing at the title and murmuring sadly ... '*Remembrance of Things Past* ... it seems now a lifetime ago since Camus and I were arguing about André Gide and Gallimard turning down this masterpiece, leaving Marcel Proust no alternative but to publish all twelve volumes himself ... *Remembrance of Things Past* ... he repeated sadly. `How appropriate a title it is now.'

Later that night, Philippe Castineau presented his daughter with a plain gold bracelet.

`If trouble comes,' he said quietly, `if danger finds you, and you need in desperation to contact me – send to me this gold bracelet, and I will know for certain the message comes from you. See, engraved inside the bracelet...'

Jacqueline held up the bracelet and read the words engraved on the inside. *The end of Paris is the end of the world.*

`To Parisians,' whispered Philippe.

Jacqueline slipped the gold bangle onto her wrist, and gently kissed his cheek. `Dear Papa, what a fool you were to think I would ever leave you or Paris. In the Resistance we shall work together, for the liberation of France.'

Philippe nodded. `Yes – Paris fallen – Paris liberated – one day it will come.'

The following morning Jacqueline rose early, eager to begin her official training in resistance work. She learned quickly, earning the surprised respect of those she worked with. She was, after all, only sixteen, but she carried out every task with calmness and efficiency and never showed any fear.

At first, when her co-Resistance members congratulated her on this, she responded with haughty coolness. `I showed no fear because I felt none.'

They shrugged and smiled at her admiringly. Perhaps her father was right. Perhaps she was truly afraid of nothing.

By day, she worked as a courier; dressed beautifully as she strolled through the streets of Paris as if she couldn't care less about the war, smiling coquettishly at young German soldiers whose eyes followed her appraisingly. Despite her age she had a certain maturity of poise that made her seem older.

Every second or third day, in various shops, coded messages

and secret addresses were casually passed to her as she paid for her purchase – scribbled on the back of the receipt. If the shop was empty, free from the danger of eavesdroppers, the message was passed on by the safer method of word of mouth.

At night she assumed her other identity, dressed as a shabby boy, leaping across from one roof-top to the next without making a slip or false move in the darkness, shinning down drainpipes, climbing walls, creeping speedily through silent streets until she reached her destination, carrying fresh instructions and new secret addresses from one Resistance member to another.

Nothing ever stopped her. The greater the risk, the bigger the thrill. Danger and excitement – that's what she loved. `For God and for France!' she always whispered as she set off on a night mission.

One night she was caught – in a silent dark street, by a lone Nazi on a motorcycle who saw a young boy out after curfew and revved up to make chase.

But there was no chase: as soon as Jacqueline heard the roar of the engine she glanced back, saw the lone motorcyclist, and immediately turned and put her hands up, walking back down the corridor of light from the glare of the bike's lamp, like a terrified child.

As she reached the motorcycle, the soldier shone a torch in her face, seeing only the large, terrified black eyes of the boy under the low brim of the peaked cap. He snapped a question in German. She held out one hand in dumb supplication as her other hand withdrew a piece of paper, shaking with fear as she handed it to him, her eyes fixed on the black swastika of his red armband.

The soldier relaxed – the boy looked harmless. He shone his torch on the paper in his hand: *Je ne peux pas parler. Je suis muet.* Underneath were written the same words in German – but even before he had finished reading Jacqueline had jumped onto the pillion of the motorcycle and pressed a gun into the back of his neck.

'Drive!' she commanded in German.

The soldier sat rigid, the cold steel of the revolver pressing into his neck, staring ahead stunned as he realised his mistake.

Jacqueline pressed the gun harder into his neck as she leaned forward a few inches and removed his gun from the holster around his waist, then kicked him viciously on the back of his black boot.

'*Fahr!*' she snapped again.

The soldier put his foot down on the accelerator and did as she commanded, speeding her away from the streets of the city towards lonely countryside.

There she made him stop the motorcycle, turn off the engine, but leave the front light on.

Slowly – holding her revolver firmly in both hands – she climbed off the bike and moved cautiously until she was standing directly in front of the bike.

'You should not have invaded my beloved Paris,' she said softly. 'And now you must die for doing so.'

The soldier was young, did not understand her French, but knew she had brought him here for his killing. Pleading, terrified, he mumbled something in German, his voice choking.

Jacqueline was not listening – she had passed judgement and sentence and now, with chilling and callous efficiency, she pointed the gun at his heart and squeezed the trigger three times.

The blood seeping over his dead body looked black in the moonlight. Jacqueline stood in the silence and looked at him without any remorse.

'You should not have invaded my beloved Paris,' she told him again, softly. 'Did you think we would not fight back?'

Calmly, in the silence, she leaned forward and turned off the bike's light.

Two hours later she was back in the city, running through the still-darkened streets with all the quiet speed of a panther, racing faster and faster towards the secret address of her destination. There, she quickly conveyed vital information to a member of the Resistance, then departed without even a farewell. The instructions entrusted to her had been successfully passed on: she was not interested in any social talk beyond that.

Utterly trustworthy, but ruthless in her determination, she took more and more risks, moving on from being a courier to active sabotage. At the end of six months, after superb and commendable service, she was given her own unit, becoming the youngest female commando in the Resistance.

Her new code name? Every commando had his or her own special code name. But even in this, as in everything else, Jacqueline refused to be like the others.

`Not a name – a number,' she insisted. `I wish to be known to others only by my number. Nothing else.'

The small group of men in the room looked at each other, then at her. It was unusual, but Jacqueline was a perfectionist in subterfuge, almost a genius, so she obviously had a good reason. She was also capable of spiteful and vengeful retaliation against anyone who dared to cross her. Even her own comrades.

`Names betray gender,' Jacqueline said simply. `Numbers do not.'

So young, so beautiful, so what drives her so insanely? Etienne Peleuvé was thinking. *And when does she sleep?*

`Very well,' Etienne agreed. `A number. What?'

Jacqueline looked at him, unsmiling, thinking of her present age: one and six made seven-a holy number.

`Sixteen,' said Jacqueline.

Three

London
July 1963

_____/

Late sunlight still shimmered on the waters of the Thames. Tourists of all nationalities still thronged the embankment near the Houses of Parliament, but for Marian there was no one else in the world at all, except herself and Marc.

Their first day together had been busy and tiring and blissful, and she wanted it to go on and on and never end.

Marc glanced at his watch: eight o'clock. He smiled at her. 'Time to wind this day up. Where shall we go for dinner?'

Marian hadn't a clue. 'You choose.'

'Me? I'm the stranger in this town, remember?'

'Yes, but—'

'Yes, but—' Marc grinned, hailing a taxi, 'we'll ask a cab driver. They usually know a good place to recommend.'

The taxi stopped, the driver turned off his yellow light. 'Where to, sir?'

'A restaurant,' Marc said. 'A place with good food, good wine, good service, and all of it French.'

The driver thought for a second, then nodded. 'Hop in. I know just the place.'

The restaurant was in Knightsbridge. A waiter handed Marian a glossy black-and-gold menu, which she opened and pretended to study, but as soon as the waiter moved away she looked up from the list of foreign words, smiled at Marc, and shrugged hopelessly.

'You choose.'

To her surprise she discovered Marc could read and speak French as fluently as a native.

51

`My mother is French,' he told her. `Spoke nothing else to me until I was three years old. So yes, I guess you could say French was my first language.'

`You're half French?'

`Half French, and born in Paris, just like my mother. But now we're both fully paid-up naturalised Americans.'

`And your father? Is he American?'

`Oh yeah ... my father is more American than the Fourth of July and home-baked apple pie. In fact, to hear him talk, you'd think it was one of his own ancestors that wrote the Declaration of Independence.'

From his tone, Marian got the faint impression that Marc did not like his father, but she was more interested in his French mother.

`So why did your mother leave Paris?'

`A whole host of reasons. But mainly the war. If she hadn't left when she did, the Nazis would have killed her. She didn't want to leave, but she did, because of me.'

Marian was rapt. `Why did the Nazis want to kill her?'

`Ah, don't ask,' Marc pleaded. `I've had my fill of the Second World War and the Nazis. There's nothing I don't know about it. I could write a book about it.'

The food arrived, and it was delicious. As they ate, they talked of this and that, until Marc finally asked her, `What about you? How much of what you told me last night was true?'

`Oh, none of it. It was all lies.'

He started to laugh. `Do you want to tell me the truth?'

Marian paused to think about it. `I've never told anyone the truth. Even Chef thinks I have a doting mother and father waiting for me at home every night.'

`But you do have a mother and father?'

`No.'

`Are they dead?'

`I'm not sure ... I'm not even sure where I was born.

Although, I suppose it *must* have been London.'

Marc listened intently as she told him her brief history, the truthful version. She told him of the day Miss Courtney had found her wrapped in a blanket inside a cardboard box just inside the main doorway of Barnardo's Reception Centre in Stepney, and of Miss Courtney's certainty that the mother of the child was a very young girl - `such a *very, very* young girl.'

`Why was she so sure of that?'

Marian remembered asking Miss Courtney the same question, on the day of her sixteenth birthday, the day she had left Barnardos.

"Because when I lifted you out of the box and opened the blanket wrapped around you," Miss Courtney had said, `you were dressed so sweetly ... little hand-knitted bonnet and booties ... but the knitting was so badly done, so childish, all plain stitches and no purl, as if that was all she knew how to do. No, she was not an adult.' Miss Courtney was convinced. `Not an experienced knitter. Yet the bonnet and booties were very pretty, a bit out of shape here and there, but the little pink ribbons sewn onto them were very neatly and carefully done. A work of love, in my opinion."

And that was not all Miss Courtney was certain of. She was also convinced that the child's father was a young soldier who had died in France. It was 1945. The year thousands of young girls knew for certain that thousands of British soldiers were not coming back.

`Marian, what you must realise,' Miss Courtney had said, `is that the World War had just ended. So many of our young men died in France. So many teenage girls were left pregnant, unable to cope. I have always believed that your mother was one of those young girls.'

Marian hesitated, and then continued.

`Miss Courtney is lovely. She has always looked after me. She firmly believes it was no accident but God's design that she happened to be in the Reception Centre in Stepney that day, because she had just been transferred to work in the Babies' Bungalow down in Barkingside. So, as we were both destined for the same place, it was Miss Courtney who took me down there on the train, just the two of us. And it was Miss Courtney who named me, on the train – Marian, after herself. And Barnard, in tribute to Dr Barnardo, the nineteenth-century founder of the Homes.'

After that, Marian explained, well, she had grown up in the Girls' Village in Barkingside – a self-contained world, surrounded by a high wall, with its own church and school. Every aspect of life was strictly regulated, because of the vast number of children housed there. Yet it was a safe world, a neat and well-ordered world, and no child ever suffered physical violence or punishment. If severe punishment was necessary, then sitting down to polish fifty pairs of shoes, instead of leisure time, was considered adequate.

Marc was listening to her intently, remaining silent when she paused. For one terrible moment she thought she saw something like pity in his eyes and – oh God in heaven – it chilled her.

'But I was very happy at Barnardo's,' she added quickly, then spent ten minutes rattling on about just how *happy* her childhood had been, such *wonderful* times they all had, lots of fun and laughter in daytime, lovely warm dormitories in winter. And well, to have had such a happy childhood ... 'I'm really quite fortunate, you know.'

'When did you leave there?' Marc asked.

'When I was sixteen. Everyone has to leave at sixteen.'

'To go where?'

'Oh, to a hostel, or a flat, anywhere we want. At sixteen we are all considered old enough to look after ourselves.' Although she tried to hide it, she was dangerously wound up now, tense and nervous.

'And that's when you became a waitress,' Marc said. 'When you were sixteen?'

`I became a waitress—' Oh God, she couldn't tell him the truth, not him, an American, he would just laugh. She couldn't tell him that although Barnardo's had kept up the age-old tradition of teaching all their girls to cook and clean and sew – all the requirements necessary for employment as domestic servants – but few people these days employed `servants' anymore, domestic or otherwise. Although the sheltered staff at Barnardo's still didn't seem to realise that.

She said quietly, `I became a waitress ... because it's something I have *always* wanted to do.'

`Jesus Christ,' Marc murmured. He sat back in his chair, irritably waving aside the waiter who had arrived to pour more wine.

Marian's hands, which for some minutes had been hidden under the table twisting the napkin on her lap, suddenly tensed even tighter, her mind flashing with a sudden and abysmal realisation.

Why had she told him the truth? Had she not learned her lesson? Two years out in the world and she had learned that illegitimacy was still considered a bastard thing. Those who created it damned. Those produced by it damned. A black mark struck against all three.

`Are you disappointed?' she asked him bluntly. `That I'm a nobody and nameless? Not a student at Oxford studying Philosophy. Although—' she added, fighting the thick numbness in her throat, `I really *would* like to study Philosophy.'

Marc suddenly looked around him and saw a number of people were smoking. `Do you mind if I have a cigarette?' he asked her.

She looked at him with surprise. `Do you smoke?'

`All soldiers smoke.'

She watched him take a pack of Camels from his jacket pocket and put a cigarette to his lips, then take it out again. `You mean you've got no family? No one at all?'

55

`Oh yes, I've got lots of people. I've got my friends, my job, and I've got Miss Courtney. She's as good as any mother could be. If she didn't live at Barnardo's, we'd live together. But we do see each other a lot. And anyway, I'm eighteen now. An adult. I don't need anyone to take care of me.'

He suddenly put the unlit cigarette back in its pack. `It's a thing I have about smoking in restaurants,' he explained. `And I don't give a damn about Oxford. I didn't last night, and I don't now.'

`What about ... me being illegitimate?'

`Marian, that's not what you are — that's just a *word*. Means nothing. Not unless you want it too.'

The look on her face was so relieved and so pleased, Marc smiled. He gestured to her glass. `Why don't you drink some wine?'

She nodded, and finally withdrew her hand from under the table, but before she could lift her glass Marc leaned forward and gently caught her hand in his own.

`You're not nobody and nameless,' he said softly. `You're Marian Barnard, and you're beautiful. And I'm very glad I've met you.'

Marian bit her lip, feeling such a welling of joy that tears started at her eyes. Because suddenly she knew it was going to be all right. With him, with Marc, it was going to be all right. She was looking straight into his eyes, beautiful dark eyes, and she saw no deception, no damnation, not even a faint shadow of it.

`You've got inner beauty too,' he said quietly. `A natural niceness. I saw that last night. The way you were with Jimmy. The way you were with me ... after we had made love.'

Marian was helpless against the blush spreading over her cheekbones. The mood was changing.

`Marc, what happened last night—'?

`Was two people who couldn't help being drawn to each other, then couldn't let go.' He looked at her questioningly, and she nodded. Yes, that was how she had felt too.

His voice became even softer. 'And what happened last night has led to me staying here for another two weeks. So now, the question is, are we going to keep on sleeping together?'

Marian blushed even deeper as she remembered the night before, in bed with Marc, lying under him, being roused to heights of passion unknown and undreamed of. She looked into Marc's eyes and knew that he was also remembering.

Both knew they would go on sleeping together. It was what they wanted to do, and inevitable.

His hand tightened around hers. 'Will you move into my hotel with me? I can change my room from a single to a double.'

'But why?' she said in bewilderment. 'There's no need for us to go to a hotel. You can come home with me. I know it's small and not very grand, but it will save you money.'

'Money?' He stared at her with a strange look of wonder. 'You want to *save* me money?'

'Yes.' She looked back at him curiously, wondering why he considered that so strange when it was a practical thing that everyone did. But maybe Americans were not as practical as the English.

'You've already had your holiday,' she said, 'so two extra weeks in a London hotel is going to be very expensive. And lieutenants don't earn a fortune, do they?'

'No,' he agreed.

'So it makes sense to leave the hotel and stay with me, doesn't it?'

Marc bit back a smile. 'Yeah, it makes sense. Okay, for the next two weeks I'll stay with you. Thanks for inviting me.'

They stopped off briefly at the hotel for him to collect his belongings and check out. When they returned to her room, as she made coffee, and while Marc took out the stack of soul and blues records he had bought that afternoon and turned on the

57

record-player, it suddenly occurred to her.

`My bed is a single bed. Does that bother you? Would you have really preferred to stay at the hotel in a double?'

When Marc did not answer, his attention on the records, she looked bleakly at her single bed, so neatly made, so unromantic.

`I suppose it is a bit cramped for two.'

Low soul music began to flow softly over the room. And now that Marc was satisfied that the volume was right, low enough for late at night, he looked at her. `Marian, that bed of yours should have a large notice on the wall above it – Last stop before Paradise.'

She smiled; he had a way of making her feel so good.

In bed, he made her feel beautiful.

She lay back on the pillows, her thick black hair tumbling around her shoulders, her dark-blue eyes smiling at him.

`God, you're heavenly,' he whispered.

His mouth touched hers. He kissed her slowly. Her arms moved around him, her heart quickening because she was so very much in love with him.

She took Marc down to Barkingside, to meet and have tea with Miss Courtney.

Marian lovingly hugged her former House-Mother. Miss Courtney was such a sweet woman, pink-faced and blue-eyed, with hair that had turned completely white, although she had just turned fifty; and, as always, she wore it pinned on top of her head like a doughnut.

But if it was true that the real beauty of a woman's face was to be found in the expression, Marian thought, then Miss Courtney was as beautiful as a summer's day. Golden-hearted and warm-eyed, she was the kindest woman alive, in her tired and often worn-out way.

Miss Courtney was delighted that Marian had brought her new American friend to meet her. She bustled around her private sitting room and kitchen, making a proper afternoon tea, chatting with Marc non-stop; asking him what was the latest on Khrushchev and Kennedy? Such a worrying state of affairs. Who could cope with another war? Especially one with nuclear weapons. Would there be another war? Did the American military know something the rest of the world did not?

Not as far as Marc knew. But then, he added with a smile, `I'm just a humble lieutenant, so who would tell me?'

`The children, you see?' Miss Courtney explained her constant fear. `If nothing else, the children must be allowed to have a future. A *safe* future, and one that simply *must* get better.'

`And it will,' Marc assured her. `No one can ever be certain, but since Cuba the Cold War seems to be thawing. Even now, a rumour is going round that Kennedy and Khrushchev have agreed to sign a nuclear test ban treaty.'

Miss Courtney clapped her hands. `Oh, that *is* good news! But just a rumour? Will it happen, do you think?'

`The test ban treaty? Yes, I think it will. If Kennedy can get it ratified by the Senate,'

`Do you think he will?'

Marc smiled. `I do.'

Marian sat silently as the two of them talked on about world affairs, losing herself in the calm and peaceful bliss of it all, the sweet smell of Miss Courtney's strawberry jam tarts, the butter melting into hot scones. Outside the window a bird was singing, and she wanted to sing with it. Marc and Miss Courtney liked each other. She could see it on both their faces. They really liked each other – her House-Mother and her beautiful lover. Occasionally they looked at her, and she embraced them both happily with her smile.

Then she watched and listened to the bird again. Life was a thing of such happy simplicity, when people liked each other.

Marc, in truth, had fallen in love with Miss Courtney on

sight. She was so incredibly English. So damned *nice*.

'Yes, she's very sweet,' Marian agreed, as they left. 'Why did you like her so much? Was it because she reminded you of your own mother?'

'*My* mother?' He stared at her. 'Marian, my mother is one of the most beautiful women in the world. There's nothing sweet and motherly about her. Not like Miss Courtney.'

Marian instantly felt sorry for him. 'Your mother is not motherly?'

'Oh, don't get me wrong. She's a good mother. She just doesn't *look* like a mother. She's thirty-nine years old, and even now half the men in Massachusetts still drool over her. Even some of my buddies at Fort Devens drooled when they first met her. Made me feel kinda sick.'

Marian tried to calculate it. 'So, if she is only thirty-nine, how old are you?'

'Twenty-two. She was seventeen when I was born. A few months off eighteen.'

'Twenty-two? You look older.' She smiled. 'You look twenty-three.'

'It's the Army,' he grinned. 'No boys allowed.'

'What is she like? Your mother?'

'Well, she's very brave, very independent ... and very rich.'

'Rich?' Marian stared at him, then snatched her hand from his, her emotions a confused tangle of humiliation and anger.

'So that's why you wanted to go to a hotel and sleep in a *double* bed? That's why you didn't want to come back to my little bed-sitter! That's why you smiled when I wanted to save you money! You were secretly *laughing* at me!'

'No, Marian, I was smiling because I *appreciated* you wanting to save me money. It was such a novelty. But I honestly didn't care where we went, your place or the hotel. Just as long as we went there together.'

He tried to take her hand again, but she put it behind her back. He pulled it away and brought it up to his mouth, kissed the palm. `Don't spoil it, Marian.' he said quietly. `Not because of money. I'm just being honest with you.'

`Are *you* rich?'

`I live on my army pay. I don't take a cent from either my mother or father. Haven't done since I joined up.'

She looked at him suspiciously, pouting.

He smiled. `Not a cent. Honest.'

`Okay,' she shrugged, walking on. `Tell me more about your mother.'

`What did I tell you about her before?'

`That she was brave, independent, and very rich.'

`Yeah, she's all those things ... she's also very religious. Joan of Arc dressed in Chanel. Her brother, my uncle Jean-Michel, is a Catholic priest out in the Congo.'

`Oh ... ' Marian's heart was plummeting again. `So she really would not approve of what you are doing. Here in London. Every night sleeping with a girl.'

`She'd go crazy.' He looked at her quickly. `But don't let that concern you.'

`What about your father?'

`My father?' He was so silent, and so thoughtful, for so long, Marian squeezed his hand and looked at him curiously.

`I hate him,' Marc finally said with quiet anger. `He's married to a beautiful woman, supposed to be devoted to her, yet he's out womanising every week of the month. He can't even look at an attractive woman without trying his chance with her. She pretends she doesn't know. My mother. Sometimes I think she *doesn't* know. But hell, the whole of Massachusetts knows.'

`Is that where they live?'

`Yeah, Harvard, Massachusetts. Not the University, that's in Cambridge. Harvard is a district about forty-five minutes by car from Boston; and five miles from Fort Devens.'

`What does he do? Your father?'

`He's a writer. A big-bear heavyweight of a self-important writer. Still thinks he's God Almighty because he won the

Pulitzer prize for his novel about war-torn France during the Nazi occupation.'

She wanted to know more, but her curiosity was not as great as her sudden concern. She did not like to see him like this, so quietly angry. One more week, that's all they had left. And he was right, nothing should spoil it. She attempted to bend the subject.

`Who's your favourite writer?'

`Oh ... ' he thought about it. `I like a few of the French writers. Especially Albert Camus. But then there's a whole lot of writers I enjoy. In college, though, I did a paper on my favourite American writer, F. Scott Fitzgerald.'

When they got back to her room, she revealed to him her secret – showing him some of her own writing, taking out a number of exercise books containing essays and poetry which she had written over the years. He read them with a silent studiousness while she made them some tea.

The tea was cold and he was still reading.

Without comment, he put down the exercise book and lifted a second one – the one with the red cover. `No, no, not that one,' Marian said quickly, realising her mistake. `I don't want you to read that one.'

But Marc was already reading.

Barkingside, 10th August, 1959.

I am now fourteen years old, but I have no identity. Nothing to sustain me. Nothing to give me a reason why. All I have is a flame that burns in me, and a hope that grows in me.

I am alone, yet not alone. There are more than a hundred here, just like me. All belonging to nobody in particular. In daytime, in sunlight, we laugh and pretend we do not care. But at night, in the silence and in the darkness, our inner loneliness is ravenous. We all know that we do not belong to anyone. Not to anyone.

'Marc...' she said pleadingly, but Marc seemed not to hear.

She put her arms around her body and hugged herself tight, as if cold, unsure what to do. She had expected him to read one or two pieces of her poetry quickly, skim through an essay, then make some appropriate comment. She had not expected him to keep turning the pages and read every word she had ever written.

Slowly, almost tiredly, she turned towards the kitchenette to make a fresh pot of tea, Miss Courtney's favourite consolation for every crisis.

When it was made, she placed the second pot of tea on the small coffee-table. There was only one armchair in the room and Marc was sitting in it. She wandered over to the window and gazed down at the tree-lined avenue, losing herself in the dark uneasiness of her thoughts.

Finally she turned back into the room and felt the teapot. Again it was cold, and Marc was still reading. Her uneasiness intensified in the silence.

Marc suddenly put down the book in his hands and stood up, looking around for his cigarettes. He still hadn't actually smoked one in the entire week he had been with her, but every so often, when something troubled him, he went looking for one.

She felt even more uneasy.

'You were not supposed to read it all,' she said quietly.

He turned to her. 'I like the way you write your words, but I don't like the way you express your feelings.'

'Why not?'

'Because I think I preferred it when you told lies.'

She stared at him. 'You're upset.'

'Damn right I'm upset. You almost had me convinced. All that crap about lots of laughter and lovely warm dormitories. So happy with motherly Miss Courtney. Not caring that you didn't have any family, not caring at all, and needing no one even now.'

`Marc...'

He looked towards the coffee-table and pointed at her exercise books. `But *there* you tell it like it *really* was. Every sentence a sharp knife cutting open the bandages, exposing the wound in a way only that the truly injured can do. Every page a young girl crying out in pain, in pitiful loneliness. And according to the dates, it went on for years. For Christ sake, Marian, one of them is dated only *three* weeks ago.'

`Oh, Marc!' she choked. `Please don't use that word!'

`What word?'

`Pitiful.'

`Well it is pitiful,' he said quietly. `It makes me want to fucking weep. A young girl asking questions that no human being should ever have to ask. "Who am I? Who are you? If I search all my life will I find you? Do I belong to the dead or the damned?"' He looked away, put a hand to his forehead. `Jesus Christ...'

She tried to speak, but felt too humiliated, too exposed, tears of shame bubbling onto her cheeks.

`Now I know why you read Dostoevsky,' he said. `You're one of his people. One of the abandoned.'

A moment later he pulled her into his arms and they were both crying. Tears silently running down his face. Tears silently bubbling down hers.

`Don't, Marc, don't feel sorry for me,' she pleaded. `That's the last thing I want. That's why I never tell anyone the truth. When I first came out of Barnardo's, when I got my first waitressing job, and the other staff asked me questions, I answered honestly, and this awful look of pity came on their faces. Every time they looked at me – this awful look of pity, until I wanted to crawl under the table. Don't make me feel like that. Marc. Not you! Not you!'

Marc gently drew back, and looked at her. `Marian,

understand, I love you. I truly do. That's why I'm feeling this. Not pity – *grief*. To know that all through the years you were hurting so bad. To know you're still wondering who and why.'

'I'll always wonder about my parents,' she admitted. 'It's something I can't help.'

'But you've got to forget the past. Break the chains. Go forward. Make your own identity.'

'But I haven't even got a proper name. Not one I can truly call my own.'

'Yes, you have. Listen—' he wiped at his eyes. 'Oh, Christ ... I haven't cried since I was a kid. I'm a disgrace to the regiment.' He gave a small smile. 'Look, let's sit down and think about all this rationally.'

He took her hand and pulled her over to the single armchair, then drew her down onto his knee.

'First, your name? You were called *Marian* by a woman who loved you so much she gave you her own first name. A woman who loves children. That's why she works with them, works *for* them.

'Second, you were called *Barnard* after a man who loved orphaned children even more than Miss Courtney. So much that he spent his life raising money and working hard to provide homes for them, Dr Barnardo. One of the great. One of the good. So, Marian Barnard, you should be proud of that name.'

She rested her head on his shoulder and thought about it. 'But my father and mother—'

'You will never know. Never find. You've got to face that, Marian. But why don't you turn the coin over and see what's on the other side. If your father and mother, whoever they were, had not come together, you would not exist. Would you prefer that?'

She shuddered at the thought of not existing, too young at eighteen to imagine life without being in it.

'Is that a no?'

`Yes, that's a no,' she agreed. `I couldn't bear not to be alive. Not now I know you're in the world. I love you, Marc,' she murmured passionately. `I love you so much.'

`Then will you do something for me? Something very special?'

`Yes,' she agreed without hesitation. `Anything.'

`From now on, whenever you think of your father and mother, think of them only with love. I'll tell you why ... I hate my father, I hate what he does to people, but deep down, there's a part of me that still loves him. Because he's my father, and because I'm glad to be alive ... Have you ever read Scott Fitzgerald's *Tender is the Night?*'

`No.'

`Well, there's a few lines in that, that go ...*Thank y'father-r. Thank y'mother-r. Thanks for meeting up with one another...*'

Suddenly they were both smiling, and then hugging each other tightly. And both knew the hug expressed more than just the love they felt for each other, but their love of life itself.

`Come on,' Marc urged. `Let's get washed and cleaned up and go out on the town. A nice relaxing French dinner. Plenty of cold champagne. Then after that' – he smiled, a dark, exciting smile –`howzabout some sexy soul smooching in the nightclub.'

As they got ready in their separate ways, Marian was sitting by her small dressing-table humming and happily chanting to herself as she brushed her black hair up into a long glossy pony-tail.... `*Thank y'father-r. Thank y'mother-r. Thanks for meeting up with one another.*'

Marc grinned, and carried it on in a pious, prayer-like, Southern drawl.

`*Thank the horse that pulled the buggy that night! Thank you both for being justabit tight ...*'

Marian was laughing hysterically by the time he had finished. She put her arms round his neck and hugged him again. `Ahhh, I love you so much I want to sing!'

Gretta Curran Browne

Four

Massachusetts
July 1963

_____/

At that same moment, although it was 7.10 p.m. in London, it was still only 2.10.p.m in Massachusetts. And at Fort Devens U.S. Military Base, Lieutenant Jimmy Overman was standing behind his desk, looking stressed.

Every day, for a full week, since he had returned from England, Linda had telephoned Jimmy from Boston, but he had managed to avoid every call, begging the operators on the switchboard to: 'Tell her I'm not here! Tell her I'm still in England! Tell her anything – but *don't* put her through.'

All Linda wanted to know was where Marc was, and Jimmy was not prepared to tell her. No way.

But now, without even asking if he would take it, the switchboard had put a call straight through to him from 'Mrs Jacqueline Gaines.'

Jimmy quickly swerved to sit down in his chair. His knees *always* trembled slightly when he spoke to Jacqueline.

She asked about his holiday in England.

'Oh, you know,' Jimmy mumbled, 'great, just great.'

She asked about his health.

'My health?' Jimmy sighed. 'Well, not so good, to tell you the truth. Last night I made the mistake of eating a bad oyster, really turned me inside out for a few hours. Almost didn't get up for work this morning.'

'And Marc?'

'Marc?'

'Have you heard from him?'

'Uh. No.'

'Why did he not return with you?'

67

`Well —'

Embarrassed and nervous, Jimmy passed a palm over his blond crew cut. This was the reason for her call and the question he had been dreading, trying to ward off the moment with a jabber of words while he got his mind straight.

`Well, Marc, you see ... he took real ill over there in England. Shaking with cold sweats and delirium and couldn't even bear to have the light on.'

Damn! – that was *malaria*, Jimmy remembered.

`And blotches!' he added quickly, rattling on nervously. `Red blotches all over him. Hands, face, arms, legs, just about everywhere that hurts. And when he was not hurting he was itching. His whole body – giving him one sore mother of an itch. Cut me up just looking at him. I would've stayed there with him, in England, but you know Marc, one independent guy, wouldn't hear of it. Told me to just head on home and explain everything to the CO.'

`Is he in hospital?'

`Uh. No-o-o.' Jimmy murmured. `But he *did* see a doctor. Oh yeah, he sure did. Saw a doctor who said it was chickenpox. He told Marc that no way could he fly back, no way could he spend nine hours trapped in an aeroplane and put other people's health at risk, chickenpox being infectious. Told him he was to go no place but bed for the next two weeks.'

`So he's still in the hotel.'

`Uh. Yeah.'

`All alone?'

Jimmy paused, puckering his eyes, trying to squint up a suitable answer while thinking of the *real* reason Marc had stayed in England – the reason Jimmy had flinched from taking any of Linda's calls – Marc had met an English girl, stayed out with her all night, stayed on with her in London, risking a helluva lot of trouble with the CO when he got back.

And as far as Jimmy knew, Marc was still staying at the hotel, and maybe the girl was there with him. Maybe the girl would answer the phone.

Jacqueline's words were cool and slow. `So, Marc is ill, all alone, in a hotel in London?'

`Well, there *is* the hotel staff, and room service ... and Marc *did* say that the doctor was going to call in on him regularly.'

Jimmy's embarrassment was making him red-faced. Lying like this caused him serious disharmony with his self-respect. And after that bad oyster, his stomach was not feeling so good either. But he and Marc had an absolute code – anything for a buddy.

`Which hotel?'

`I uh ... can't remember the name exactly—'

She sighed, a loud sigh full of irritation, but her voice was as cool as ice.

`Which hotel?' she repeated.

`Well ... it was not too far from Marble Arch ... on the Edgware Road-'

`The *name*, Jimmy.'

Jimmy swallowed; he had tried so hard, but he knew it was hopeless, because he knew Jacqueline.

`Metropole.'

She clicked off without even a thank-you or goodbye.

Five

London
July 1963
_____/

The sun churned above the roof, up towards its zenith, heating the avenue with the smell of summer gardens, but Marian was still in the dark, curled up under the disordered bedclothes, lying between sleep and wakefulness, the tiredness in her body bringing back hazy memories from the sleepy distance of the night before.

Slightly woozed in the nightclub ... Music and fire, warm red wine. A beautiful black girl dancing by herself, wanting no partner, just music, music, music, sweet and hot. Leaving the club in the small hours. Coming home to bed and bliss ...

A hedge-clipper was snapping furiously in the street below. Her eyes twitched, her head rolled back on the pillow, her body slowly stretching, luxuriating in the wide space of the bed. Vaguely she began to realise that she was alone in the bed. Sleepiness still clogged her brain as she slowly sat up and looked around the room.

Marc was gone.

Oh God, she thought. Oh God!

She abruptly put a hand to her face as if she had been struck violently. She threw back the covers and got out of bed. What time was it? She looked towards the clock. After twelve. The heat of the day was already high; her body felt warm and damp. What had made her sleep so late?

Then she saw it – a note on the coffee table. Her fingers shook as she picked it up, but it was only two lines:

> *Be back in an hour or so.*
> *Love, Marc.*

She smiled in delighted relief, hardly able to bear her happiness as she stared at his writing in wonder.

Love, Marc ... Love, Marc ... Love, Marc ... Her first love-letter. She kissed the words, then moved to the chest of drawers and put the letter away in a special box.

Her first love-letter.

Even Miss Courtney's letters throughout the past two years had always been signed with the usual *God bless*.

She sang as she bathed in the small adjoining bathroom ... *some kind of wonderful* ...' She dabbed herself with cologne, wished it was real perfume, shrugged, brushed her hair up into a ponytail and dressed.

It was not until she returned to her room, while she was making coffee, that she began to wonder where he had gone?

Only minutes later, her heart began to beat excitedly as she heard his footsteps on the stairs. He smiled as he entered.

`Hi,' was all he said.

Then he handed her a large dark-blue carrier-bag with the words *Hatchards* printed on the outside.

She stared at the bag, amazed. `You've been all the way into town, to Piccadilly?'

`I caught a cab. Told the driver what I wanted and he took me straight to Hatchards bookstore in Piccadilly. Aren't you going to look inside? I got them for you.'

Inside she saw books. She took them out one by one. Beautiful books. American. English. Irish. French translations.

She looked at him - smiling astonishment in her eyes. `Why?'

`Dostoevsky,' he said, convinced. `That's where you've been going wrong, Marian. That's what's been making you so gloomy and introspective these past years. Your choice of reading. Too dark. Lighten up. Stop reading the Russians. See this—' He moved over to her small pile of library-books on the chest of drawers and lifted up Tolstoy's *Anna Karenina*.

`Now, when you're all alone and feeling sad - this is one truly comforting book to read – the story of a woman who committed suicide! Really make you feel good.'

He lifted another library-book. 'And this, Tolstoy again. *Memoirs of a Madman*—' He opened a page at random. '*"I am always with myself, and it is I who am my tormentor"* — Oh, Christ.'

She was not angry, she was smiling. 'And that is why you have bought me all these books? To cheer me up?'

Marc sighed. 'Marian, honey, you're only eighteen. Too young to be seeing the world so black.'

Marian was still smiling as she looked at the worried expression on his face – seeing only the sunshine gold of her happiness.

'What you need to do,' he advised, 'is start reading books with a bit of bright philosophy in them. Books with a bit of wry humour. Don't read about the mad or the suicides, Marian. Read about the people who went out there and conquered the world. Did their own thing. Took no shit. Never got beat.'

'Such as?'

'Well ... some of the *writers* themselves. Here, Oscar Wilde, a biography.'

'Oscar Wilde was a homosexual. I'm not sure if I'm ready for him.'

'Oscar Wilde was a *writer*. One of the greats.'

He looked at her thoughtfully. 'You see, Marian, all the great American and European writers – and here I mean the *truly* great – always gave their readers something more than just a book. Always gave them one of two small literary gifts to take on with them after the last page. Random sentences, words that come back time and again, helping you to cope, helping you to see life just that bit differently. Maybe only a slant, but still, the view widens.'

'That's what Dostoevsky does for me.'

'Yeah, but Dostoevsky – He's not right for you, Marian, not at the moment. Like I say, read someone cheerful. Someone indomitable. Someone who took no shit.

`Such as?'

`Well, for example, here in front of you, the words of Oscar Wilde, vilified and imprisoned: `"*Two men looked out from prison bars. One saw mud, the other saw stars.*"'

She smiled. `I like that.'

`You see, Marian, what Wilde is saying there, is that life all depends on how you look at it. Up at the shining stars, or down at the stinking mud. Oscar Wilde never looked at the mud – not even when they were throwing it at him.'

Instantly she was inspired. `I want to read about him.'

`Hey – not now! When I've gone back to the States.'

`Okay.' She smiled. `I'll wait.'

He looked at her with thoughtful seriousness. `You could be a writer, Marian'.

`Don't be silly.'

`I'm not being silly. I've read your essays and poetry.'

`To be a writer, Marc, you have to be highly educated, go to university.'

`Ah, crap! You can do it without. You've got a natural gift for telling it like it is. Just like Capote.'

`Capote?'

He lifted up another book from the pile on the coffee-table. `Here – one of the Americans. Truman Capote. Another orphaned child, in a way. Farmed out to relatives here and there. Never really knew where he was at. Never went to college, never went to writing school, yet wrote a masterpiece. Another outsider who refused to stay out in the cold. Took no shit. Never got beat. *Still* ain't beat.'

She opened the book he handed to her, and silently read the first line: *Now a traveller must make his way to Noon City by the best means he can ...'*

She wanted to read on.

`Not now – when I've gone back.'

Marian was silent, wishing he would stop reminding her that he would soon be going back to America.

`When you're feeling lonesome, Marian,' he said quietly, `read a book that will make you feel better, even make you laugh. Wilde will make you laugh. So will Capote. Hey, even Dickens couldn't help being funny at times. Not so the Russians, though. Must be something in the vodka.'

He moved over to the kitchenette to pour himself a mug of coffee. He liked it strong and black and that's how she had made it.

`Did you know, the Russians have the highest suicide rate in the world?' He looked at her and nodded. `It's true! And can you blame them? Living under the Commies. No freedom to do this, no freedom to do that. I mean – what kind of mentality erects an obscenity like the Berlin Wall? Keeping people in, keeping others out. When I was over in Germany last November, it made me sick just looking at it.'

`Are you very anti-Communist?' she asked.

`Yes, I am,' he admitted bluntly. `If you mean the type of communism that built the Berlin Wall, then yes, I'm dead against it.' He sipped his coffee. `I believe in civil rights. Martin Luther King. Desegregation in schools. And no more black people having to sit at the back of the bus.'

Her blue eyes widened. `The back of the bus?'

`By law, in some states.' Marc leaned back against the open louvered door of the kitchenette, coffee-mug in his right hand and the thumb of his left hand hooked round his belt. For a moment there was a silence between them, as if both were imagining what it must feel like to be told to sit at the *back* of the bus.

Marc sighed. `That's why I love Bobby Kennedy – his fearless commitment to civil rights. That's why I love John Kennedy – the first President since Lincoln to propose a sweeping civil rights bill. Lost all his Congressional support on that one. His enemies have it log-jammed and tied up tight with red tape. But Kennedy's commitment to civil rights is like stone. He won't budge ... Hell, I just don't *care* what those muck-rakers say about him, I love that man. He's my kind of President.'

`I love him too,' Marian decided. `From now on, when anyone asks, I'll tell them I *love* President Kennedy.'

He laughed at her earnestness. `You can't love him just because I do.'

`Well, I do!' she said, determined. `I love everything you've said about him.' She frowned. `It seems strange now, but before I met you I never so much as *thought* about America. Never really thought about *anywhere* outside England. Never knew about Cuba or Khrushchev or even the Berlin Wall.'

She wondered.

`So how much more don't I know about this world I live in? Certainly not as much as people who occasionally read the newspapers, because I don't read them at all.'

She nodded her determination. `That's all going to change. I'm going to start taking more interest in politics and the people who make them ... And yes, I've made up my mind, I *love* President Kennedy.'

`And Bobby,' said Marc, grinning. `If you're going to support the Democrats you've gotta love Robert Kennedy too. Hey, everyone loves Bobby. That guy's got one razor sharp intellect. And frightened of no one. Not even the Mafia.'

He put his mug down and moved across to the solitary armchair. `Shall I sit down first?'

Marian nodded, waited for him to sit down, then sat on his knee. Sharing the chair was the only way they could both sit at the same time, unless one of them sat on the floor, or both sat on the bed.

`And listen,' Marc continued, `getting back to writers – *great* writers – there's a line or two that Bobby Kennedy is always quoting, not exactly verbatim, but more or less ... "*I may be just one man, but at the end of my life, I'd like to think I made a difference.*"

Marc sighed. `Now every hand-on-heart patriot is saying it, "I want to make a *difference!*" As if those words came from the

Constitution of America itself, and not the pen of a foreign writer.'

`Who?'

`A Frenchman.' Marc remembered his mother's description of that gaunt and intense young twenty-seven-year old who had seemed unable to get through life without a cigarette in his hand.

`Albert Camus. An Algerian-born Frenchman. One of the intellectual leaders of the Resistance movement in Paris during the Nazi occupation. Albert Camus. A man who really *did* try to make a difference.'

Marian smiled, and pronounced it as he had done, `Alberr Camuu.' She suddenly put her arms around his shoulders and looked into his face, gravely serious.

`You're quite extraordinary, Marc, do you know that? You may be just one man, but you've made a very big difference to my life.'

And so it went on. The love affair that changed Marian Barnard's whole life, her whole personality. From her youngest days she had always felt an inner sense of alienation, always felt as if she was someone not entitled to move beyond the edge of the crowd.

But now, Marc Castineau Gaines had changed all that. Marc made her feel as if she was the most precious person in the world.

In Regent's Park, he made her stand under a tree while he took her photograph.

`To take back with me.'

He took reels of photographs of her to take back with him to America.

Then came his last night in London.

They didn't go out, stayed in, and the only records they played were the Blues. He finally smoked a cigarette.

Sighing, he moved away from the open window and over to

the solitary armchair. She sat on his lap and buried her face in his neck. She was aware only of his body and his arms around her, strong and warm and alive.

Tomorrow he would be gone.

The Blues played on.

When they talked at all, they talked small. No words could express their thoughts or feelings.

`Let's go to bed,' he suggested. `Let's make love all night without stopping.'

They made love with a passion so heightened, every touch seemed edged with their own inner pain. He did things to her that night that he had never done to any other woman. And she did things she had not known were done, but came to her instinctively from her need to possess every part of him.

A maelstrom of lovemaking. Sometimes he was in her, and then she was in him, her breasts in his mouth, the skin of her inner thighs trembling under his hot tongue, until she felt she was being turned inside out, a flower opening for him, young inhibitions breaking down in the heat of love, and it was wonderful.

Exhausted by their passion, still they fought off sleep. Marian ran a hot both full of relaxing scents and foams, and together they lay in the water's warmth, she lying with her back against his chest, he with his arms around her, and there they both lost the battle and fell asleep.

Even when the coldness of the water awakened them, they did not move. They lay staring in cold silence at the grey light of dawn on the window. His flight was at ten o'clock.

`It was just a dream,' she said tiredly.

`It felt real. It felt right.'

`Now it will all start to go wrong,' she sighed.

`Whatever else goes wrong, it will stay all right with us. I'm certain of that.'

`It's the end.' She closed her eyes. `The end of my American dream.'

'It's not the end. I'll be back. As soon as I get my next leave, I'll be back.'

'But every minute is going to seem so dead and dull without you.' She slipped lower into the cold water. 'I won't be able to survive the deadness for even a day.'

'You won't be alone. I don't want you to feel alone. Every hour I'll be thinking of you, Marian. Every hour. As long as the day lasts.'

'I don't want to remember,' she whispered. 'I want to drown in unremembrance.' She slid down under the cold water until her face was submerged.

He pulled her back up. 'Don't do this to me.'

'It was you who walked into my world. You who started it all.'

'I couldn't help it. I'm like Gatsby. I believe in the green light.'

'You took photos of me. I have none of you.'

'I'll buy you a camera in the States and bring it back with me next time.'

'I don't want a camera. I want *you!*'

She turned her face into his neck and cried like a baby. He rested his face against her head and looked towards the brightening square of window.

'It's trite, but it's true,' he whispered. 'Love hurts.'

At the airport she kissed him with trembling lips, her hands tightly clutching the lapels of his leather jacket.

Nervously she looked into his face and asked the question she had wanted to ask him for days. 'Do you have a girlfriend in America?'

'Ah, Marian,' he pleaded, 'don't even think about it.'

'But I *do* think about it. And I *will* think about it. I want to know. Please tell me, Marc, tell me the truth. Do you have a girlfriend in America?'

'Yes.'

'Have you slept with her?'

'Yes.'

That hurt. A sudden feeling of terrible hurt, then abysmal pain.

'Are you in love with her?'

'No, I'm not in love with her. How can you even ask that? How could I have spent these last two weeks with you if I was in love with someone else?'

'Is she in love with you?'

'Ah, Marian, please— '

'Tell me, Marc, tell me the truth. Is she in love with you?'

'No, no, I don't know, I don't think so.'

'But you and she made love together.'

'We've never made love.'

'But you said—'

'I said we slept together.'

'And is that all you did – just sleep together?'

'Oh, stop!' He was getting angry. 'Stop asking these questions.'

'I can't help it.'

'Marian, I don't want to talk about this.'

'I want to know!' she burst out. 'I've got to know! Marc, tell me the *truth*. Please!'

'You want to know the truth?' He pulled her over to a quiet corner, roughly, angrily. 'You're spoiling it all.' he said quietly.

'Our last few minutes together and you want to talk about something that's got nothing to do with us.'

She began to cry. 'I know, Marc, I know. But I love you so much. I can't bear not knowing the truth. I can't believe all you did was sleep with her.'

'Okay, here's the truth. Every time we slept together, I fucked her. Because that's what she wanted me to do. That's what she *said* she wanted me to do. But I've never made love with her. There's a big difference between the two.'

Shock took her breath away. His awful words were like a douche of cold water. And she had not known there was a difference.

'I'm sorry,' he said. 'I didn't want to offend you.'

'Will you sleep with her again when you go back?'

'No.'

'Do you promise?'

'I promise.'

'Marc ... tell me again, do you love me?'

He caught her in his arms and held her tightly. 'I love you, Marian. Oh Christ ... why don't you *believe* me?'

'I believe you,' she said, pressing her lips to his.

Seconds ticking away, slipping away. Soon, even this moment, this last tender moment full of kisses and loving whispers, would be part of the past. Part of the once-upon-a-time.

'I bought you a present,' she said shakily, opening her shoulder-bag and taking out a flat brown package neatly wrapped,

He looked at it in surprise. 'When?'

'Yesterday. When I went to the supermarket to buy the eggs for breakfast. I also went to the bookshop. It's a book,' she said unnecessarily, tears beginning to fall. 'You bought me so many, I wanted to buy you one.'

'I'll treasure it,' he whispered.

'And a letter,' she said, opening her bag again. 'I wrote you a letter to read on the plane. My first love-letter. I'm so glad it's written to you. Not somebody else.'

She took a tissue out of her bag and wiped her eyes. 'You'll wait until you are up in the sky before you read the letter, won't you?'

He nodded, unable to speak – he knew she was convinced it was the end.

The last call for his flight came over the tannoy. It was time to go.

As he walked through the barrier gate, he suddenly turned round again, caught her arm, and stretched across to kiss her lips, his dark eyes looking into hers.

'I'll be back, I promise, so don't cry anymore.' He had tears in his eyes.

She cried all the way home.

'Look at the clouds! Look at the clouds! All soft and fluffy like white cotton wool! Oh, it's so beautiful up here!'

Marc didn't even hear the excited child yelling at her parents a few seats behind. He was staring at the book Marian had bought him. The one he had told her was his favourite book of all time. A hardcover edition of Scott Fitzgerald's *The Great Gatsby*.

He saw again the morning when he had told her about Gatsby ... a lazy morning when they had delayed getting up, and had just lay in bed together talking.

Books were something they both loved to discuss, and she had asked him which was his favourite – 'You know, the one book you would choose to take with you to a desert island.'

When he told her about Gatsby, she wanted to know why.

'Gatsby,' he had said, 'is an exquisite novel. A young man's novel. Dreamlike. Restless young men dreaming about the green light and the orgiastic future. One young man, Jay Gatsby. A soldier at the start, a rich man in the middle ... always hundreds at his house when he was full of money ... but at the end, when the party was over ... Oh, the end is painful—'

'Do you often read it?' she had asked.

'I used to. But not since I signed up. My copy got lost somewhere after I left Harvard.'

Now she had bought him another copy.

Finally, he opened the envelope and read her letter.

Dear Marc,
One summer's night, long ago, in 1963 – If ever I write about

my American Dream, one day, some day, in the far distant future, that's how it will begin. There were many things you said and many things you did in the past two weeks, which made me love you deeply. But, only in a letter, can I thank you profoundly for helping me to find my father and mother. I know they are still lost in name, and I still don't know who. But at least now I understand why. Now that I know what it's like to lie in the darkness with someone you love.

And now that I also know the pain of having to say goodbye to someone I love, I find myself thinking of another girl in another long-ago, lovingly sewing pretty pink ribbons on a poorly-knitted bonnet. Young and desperate and afraid, I no longer believe she discarded me. I believe she loved me, but sacrificed her own love in order to give me what she could not provide: a warm and safe home at Barnardo's. How many lonely nights did I suffer thinking about her. How many lonely little deaths did she suffer thinking about me? From now on I will think of her only with love. And somehow, Marc, I know it's all thanks to you.

All my anger is gone. Thank you for crying with me. It helped me to bear my own hurt, and see how blind with self-pity I was. Thank you for loving me. It helped me to understand. Thank you for everything, but most of all, thank you for helping me to love my father and mother – if nothing else, the last two wonderful weeks I've lived and loved with you, have made me so grateful for being born – which all explains my dedication to you inside The Great Gatsby.

Goodbye, my darling. I don't know if you will come back. But if you don't, I'll still love you, and I always will.

Marian.

Somewhere in the far distance, he could hear the soft sonorous roar of the plane's engines. He had not opened *The Great Gatsby*. He opened it now, and saw her handwriting. More words from Scott Fitzgerald: *For Marc – Tender is the Night.*

No signature.

A stewardess appeared from nowhere and spoke to him, bending and smiling, asking him if he was comfortable, if he would like a drink, but he answered 'No, no' quickly and turned to the first page of his book, lowering his eyes as if wishing only to be left alone to read.

He was still staring down at the first page when she returned an hour later with his lunch tray.

Six

London
July 1963

_____/

For Marian, the first night was the worst.

The bed, which for two weeks had felt just a bit cramped but always lovely and warm, now felt as wide as the ocean and very cold. Lying alone and lonely in the dark, listening to the silence, listening to her own heartbeats, remembering sweet music, tasting salty tears.

The first morning was the worst. Blinding daylight. A silent room. The empty present. A lukewarm bath.

Pulling on pants and bra. Pulling on blue jeans. Forgetting to put on a top, walking on the worn carpet in bare feet. Lonely wanderings back and forth to the record-player. Switching on, switching off. He had left behind all his records. She couldn't bear to play them.

The first afternoon was the worst. The restaurant noisy and hungry. Chef looking at her suspiciously; worriedly.

Twice Chef found her in a state of dazed absent-mindedness and touched her arm roughly to bring her out of her daydreaming.

After that she kept away from her thoughts. Kept her hands busy. Kept everyone satisfied. Kept away from the kitchen until near closing time – until Chef called out to her in a voice singing with cheerful relief.

`Mari-annn! Tele-phonnne! Long-distannnce! From Americaaa!'

She dropped whatever was in her hands and ran towards the kitchen as if a pack of grotesque monsters were chasing her. She grabbed up the phone and held it to her ear, her voice breathless.

`Hello?'

`Hi,' was all he said.

Tears rose into her eyes, tears of triumph and happiness. `Oh, Marc, I've survived the first day, I've survived....'

Chef gave a sigh of nostalgia, vaguely remembering what it was like to be young and passionate and full of love ... He turned away and went out to the restaurant to add up the till receipts.

Marian watched him go, her eyes moving around Chef's kitchen, over the racks of copper pots and stainless-steel pans that shone to perfection. Then the room dimmed all about her as she listened with heart beating to the distant voice of her lover. His voice was quiet, but she heard every word. She bent more closely over the phone and spoke back to him softly.

When she finally put down the phone, she turned and saw Chef standing there, his brown trilby hat sitting firmly on his head, his overcoat on.

Every night, from that night on, Marc telephoned her from Massachusetts, just to let her know he was thinking of her.

`As long as the day lasts, Marian, I'll be thinking of you.'

He always phoned her at the restaurant, because there was no telephone in the house. He knew exactly the right moment to call, in those quiet minutes just before eleven o'clock when the restaurant was closing.

Even Chef became used to the nightly calls from the American. As soon as the phone started to ring, Chef would glance up at the clock, see it was almost eleven, and utter only one word, `Valentino,' then sigh and leave her to answer it.

One night, after two weeks, she told Marc an astonishing truth which she had discovered that day.

`I don't stare into the mirror anymore. I know who I am.'

She knew Marc was smiling.

`My girl.'

Then she wondered again – and finally asked him. `Have

85

you seen her? Since you went back. The girl in America?'

`Ah, Marian, don't even talk about it. It's over.'

`Is it?'

`Yes. I can't even stand the sight of her now, honestly.'

`Did you tell her about me?'

`No. I just told her goodbye.'

`What did she say?'

`I didn't stop to listen.'

`Why?'

`It was too blue.'

`What was?'

`Her language.'

Marian suddenly felt an overwhelming sense of sympathy and guilt. `Oh Marc, I feel awful, the poor girl.'

`Poor girl? No, she ain't that. She's one of the richest girls in Boston. I think my father was more upset than she was.'

`Why?'

`Money. Good family. All that crap.' He sighed. `Marian, what say we shut down this subject once and for all.'

Marian glanced round; saw Chef standing with his brown trilby on. It was time to go.

Gretta Curran Browne

Seven

Boston
August 1963
_____/

`*R oll me over, in the clover, roll me over and do it again!'*

In a back-street hotel, Alexander Gaines looked at the drunken, singing woman in the bed beside him, and wondered why he had bothered doing it once. He had not got any real satisfaction from the encounter, just a few minutes of fantasy. It wasn't the woman he had wanted, but the warmth and reassurance of human contact. Well, he had got that all right. A little human contact, a little romantic fantasy – and now he had to endure this ear-splitting caterwauling.

`*Roll me over, in the clover, shove me down —*'

`The goddamned fire-escape if you don't shut up.'

`Ah, Bill ... whassa matter?'

`Chrissakes, do you have to keep drinking? Didn't you have enough in the bar downstairs?'

The woman was a blonde, about thirty-five, and she seemed nice enough before she had a few too many. He moved away from her to the edge of the bed. Her body had begun to sweat, and the odour did not mix well with the smell of the bourbon.

Not like Jacqueline. Even the fresh flowers of a beautiful spring morning could not smell as fresh or divine as Jacqueline.

When had he begun to betray Jacqueline? Hell, he had never betrayed her! He was as true to her now as he had always been. These little interludes were just ...' He sighed and scratched his chest.

Separate rooms, separate beds, a mere pretence of a marriage. That's all he had now with Jacqueline. And all because ... and all because ... Alexander shuddered coldly as he remembered ...

87

And *dammit* – it was so unfair! Because none of it had been *his* fault. He had been an innocent bystander, had done nothing wrong. But ever since then, ever since that night, Jacqueline had—

`Bill?'

Alexander turned round, stared at the blonde in the bed abstractedly.

`Come on, Bill, what you doing?' She giggled and grabbed his hand. `Gis a kiss?'

Alexander wrenched his hand away and sat up. `Listen– what did you say your name was?'

`Louisa.'

`Well, Louisa, I hate to do it, but I gotta go. It's been nice knowing you and all that, but— '

`You gotta go back to your wife.' She pouted carelessly. `That it, hun? Gotta rush home to the meat roast and the nice little lady who bores you sick?'

Alexander pulled on his clothes, agitated. `My wife is a lot of things, but *boring* is not one of them.'

Louisa shrugged, lifted the bottle of bourbon from the locker, refilled her glass and took a gulp with her luscious mouth. She licked at the few golden drops on her lips, her eyes narrowed.

`You're not so hot in bed, d'you know that, Bill?  Is that the problem? Get your kicks elsewhere, but rush home for a respectable dinner with the family and lady wife, huh?' She grinned sarcastically. `Or do you still love her?'

Alexander went still, quivered slightly, `I hate her,' he replied.

And as he got behind the wheel of his car and began the forty-five minute drive from Boston to Harvard, Alexander stared at the lights of his headlamps shining on the dark road's smooth surface, and wondered if what he had said was true?

Did he hate Jacqueline? Or was his obsessive love for her so dammed up in her emasculation of him, it was just beginning to *feel* like hate.

Eight

_____/

Every slow and sluggish minute seemed like an hour. Marian had never known such a long Thursday in all her life.

Today, four weeks after leaving, Marc was coming back to London.

`My plane is due in at twelve noon,' he had told her on the phone last night, `so I'll see you at the house around one o'clock, probably nearer to half past.'

But now it was almost sunset, the sky a dark copper, and she had been standing by her window all afternoon, waiting with a gnawing restlessness as she kept watch over the quiet avenue.

A sickening panic turned her away from the window and sent her over to the bedside table where she again looked despairingly at the clock: almost seven! He was not coming. He had changed his mind or missed his plane.

Then she heard it – the unmistakable diesel sound of a black taxi-cab outside, its engine rumbling on rhythmically even though it had drawn to a halt.

She turned swiftly back to the window: the taxi was stationed on the opposite side of the street and Marc was paying the driver. Her mood of misery pyramided into a smile of bursting delight.

She rushed across the room-detouring long enough to check her appearance in the wardrobe mirror – her blue jeans neat and crisp, her new sweater soft and pretty, her long black pony-tail gleaming. She turned away quickly and opened the door, skipping frantically down the stairs. She heard the bell ring below. Someone opened the front door to him.

On the second flight of stairs she saw him, pausing in his

climb to look up at her, his dark eyes smiling apologetically.

She ran down the few steps between them and threw her arms around his neck, babbling incoherently, her lips moving frenziedly over his face. He dropped his bag and hugged her so hard she could barely breathe. She closed her eyes, weak with happiness, feeling secure again, alive again.

Someone coughed behind them. They smiled and moved on up the dim stairway.

As they entered her room, she paused in surprise, pointing to a beam of sun dancing on her dressing-table mirror. `Look – I thought it was sunset, but the sun's still shining.'

`That's because your room is facing west.'

`No, it's because you are here.' She stood smiling in wordless bliss as she felt the magic return, the dull silence gone. Even the old flowered wallpaper looked bright and cheerful, less faded – her one-room world idyllic once more.

Minutes later sweet soul music vibrated low on the record-player. She watched Marc take off his jacket. He was wearing a dark-blue T-shirt with his jeans and she saw again the strength of his male body, lean and very fit. His hair seemed even blacker, his smile even warmer, and she stared at him when he took a package from his travelling bag and held it out to her.

`For you.'

She felt strange as she fumbled with the present, tugging at the paper, so prettily wrapped.

`Was it you who wrapped it up so nicely?' she asked.

His eyes widened. `Are you kidding? I asked the woman in the store to do it. Told her it was for a very special girl in England, so she went to town on it.'

The paper opened – a beautiful camera. Three rolls of film.

`For you.'

French perfume. Chanel.

`Chanel? The same as your mother wears?'

`Not perfume – not Chanel. She *never* wears Chanel perfume. But Marilyn Monroe loved it. That sweet babe. So why not you?'

`I love it.'

`For you.'

A beautiful watch ... white gold ... *Cartier*.

She stared at him. `Oh, Marc!'

He smiled, but there was a faint shadow of something dark in his eyes. `I'd like to buy you the world, Marian. Anything you want. Everything you need. I'd like to pack it all up in a gold box and just hand it to you.'

`Oh, Marc ... I don't want the world. I just want *you!*'

Later, she tried to make some coffee but was too busy laughing as he told her about a rotten trick which he and some of the other guys had pulled on Jimmy a few days earlier.

Jimmy, deadly serious, a career officer, walking along the corridor at Fort Devens, bumps into Marc who pauses and catches his arm urgently. `Say, Jimmy, would you help a guy out and do me a real big favour?'

`Sure, Marc, anything for a buddy,' Jimmy replies innocently, and takes the buff folder Marc hands to him.

`The colonel wants this security file urgently, Jimmy, wants it on the double. But I've got to go and see the First Sergeant about something else. Will you take it for me?'

`To the colonel – sure thing!" Jimmy says, and rushes away officiously with file in hand.

Ten minutes later, Jimmy comes rushing back, red-faced and yelling with rage as everyone creases up laughing.

`*You bunch of bastards!* There was nothing in that file but a nude centrefold! Fell right out onto the colonel's desk. Almost gave him a heart attack!'

Marian fell back against the open door of the kitchenette laughing. `Poor Jimmy!'

They went out to dinner in a small local restaurant where Italian waiters smiled as they ordered champagne and held hands in the candlelight. She ended up laughing again as he did an imitation of his mother tasting champagne, her nose delicately sniffing, her French eyes smouldering if it was not the very best.

`This is a long way from the best,' Marc said, putting down his glass. `Tomorrow night we'll go to the French restaurant in town.'

It was dark when they walked back through the silent streets, both suddenly very quiet, all humour gone.

A beautiful summer's night, mid-August. She looked up at the magical moonlight and felt a small stab of agony at the realisation that their time together was so short. He had come back to London on a four-day pass, which – deducting travelling time – gave them only two-and-a-half days together.

The silence between them continued as they entered her room. She switched on the small lamp by the bed, and turned to him.

He embraced her, and kissed her. The kiss made her tremble so violently, she gave no resistance when he started to undress her. She watched his eyes as he undid the metal buttons down the front of her jeans. His eyes were hazy. His fingers were trembling. She reached up and undid her ponytail, letting her dark hair tumble over her shoulders as his hands gently pushed her jeans downwards.

In bed, under the soft glow of the lamp, she touched his face in silent love.

His mouth lowered to hers, and the ecstasy began.

Hours of speechless tenderness and wordless lovemaking. Welcoming him back with hugging arms, loving lips. The bed, a magic carpet, floating towards the stars.

The following morning they woke early, went out early, breakfasting on hot croissants and coffee, before going to the American Embassy for some reason which he didn't bother to explain – something to do with his passport.

When they came out, she held up her new camera and took

his photograph on the steps of the Embassy.

He explained to her then about his leave.

Apart from normal time off, every soldier, from the lowest rank to the highest, got thirty days' holiday leave a year. It could be taken in days or weeks or however. But every time an extra day's leave or a full week's leave was requested, that time was deducted from the thirty days. After that, no leave, until the following year's allowance. He would have to ration his leave-days carefully, so they could see each other regularly.

She took another photograph of him as they walked along. `What about the two weeks you stayed behind with me? Will they be deducted from the thirty days?'

`No. I managed to get that put down as sick leave.' Marc grinned. `But nobody believes I had chickenpox. Especially my commanding officer. "Gaines," he said, "I can't prove it, but I know you ain't telling the goddamned truth. I don't care about no prissy English doctor in Harley Street. He's not a military doctor, so his fancy note don't count."'

Marian was concerned. `Was he very angry with you?'

`Nah! He's a sound guy. He was just born with a cynical mind and mouth, but he's okay. By rights – without a military doctor's letter confirming my illness – he could have thrown the Harley Street note in the trash-can and debited the two weeks as leave, but he didn't, he accepted it, after a long cynical smile letting me know he was no fool.'

Marian looked silently at his smiling handsome face; inwardly adoring him and wishing she could chain him down in England and never let him go back. She held up her camera and snapped another photograph.

`Will you put that thing away!' Marc protested.

Too soon the day moved on, too short the time they had. They did only the things they enjoyed doing. A slow walk in Regent's Park. More laughter as they talked. Then looking up at the cloudy sky: maybe rain, maybe not.

The silent darkness of an afternoon cinema: *The Pink Panther*.

Marc laughing hysterically at Peter Sellers' comic portrayal of a bumbling French police inspector with a ridiculous French accent – "I am an officer of the *luh!*"

Outside a shower of summer rain. A taxi to the French restaurant. Delicious food. Cold champagne. Candlelight.

Home. Soft music. Sweet feelings. A long luxurious night of skin-soft hours of love. Floating, undulating, a slow erotic dream that went on and on, while outside the black window a pale August moon roamed through the night sky.

At the airport, a plane took off towards the sky, its roar deafening, leaving two rivers of smoke behinds its flashing lights. She bit her lip. His plane was the next to leave.

`I'd like to go up in an aeroplane one day,' she said quietly. `Really fly up there, physically, amongst the clouds.'

`I'll take you,' he promised. `One day.'

They turned into each other and hugged in long silence.

`Will you, Marc?' she asked at length. `Take me up there with you, in an aeroplane?'

`One day,' he promised. `I'll take you, Marian. I'll take you to America. Better still, the way things are going over there at Cape Canaveral, I'll soon be able to take you to the *moon*.'

She smiled. `I don't think you would like the moon, Marc. There's no electricity up there. No record-players. No soul music.'

`Yeah, guess you're right ... kinda dull and quiet. Dusty too. Maybe we should give the moon a miss.'

Alone, he went back to Massachusetts.

Alone, she stood by the glass of the airport window and watched that silver bird cruising down the runway, roaring, roaring, faster and faster, then lift-off – up into the vast expanse of sky – back to the USA.

She looked down at her new Cartier watch. Now the minutes would slow into hours. Now the waiting game.

Just a couple of days a month – that's all the time they could have together, all they could share. The long days in between sustained by his nightly telephone calls to her: and her regular letters to him at Fort Devens.

He had not offered her his home address, she realised, even though she knew he often stayed there at weekends.

Still, she did not spare more than an occasional random thought on it, did not want anything negative to spoil what they had, too engrossed in the magic of reality when they were together, and the bliss of daydreaming when they were apart.

As his plane soared ever upwards, Marc sat back in his seat and wondered how long they could go on like this. Marian thought all their problems lay with Uncle Sam, lay with him being locked up in the Army for three more years. But what she didn't know was that *his* main problem waited for him back in America, back in Harvard, Massachusetts.

She didn't know about Jacqueline.

Nine

Massachusetts
September 1963

_____/

As soon as Marc got back to Fort Devens, he telephoned Jacqueline.

`Hi,' was all he said, but she knew instantly who it was, her voice coming alive with joy.

`Marc! *Oh, mon chéri,* it must be telepathy. I was sitting here thinking about you when the phone rang. *Comment çà va, chéri?*'

He couldn't tell her. Not when she spoke to him in French. Always with him, and only with him, she preferred to speak in French. It was something that kept them private and separate from the rest of the world. `Our own language,' she liked to call it. `Just between the two of us, *mon chéri, mon fils, ma vie.*'

`Don't speak in French,' he said.

`*Je n'y peux rien!*'

And he knew that was true. So he let her speak on in French, and answered her likewise, and was unable to tell her about Marian.

When Jacqueline finally and reluctantly put down the phone, she slowly lifted her beautiful dark eyes and saw Alexander standing by the open door of the library.

`Jacqueline ... we have to talk.'

Jacqueline glanced at her watch as she rose from the chair. `Not now, Alexander. I have an appointment.'

`No wait ... wait,' he pleaded as she moved to walk past him. `It's important, Jacqueline, very important. You see, I've been thinking— '

`*Thinking?*' Jacqueline smiled coolly. `You know the doctor warned you not to do anything very painful.'

Alexander was left staring after her, eyes blinking as he watched her walk down the hall, as graceful as a cougar, one beautiful woman.

'Jacqueline!'

Indifferently, she lifted her car keys from the hall-table and ignored him.

God Almighty! What had he ever done to deserve this?

'You know something?' he shouted after her, 'I never knew you and I still don't! Not even God Himself could understand a woman like you!'

But she had gone.

And once again Alexander felt a feeling of real *hatred* for her. It comforted him. Hating her he could understand. It was still loving her so much that often baffled him.

Ten

London
October 1963

_____/

'**B**uckingham Palace?' the customer asked as Marian set down two plates of food. 'How far is it from here?

Marian waved her hand as she gave directions, pausing momentarily when she saw Marc walking into the restaurant—the first time she had ever seen him in his military uniform, and oh—he looked *gorgeous!*

It was just a daydream, of course. Her imagination playing silly games with her. She turned back to her customers and continued answering their questions.

He touched her arm. She almost jumped out of her skin; turned and stared at him. 'Marc! You look incredible! Almost real!'

'I've no time for wisecracks, Marian. My pass is only for twenty-four hours.' He pointed to his watch. 'I've only got three hours left then back to the airport. I've already wasted an hour going to the house. I thought you didn't start work until four.'

'Yes, but one of the other girls is off sick so I offered to come in and do the lunch period ... Marc, what are you *doing* here?'

'It's too long to explain. The thing is, I'm here – so can you get away now?'

'No ... I don't think so...' She looked around her in flushed confusion. 'We're so busy. Chef will be very angry if I even ask him.'

'Is he in the kitchen? Oh, sure he is.'

'Marc, no!' Seconds later she was chasing after him towards the kitchen. There would be murder! Chef never allowed any non-staff in his kitchen.

Chef had a large carving-knife in his hand when Marc

entered. Marc approached him fearlessly, a winning smile on his face.

`Hi, Chef. How you doing?'

`My dear boy!' Chef's face lit up with a surprised smile. He and Marc had met three times before, but never in the kitchen. Chef didn't seem to notice. He turned the knife on his not-so-new assistant. `Peter, lift those eyes from those avocados and meet Valentino.'

`Peter, my name is Marc, nice to meet you.'

They shook hands. Peter smiled.

Chef frowned. `Are you *sure* you're not from Alabama? It would make me very happy if you were. Massachusetts is not my kind of place, you know. When it comes to America, you simply cannot beat the South. It's the women, you see. There's something rather special about those Southern women.' He hummed a sigh. His shoes began to make a tapping sound.

`Chef,' Marc explained. `It's like this...'

One minute later, Chef sighed again. `You Americans! You have the cheek of John Boyle O'Reilly. First you get Marian into close-quarter combat. Then you take away her innocence. Now don't deny it, Valentino, because I know you did. I can see it in her eyes. All her innocence lost to carnal knowledge. Then you give her a rather strange dose of chickenpox and keep her away from work for two weeks. Then you keep her on the phone for hours every night. And now – *now* you want to take her away during one of our busy periods. Americans!' Chef laughed affectionately. `Take her away.'

Outside on the street, Marian was still amazed, shaking her head. `I don't know how you did it. I really don't.'

`Just between the two of us,' Marc confided in a low voice. `I think it's all thanks to that red-haired Mama down in Alabama, whoever she is.'

`Only three hours? What shall we do? Shall we go back to my room?'

`No, not enough time. If you'd *been* there, we could have

stayed there. But now it's too late. Anyway—' He seized her hands, briefly kissed the knuckles, `you know what'll happen if we go back to the room. I'll get chickenpox again. But this time Uncle Sam won't buy it – no, sir, ya gottit right! I ain't buying *that* one again!'

She grinned guiltily.

He looked around him at the busy street. `Let's take a cab to Regent's Park.'

He smiled at her. `It's something I really like – walking with you in the park.'

Above Regent's Park, any threatening clouds had moved on to make way for the sunlight. Marian looked up at the trees – the first week of October and already the green leaves were drying and discolouring at the edges in readiness for the brown falling of November. Still, it had been a long and beautiful summer.

`Why did you do it, Marc? This crazy thing? Flying over to London for just a few hours. For just a walk in the park?'

He looked at her, and once again that shadow of something dark was back in his eyes.

`Do you ever read the Bible?'

`Yes, but not so much nowadays. Not since I left Barnardo's.'

`Well, there's a few lines in the Bible that tell us, for everything there is a season, everything there is a time—' He gazed up at the trees, watched a bird take flight with an excited beating of wings. This is our season, Marian, our time on earth, our little volume in that great big book of the Universe.' He looked at her. `I don't want to waste any of it.'

Was it then? Or was it before? Or was it afterwards? That she realised it was Marc who should be a writer. Not her. His love of words, his love of books, his love of other writers. The solace and encouragement he seemed to find in their literary intelligence.

Even the dead, even those from another time – their words kept coming back to him in a bequest of enlightening literary gifts, widening his vision, calming his confusion. Life was life, and they had been through it too, the writers, before they had moved on from this never-never and forever land, they had been through it too.

`You should be a writer,' she said bluntly.

`Me? A writer?' He looked surprised, then strangely angry. `No way!'

`Why not?'

`Why should I?'

`Well,' she said, surprised by his response, `you're always quoting from books.'

`Yeah ... gotta stop that. But I can't help it. *Je n'y peux rien.*' He suddenly grinned. `Now you've made me feel ashamed.'

`Why?'

`Pointing out my habit of randomly quoting from books. And there you see –' he shook his head in genuine admiration, `Mr F. Scott Fitzgerald got even *that* right. "The intimate revelations of young men," Fitzgerald said, "or at least the terms in which they express them, are usually plagiaristic."'

He smiled deprecatingly. `See, I'm quoting again.'

No, like Uncle Sam, she was not buying it. There was a vast difference in the way he absorbed and remembered a writer's words, to those young men who only used them to impress.

No, there was something else behind his initial anger at her suggestion that he should be a writer. Something in his past. Something that had made him drop out of college and turn his back on it all. Something that had made him walk to the opposite side of the road and sign up with the Army.

`Marc, why did you join the Army?'

A sigh, a far-away look, a shrug, then a swift change of subject.

`Was it something to do with your father? The writer?'

`My father's not a writer, Marian. Not a *real* writer. Not in my opinion.' He shrugged again. `He's just one of those lets-make-a-fast-buck merchants. And in twenty years he's only ever written one book. Does a singer sing only one song? Nah! He's not a writer. But what he is, is a *great* reporter, a *great* journalist, a man who can spot a good story a year away.'

`But, Marc, his book won the Pulitzer prize?'

`Yeah, and wasn't that a shame. Led him into a long life of self-deception. Been living on the glory ever since. Mr Pulitzer Prize. Mr How-Great-I-Am. Mr Bullshit.'

He turned and looked at her. `Let's sit down and I'll tell you the truth about that Pulitzer.'

They sat down on a park bench, both gazing ahead. The autumn sun seemed to be slipping behind the trees.

`The truth,' Marc said, ` is that my father may have won the Pulitzer prize, but he didn't write that book. My *mother* did – it was *her* story, *her* war, *her* France. All the drama, all the horror, all the pain, all the loss – all hers. Once she had left Paris and arrived in America, it was like some sort of healing therapy for her, talking about it, reliving it, while my father hung on every word. And every word she spoke, he wrote it down. Not in front of her, of course. No, he waited until he was back in his study then scribbled away like a maniac. Every word she had said.

Marian listened to him silently.

`He was there, my father, when Hitler entered Paris. And like the Parisians, he saw it – saw the indifferent way Hitler looked at the city of Paris, its pride, its beauty, its architectural magnificence.

`Of course, Hitler knew the eyes of the world were upon him. It was not just his own Nazi photographers who were there in Paris capturing him on camera and newsreels. So were the whole of the Associated Press.

`But *then*, at last, came Hitler's moment of true glory. The moment he stood on the ramp in Invalides chapel and looked down on Napoleon's tomb – the great Napoleon, the Eagle of France – Hitler stood in his city and looked down on his tomb and maybe Hitler would have smiled, if the cameras had not been there. But they were – the world was watching. So Adolf Hitler took off his hat to Napoleon Bonaparte, held the hat against his heart, and bowed his head in silent respect. As if to show one great soldier respecting another.'

Marian's eyes were fixed on Marc's face, but he was gazing darkly ahead, still seeing his own vision of Adolf Hitler standing with head bowed in silent respect.

'That fucking hypocrite. That reincarnation of the Devil. That murderer of so many French children and French Jews.'

'Marc ...'

'And so my father reported it. That's all. He saw it, he reported it, but he didn't *feel* it. Not like the Parisians felt it. To know that Adolf Hitler was standing in Invalides chapel, looking down in triumph on the tomb of Napoléon – no, my father couldn't feel it, not like the French did. And he certainly couldn't *tell* it – not like it truly and tragically was. He had to wait for *her* to do it for him, in his book.'

Marc turned and looked at her, his eyes and voice contemptuous.

'He couldn't even tell the difference between a German and a Nazi. Many of those German soldiers were anti-Nazi, sons of parents who were also anti-Nazi. But they were called up, drafted, just like the British boys. He never even suspected that some of those Germans hated Hitler as much as the rest of the world. Polite, well-brought up, very correctly mannered German boys who found themselves in the midst of a nightmare. Some tried to help, risked their lives, worked secretly with the Resistance to bring down Hitler. Good Germans. All found out. All shot by the Nazis.'

Marian kissed him. She put her arms around his neck and kissed him, because he was angry and upset and she didn't want him to be.

'So now you know the truth about the Pulitzer,' Marc said quietly. 'His name, but her story. Her words, but his glory.'

'And yet –' Marian was slightly confused. 'And yet, they are

103

still married, still together.'

`Well, *he* will never leave her. Because he still loves her. Despite his other women, he still loves her. And not only that, he's terrified of her. He wouldn't dare walk out on that marriage, even if he wanted to.'

Marc sighed, and gazed around the park, but she knew he was still thinking about his parents.

`They should never have married in the first place,' he said. `But she was just seventeen, all fired up with passion for the resistance, and one night that passion spilled over and she went to bed with him. And so I was conceived. They married as soon as she knew she was pregnant.'

He gave an ironic smile. `Even in the midst of a war, in a Paris under siege, she was not prepared to destroy the moral respectability of the name of Castineau. Not while her father was alive.'

`So why does she stay with him now? In America?'

`Ah, well, now you're turning up the other side of the coin. The other side of Jacqueline Castineau. Like her father, she's a devout Catholic; her brother is a priest, so no divorce. But that's not the *only* reason. There's also the matter of keeping up appearances. They mix in a very rich set. Country club dinners. Weekends in New York at their suite in the Plaza. Shows on Broadway. Carnegie Hall at the personal invitation of Frank Sinatra: a few drinks with "Francis" afterwards ... I suppose the best way to explain it, is to say that my mother is a bigger snob than any American WASP.'

`So ... so...' Now Marian was still feeling confused, and desperately worried. `So if your mother knew you were in love with me, a waitress who lives in a room, how would she feel?'

He glanced away, didn't meet her eyes, but he squeezed her hand so tightly it almost hurt.

`If she met you, Marian, she would love you.'

Marian was beginning to feel very uneasy. And another question that puzzled her.

`Why is your father terrified of her? He wasn't too terrified to steal her story and sell it as his own literary creation.'

`Because the poor sonofabitch still doesn't fully realise what he did. He truly believes that *he* wrote that book. Just because he physically wrote it down and typed it up. He was there, wasn't he? In Paris. Saw it all. Saw Hitler. Hey, another slap on the back for good old Alex. Another bottle of champagne for the war correspondent. By the time the book was printed he truly believed his own publicity. But when *she* saw it, and read it, she knew.'

`So why then,' Marian asked again, `is he terrified of her?'

Marc hesitated, looked at his watch. `Marian,' he said tiredly, `I came to London to see you, not to talk about my parents. How did we get on to this subject anyway?'

At first Marian couldn't remember. Then she did. `I wanted to know why you had joined the Army?'

`Oh yeah—' He smiled vaguely. `The reason I joined the Army, is because I wanted to.'

`That's not an answer.'

`It's the only one you're gonna get. I'm beginning to wish we had gone to your room.' He took her hand and pulled her up. `Come on, let's go see the chimps.'

But she was not in the mood for the chimps, and when she glanced at his face as they walked on, she knew that neither was he. The silence between them was grave and unusual.

`It's all spoiled,' she said quietly. `The lovely surprise, the whole afternoon, all spoiled. After you flying all the way from America too. I wish we hadn't come to the park.'

`Ah, Marian, don't blame the park.'

`I'm not, I love the park. But I wish we hadn't come here today. I wish we hadn't talked of Adolf Hitler, or your father, or your mother ... I wish we'd gone to my room and made beautiful love and not talked at all.'

He looked at her. `Do you still want to?'

She stared back at him. `Go to my room?'

105

`No, not there, not enough time...' he glanced at his watch, `but we've still got an hour or so before a cab back to the airport. We could go to some nearby hotel.'

Marian felt her heart beating faster as he smiled-that darling, lovely smile. `Do you want to?' he asked.

`Yes.'

And suddenly they were both fired and smiling with excitement, realising it was possible. Quick, but possible.

They left the park and caught a cab.

Fifteen minutes later they were in a comfortable and well-heated room in the Russell Hotel in Russell Square, kissing ... kissing as he unbuttoned the top of her dress and pushed it from her shoulders. She freed her arms and tugged at his tie, couldn't undo the knot. He undid it himself.

An eternity later they were in the wide warm bed, and she lay smiling up at him as she lightly fondled his hair.

`It's not all spoiled,' she whispered. `I'm happy again, Marc. Happy because we're together and it's all beautiful again.'

`Ah, babe, it's always beautiful with you.'

`I love you, Marc ... I love you ... I'll never love any other man but you ... never...'

Was it that day their child was conceived? Marian later wondered. Or was it before?

Less than two weeks later, she had a sudden and awful suspicion that she was pregnant.

Day after day she waited with growing anxiety, but her period— always regular as clockwork —failed to show.

It was still very early, but she knew.

In the darkness of the night she lay for hours with her hands on her stomach, and she knew.

They had both been foolish. Crazily in love, unthinking in their passion. And now the consequence ... Now the rose-tinted glasses must come off as she considered the situation carefully.

If she told Marc, he would marry her. She was sure of that.

Or was she?

He had still not offered to give her his home address. She knew he spent some time there, at weekends, evenings, normal time off, but he obviously preferred to wait until he returned to his quarters at the base to receive and read her letters.

She fretted and frowned about it.

He was in love with her now – but *now* there was just the two of them: romantic interludes in a cosy room high up. Walks in the park. Candlelight dinners. Rainy afternoons at the cinema. All the things people did on holiday.

Yes – now she could see it clearly – those times that Marc spent with her were short holidays for him, wonderful and romantic. But what of later – after he had been forced to marry her – *forced*.

He couldn't leave the Army, so he would have to take her to America. Then he would find himself tied down in married quarters, away from his friends, coming home to a crying child and buckets of soiled nappies everywhere. And he would *hate* it. And then he would slowly begin to hate her, too ...

Oh no, she could not bear that. To find herself looking at Marc one day and seeing that he despised her.

`And what then?' sang Plato's ghost. `What then?'

Marc's words about the girl in America came back to her ... `I can't even stand the sight of her now, honestly.'

Maybe he would also despise the child?

Maybe that's why her own mother had given her away?

By the time another few days had passed, she had convinced herself of all these things, and had decided what to do.

Throughout the following two days she was so upset and confused, she felt too despondently sick to go into work, staying at home, just wandering around her room in a thought-saturated daze, wondering how she could survive this life without seeing Marc again.

There was something about him – *everything* about him – that was so perfect in her eyes. As if he had been designed by God just for her. He understood all her thoughts, all her feelings. And when she was up there, blissful, drooling over a piece of poetry or the words of some great writer, he understood, agreed with her, felt it too. The genius of Wilde. The tragic magic of Capote. The haunting splendour of Scott Fitzgerald. The unique *wisdom* of Shakespeare. The terrible beauty of Yeats.

There was so much they had shared, not just love, but so much else. Every moment together was sheer, *sheer* happiness, for both of them.

Unable to think anymore, she flung herself onto her bed with such a despairing cry the whole bed seemed to shake as she heaved in a convulsion of crying ... `Oh G-G-God, why weren't we more ca-ca-careful? Why did I have to get preggg-nant? I love him s-s-so much! How am I going to t-t-tell him goodbye?'

She told him the following night.

Drained and white and empty, she assured dear worried Chef that she was better now, her sickness completely gone, an upset stomach, nothing more.

Then she watched the clock and waited for Marc's call.

`He's been very worried,' Chef told her. `Valentino. Very worried. Especially when you didn't come into work the second night.'

Marc sounded just as worried when she later answered the telephone.

`Marian? Are you okay?'

Now the lies – something she was well practised in. Now to adhere to that old proverb: sometimes you've got to be cruel to be kind.

`Yes, Marc, I'm fine.'

`Chef said you called in sick. I wish there was a goddamn phone in that house.'

Although the kitchen was empty, she cupped her hand around the phone's mouthpiece and spoke to him furtively.

`I wasn't sick, Marc. I just said that to Chef to get time off. You know? Same as you and I did with the chickenpox.'

'You weren't sick? ... So why did you need time off?'

She swallowed nervously. 'Marc ... I've met somebody else. Another man. Just the other day. But we fell in love straight away ... That's why I wasn't in work the last two nights. I was with him.'

'What?'

'Three days ago,' she babbled on, 'after a lunchtime visit to the library. He came back with me to my room. Just for a coffee. You know? But, well, he stayed, because I didn't want him to go, so he stayed with me, for the past two nights.'

After a silence, Marc said quietly, 'I don't believe you. Why are you saying these things?'

'Because it's *true*. Oh, Marc, I'm sorry ... it's so hard for me to tell you this, because the last thing I want to do is hurt you. You've been so good to me. But it just *happened*. I couldn't help it. We met, a chance encounter in the library, but after a few hours in his company I suddenly realised that I was no longer in love with you.'

The silence was so long, she thought she was going to faint.

Then he spoke again, very quietly, but she knew his mind was suspended somewhere between disbelief and devastation.

'Marian, I don't believe you. Why are you doing this to me? You can't have fallen in love with somebody else. You love me. I know you do.'

'No, Marc, I *did* love you. And I still do – in a way. And I always will – in a way. But now I see it was just a wild infatuation, because you were my first ... my first lover. But, my new boyfriend ... we have so much more in common. He's English, lives just down the street, so we can see each other every night, not just two days a month— '

'Marian, I don't believe any of this shit! Do you honestly expect me to believe you fell in love with some guy just because he's English! Because he lives down the street! I don't believe you. I don't believe he stayed at your place. I don't believe you went to bed with any guy a few nights after meeting him.'

`I went to bed with you only a few *hours* after meeting you!' she screamed, angry, angry, angry, because he was making it so hard, because he was breaking her heart.

`You started it all, Marc. You're the one who seduced me - even though you knew I was a virgin. You're the one who made me like making love.'

`You've made love with this guy?'

`Yes.'

`Now let's be clear about this, Marian. Did you make love with him? Or did you just *fuck* with him?'

`We made love.'

`In our bed?'

`Yes – in *my* bed!'

The silence was so long, the pain so strong, she had to say something to stop herself thinking of the hurt and disbelief he must be now feeling. Now he believed her.

`I'm sorry, Marc. I don't want to hurt you, but it's only fair to tell you the truth. I don't want you to come to London again, or to phone me again. I want to say goodbye. I'm sorry, Marc ... I hope you'll forgive me.'

`Forgive you?' he said quietly. `In a pig's ass I'll forgive you.'

Five minutes after he had slammed down the phone, she was still standing there: motionless, staring, and chillingly cold. As if a small part of her had just died. Someplace round about her heart. She was aware of no feeling, no emotion, just a cold and empty deadness.

Eleven

London
November 1963

_____/

One week, two weeks, three weeks, four weeks ... Marc did not call her again, did not come back to England, did not try to contact her in any way.

She now knew that he had meant his final words: he would never forgive her for what she had done - slept with another man in their bed – made love with another man in their bed – betraying him – betraying the love he had once so deeply felt for her.

`What now?' sang Plato's ghost. `What now?'

Now the pain hurt so badly she could barely function, walking through the days and performing her duties like a programmed robot. `Yes, sir. No, sir. Coffee coming right up. Oh, you ordered tea? So sorry.'

Vaguely, she was aware of Chef watching her. Vaguely, she answered his questions. Vaguely, vaguely, she wandered through life. Every day the same, dead and dull, the heartbreak numbing. No more immature, girlish dreams. She had made a sensible woman's decision, and now she felt very old and very cold.

And vaguely, on the evening of Friday the 22nd November, she became aware of a sudden commotion in the restaurant, saw the stunned faces all around her, then finally heard what the strange man who had rushed into the restaurant was shouting: `President Kennedy's been shot! In Dallas! President Kennedy – shot!'

`My God,' said Marian, whispering, the tray in her hands beginning to shake; `Oh, my God ... '

Questions. Answers. More questions. The place buzzed all around her as she stared at the man in disbelief. But it was true,

111

horrifyingly *true* – President Kennedy had been shot.

'Is he dead?' someone asked.

The man didn't know for sure. 'But he *must* be,' he decided. 'They say the blood from his head went all over Jackie's suit!'

'My God ...' Marian ran into the kitchen and told Chef. He stared at her – turned white and motionless for a few seconds – then rushed to turn on his radio.

Immediately they heard the report ... the motorcade, the open car, John and Jackie Kennedy sitting together, both smiling, the sudden bullet – reports of more than one bullet – Governor John Connally had also been shot, severely wounded.

'...*We are now switching to a live report from Parkland Memorial Hospital in Dallas, where President Kennedy was taken immediately after the shooting* ' Then an American voice ... '*All we can say at this time, is that the President's condition is critical.*'

'Khrushchev!' said Chef angrily. 'It's that midget Khrushchev who's behind this! It's the Russians! They've never forgiven Kennedy for standing up to them during the Cuban crisis.'

On the radio, pundits were already voicing their speculations: The attack had happened in Dallas, so it was obvious – Kennedy had been shot because of his commitment to civil rights for black people – '*For all Americans*' as President Kennedy had so often stated.

An interruption by the newscaster: '*We are going live to Washington for an official report ...*' Then another American voice, halting and husky, attempting to choke back tears:

'*Today, in Dallas, Texas, President Kennedy died at 1 p.m Central Standard time, 2.p.m. Eastern Standard time ... some thirty-eight minutes ago ... Vice-President Lyndon Johnson has now left the hospital.*'

Marian sagged against Chef's table like a limp doll. *Oh, Marc, poor Marc!* He had loved President Kennedy so much, admired him so much. The grief – the terrible *grief* that Marc must be feeling now.

The whole of America and most of Europe grieved. In West Berlin, Germans openly wept. Only a few months earlier, Kennedy had received a rapturous welcome from the West Berliners when he had publicly denounced the Communists for building the Berlin Wall.

On Saturday, everywhere Marian went, into shops, sitting on the tube-train, people were talking of nothing else, but the death of Kennedy.

When she arrived at work, Chef had brought in a small portable television and set it up in the kitchen. At every opportunity they watched the reports – all other programmes had been cancelled – and all they could see were non-stop images of Americans weeping. Some were just standing in stunned immobility. Others hugged each other as they wept. Strangers embracing in the street.

The sorrow, the loss, and the anger - the whole of America seemed to be united as one grieving family. Someone had killed their President, and they wanted to know who?

Lee Harvey Oswald, an ex-Marine and a Marxist who had spent some time in Moscow, was arrested for the murder. He had shot a Dallas policeman in the process.

Throughout Sunday, they watched the television as more than two million Americans, in a stretch more than two miles long, queued to pay their last respects and say farewell to a President lying in state. Not even Abraham Lincoln had been so mourned.

Oh, Marc, my Marc, was all Marian kept thinking. Was he crying too? Were all the military at Fort Devens grieving? The Kennedys were from Massachusetts. The President a Boston boy. The whole of New England was probably in mourning.

`Valentino must be sad,' Chef said suddenly. `The President of the United States is also Commander-in-Chief of the Army.'

`Chef— '

`Hush!' Chef held up his hand to silence Peter's question – a news flash on the television – `*Lee Harvey Oswald, the alleged assassin of President John Kennedy, has himself been shot and killed during a jail transfer.'*

Chef shook his head and sighed. `America is in a turmoil over this.'

Marian could bear it no longer. As soon as she got home she wrote a short letter to Marc at Fort Devens. Her hands were shaking. She couldn't think of the right words, and frowned as she expressed herself awkwardly.

> *Dear Marc,*
> *Just a few words to say how sorry I am about President*
> *Kennedy. I know what his sudden and awful death must*
> *mean to you, and how it must be affecting you now.*
> *A tragedy like this makes me keep remembering some words I*
> *read only last week by Albert Camus – Death darkens all our*
> *futures, so each day must be a celebration of life.*
> *My sincere condolences.*
>
> *Marian.*

She posted the letter on her way to work the following day: Monday, 25 November, the day of President Kennedy's funeral.

The television was on when she arrived. Chef's eyes were glued to it as he continued to do his work expertly without the benefit of sight – just an occasional glance now and again, then back his eyes would go to the television screen.

Customers were left waiting for their food as, in the kitchen, they all stood watching the funeral ... It was awful and magnificent. The continuous beat of the sombre drum, the flag-draped coffin, the riderless horse ... Bobby and Jackie Kennedy walking side by side behind the coffin, a brother and a wife, both in black, and both symbolising everything the Kennedy Presidency had seemed to represent: youth, courage, and a cultured intellectualism.

`Such dignity,' Chef said, looking at the faces of Bobby and Jackie, then wiping his eyes quickly with his apron. `Such dignity, such grace.'

Then it was all over.

Chef switched the set off, quickly wiped his eyes with his apron again, and brusquely ordered everyone back to work. He unplugged and took the television back home that night; and from then on contented himself with listening to his radio and kept his eyes on his work.

A week after the funeral, a week after posting her letter, Marian began to wonder if Marc had received it, and if ... perhaps ... he might phone her. She hoped desperately that he would. Just to hear his voice again. Just one more time. *Oh, Marc, I miss you so unbearably.*

But another week passed and, as the hands on the clock moved up to eleven, the telephone remained silent.

Twelve

Massachusetts
December 1963

_____/

It was the deer-hunting season again.

Alexander Gaines had spent the past three days over at Bolton Flats with his shotgun and his friends, doing some shooting. But now it was Saturday night and he was home and he was tired and he would have preferred a quick meal in the kitchen before going to bed. But no – even during the twelve days of the hunting season – Jacqueline insisted that dinner be eaten at the dining table in the dining room, as always.

The dining room was warm and quiet. Alexander watched apathetically as the housekeeper silently cleared away the dinner plates. He eased further back into his chair, a lack of focus in his eyes as he turned his gaze to the fireplace where the flaming logs had now waned to a passive simmer.

Mrs Edwards returned, carrying a tray of desserts. 'Snow's in the air,' she announced, setting down a plate of chocolate gateaux and a jug of cream. 'Feel it in my bones. Can you feel it Mr Gaines?'

Alexander looked round. 'Feel what, Eddie?'

'Snow!'

'Well ... maybe.'

'What about you, Mrs Gaines?' the housekeeper asked. 'You think I should tell Cal to get out the snow chains for the car wheels in case it comes in the night?'

They both looked down the long table at Jacqueline who was sitting with her chin resting delicately on the palm of her hand, her mind miles away, unaware of their existence.

Alexander said loudly: 'Jacqueline?'

Jacqueline came out of her trance, looked at them both

116

blankly, then smiled and nodded. `Yes, Eddie, we would like coffee now, thank you.'

Mrs Edwards exchanged a glance with Alexander, then ho-hummed back to the kitchen where she informed Cal the chauffeur, `She's thinking of him again. Never stops thinking of him.'

`Who? President Kennedy?'

`No, you dope – Marc! He was supposed to come home to dinner tonight, wasn't he? But he doesn't come. Rings to say he'll be over for lunch tomorrow instead. So she's upset. Doesn't eat as much as a forkful of the delicious dinner I specially prepared. Marc doesn't come, so she doesn't eat.'

In the dining room, Alexander was looking at his wife and saw that she had lapsed into her own thoughts again.

And as he looked at her, Alexander wondered with resentment why Jacqueline had grown even more beautiful with age. It was a sad thing to observe, because he had hoped - *desperately hoped* – that by the time she neared her fortieth birthday her looks would have faded and fattened, and then, perhaps, maybe, he might have been able to look at her with total disinterest, and finally walk away.

But no, if anything, age had improved her. Her body was still as lithe and energetic as a young girl's. Her black hair was still long and curling around her shoulders. Her black eyes still sensuously expressive. And every time he made love to another woman, in his mind he imagined he was making love to Jacqueline Castineau.

Only her image could make it happen. Only the pretence that he was making love to his wife gave him the excitement he needed.

Oh, the irony of it! In New York and Boston she was liked and admired by everyone, for her charm, her exquisite taste, and her beauty. All his friends envied him, thought he must be loco to go with other women. But they didn't know ... *they didn't know* ... they didn't know Jacqueline.

117

He looked at her now, still lost in her thoughts, and wondered if he spoke to her, would she even hear him? 'Jacqueline,' he said – as *if he didn't already know* – 'what are you thinking about?'

She shook her head, regretful, sad. 'I don't know what to do, Alexander. It seems almost like I don't know him anymore. He's like a different person. Something is wrong with him.'

'You can say that again! Was he a fool or what, to break up with Linda? That girl had everything-damn well *everything* a guy could wish for. Money. Good looks. Good family-the cream of Boston society! And he just throws it all away. For what? For what? Last week I asked him again, but what did he say? He just ignored my questions and walked out of the room, out of the house.'

'I loathed that girl,' Jacqueline said softly. 'I'm glad he finished with her. '

She made a helpless little gesture with her hands. 'I don't know what it is, Alexander. All I know is there is *something* constantly on his mind. And yes, when I tried to talk to him, he walked away from me too. Just drove away, back to the Base. Have you noticed how withdrawn and restless he's been these last few weeks?'

Alexander nodded his head, surprised and strangely happy that she was asking his advice for a change.

'It could be Kennedy,' he suggested. 'Like us all, he could still be upset about the death of President Kennedy.'

'No, it's not that.'

'Or maybe – you never know – maybe he's having second thoughts about the Army. Maybe he's now realising that I was right, that he should never have left Harvard, never decided to be a soldier instead of a writer. But there's still time for him to change course again. Oh yes, still plenty of time.'

Jacqueline was about to agree – every thought of Marc wasting his life and talents in the army filled her with frustrated despair.

But then she looked directly at the man who had driven him to it, driven her son to sign up, and her eyes flashed with malefic contempt.

'Oh, you would like that, wouldn't you, Alexander?' she said coldly. 'For Marc to follow the career of *your* choice, marry a person of *your* choice. But he is not going to.'

'No,' Alexander replied bitterly. 'Because if ever and whenever Marc does marry a girl, you are determined the choice will be *yours*.'

Jacqueline contemplated him gravely. 'Marc is not going to marry anyone. Not now. Not yet. Not for a very long time.'

Impatience edged her voice. 'For goodness sake, Alexander, he is only twenty-two. What do you expect him to do? Marry early into a good Boston family for *your* benefit? Sit all day in a study writing books for *your* benefit?'

'Dammit, the boy is talented!' Alexander argued. 'Every teacher he's ever had told me so. The boy is *gifted*. Well, I allowed him to throw Linda away – that poor girl cried on the phone to me for almost an hour. Well, I allowed him to do that. I allowed him to get away with that. But I am *not* going to allow him to throw away his talent. Chrissakes, he was even *named* after a writer – Marcel – after Marcel Proust, your father's favourite author.'

An old anger flared again in Alexander's chest. 'But of course, *I* had no say in the matter, did I? In the choice of my own son's name. You and Philippe decided it between you. You both *knew* I hated Proust! You both *knew* I agreed with Gidé and Gallimard for turning *Remembrance* down. It's as boring as a shopping list.'

'Alexander, I am tired of this battle. Always, always, you must hammer a point like an angry carpenter. And *always* you blame my father or my son for everything.'

'No, Jacqueline, I blame you! *You!*'

'Then blame me,' she said coldly. 'But do *not* keep blaming my son! Is it any wonder there is such a gulf between you two?

119

When even as a child you let him know that you hated even his *name*.'

'That's not true! What I hated was having no say in the matter. But I don't hate *Marc*! Chrissakes, Jacqueline, he's my son, my boy—' But she cut him off.

'He is *my* son,' Alexander.' She stood up, haughty and proud, her beautiful eyes dark with warning. 'Make sure you never forget that.'

And she was gone, leaving Alexander staring after her in a state of chilling recollection.

That *look* in her eyes – that dark look of warning – it was the same look she had given him that awful morning in Paris, in the apartment on rue de Berri, in 1943 ...

Sunshine coming through the lace-curtained windows.

Alexander remembered the sunshine because it had seemed so at variance with the way the two SS officers were dressed: black leather coats down to their ankles, thick uniforms underneath.

They had come to speak to Philippe Castineau, they said. Nothing important, they said. Merely routine. They had no suspicions, or so it seemed, that Philippe was one of the leaders of the Resistance.

Jacqueline welcomed them graciously – as friendly as a collaborator – smiling as she poured them coffee from a silver jug. Her father, she told them, would be back very soon.

After half an hour of stiff pleasantries, the two SS announced they could wait no longer and decided to search the apartment.

'Very well,' Jacqueline agreed, still gracious. 'You may search in every room from top to bottom, but I would ask you not to enter this room—' She walked to a small room off the main salon and opened the door just wide enough for them to see the sleeping child in a cot inside.

'My son is asleep,' she said. 'He is only two years old. He has been sick these last few days, but now he is sleeping, I will not allow you to disturb him.' She closed the door quietly.

Their smiles were surprised and mocking, and in that moment Alexander saw Jacqueline as they were seeing her: not yet twenty years old, a slip of a French girl telling the *SS* – the Nazi Special Police – what she would, and would not, allow them to do.

Both withdrew their revolvers. 'Stand aside, Madame. We have our orders. We must search the room. We will try not to waken your son.'

'No,' Jacqueline said defiantly, barring their way. 'I will not allow Nazis with guns to enter the same room as my baby son.'

Only then did one of the SS officers turn to Alexander and snap a command. 'Herr Gaines, remove your wife please!'

Alexander did so, strongly pulling Jacqueline aside and asking her what the hell was she doing?

The SS entered Marc's room as he tugged her back into the main salon and whispered to her. 'You know what they're searching for – the gold and diamonds missing from your father's jewellery salon. They know Philippe has them hidden somewhere. But they'll find nothing in Marc's room, or any other room, you know that. So why all the fuss? Just let them get on with it, and then they'll go!'

She stood very still, her composure calm, but the look in her black eyes was chilling. 'There are two Nazis with guns in the same room as my baby son,' she said softly. 'I told them I would not allow it.'

She turned so swiftly he was unable to stop her. All he saw was the revolver coming out of a pocket in the deep folds of her skirt. Then she was standing at the open door of Marc's room with the gun held outstretched in both hands. Two quick shots, and it was all over. Without a moment's hesitation she killed one, then the other. Both slumped in black leather heaps when Alexander entered the room.

'Jacqueline!' he gasped.

The two explosions had woken Marc with a fright; the boy

was sitting up and sobbing as he stared at a stream of red blood running down the wall right next to his cot. The blood that had spurted from one of the SS officer's head.

'That pig! He was standing by the cot,' Jacqueline said. 'About to search under the mattress and disturb my son. How dare he?'

'Jacqueline!' he gasped again.

She was lifting Marc out of the cot, not a trace of remorse in her voice. 'They entered my son's room with guns in their hands. Two Nazis. I told you, Alexander, I will risk anything for the resistance, but I will not risk anyone harming my son.'

Alexander was still staring in petrified disbelief at the two dead SS officers. 'What about the bodies?' he asked her, and suddenly realised why men in the resistance, men much older than her, were prepared to take orders from her.

'The bodies?' She looked back over her shoulder as if looking at two heaps of rubbish. 'Tonight, after dark, I will arrange for Resistance members to throw them in the Seine. We will deny they ever came here.'

They were not the first Nazis she had shot, or bombed, or knifed – but only the Resistance truly knew how many Nazis she had killed, how many bodies found floating in the Seine.

'*The black-eyed boy.*' For a long time the Nazis had searched for '*The black-eyed boy*' – a cold and ruthless killer. But it was not until near the end, they discovered 'the boy' was Jacqueline Castineau.

It was all in his book.

Alexander did not realise he had wandered into his study and picked up his own prized book – *Behind Lace Curtains* – his novel about the Parisian arm of the French Resistance during the Nazi occupation.

All the names had been fictionalised. In the original draft he had changed Jacqueline's name to Yvette, but she had stared at the finished script in horror and insisted, 'No – my name must be *Jeanette*.' And he had sighed and complied because he knew her heroine was Joan of Arc.

Some joke that turned out to be! At least Joan of Arc had a heart. A God-loving heart. But Jacqueline was cruelly and utterly heartless. As cold as the Nazis she had despised.

At least, that's how she seemed to him.

Cold and heartless – *particularly* with him.

Desperately he forced himself not to care. Truth was, he only stayed with the bitch because she was rich.

Chrissakes, who was he kidding?

He liked the money, yeah, sure. Liked the easy life-style it provided. Allowed him to sit back and be his own boss, work on his new novel in comfort and leisure. But – he sighed helplessly, like an addict still craving for a fix – he still missed Jacqueline's scented sheets and soft touch. Missed her smouldering beauty in the heat of the night. Missed her radiant smile when she was genuinely happy.

Breathtaking.

Hell, all those Castineaus were fantastic looking – Philippe, Jacqueline, and Marc too. Oh yeah, Marc was a Castineau through and through, sad to say. He would have liked to have seen some sign of his own family in his only son; but no, Jacqueline had beaten him on that one too. Her son, as she so often boasted, was a true Castineau.

Alexander slowly moved out to the hall, and looked around him bleakly. This house ... this house was the only thing she hadn't beaten him on. This beautiful old country house had been in his family since the turn of the century, a time when his own ancestors had been fairly wealthy. Jacqueline had decorated and refurbished it with exquisite style, but she had always hated it.

No, even this house of his was not good enough for her. Too lonely. Too out of the way. She much preferred to spend her time at their town house in Boston, lunching every day with her friends. When Marc was studying at Harvard she had even moved to Boston permanently, refusing to live too far away from her beloved son.

Alexander had resisted the move, argued his damnedest, but in the end he had joined her.

And then – when Marc turned rebel and joined the Army, stationed at Fort Devens only five miles away, then it all changed, then this house became her favourite abode, because it was close enough for Marc to visit, stay over at weekends. Truth was – and no one knew it better than he – *any place* would be heaven to Jacqueline, just so long as she was close to Marc.

Thirteen

Massachusetts
December 1963

_____/

Jacqueline was watching from her bedroom window when Marc arrived for lunch the following day. As soon as she saw his Lincoln turn off the country road into the lane that led up to the house, she rushed downstairs to greet him.

Alexander beat her to it. As she approached the front door she saw Alexander on the porch, his arm around Marc's shoulder in that buddy-buddy way of his.

'Thought you'd be out hunting today,' Marc said.

Alexander's head shot back in surprise, eyes wide. 'You know hunting of any kind is prohibited on Sundays!'

'Oh yeah,' Marc nodded his head distractedly. 'I forgot that.'

'Marc ...'

Alexander instinctively stepped back a pace as Jacqueline moved towards her son – her hands going up around his shoulders, a kiss on both cheeks – then her radiant smile. '*Ça va, chéri?*'

Marc shrugged, 'Oui, *comme ci, comme ça.*'

'No frigging French!' Alexander exclaimed, then laughed, and laid claim on his son again, hand slapped on the shoulder, steering him away from Jacqueline and monopolising the conversation from that moment on.

Throughout lunch, Jacqueline sat silently while Alexander talked "man-talk" with Marc. Any subject she had no interest in, could make no contribution to, Alexander talked about it.

'It was guys from the Army, Marc. I know it was. And you know what – it was frigging disgraceful! Now we all know the rules – every citizen in this county knows the rules, and that includes every serving soldier and officer over there at Fort

125

Devens.'

Alexander laid down his fork, sat back in his chair, and began to count off the rules on his fingers.

'Number one – no shotguns to be used until the archery season is over. Number two – no crossbows are allowed on the deer, and no fully-automatic firearms. Number three – no chasing down animals or carrying loaded weapons in motor vehicles, not even in snowmobiles. Artificial lights, baiting and decoys are also prohibited.

Alexander laid his palms flat on the table. 'So, those are the rules, and everyone knows them. No fully-automatic weapons and no shooting from motor vehicles. But these guys, Marc,' – Alexander still couldn't believe it – 'they came over in a frigging *helicopter!* Firing a frigging *machine gun!* Now you tell me they were not Army!'

Marc looked at his father dubiously. 'Was it an Army helicopter?'

'No, it was a private helicopter, white with blue lines, but I know the guys inside were Army. I know it!'

'Why?'

'Because of the *machine gun!* Who else but the Army has access to machine guns?'

'Thousands,' Marc replied. 'If you have the money, machine guns can be bought just like any other weapon.'

'Well whoever it was, they broke the law. And everyone is furious about it. First thing Monday – tomorrow that is – we're going over there to Fort Devens to make an official complaint. We want to see somebody kick ass over this. We want to see court martials! I mean, Chrissakes, *we're* not allowed to trespass on Army lands, are we? Yet their guys can fly over our wildlife areas and mow down our deer with frigging machine guns!'

'Okay, Dad, you do that,' Marc said patiently. 'You go over there and raise all the hell you want. But the Army won't allow any civilian in the three towns to blame its personnel, not if an investigation proves that none of its personnel were responsible.'

`And that's what they *will* say! The Army. They'll close ranks as always. But we're going to fight them on this.'

Alexander leaned forward and poured more wine.

`You see, that's what's wrong with this place, son. The three towns, Harvard, Ayer and Shirley, should work together more for the common good. Town officials and citizens working together, but everything we try to do is subjected or frustrated by too many outside influences – the Army, the state, the federal government.'

Even when lunch was over, Alexander followed Marc from room to room; talking, talking, talking ... Marc attempted to escape to his room.

In his room he lay down on his bed, put his hands behind his head and closed his eyes, but Alexander was still there, sitting on the side of the bed, still talking to him.

`And while we're on the subject of the Army, son ... You know that land up by the South Post? Six hundred acres of unused land up by the South Post. You know it?'

Marc sighed. `Yes, I know it.'

`Well we think the Army should decommission that land and allow the citizens to use it for horse-riding and major equestrian events. Some of us are going to look into it. Raise the matter with the Massachusetts Government Land Bank. Bill Simons, over in Shirley, he's already spoken to the Land Bank's—'

Marc groaned and swung off the bed, grabbed a sheepskin jacket from the back of a chair. Alexander caught him at the bedroom door.

`Where you going, son?'

Marc took a deep breath. `For a walk, Dad. A short walk.'

`Shall I come with you?'

`No, no,' Marc said quickly, `I prefer to go alone. Company spoils the poetry.'

`Poetry?' Alexander's eyes widened in delight. `You writing poetry now?'

`No! It's a joke, a joke! An expression, nothing more.' Marc tried to shove past him to get out, get some air.

Alexander clung to his arm. `Marc, what the hell is wrong with you? I'm your father, for Chrissake! So why won't you *talk* to me? It's not true, you know? I don't hate your name. I hate the fact that *they* chose your name. If it had been left to me, I would still have named you after a writer. An *American* writer.'

Marc's dark eyes, exactly like Jacqueline's, looked despairingly at Alexander. `Dad, I'm asphyxiating here, I need air, so please, just let me pass.'

`Maybe even Scott Fitzgerald,' Alexander said, as Marc walked away. `Or maybe even ... Alexander Gaines ... Junior.'

Although the house was set in five acres of beautifully landscaped gardens, Marc chose to walk towards the woodland lanes that would give him privacy and an opportunity to clear his mind and think.

The air was sharp and cold and yes, Eddie was right, there was definitely snow in the air.

He had not walked far when he heard a voice behind him, calling to him. He looked back and saw Jacqueline running after him: she too had donned a warm sheepskin jacket.

As soon as she reached him, she put her arm through his and smiled as they walked on. `Alone at last. I did not think he was going to allow me a chance to speak to you at all.'

Marc sighed. `Why does he do it?'

Jacqueline hesitated: the truthful answer was that Alexander genuinely loved his son, even more than Alexander himself realised. She had known it for years, but today, a silent observer, she had seen it so clearly. The way Alexander's eyes never seemed to leave Marc's face. The way he followed Marc from room to room. The incessant talk was merely a camouflage for his own feelings – just another of Alexander's desperate attempts to get Marc to talk to *him*. But in this, as in everything, Alexander was his own worst enemy.

'I only came today because I thought he would be out,' Marc said quietly. 'I can't cope with him anymore.'

'Then let's not talk about him.' Jacqueline squeezed his arm and snuggled closer in the cold. 'Let's talk about you.'

'No, I want to talk some more about him.' Marc stopped and turned to her, as if he had suddenly come to a decision.

'I want you to tell me the truth. I left Harvard and joined the Army to get away from Massachusetts. Hopefully, thousands of miles away. Hopefully, somewhere in the Pacific. Yet I end up only five miles from home at Fort Devens. Even closer to home than when I was at Harvard.'

He looked at her questioningly. 'So? Was it him? Did he go to Army Headquarters in Washington? Did he make the phone calls? Did he pull the strings to get me stationed at Devens? Just tell me the truth. I won't say a word to him, I promise. I just want to know the truth.'

'No,' she replied truthfully. 'Your father did none of those things, Marc. He did not go to Washington. He made no phone calls. And he pulled no strings to get you stationed at Fort Devens. You can take my word for that, Marc.'

Marc looked genuinely surprised. 'So, it was just a coincidence?'

Jacqueline smiled faintly. 'Life is full of coincidences, Marc. And usually they have a purpose, and work out for the best.'

There was a silence between them as they walked on, and Jacqueline was glad of it. Now she realised how very important it was that Marc should never find out that it was *she* who had made the phone calls and flown to Washington to ensure he was stationed close to her at Fort Devens.

She had a number of political friends in Washington. A successful fund-raiser for the Democratic Party, she had worked tirelessly during Kennedy's election campaign, hosting dinners and parties in New York and Boston and contributing half a million dollars of her own money to JFK's funds. And she had received her favour in return for services rendered, and that was all that mattered now.

When it came to her son she had no regrets, no conscience about anything she did. She loved him even more than she had loved her father, and no daughter in the world had loved a father as much as she had loved hers.

`*Chéri*,' she said softly. `I need to talk to you.'

`About what?'

`About this girl of yours in England.'

It took him some moments to reply.

`I have no girl in England.'

`But you did, didn't you?' She put the question gently.

Marc let his gaze wander over the trees. `What makes you think so?'

Jacqueline smiled. `Oh, I have always enjoyed puzzles. But this one did not take me long to work out. First, Jimmy returns alone, insisting he had left you behind in London suffering from chickenpox ... unlikely ... you had that illness in childhood. Also, you had checked out of your hotel, but were not registered at any other hotel in London. I telephoned every single one. After two full days on the telephone, I finally concluded that you must be staying at some private address. Therefore it had to be a girl.'

She shrugged. `Then when you returned and immediately ended your association with Linda, followed by your trips back to England.'

After a silence, Marc turned his head and looked at her. `Well, go on. You know so much. Tell me more.'

`No,' she said softly. `You tell me, Marc.'

`There's nothing to tell.'

`So, your relationship with this English girl, it is over now? It was just ... a brief romance?'

Marc glanced at his watch and turned. `We'd better head back. It'll soon be dark, and I have to get back to the Base.'

Another silence followed as they strolled back. Eventually Jacqueline spoke again, very softly.

`Darling Marc, I wish you would tell me about her.'

`Why?'

`Because I know you are troubled. And I wish to help you.'

`*Maman*,' he said, speaking to her now in French, `I know you mean well. But my private relationships are no concern of yours.'

Jacqueline accepted the rebuke calmly, squeezing his arm as if to say yes, she understood that to be so. `But,' she said after a few minutes, `I was so pleased for you when you returned from England. You looked so happy. This English girl, I thought, must be a very nice girl. Very special.'

`Yes, she was.'

`And beautiful?'

`To me, yes.'

`Yes, she made you happy. She was good for you. Oh, I think I would have liked her. Were you in love with her?'

`Yes.'

Jacqueline sighed wistfully, `Oh, I wish so much I could have met her. What were her special qualities, this special girl? I am a romantic, so I would like to know what it was that made you like her so much?'

`Well, she was very gentle, very feminine, and ... ah, I can't explain it in words...One thing, though, that I particularly liked ... she was never aggressive. Not even when she was angry – I can't stand aggressive women. I get enough of all that in the Army.'

`Did you sleep with her?'

He shot her a wry, sideways glance; but gave no answer.

She squeezed his arm mischievously and giggled. `*Chéri*, I am not a prude. I know what goes on with the young. I *know*. And so ... on the last night, you could not bear to part from her, this special girl, and so you went to her room and slept with her. Yes? Am I right?'

`No. We went to her room on the first night we met, and slept together every night after that.'

`Ah. Instant passion.' She smiled. `So French! But the English.... were her family not shocked?'

`She has no family.'

`No?'

`She lives alone.'

`And what does she do? How does she earn a living?'

`As a waitress. That's where I first saw her. In the restaurant.'

`And now? Why is it all over now?'

Marc seemed to think about that for a long time. They had reached the gardens of the house before he finally answered. `She met someone else.

Jacqueline glanced away with a silent sigh of relief. Well thank God for that!

`You're very clever, aren't you?' Marc murmured. `I should have known that somehow you would persuade me to tell you what you wanted to know. So? Now I've told you everything else, don't you want to know her name?'

`No. Her name is of no importance,' Jacqueline said decisively. `You and she are finished now. So it is best to forget her.'

She turned to him suddenly. `It is best, Marc. To forget her. And try never again to think of her. In the end, she would have made you very unhappy. Someone like that. Now don't frown. You know it is true.'

`No,' Marc replied, `I don't know it's true. I don't know what the hell you're talking about. And *you* don't even know *who* you are talking about!'

`Marc,' she said angrily, `I don't need to know who. I don't need to know anything more. And please do not speak to me like that. I do not deserve it, because I am thinking only of you. Already this girl has made you very unhappy. These last weeks you are like a different person, a stranger. You are so *rash*. So *unpredictable*. You break appointments with hardly any notice.

You lose your temper at the smallest thing. This girl is not worth such anger. Your pride is hurt, I understand that, because this girl was stupid enough to choose another man instead of you.'

Her dark eyes flashed – it was an insult to herself as well as her son. This slut of a waitress – to turn up her nose at the son of a Castineau!

'Someone like that,' she said with contempt. 'How dare she? Someone like that – to think she is too good for someone like you.'

'Now wait a minute! *What* do you mean? "Someone like that!"'

'Very well,' Jacqueline replied coldly, 'if you are too young, and too blind to see it for yourself, I will explain this girl to you. She works as a waitress; so she is obviously not very intelligent. She slept with you, a stranger, the first night she met you; so she is obviously highly immoral. Or as the Americans would say—a tramp, a slut. Do you think your father or I would allow you to become seriously involved with someone like that? You deserve better, Marc. You are well rid of her. Thank God she was stupid enough to find someone else.'

Marc stared at her as if she had knifed him. He tried to speak, but she gave him no chance.

'No, Marc—' she held up a quietening hand. 'I will not allow this subject to cause any more discord between us. You are my son, and I love you with all my heart, so I will not allow you to destroy your life. One day, in the future, when you are happily married to someone more suitable here in New England, you will come to me and apologise and tell me that I was right.'

'I doubt it.' Marc's eyes and voice were now as cold as hers. 'Because everything you have concluded about her so far, is wrong, wrong, wrong.'

He turned and walked away from her. She took a hasty step after him, called his name, but he ignored her. By the time she had walked back to the front of the house, he had already driven away.

`What made him go?' Alexander looked crestfallen when she returned to the house alone. `He never even said goodbye. What made him drive off like that?'

`You did,' Jacqueline said quietly.

`Me?'

`Yes, *you*!' She turned on him with venom. `All your talk about Linda! Almost *pushing* Marc into an early marriage with her. If you had not done that, he would not have been so ready to fall in love with the girl in England. He would not be so upset now!'

`The girl in England?' Alexander immediately stiffened with alarm. `*What* girl in England?'

Jacqueline sighed, then suddenly patted Alexander's arm in a comradely fashion. Yes, yes, in something like this, at least, she and Alexander would be allies.

`Alexander,' she said softly, `I am very worried about our son. I need your advice.'

Alexander almost collapsed, especially when she sat close to him on the sofa, lifted his hand gently in both of hers, and spoke to him softly . . .

Five minutes later, Alexander reacted as Jacqueline had expected. Jumped up and – as the Americans say – blew his top!

`Is he crazy? Is he on drugs? A two-bit waitress? No family! Oh, wouldn't Linda's parents laugh at something like *that*! Chrissakes – this frigging generation!'

He suddenly paused, frowned. `But, listen, wait a minute – if this girl in England has now moved on to another guy, where's the problem?'

`He is still in love with her,' Jacqueline said. `He is still thinking about her. And now he has his own money from my father's trust fund, he can afford to fly back to England whenever he likes, at a moment's notice ... ' A shiver seemed to ripple through her entire body.

'Alexander, we must somehow make him realise how very unsuitable this girl would be.'

'Yeah.' Alexander stood for a moment looking thoughtful. 'Yeah!'

He sat down beside Jacqueline again. 'It's what? Three weeks to Christmas. So what we'll do,' he said cunningly, 'is get him to join us for dinner here and there over the Christmas period. Good restaurants, good food – but we'll treat the waitresses like *dirt!*'

Jacqueline closed her eyes. Such lack of subtlety had always appalled her. She opened them again and smiled ingenuously at her husband.

'No, Alexander, we cannot be so obvious. But perhaps ... a little subtle scorn? Marc, as you know, is a very proud young man. And few young men of pride can tolerate scorn, especially in their choice of women.'

Fourteen

London
December 1963

_____/

`Seven weeks,' Chef said to her suddenly one night. `It's now seven weeks since Valentino last phoned us. What happened between you two?'

Marian looked vague, and pretended not to hear him, wandering back into the restaurant with a frown on her face – seven weeks? It seemed like seven months.

Months ... months ... she still did not know how many months pregnant she was. Was it two? Or was it almost three? If it happened the day of the park – it was two. If it happened before – it was nearer three.

She knew she should go to the doctor, but she was too frightened to go to the doctor. He might tell the authorities – a Barnardo's orphan – unmarried and pregnant and cooped up alone in an attic – they would send their spies up to see her, women with smiles as mushy as mashed potatoes. `We want to help you, Marian. We want to help you.'

Then as soon as the baby was born they would take it away, and tell her it was all for the best ... the best for the child.

And what would they give her in return? Counselling. It was their answer to everything – counselling. Even when she was in the hostel, after she had left Barnardo's, they had insisted on giving her regular counselling.

She didn't need any more counselling. She needed more *books!* The answers to all life's problems were to be found in books. The writers and publishers made sure they were.

So began her morning trips back and forth to the library: she knew all about babies, but how were they delivered – the

136

technicalities – that's what she needed to know. The books would tell her.

'I'm studying to be a midwife,' she nervously told the librarian, as she checked the pile of books out.

'How nice, dear,' replied the librarian, and immediately passed on to the person behind her, stamping more books as Marian breathed a sigh of relief.

Earnestly she studied, frowning as she read about the three stages of labour: not pushing too fast or hard at the end. Breathing evenly and deeply, and when the moment came, letting the baby's head come out carefully. The breathing was very important

She would have to do it in a semi-sitting position, she decided, sitting on a towel on the floor, so she could lean forward and hold the baby's head as it came out. Then after the baby, the placenta, then cutting the umbilical cord and clamping it.

Clamping it? She looked at the picture and decided she would use an ordinary clothes peg.

Then what?

She closed her eyes, frantically massaging her temples with her fingers, and tried not to think about it any more. If she did, she would only get more confused. All she knew for certain was that she was going to have a baby, and no one must know about it.

She stood up and studied herself sideways in the mirror – but, no, nothing showed. Not yet. As soon as it did, she would buy herself a strong girdle and keep her stomach squeezed in for as long as possible. Maybe it would be only a little baby and not show much at all, not until the last few months – a little girl.

A girl? So why did she keep thinking of it as 'he'? Well it didn't matter. Whatever it was, it was a good baby. She had not yet suffered one morning of sickness, no nausea at all, just a slight heaviness in her breasts when she awoke, but it soon passed.

Meanwhile she would save up every penny until she began to noticeably put on weight; then she would tell Chef she was going to live with Marc in America. After that, she would stay at home in her room until the baby was born. She would deliver it herself, with the help of the books; then she and the baby would go away somewhere. To some big seaside town like Blackpool where they had lots of strangers and lots of restaurants and she would quickly get work.

A sensation of misery slowly swept through her as she stood looking around her room – the photographs she had taken of Marc now stood in frames on every surface – *Oh Marc, how could you believe that I would ever love anyone else?'*

Because that's what she had told him. So believably. It had seemed the right thing to do at the time. So why did it not seem so right now?

An hour later she put on her warm navy coat and black knitted gloves and started the journey into work. Less than two weeks to Christmas. Bright decorations were beginning to twinkle everywhere.

What would she do at Christmas?

She would go back to Barnardo's for the day and spend it with Miss Courtney. Christmas Day at Barnardo's was always wonderful. The staff did everything possible to make the day very special for the children. And bags of fabulous presents were always sent in by the local community. Every window was decorated with lights, and after the traditional dinner there would be a big party with lots of sweets and games.

As she descended into the underground, she smiled at the thought of Christmas Day at Barnardo's. She had always loved it. And Miss Courtney always looked very tired at the end of it, but her blue eyes would be sparkling with satisfaction.

She sat on the tube-train and found herself staring at her reflection in the blackness of the opposite window. A dark-haired girl in a navy wool coat surrounded by a dreary yellow light. She was a disgrace. Only two years out in the world and already she was pregnant. After all their care and training, she had let them down. Miss Courtney and everyone at Barnardo's. They must never find out. They must think she had gone to a new life in America.

`Dear oh dear,' said Chef when she entered the kitchen, `what's the matter now?'

`Matter?' She looked at him in puzzlement. `Nothing is the matter, Chef.'

`Oh I *am* glad!' Chef exclaimed, inserting two halves of peeled garlic inside a piece of steak. `I only asked because I do like to assure myself, now and again, that you are not unhappy.'

She smiled affectionately at him. `I'm happy, Chef, I'm happy.'

`You don't *look* it,' Chef said quietly, trimming his steak. `In fact, since Valentino stopped calling, you've looked, well – shall we say – terminally ill? Is it a broken heart, I ask myself. Or is it something else?'

He put his knife down, lifted the steak off the meat board and carried it over to his grill.

`Even my darling Sofia has noticed it,' he went on. `She noticed it when she came in here last week to show me the Mass card and ten-page letter of sympathy she had finally finished writing to Mrs Kennedy and wanted me to check the English. Do you remember that, Marian?'

`I remember,' Marian said, reluctantly smiling as she remembered Chef telling his lovely warm-hearted Italian wife that she could not punctuate every sentence to Jackie Kennedy with the word *Dio!*

`Well,' said Chef, keeping his eyes on the flame of the grill, `when I arrived home later that night, Sofia said to me, "*Angelo mio* – can't you see that Marian is not well! Her face is white and she has lost all her smiles. *Si, Alberto* – she is either ill, or

139

her heart is suffering from some tragic *amoré*."'

Marian attempted to giggle it off. 'Sofia has always been too dramatic. I'm not ill, Chef, not even a little bit. It's just winter that makes me go white and feel so cold.'

'But *cara*, I said to Sofia,' Chef continued as if she had not spoken, 'what can I do? How can I help our poor white-faced Marian? Shall I feed her on steak and forbid her to eat so much salad? Peter – why are you crying?'

'It's the onions, Chef, it's peeling all these bloody onions!'

'Ah,' Chef sighed, 'how lucky you are to have only onions to cry over. How lucky, dear boy. Get down on your knees and thank God for being so kind to you! A plate, please, Marian.'

Marian handed him a large white plate on which he started to arrange some bright green baby-lettuce.

'Yes, I said to my Sofia,' Chef continued as he worked, 'our Marian looks like a sad picture of doomed youth, all her hopes dashed, all her smiles gone. But what can I do? Shall I phone up Valentino at that military base in Massachusetts and ask him why he took away her innocence then broke her heart? Shall I do that, Sofia? Shall I phone Valentino? And do you know what Sofia said? Oh, she was very angry. As angry as a Mafiosa Godmother. She said "*Si, Alberto!* Phone up that *figlio de putana* and ask him why he de-virgined a nice young girl then heartlessly told her *arrivederci*."'

'Oh, Chef, stop!' Marian said irritably. 'I know you're playing games with me, and I know Sofia said none of those things, and it's *not* funny! And – and,' she shouted, suddenly furious with Chef, '*I don't know anyone called Valentino!*'

She rushed into the staff-kitchen, put on her apron over her black sweater and skirt, washed her hands and tightened her pony-tail, then walked back through the main kitchen without even glancing at Chef.

She would ignore him all night. She would hand him the food orders, and collect those that were ready, and refuse to speak a word to him. She would make him sorry for amusing himself at her expense.

Less than an hour later, she felt her first wave of nausea. Someone had stubbed a number of cigarettes out on their plate, even though a clean ashtray was provided, and the sight of the black ash and twisted filters stuck inside a mashed-up tomato turned her stomach.

She sat down at the empty table and drew a number of deep breaths; calm, calming breaths – until the unsettling wave of nausea passed. She quickly stood up and removed the plates into the kitchen.

When Chef saw the plate it was too much for him also. He furiously struck his knife into the meat board with a thump.

`How could anyone behave with such disgusting table manners in my beautiful bistro!' he demanded to know. `How could they have so little respect for those who have to clean up after them!'

She refused to answer him, refused to share his rage. She even refused to feel sympathy for Peter who wiped his eyes and said tearfully, `I've done all the onions.'

She walked back into the restaurant, still feeling slightly faint from the sight of the awful plate.

She looked around, saw she had no customers waiting, and wandered over to a small table for two at the back of the restaurant.

She sat down and clasped her hands together on her lap, gazing out the window and wondering what she could buy Miss Courtney for Christmas? Nothing expensive. She had to be very careful with her money now ... Perhaps some nice writing paper and envelopes? That would be useful. Miss Courtney kept in touch with all her ex-Barnardo children and spent half her life writing letters to them all.

`Just once or twice a year, to keep in touch,' Miss Courtney would say. `And we do like to know if any of them intend to get married – so we can send a representative from Barnardo's to the church with a small wedding gift.'

Marian nodded to herself. Yes, writing paper, that's what she would get for Miss Courtney. And what for Sofia?

As she wondered about this, she had a moment's dizzying vision of Marc walking into the restaurant, black leather jacket and jeans. She felt the old familiar rushing of excitement, then sighed heavily and turned her eyes back to the window. She was always having that vision, almost every day, gazing at the world with dream-dust in her eyes, and seeing Marc walk into the restaurant in a haze of wishful thinking.

He sat down at the table, on the chair opposite her, and looked at her silently for a long moment. 'I could kill you,' he said quietly.

She sat looking back at him with a puzzled frown, her brow puckering, then her eyes slowly widening as she realised it *was* Marc – there – in front of her eyes, not some regular figment of her imagination. Her heart began thumping in the way it always did when she saw him. His eyes were absorbing every detail of her face again, but this time he looked very angry.

'I've got a taxi waiting outside,' he said. 'Get your coat.'

'I can't...' she said faintly. 'I can't just leave...'

'Oh, you want me to go see Chef again? Okay, I'll do that.' He stood up and strode towards the kitchen. She made no attempt to follow him, too stunned to do anything but turn her head back and sit staring down the restaurant as if staring through a thick blanket of fog.

He came back into her vision, holding her navy coat. Chef must have got it for him, or told him where to get it, or maybe Chef had sent Peter to get it. Marc threw the coat onto her lap. 'He said you can go.'

'No, I ... I must speak to Chef myself.' As she moved to stand up something clicked in her knee and she almost stumbled. Her coat fell to the floor. The fog was still floating thickly before her eyes.

Marc bent and picked up the coat and roughly shoved it into her hands. 'There's no need to speak to Chef. I've just done that.

Put your coat on.'

He made no move to help her as she struggled into her coat, but once it was on, he caught her elbow and she found herself being steered towards the door and out to the street. She stopped in the cold air and turned to look at him in bewilderment.

`Marc—'

He didn't answer her, just pushed her on in front of him towards the waiting taxi, and she almost stumbled again.

`You mustn't push me like that!'

`I could kill you!' He opened the door of the taxi and pushed her again, inside the cab, and as she fell onto the seat she began to feel frightened of him.

`Why have you come back?' she faltered.

`I don't want to talk until we get to your room,' he said quietly. `So until then why don't you be a good girl and just shut the fuck up.'

`Don't *speak* to me like that!'

He didn't answer her, didn't apologise — and she knew he was as resolute as she had been earlier with Chef. They sat apart in the back of the taxi, looking towards their own side-windows in silence.

`I've left my shoulder-bag in the restaurant,' she said with sudden realisation. `And my gloves. Can we go back and get them?'

`No.'

She remained silent, pale, staring out at the passing traffic, dreading to think what might happen once they got back to her room. He hated her. He was still not prepared to forgive her. So why had he come back?

Then it slowly dawned on her — Chef *had* phoned him. Chef had found out the number of the military base in Massachusetts and phoned him. And that's what Chef had been doing earlier in the kitchen – not playing games – but trying to warn her. He had phoned Marc, and knew that Marc was on his way.

When the taxi stopped, she climbed out reluctantly, feeling afraid, although she was not quite sure what she was afraid of.

While Marc paid the driver, she walked quickly to the front door, then had to wait and ring the bell because without her bag she had no keys. The old lady from the ground-floor flat opened the door to her – a few moments of polite chitchat – then Marc followed her silently up the stairs.

Step by step they walked up the five flights in silence. It was very dim and very quiet and she could hear the sound of her own breathing.

When they reached her own private little landing, she remembered again that she had no keys, and went into the bathroom, her hands trembling as she removed a spare set of keys from an empty bath-salts jar.

Marc was leaning against the door-frame of her room when she came out, his eyes fixed on the floor. She could sense a fierce tension in him, like an angry animal waiting to spring. She began to feel frightened again.

`Marc—'

He sighed irritably, snatched the keys from her hand, opened the door, and pushed her inside.

`Don't *push* me like that!' she said again, backing away from him as she suddenly realised he had come to kill her. He was half-French. This was going to be a *Crime Passionnel*. Her imagination spun into overdrive as she watched him looking silently round the room, his eyes seeing all the framed photographs of himself.

`Your new lover blind, is he?'

`No.'

`No?' He abruptly swung round and seized her shoulders, gripping them so tight she thought her bones would break. `No! He's not blind or anything else – because he doesn't exist! Does he?'

`No.'

`So why did you say all those things? All those lies! Why did you do that to me?'

'I don't know! I don't know why I said all those things. I was confused and upset and it seemed right at the time. But then – when I began to miss you so unbearably – it didn't seem so right any more.'

'Why did it seem right in the first place?'

'Because I didn't want you to end up hating me. I couldn't have borne that ... But all I did was to make you hate me anyway.'

'I don't hate you. But I'm having a tough time trying to understand you. Marian – just what in the name of sweet Jesus are you *talking* about? I know I'm jet-lagged, and I can hear what you're saying, but not one word of it makes sense.'

Now she became as confused as he. 'Don't you know? Didn't Chef tell you? Isn't that why he phoned you? Because he knew? Because Sofia told him. Italian women always know these things,' she said, beginning to talk to herself. 'It must have been Sofia. That ten-page letter to Jacqueline Kennedy – that was just a ploy. Although there *was* a ten-page letter to Mrs Kennedy, but I remember thinking it strange that Sofia should come all the way into town just to get Chef to check the English. It's something he would do at home, not at work. No, Sofia came in because Chef asked her to come in and spy on me. I remember now, the way she kept watching me—'

'Oh Christ – I can't breathe – you're as bad as Jimmy – as bad as Chef and his mad Italian wife – as bad as my father and mother.' He walked over to the sash-window and quickly pushed the lower half open. 'All the time,' he said, bending to breathe in the air. 'people talking to me, talking, talking, talking, saying ridiculous things, and none of it making sense.'

'Marc, it's freezing! Please close the window.'

'But I would get some sense from you, I thought,' he continued, looking down at the street. 'Or would I just get more lies? I didn't know. But I get here – and what? You're as mixed-up and crazy as the rest of them.'

'Insult me now. Go on. Keep doing your worst!' she said, beginning to shiver with indignation as well as the cold. 'First you drag me out of work, then you push me, then you swear at me, and *now* you're trying to give me pneumonia.'

'I'm *trying* to find out what's going on.' He turned and looked at her. 'Just for my own satisfaction, you understand?'

'Didn't Chef tell you?'

He looked up to heaven for patience. 'All Chef told me was that there was no other man in your life. Never had been. Accused me of treating you shamelessly. Demanded to know why? Man to man? A straight answer. Wouldn't even believe me when I said it was *you* who had said goodbye to me. Just went on and on about his poor girl looking so white, so haunted, her sad, beautiful face, so broken-hearted ... and all because I didn't phone anymore, because I didn't come to London anymore. Then his wife came on the phone shouting abuse in Italian—said I was a heartless American something-or-other who had de-virgined a nice English girl and if I came back to London she would get Chef's knife and cut off my *cazzo*!'

Marian's burst of laughter came without warning.

Out of the relief of Marc returning, and the knowledge that Chef and Sofia would go to such lengths on her behalf, burst a flood of hysterical emotion which had been bottling up inside her for endless weeks.

She collapsed into the chair and laughed so much he had to slap her face. And when he did that she began to cry, heaving in a paroxysm of suffering that blinded her vision. He was talking to her, but she couldn't hear him through her sobs. All she could feel was the cold, her body shivering uncontrollably.

Marc quickly shut the window, closed the curtains, lit the gas-fire, then began to rub her arms and back vigorously. She could feel the warmth coming back to her blood, but she was still shivering and crying. 'It's – it's – it's the shock,' she said shakily. 'You just c- c-coming back without w-w-warning.'

'Are you feeling any warmer?'

'I'm going to have a baby,' she said timorously.

He reacted as if he hadn't heard her at first, his hands still rubbing her arms and back in the way he must have been trained to do when faced with someone cold with shock. Then slowly ... slowly her quiet words connected their meaning to his mind, and he went very still, drew back and stared at her wet face.

'I think I'm going to have it in June,' she said, pulling a tissue from her coat pocket and wiping her eyes, 'but I'm not sure. If it happened the day of the park, then it will be the end of June. But if it happened before, when you came on leave, then it will be two weeks before. I don't really know when.'

He moved away from her, turned his back on her, stood for a moment with a hand on his head, as if trying to control his anger.

'I could kill you,' he said again. He swung round to face her. 'You mean you put me through all that – put yourself through all that – because you're *pregnant!*'

'Well—'

'What kind of a mixed-up crazy person are you? Why couldn't you just tell me?'

'Oh yes – shout at me now!' she shouted angrily. 'I knew you'd blame me. That's why I didn't tell you. I didn't tell you because I didn't want you to feel forced to marry me. I wasn't going to tell anyone. I was just going to have my baby in secret and then go away somewhere.'

'Wait ... wait a minute.' He now had both hands on his head as if still trying to get his mind around all this. 'What do you mean, you were going to have your baby in secret? How can you have a baby in secret? Have you been to a doctor?'

'I need a cup of hot tea,' she said quickly, standing up unsteadily. 'Tea is the best cure when feeling cold. Heats you up from within.' She moved towards the kitchenette. 'Would you like some tea?'

'I'd like to kill you – if having your baby in secret means what I think it means.'

She turned round indignantly, and her knee clicked again, she grabbed onto the back of the armchair. 'That's about the *tenth* time you've threatened to kill me since you came back.' She clenched her fists angrily. 'Well, all I can say is ... I'm glad I didn't tell you before!'

'Marian ...' He tried to speak very calmly. 'Marian, I just want to know—' He frowned. 'Why are you hanging onto that chair as if you're about to collapse?'

'It's my knee,' she explained. 'Something keeps going wrong with my knee.'

'Let me see?'

'See what?'

'Your frigging knee.'

'At least the swearing has now modified,' she observed, hopping round the chair on one foot and sitting down. She no longer felt upset, but very bad-tempered. 'Do you have any medical experience?'

'No, of course not. If ever I find myself in a combat zone with an injured buddy, I'm trained to tell him a bedtime story and kiss him goodnight while waiting for the helicopter to arrive.'

He was squatting down in front of her, his hands examining her left knee. He pressed with his fingers. 'Does that hurt?'

She winced. 'It didn't before *you* came back! There's never been anything wrong with my knee until today.'

'You're so childish at times,' he said, his attention on her knee, 'childish and womanly and adorable, and your legs are very feminine. I could kill you, and eat you, then kill you again for almost driving me out of my mind.'

'Do you still hate me?'

'I've always loved you.' He pressed his fingers hard – her knee clicked – she gasped. 'Stand up,' he suggested. 'See if it's okay now.'

He lifted her arm and put it round his neck, then drew her up to standing position. She stamped her foot, and looked surprised. 'You've fixed it.'

It happened before either of them could think about it – a sudden clinging together in trembling love, his mouth on hers, his hand touching her face and hair. He spoke to her, softly, emotionally, incoherently, and she agreed with him, her own mutterings as incoherent, her hands caressing him, reassuring him ... she loved him ... she loved him ... she did not realise how much she had hurt him.

'It was the baby. I didn't want you to despise me or the baby.'

'That's just it,' he said, drawing back from her a little, 'that's what I don't understand. That's why it never once occurred to me that you might be pregnant. If you were to get pregnant, I thought it was something you would tell me straight away. Something you would want us to face together.'

He looked sadly and searchingly into her face. 'Why should you think I would despise you or the baby?'

She started to tell him her reasons, and as he listened, he began to understand what she was trying, sometimes inarticulately, to explain.

But he disagreed.

'No, you weren't being grown-up and sensible; you were being damned unfair in your assessment of me. Credit me with some intelligence, Marian. I knew the risks we were taking. And I gave thought to it. And if it happened, well then it would be our baby, and my responsibility.'

'Oh, Marc, don't you understand, that's just what I *don't* want to become – your *responsibility*.'

'Well you are, whether you want it or not, you *both* are. You and the baby. Have you been to see a doctor?'

'No, I was too frightened to see a doctor, because I thought they might try and take the baby away.'

'Who? Who's they? Who's *they*?'

`The authorities – they do that kind of thing. They come when you're not expecting them and take the child away. They did it to a child in Barnardo's. Just walked in and took her from her mother. She cried for days after they brought her in. And she was *six years old*. Crying and crying and wanting to know why the smiling women had taken her from her mummy. They wouldn't even let her finish the boiled egg her mummy had cooked for her. But that's what they did – just took her – the smiling women. Gave her to Miss Courtney and Miss Courtney gave her a boiled egg and I gave her some sweets.'

`Marian, listen,' he said tiredly, `no one's going to take the baby away. So forget about that. Put it out of your mind and don't think of it again. What we've got to do now, is sit down and talk this through rationally.'

`Shall I make some tea?'

`I'd prefer coffee.' He smiled slightly. `We're not too fond of tea in the Boston area, you know.'

`Oh ...' she said, and did not make the connection until a few seconds later. `Oh yes, the famous Boston tea party – well, I think it was a stupid thing to do, dumping all that tea in the river. We never wasted *one single leaf* of tea in Barnardo's. I remember saying to Miss Courtney how *stupid* the Americans were – because King George didn't care about all that tea being wasted – didn't give a hoot!'

He smiled again, his eyes slightly bemused. `Shall I gag you now or later? What is it - all this sudden and ridiculous talking of yours? You weren't like this before. Is it something to do with being pregnant?'

She compressed her lips and looked back at him with tears glistening in her eyes. `It's excitement,' she confessed. `And nerves.'

`Nerves?'

`Yes, *nerves!*' she cried, erratically holding out her two hands in front of her so he could see they were shaking.

`I'm all excited and a bundle of nerves because I still can't

150

believe we're really having this conversation! I still can't believe you came back! That you're really here! That you still love me! I can't believe—'

`Sh-sh-sh!' He caught her into his arms and held her tightly. 'I can't believe it either,' he said softly. 'My lost love ... my pregnant girl ... when I walked into the restaurant and saw you sitting there, my heart just turned over. You looked so beautiful, but so pale.'

He stood for a time just holding her. 'Marian, you're everything I want. Everything I love. Exactly as you are. These past two months I've suffered. And it just got worse instead of easing. So I know. I know who I want.'

The love and tenderness in his voice was almost too much for her. 'Marc, please don't make us talk things through rationally tonight,' she pleaded. 'I'm too tired after all my hysterics. I love you so much—' she kissed him. 'and all I want to do tonight is lie in bed with you again, and feel close to you again, and for us to go back to where we were.' She looked at him honestly. 'It's the only way I'll stop feeling so nervous.'

He looked over her shoulder at the bed – *the bed* – the one she had told him she had slept in with some other guy. It suddenly occurred to him that not once, since the first night they had met, had he ever refused her anything.

But the time had come.

`No,' he said firmly. 'No, I'm not sleeping in that bed. Not tonight. Not till I get my mind back in order. Not till we put things right between us.'

`Why?' she asked.

`Because, because,' he replied off-handedly. 'I don't want to.'

`You don't want to sleep with me?'

`Oh yes, I do!' he assured her quickly. 'But not in that bed. Look – just for tonight, let's go back to that hotel? The one we went to the day of the park.'

`The one where you made me pregnant?'

`Did I? That hotel? The day of the park? Okay, let's go back there and I'll make you pregnant again.'

She didn't think it was funny. 'To think of it!' she said in the taxi, having worked out why he wanted to go to a hotel. 'You *still* believe I had another man in our bed.'

'No, I don't! But I *did*.'

'Don't you know I would rather *die* than—'

'Marian, will you please shut up about it. That's the whole point of going to the hotel. To put all past thoughts behind us, while we make things right again. *Then* we'll sleep in the frigging bed.'

'You used to *love* that bed!'

'No, no, it was *you* I loved in that bed. Not the bed itself. Oh, Christ ... if I'd known you were going to get so upset about it.'

'And I still haven't had any tea,' she murmured.

'I'll get you some at the hotel. I'll get you a five-course dinner if it'll make you feel any better.'

She thought about that. 'I couldn't eat five courses. But I wouldn't mind a sandwich. Could you not just arrange for them to send up a pot of tea and a plate of sandwiches.'

'I'll do that.'

'And maybe some fruit?'

'And some fruit.'

'Thank you.'

'You're welcome.'

'Do you think ... if you asked them to just send up a tray of cold things, sandwiches and fruit, they might also put a few chocolates on the tray?'

'Chocolates?' He looked at her curiously. 'Do you *want* chocolates?'

'No,' she said quickly.

'Good. Because I don't think they'd serve them anyway.'

'No ... so it's a good thing I don't want any.'

She sat back and chewed her lip

After a long moment, she sighed dreamily. 'In the Savoy Hotel—I was reading this in a magazine, oh, just the other day—that in the Savoy Hotel, in all their rooms, in all the little cocktail bars, they don't just have drinks, but a box of chocolates in every one. And you don't even have to pay for them – the chocolates – they're on the house.'

`You *do* want chocolates.'

`No.'

`So why are you looking so dreamy?'

`I was thinking of the Savoy Hotel ... the sort of people who go there ... people who *would* like to have chocolates provided for them.'

`People like you?'

`Me?'

`Yes, you. You'd love to go to the Savoy, wouldn't you?'

`Me? The Savoy?' She stared at him, astounded. `Don't be ridiculous.'

`I knew it. Women always say that in a sneering way when they mean yes — "Don't be ridiculous!"' He leaned forward and slid open the driver's window. The driver tilted his head back while keeping his eyes on the road.

`Yes, sir.'

`Forget Russell Square. Go to the Savoy.'

`The Savoy? Right you are, squire.'

`Marc, what do you think you are doing?' she whispered.

`Celebrating. We're going to have a baby, aren't we? That's what people usually do. Go out and celebrate.'

`Do they?'

`Yes, they do. Only last week one of the girls at Fort Devens – a civilian who works for the military in one of the offices – she announced she was pregnant and everyone was congratulating her. Then her husband comes along, weighed down with flowers and grinning like a mad dog, showing all his teeth – like he'd just pulled off something real smart. So yeah, people do celebrate these things. And if *we* don't celebrate this baby's creation, then who else will?'

She looked at him sideways. `You're being very mature

about all this.'

'That's because I am mature, Marian. A lot more than you, thank God. I've always believed in being positive about things.'

'Oh yes, very positive,' Marian said. 'Is that why you didn't contact me for two months?'

A look of affront. 'Now, hey – that's unfair. I was *positive* you were with another guy. I didn't know you were all alone and pregnant. But I'm making up for it now. I'm taking you to the Savoy.'

She sat thoughtful. But what was he trying to make up to her? She was the guilty party. She was the one who had foolishly caused all the heartbreak. No, she could *not* let him spend all his money on taking her to the Savoy Hotel. There was simply no need for such extravagance. No need at all.

She turned to him.

'Marc ...'

He looked at her serious face and smiled.

'Marian ...'

'I don't want to go to the Savoy.'

'Too late.' He glanced out of the window. 'Because that's where we're going.'

By the time they reached the Strand, Marian was beginning to look desperate. 'Can you *afford* the Savoy?' she asked.

Marc's expression was doubtful. 'Probably clean me out. Leave me broke. But still,' he grinned, 'you *did* say the chocolates were on the house, didn't you? So I won't have to pay for them.'

'Oh, Marc – *look!*' She shrank back in her seat at the sight of one of the Savoy's doormen moving forward to open the door of the taxi. 'Look at his top hat! Look at his uniform! Look – he's wearing *white gloves*!' She shrank back even further. 'No, no, I can't go in there.'

'Why not?'

'Marc, only a few hours ago I was waiting on tables and cleaning away dirty plates. I can't go waltzing in there.'

'Now, hey, listen, ' he said, slightly angry. 'don't let these people intimidate you. You may be a waitress but what is he? – a doorman in a fancy uniform. All of them – all employees just doing a job like everyone else. So come on!'

He pushed her again, more gently this time, out of the taxi. Her outstretched hand was suddenly enfolded in a soft white glove, and she found herself looking into the face of the doorman who had one of the friendliest smiles she had ever seen, like Father Christmas.

'Welcome to the Savoy.'

In the foyer, Marian noticed the way Marc moved through the plush hotel as if he had been born to live in such places.

In the lift going up, she whispered to him, 'Did you order my tea and sandwiches?'

'Yes,' Marc said, refusing to whisper. 'I ordered a cold tray, a bottle of chilled Roederer's Cristal, and a pot of tea.'

'Oh, good,' she whispered, glancing nervously at the stiff back of the uniformed lift-attendant, then looked around her and whispered to Marc again, wondering if their room would be as large and elaborately-decorated as this lift?

'Elevator,' Marc said. 'In America we call it an elevator.'

'In England we call it a lift,' she replied pertly. 'And in England we are.'

Marc smiled. 'Touché.'

She whispered again. 'Did you book us in as a married couple?'

He nodded.

She strained even closer to his ear and whispered again. 'What's our name?'

'Would you believe?' he said out loud. 'I registered under the name of Gaines.'

She glanced up at the ceiling and decided that from now on, it might be prudent to keep her mouth shut until they got to their room.

As soon as they entered the room, her mouth opened in a

gasp. A beautiful room, with a sofa and matching armchairs, a huge vase of fresh flowers on the coffee-table ... floor-length windows, overlooking the river, blue velvet curtains ... utter luxury ... but there was something wrong.

`Where's the bed?' she asked Marc as he closed the door behind the bellhop.

`Probably in the bedroom.'

She turned then and stared at the two doors adjoining the room: one was half-open, and clearly a bathroom. The other, when she opened it, led into a room that looked like something out of a French palace – blue brocade chaise-longue, eighteenth-century furniture, and a luxurious bed.

`You ordered a suite!'

`Yep. A suite for my sweet.' He laughed. `Trust an American to be corny.'

`Oh, Marc, it's not corny, it's ... it's...' Her face screwed up as she tried to find the right word.

`Fitting,' Marc suggested, bending down and opening the door of the drinks cabinet. `After all, that's my son or daughter you've got in there, and in years to come I want he or she to know we celebrated the news of their existence in style.'

`Ah. Indeed!'

He turned his head and looked at her.

She smiled. `That's what Chef would say in answer to what you have just said. "Ah. Indeed!"'

`Here's your chocolates.' he said, taking a box from the lower shelf of the drinks cabinet and holding it out to her.

`Chocolate truffles! Oh Marc, how did they know – I *love* chocolate truffles!'

`And pistachios,' he said, handing her a jar of nuts. `Would you like a drink?'

`Yes, a nice hot cup of tea.'

Marc sighed. `You English.'

Outside in the corridor the overhead lights were sparkling.

Occasional noises. Occasional footsteps passing by unheard. Not quite eleven o'clock, life in the hotel still buzzed. Diners were still lingering over their coffee in the dining-room. Laughter and bright-eyed conversations still going on in the bar.

Inside the suite, the sitting-room was in darkness, the cold tray of smoked salmon and cheese and fruit, barely touched. The bedroom was warm and dimly lit, just one small light on the headboard, throwing a shaft of golden light down the centre of the bed like a ray of a setting sun.

Their lovemaking was gentle. He whispered over and over how much he loved her. She covered his face with soft kisses and promised undying love, and all the loneliness and pain of the past few months faded away.

Finally they lay close and relaxed and on the edge of sleep. As Marc lifted his hand to turn off the light, she whispered, 'You're the only man I have ever loved,' and Marc knew that was true.

Some time later she awoke and left the bed silently without waking him. She removed a pair of summer pyjamas from her overnight bag and covered her nakedness, then went to the bathroom. Only minutes after leaving the bed, she was back under the warm covers, fast asleep.

Then the dream began ...

She fell out of bed with a thump. Marc instantly awoke.

'Marian?'

He switched on the lamp then rolled over, and saw her sitting on the floor in a pair of blue pyjamas, her long hair tousled.

'Marian?' he whispered. 'Are you okay? Are you hurt?'

She didn't seem to hear him. She suddenly went down on her hands and knees and began feeling around the floor, as if searching for something. She seemed to be in a state of great distress as she searched, lifting up the cotton valance to look under the bed and muttering to herself.

`The peg? Oh crikey – where's the clothes peg? I need it for the clamp. Where's it gone? On the floor ... I *know* I put everything on the floor—' She began to sob herself. `It's gone! The peg – it's gone! Oh God....'

`Marian!'

She knelt up and looked at him, then scrambled back into bed, still muttering. She lay her head down on his arm and he gathered her legs towards him with his other arm. She sank into him, and was asleep again within seconds. He was not sure whether she had ever woke up.

He frowned. Why was she looking for a clothes peg? And when did she put on the blue pyjamas?

He glanced at his watch: ten minutes to four. They had gone to bed before midnight, but he had no idea what time they had gone to sleep. The warmth of her soft body began to seep into him, her warm breath blew gently on his neck, and he too drifted back into the oblivion of sleep, but even then he kept his hand on her so that he awoke whenever she moved.

The next time he awakened fully he saw daylight. He glanced at his watch: five past eight. She was still asleep at his side. He looked towards the window. Rain was falling now, spattering against the glass.

Unwilling to wake her, he continued watching the rain and thought about her, as he had done so often in Massachusetts. She was the one he wanted. As soon as he saw her again, he had recognised his certainty.

She was an idiot. A baby. A child. A beautiful and highly intelligent girl, and a gorgeous and womanly lover. She was elusively original.

His mother had never been more wrong.

A complicated childhood, a complicated life, he did not want a complicated love affair, but a love that gave him contentment and peace. With Marian he had found it. With Marian he had discovered a new and never-known experience — what it was

like to feel and touch happiness. And with Marian he always
slept peacefully, and never dreamed of blood on the walls.

He had no desire for tempestuous bouts of sexual combat
and intellectual conflict. He had no interest in other people's
glories or vainglorious wealth. He was not like the child who
had begged his parents to buy him the sun. He had never cried
for the moon. But in the blue of an English summer night, he
had found his own star.

At the end of his youth he had discovered the truth, and
realised that all he wanted was to live his own life and navigate
his own destiny. He had looked up at the sky, saw it was too
high, and walked on.

He had once walked all the way to Tennessee. One summer
day he had just closed the door behind him and started to walk,
hitching lifts at night, and walking in the day. He could have
caught a bus or a train, but he had no idea where he wanted to
go. So he just kept on going to wherever the trucks were going.

He was gone for months. Every now and again he phoned
home just to let them know he was okay, but any question to
him beyond that received only the click of the receiver, line
dead.

He made friends with innumerable strangers, slept in some
strange motels, cracked beer with cowboys in smoky pool-
rooms. And one night, in a deserted shack by a lonely creek, he
had eaten dinner with a cheerful black family, then he had gone
outside with them to a cluster of rickety old chairs, and sat
back under the stars and listened as the father played a guitar
while his wife sang about Jesus; and then, later, their son Leon
sang the Blues.

It was the start of his philosophical redemption, that journey.
When he returned home his mother performed a long tragedy.
The sorrow and the weeping and the drama of maternal love.
His father had played the masculine role – thumping the table
with an angry fist and roaring like a bear.

And then everything grew calm. He had stood watching and

listening to them in silence, and finally his silence had calmed them. His mother stopped weeping. His father stopped complaining. They may as well sit down to a nice family dinner together and forget all about it, his father decided. Since, after all, he was back now.

And nothing had changed.

His father still monopolised the conversation during dinner, telling him what he had said to this neighbour or that acquaintance about `My son.'

His mother had sat looking at him with red-rimmed eyes, and the expression on her face had filled him with pain and frustration. She was still seeing him in only one perspective – her own – seeing only *her* child, *her* son. Not the man that he was now. Not the man he had become.

Marian stirred beside him, but she did not wake. He could feel the slight undulation of her breast against his side as she breathed. He raised himself on his elbow and looked at her face. The bad dream that had troubled her in the night was gone now. She looked as peaceful as an angel slumbering on a cloud.

He stroked her hair and whispered softly, `C'en est fait des mauvais rêves, ah, c'en est fait,' then he put his lips on her beautiful mouth.

She awoke slowly, her eyes and smile radiant with warmth, her face rosy from the richness of her sleep.

`Marc—' her blue eyes opened wider with a faint look of surprise. Then her arms came up to hold him, drawing his mouth back to hers and kissing him, a wild, hungry kiss. She was holding him so tightly he could not have drawn back, even if he had wanted to.

He seized her around the body as they both became lusty again. His lips descended to her neck, her shoulders. He undid the last two buttons of her pyjama top and gently bared her breasts.

Afterwards, he whispered to her, `You're like two different

160

girls, childishly vulnerable and sexually beautiful.'

She smiled and rubbed his face with her palm. `I'm not childish.'

`No, no, you're not. Just in ways, sometimes, little ways. Will you marry me?'

The question seemed to catch her off-guard.

`Marry you?'

`Yes, marry me. Be my wife. Come back to America with me.'

She lay for a minute gazing at him thoughtfully, a sudden dark-blue look of sadness in her eyes, and then she quietly gave him her answer:

`No.'

At the airport Marc was still confused, still unable to comprehend her reasoning as she endeavoured to make him understand.

`I don't want you to do anything you will regret later.'

`Marian, you're going to have a baby in six months! Decisions have to be made. Arrangements have to be made. These things can't wait until you have finally made up your mind.'

`I've already made up my mind. I don't want us to marry, just because I'm pregnant. I want us to wait until after the baby is born, and then – then you can see what it would be like to be tied to a wife and a crying child.'

`After the baby is born – how long after?'

`I don't know...' she shrugged, and looked at him helplessly. `Maybe six months ... Maybe never ... if you finally decide you don't want to.'

He was so angry he turned away, his dark eyes ranging over the crowds of other passengers wondering if the whole world was mad.

He turned back to her. `Is that what you really want?' he snapped. `To be like your mother? A sad young waife with a babe in arms. Doing the best thing for one and all. You think

161

that's noble? Something to aim for? Christ, Marian, this is the sixties – no one marries anyone unless they want to anymore. When the fuck are you going to grow up?'

She covered her face with her hands and cried silently, her shoulders heaving. 'You don't understand ... I have to be sure ... I have to be sure that your decision to get married is a free one made by *you* – not forced on you by circumstances.'

Marc sighed. 'If you're not sure about me now, then you never will be.'

The last call for his flight came over the tannoy. Her head jerked back and she stared at him tearfully.

Marc sighed again, and took her in his arms. She lifted her hands and clung to him tightly, and the void between them was bridged.

'I will never love any other man, but you only,' she whispered, kissing his lips, softly at first, then hungry and passionate.

'Marian—'

But there was no more time, and Marc was forced to leave England feeling as confused as when he had arrived.

On the plane he tried to think about it rationally, consider the situation from her point of view, but still none of it made any sense to him. They were in love and expecting a child, and what they should do now was as clear to him as the blue sky.

He was still thinking about it ten days later as the seasonal cheer of Christmas buzzed noisily around him, but as the year came to an end, he gave up the quest and wrote in his private journal:

> *31 December 1963*
>
> *I am still at a loss to understand. Her letters and my telephone calls have solved nothing. The future remains unresolved. I cannot force her. She thinks it is me who is being forced. I cannot persuade her. She needs more time*

to persuade herself. Whenever I think of her alone in that room, I feel depressed. Before I left she allowed me to buy her a small television set. At the airport, as we said goodbye, she said: `Just keep coming back to me with love in your eyes.' Marian, oh Marian, you are mad.

Fifteen

London
July 1964

_____/

`I must have been barmy!' Marian thought feverishly, and gave another racking scream. `Insane to think I could go through this on my own!'

Someone pushed the gas-and-air mask back over her mouth. She clutched it and sucked deeply, but it didn't help, *didn't help!*

Outside the hospital it was a very warm July day, and the baby who should have been born at the end of June was now eight days post-mature. `Quite normal, quite normal,' she had been assured. `First babies usually come late.'

She screamed again, slapped away the hand holding the mask to her face, making small animal-like cries as her hands viciously thumped and threshed the sides of the delivery-bed. Red-hot knives were cutting up and down her lower back with no respite, and she could endure no more. No more! No more! She also knew something was very wrong.

So did the midwife. `Fetch the doctor,' she snapped at the nurse. `Her labour has gone on far too long, and there's still no sight of the head.'

The doctor came. The midwife explained quickly to save him looking at the notes. `Primigravida. Eight days post-mature. Labour induced with pessaries. First stage commenced twenty-six hours ago. Fully dilated...'

Marian's screams drowned out the midwife's voice. Her hair and face were soaking wet, her entire body on fire with pain.

`Pethidine,' the doctor said gently, then inserted a needle into her thigh, `I'm giving you a small shot of pethidine to take the edge off the pain.'

The doctor then sent for the obstetric consultant – a tall lady of middle years wearing a green gown and green theatre cap. 'Hello, Marian,' she said kindly, taking Marian's hand in both of hers and patting it tenderly. 'Having a hard time, are we?'

Marian stared at her with slightly-glazed eyes, and instinctively knew that help was at hand and she had found a friend. Or was it just the peth-a-something the doctor had given her, which was now easing the pain.

'Marian,' she said gently, 'baby is post-mature and very big. We think your pelvic canal may be too small for a normal delivery. The monitor is also registering rapid distress in baby's heartbeats, so we are going to put you to sleep while we give you a Caesarean section. Is that agreeable to you?'

'Put me to sleep? Take away the pain?' Marian grabbed the consultant's hand and covered it with frenzied kisses. 'I love you, I love you ... You're the best doctor in the world...'

Someone was pulling her wet hair back from her face, placing a cap on her head, her face was being wiped with a cold sponge, and a moment later she felt the hard stab of a needle going into the back of her hand.

'Marian, start counting from one to ten,' somebody said. And she did so, but blacked out on 'three....'

The light was blinding, making her blink and forcing her to close her eyes. Again and again, someone whispered to her.

She opened her eyes again and saw that the light was sunlight. She was in a room with flowered curtains on each side of the window. And now the only sound she could hear was blissful silence. Gone was the electronic ping of the cardiac monitor, the bustle of nurses and doctors, the clinking of instruments. All that had stopped when they asked her to count to ten.

Gone also was her pain, and the doctor, and the consultant in green, as if they had never been. As if it had all been a dream.

She stirred, and looked round the pleasant private room, then turned her head and saw Marc sitting beside the bed. He was holding her hand, but she was so groggy she had not known it.

'How do you feel?' he asked her.

'I feel ... like I died and was just reborn.' Her mouth felt dry, making her speech thick.

Marc poured her a glass of water, holding her head up while she drank it. The water refreshed her, clearing her mind as well as her mouth, and brought her back to life.

She looked at him curiously. 'When did you arrive?'

'A few hours ago. Miss Courtney telephoned me yesterday. She's still outside in the corridor.'

He gently kissed her face. She put her arms around him in her usual loving way, and then slowly she became aware of what had happened and why she was here. She broke away from him, tried to sit up, felt the soreness in her lower abdomen.

'Where's the baby?' She looked at the crib beside the bed and saw it was empty, turning back to stare at Marc with incipient fear. 'Where's the baby?'

Marc was smiling, his dark excited smile. 'Oh, he'll be back in a while. He's had a hard time too, so the paediatrician has taken him away to do a few tests.'

'Him? A boy? Are you sure?'

'Yeah, I think by now I can tell the difference.' Marc's excitement washed over her, bringing a delighted smile to her face.

'One hell of an angry little boy,' Marc grinned, 'screaming in fury when they took him away.'

'I want to see him,' she cried eagerly, pushing at Marc's shoulders. 'Go and get him, Marc.' She pushed again. 'Go and get him!'

There was no need. As soon as Marc reached the door, he heard the baby in the corridor, still yelling, and opened the door wider to admit the paediatrician, followed by the midwife.

'He's got healthy lungs,' smiled the paediatrician, a young man in a short-sleeved white tunic. 'And everything else seems just as healthy.'

'Eight pounds, eight ounces,' said the midwife. 'And I think he's going to be tall when he grows up. A six-footer I'd say.'

'Give him to me—' Marian pleaded excitedly, reaching for the baby. The paediatrician seemed relieved to hand the boy over to his nineteen-year old mother, and as soon as he did, the yelling stopped.

Even Marc stared in amazement as the baby's screams suddenly subsided to a trembling whimper, then stopped altogether as Marian held him close against her breast.

'He knows who I am,' Marian murmured. 'He knows I'm his mummy. He knows he is safe now.'

Then tears were suddenly slipping down her cheeks as she stared at her son, because his eyes were very black and his hair was very black, and she knew it was Marc who had been reborn.

'He's not big at all,' she said. 'He's tiny and fragile, and he was frightened ... My own little boy ...'

The paediatrician and midwife had seen it all before, but the miracle of new life was just beginning for Marian, overwhelming her, shutting out consciousness of all else as she covered the tiny face and tiny fists with loving little kisses, and still the baby did not cry: he yawned and closed his eyes contentedly, and let her carry on.

She was not aware of the paediatrician and midwife leaving the room, or even of Miss Courtney entering.

'Oh, how adorable,' Miss Courtney said, and then just stood for a long time just staring at the baby with a dumb adoring smile.

Finally, an eternity later, Marian laid the sleeping baby down in the crib at her side, and turned to see only Marc in the room.

'Isn't he wonderful?' she whispered. 'Oh Marc – how can I thank you for giving me such a treasure. Isn't he wonderful?'

167

'He's wonderful,' Marc agreed, and once again her arms came up to hold him, and for a long moment they remained close in silent joy.

'Okay, that's it,' Marc said suddenly. 'Now I've seen him and heard him yelling. Now I know the score. Now will you marry me?'

Marian smiled guiltily. 'I've been a bit barmy, haven't I? Stupid and childish and—'

'Yeah, yeah, I know all that,' Marc interrupted. 'But what I want to know now is – will you marry me? Make an honourable and decent man of me?'

Marian laughed. 'I can't wait.'

She lay back on the pillows, radiant in her happiness. 'Marian Gaines. I'll have a real name. A husband and son. A real family all of my own.'

She glanced at the sleeping baby in the crib. 'What shall we call him, Marc? You choose.'

'Philippe,' Marc decided. 'After my grandfather, Philippe Castineau.'

Sixteen

Massachusetts
July 1964
_____/

Three days later, a horrible feeling of impending disaster hit
Jacqueline. She knew it as soon as Marc walked in the door,
halfway through the day, when he should have been at the
Base. Now she knew that Jimmy had lied to her--that Marc
hadn't gone to Washington on an Officers' Course after all. She
knew it as soon as she saw that Marc was not in uniform. As
soon as she saw a *British* airline label on his travelling bag.

`You've been to England,' she said, her eyes wide with
realisation. `You've been to see that girl. The waitress. Yes?'

Marc nodded. `Yes.'

`I thought that was over. I thought you had recovered from
that ridiculous madness.'

`No.'

Something in his tone – something in his expression –
Jacqueline's face blanched as she realised something very
serious had brought Marc here today – something that had
made him come here straight from the airport, even before
reporting in back at the Base.

`I'm going to marry her,' Marc said. `I'm going to leave the
Army, buy myself out. Then I'm leaving the States and going
over to live in England for a while. But first I'm going to marry
her, and bring her to America to meet my family. And I want
you to welcome her.'

`No!' The awful shock in Jacqueline's eyes stunned him.
`Marry that girl and live with her in England? No!' she gasped.
`*No!* I will not allow you to marry her. I will *not* allow it!'

`I don't need your permission,' Marc reminded her quietly.
`Only hers. And now she has given it. So I'm going to marry

169

her. In a few weeks. And as soon as I can get her a visa I'm going to bring her here to Massachusetts and I want you, my mother, to welcome her into this family.'

'No!' Jacqueline repeated fiercely. 'No! Do you think I have suffered all I have suffered just to let you end up marrying someone like that!'

Alexander, who was supposed to be locked away in his study writing his new novel but had actually been having a snooze, came out to see what all the fuss was about.

'What, what? he mumbled, Then he blinked. 'Marc, what're you doing here in the middle of a weekday?'

'He's been to England,' Jacqueline snapped. 'To see the waitress. He says he is going to marry her.'

'Like hell he is!' Alexander instantly became fully awake. Jacqueline shot him a glance, which spurred him on.

'You must be crazy! Crazy if you think we're going to let our boy get caught up with some two-bit waitress in England – a nobody with no parents and nothing else.'

'Marc—' Jacqueline said more calmly, 'Marc, this romance with this girl – all young men, soldiers, on leave, in a foreign place, they meet a girl and think it is love. But when they marry, and the novelty wears away, they begin to feel –' she held out her palms and shrugged her shoulders in a French gesture – 'rien.'

'No,' Marc insisted, 'I could never feel that about her – not *rien* – not nothing. She means *everything* to me.'

'You say that now,' Jacqueline said. 'You think that now—'

'Please,' Marc begged, 'just agree to meet her. Both of you – just agree to meet her. If you don't want me to bring her here at first, well, then, in a week's time I'll be going back. So both of you – fly back with me to London, just for a week, or even a few days. Treat it like a holiday, stay at the Savoy – you both love the Savoy – and while you're there I'll bring her to meet you.'

'No!' Jacqueline's eyes flashed with volatile fury. 'No, I will *not* agree to meet her! I've already told you! I don't even want to know her name!'

She walked swiftly out of the room with an expression on her face that Alexander had seen only once before, in Paris, when she had walked swiftly away and seconds later had killed two SS officers, because they had dared to enter the same room as her son.

`She's feeling murderous,' Alexander said, and looked at Marc with blame.

And in that moment, Marc realised that Marian would never find any welcome in this house. Not from his mother or his father. Neither of them were prepared to give her even the smallest chance. Without even meeting her, both had decided that she was not good enough for them, didn't fit the bill, cut from the wrong cloth, all the sad, sad things that New York and Boston society bothered about.

`So, that's it,' he said resignedly. `I may as well go.'

`Go where?' Alexander demanded.

`To the Base.'

`I don't know why you joined the Army in the first place,' Alexander snapped, unaware of Marc's decision to leave it. `You've never said why. And you've never given a damn about how we felt about it – you throwing away your education at Harvard to join that bunch of bozos! Do you know how much you hurt your mother when you did that? Left Harvard and joined the Army. Broke her heart!'

Marc slowly looked at him. `You know why I joined the Army, Dad? To get away from you.'

`Me?' Alexander was astounded. `Why?'

`Because you're another Adolf fucking Hitler! Because you've been banging my brain since I was ten years old! Trying to turn me into a replica clone of you. But you'll never do it, Dad, know why? – *because I'm the grandson of Philippe Castineau.* And like him, no bullying Nazi will ever be given the chance to break *my* balls!'

Alexander was genuinely shocked. 'Marc ... Marc ... I only wanted the best for you. I only wanted–'

'You only wanted the best for *you!* Not for me. For *you* – Alexander Gaines, the great award-winning writer and war correspondent. I'll tell you what you've *really* wanted all these years, Dad. Not a son – just another fucking Pulitzer Prize.'

'That's not true ... That's not true ... Is it so terrible for a father to recognise his own gift reborn in his own son? And you *do* have the gift, Marc! You *could* be a great writer.'

Marc had heard enough, heard this a thousand times before. He turned and walked towards the door.

'A great writer,' Alexander repeated. 'They even said so at Harvard. Told me straight out! That Mr Whatsisname? The one with the red beard. Said you could be—'

'As good as you.' Marc smiled with faint contempt. He had paused at door, looking back. 'But that's not what I wanted, Dad. To be as good a writer as you or anyone else. I just wanted to be a man. My own man.'

'And so you joined the Army?' Alexander said sneeringly.

'And so I joined the Army,' Marc agreed.

'Trained to kill. Paid to die. Only a fool would join the Army, son.'

Marc walked out.

He went up to his room and dragged out a suitcase from the bottom of a closet. Then he went to his desk, took a key from his pocket and unlocked a drawer, removed all his private papers and diaries. Then to his bookcase, removing books, just the ones he didn't want to leave behind, packing them carefully on top of the papers.

His father entered the room.

Marc ignored him, and kept on packing.

'What are you doing?' Alexander asked. 'Why are you packing those things?'

'I'm clearing out,' Marc said. 'I'm taking only my personal

stuff and I'm clearing out. And this time I'm not *ever* coming back.'

'No, no,' Alexander said quickly, alarmed. 'No, don't do that, Marc. Don't leave. Think of your mother.'

'No. Not anymore. If you two are not prepared to give Marian a welcome in this house, then it's not a place I want to be. It's a place I'm *ashamed* to be.'

'Marc,' whispered Alexander, stunned, incredulous. 'Don't do this. You're all we've got now. You're the only reason we've stayed together all these years, your mother and I. You're the only thing we have in common. And that's why we've stayed together, because of you. Because we both loved our son.'

'Oh, come on,' Marc sighed. 'The only reason you've stayed around, Dad, is because of the Castineau money, and because you're still in love with my mother.'

'I sure wouldn't mind going to bed with her now and again,' Alexander admitted bluntly. 'Your mother is still one beautiful woman. She's got more sex in just a look from her eyes than any other woman I know. But well, she doesn't do that kind of thing anymore. Not for years. As celibate as a saint. Offers it all up to God instead. Some kind of penance.' He shrugged. 'But dammit, I don't care. At the end of the day, as Kipling said, a woman is only a woman.'

'But you still love her,' Marc said quietly. 'My mother.'

'Well, you know—' Alexander sighed heavily, 'she's impossible to live with. Your mother. One goddamned bitch. Cold as frost one minute, flashing fire the next. Sometimes I think perhaps I *do* still love her, but most days I hate her like hell.'

Marc impatiently slammed his case shut, wondering why he was even bothering to listen. His father was the one who was impossible to live with, always had been. He was arrogant and sarcastic and thought he was entitled to be a snob. But without the Castineau money he would have been forced to sell this house years ago, and get a job or live on welfare, because he had hadn't written a word worth reading in years. Not since his one-book wonder. Only the Castineau money allowed him to keep living in the comfort he was now accustomed to. He should at least give his mother some credit for that.

Alexander was leaning forward, staring into Marc's face, seeking a reaction.

Marc blinked out of his thoughts. `What?'

`You can see that, can't you, Marc? This girl in England, she's—'

`The person I intend to share the rest of my life with,' Marc interjected.

Alexander couldn't hide his exasperation. `Why, son? Why does it have to be that particular girl? Tell me – why the hell her?'

`Because she's my *type*. She's from the same intellectual and spiritual tribe as me. We get along without any effort.'

Alexander shrugged, unimpressed. `Bill Simons and me, we get along without any effort too. Doesn't mean we want to get married. Sounds to me like all you share with this girl is some kind of natural friendship.'

`And a whole lot of love,' Marc said softly, turning away to make a last examination of his bookcase. `You know the kind of love I mean? No other addiction like it. Big time and better than marijuana. The once-in-a-lifetime kind.'

On the top shelf he saw he had missed a masterpiece and lifted down his French original of *Madame Bovary*. `There's something else we share too,' Marc murmured. `A son.'

`A what?' Alexander jumped with shock, stared like an owl at Marc's back. `What's that you said?'

Marc glanced back at him. ``Born three days ago. In London. My son.'

Alexander's heart faltered for a second. `Don't you dare say anything like that to your mother,' he snapped. `You hear me? Don't you dare say anything like that to *her!*'

Marc was about to answer, changed his mind, turned to the

suitcase and carefully placed the book inside.

Alexander stood glaring at him. `Is that what she told you? This two-bit waitress. That her kid was your son? How do you know that? You spend most of your time at Fort Devens. But *she* knows that you come from a family with money. Right? *She* knows she'd have a rich ride and easy meal-ticket if she could get you to marry her. Oh, Marc, Marc, you may be a man but you still have a lot to learn. It's an old trick, that. The oldest trick in the world. Especially with two-bit white trash.'

Marc's fist crashed backwards across Alexander's face, propelling him against the chest of drawers.

Alexander stared at him, stunned, a hand touching his bloody lip. `You sonofabitch,' he stammered.

`Apologise!' Marc demanded, his eyes blazing with fury. He lunged forward and grabbed Alexander. `Come on, you fucking despot – down on your knees and apologise to me for what you just said.'

`Marc ... Chrissakes – you're choking me!'

Marc's hands were almost around Alexander's throat, the strength of his fury pressing down on his shoulders.

`*He* is mine! *She* is mine! And they are *both* my family now. So you'd better get down on your knees and apologise to me for trying to belittle the three of us!'

Alexander collapsed onto his knees, his eyes rolling in mortified rage. `I'll be damned if I'm going to be demeaned by my own son! I'll be damned if I'm going to be forced onto my knees like a dog! And all because of some bitch that—'

Marc struck a stinging back-hander across Alexander's face. `If you insult her again, so help me, I'll kill you!'

`God ...' Alexander gasped, and spluttered for help. `*Jacqueline!*'

`Ten seconds!' Marc held Alexander down on his knees with an iron grip. `You've got ten seconds to apologise, because dammit – for the first time in your life – you are *going* to apologise to me. Now do it!'

Alexander's rage suddenly melted into self-pity, certain of
his right to feel persecuted and grossly wronged. `This is so
unfair, so *damned* unfair. Marc ... I'm only forty-eight years old,
but already I've had a vein taken out of my leg and an
operation on my heart. And you know why? Because I've lived
one hell of a life with your mother. I mean one shit-awful life. I
can take it from her. But not from you. Chrissakes, Marc, the
last thing I want to do is fall out with you.'

`Two seconds!'

`All-fucking-right!' Alexander shouted. `I apologise! There!
Are you satisfied? Do you feel like a man now? I apologise!'

Marc let him go. Alexander fell back against the chest of
drawers; his breathing ragged as he pulled a handkerchief out
of his pocket and put it to his lip. He watched Marc grab up the
suitcase and walk towards the door.

`Marc, listen to me!' Alexander urgently rasped. `I know I'm
the devil incarnate in your eyes, but I'm still your father, and I
can't take any more today. So Marc, *please*, when you go
downstairs, don't say anything to your mother about any
bastard kid.'

It had grown warmer, windier, the air heavy with threat of a
storm.

Jacqueline had sought to cool off in the garden, but her anger
was still as fierce, and her resolve still as strong. Everything
and everyone else in the world meant nothing to her. Only
Marc. His happiness, his welfare, his life – ensuring he ended
up with the best of everything – was all that mattered to her
now. So how could she prevent him from making this terrible
mistake?

When a solution came to her, it was so detestable she almost
rejected it. A sulky pout settled on her mouth as she
contemplated it.

She hated the Army, hated the hold they had on Marc, hated
their authority and power, so much greater than her own. She

had been determined to beat them, win her son back, and at every opportunity she had used every subtle method to persuade Marc to buy himself out. But now – to keep him in America and prevent him from going to live in England, prevent him from marrying that girl – could she really do it?

Her eyes narrowed like slits, her emotions forceful and passionate. *Yes!* – she would do *anything* to keep him close to her and stop him marrying someone like that! It was bad enough that she, a Castineau, had married someone like Alexander. But Marc – *no* – for Marc she would accept only the best.

She walked slowly back into the house, her arms folded, her mind reflective. She met Marc in the hall, and looked solemnly at his suitcase.

`Don't,' Marc pleaded quietly. `Don't make me fight with you too.'

Jacqueline smiled, but it was an effort. `You and I never fought before you met this girl,' she said softly. `We have always been very close, you and I.'

`Yes, but—'

`But now you want to go away and lead your own life, yes?'

He stood looking at her in the same reflective way. `I've been leading my own life for years. You know that.'

`And it was I who gave you that life, Marc. Am I no longer allowed to be a part of it? Or have a say in it? You may be twenty-three, but I am still your mother.'

`Yes,' Marc agreed, unwilling to argue or quarrel with her. He truly did love his mother. And now, looking at her face, it hurt him to see her so whitely devastated.

He said quietly: `I can only say this to you: I don't want to hurt you, but nothing you say or do will stop me from marrying her.'

`Very well,' Jacqueline agreed calmly. `Marry her, as you wish. But before you do, Marc, will you do something for me? Now, before you leave?'

Marc was stunned by her capitulation. Slowly the expression on his face softened as he began to feel a marvellous relief. 'Of course. Whatever you want.'

She smiled and touched his arm gently. 'Come with me into the library.'

In the library she took a medium-sized leather-bound book from a glass case. He did not recognise it at first – not until it was too late – not until she had grabbed his hand and pressed it flat on top of the book.

'Your grandfather's Bible,' she said. 'Philippe Castineau! It has his fingerprints all over it, stains of his blood. You know all about this bible, Marc. You know he was reading it the night he died! *Philippe Castineau!* You cannot forget him! I will not allow you to forget him and what he did for you! The French must *never* forget the men and women who served and died in the Resistance! And so I remember – that night, only hours after he had tucked you up in bed, he was sitting in his chair in the salon, reading this bible and praying – *holding this bible and praying* – not for France, but for his family. Praying that you would have a better life than he had. Now swear on it, Marc, swear that you will not marry this girl until you have served out your time in the Army.'

'No!' He tried to drag his hand away, but her grip was as fierce as a tiger's. 'You have no right to ask me to do this. Christ—*you have no right!*'

'I have every right, Marc. For you I have done everything, suffered everything. For you I even killed two men to save you from harm. I have given you everything. What have I ever denied you? You have lived in luxury and received the best education that money could provide. Was it all a waste? Was it all for nothing? Are you now ready to turn your back on your childhood and pretend the boy I raised no longer exists? I not only gave you my love – I gave you my life!'

Marc could hear the torment in her voice, the despair and the anger. He felt a chill dread coming over him, and knew he

178

couldn't deal with this.

`And now, all I ask in return, is that you stay in the Army and serve your full time. Only twenty more months. That's all. So I ask you to wait – *wait* before you marry this girl – *wait* until you leave the Army.'

`I can't wait ... You don't understand—'

`I do understand. I once truly believed I loved your father. I married him hastily because I was expecting a child. I have lived to regret it. Long, long years of regret. I don't want the same to happen to you. If you truly love this girl, it will last for another twenty months. That's all, Marc, less than two years. And if by that time, you still love this girl then, believe me, I will welcome her into our family with open arms. I will love her and cherish her like a daughter. I will even ask your Uncle Jean-Michel to come back from the Congo and be the priest at your wedding.'

Her lips trembled with passion, but her dark eyes held his resolutely. `That's all I ask of you, Marc, to wait twenty months. A short enough time, but long enough to assure me that you are not making a mistake.'

He couldn't speak, couldn't argue, couldn't fight her, not with his hand on Philippe's blood-stained bible...

`If you refuse me this one request,' Jacqueline said, `the only request I have ever made to you in my life – if you deny me this, if you refuse to swear, if you refuse to wait – then I will know I have wasted my life on you, and you were not worth an hour of it.'

Seventeen

London
July 1964

_____/

The spacious, ground-floor apartment in Hampstead felt like home to her now. It had two large bedrooms, an enormous living room, and a white kitchen with honey coloured furniture and cupboards. It even had automatic heating, so every room was cosily warm, and she no longer had to worry about stacking up coins for the gas meter to light a gas fire.

Marc had bought her the flat when she was seven months pregnant, refusing to allow her to go on climbing that Everest of stairs up to her fifth-floor room.

He had given her no warning, just took her out one Saturday afternoon to show her something interesting.

It was the flat. In a red-bricked modern apartment block in trendy Hampstead. She had simply gaped as she walked from room to room, each one entirely bare of furniture or carpets.

`Ground floor,' Marc smiled. `And look – it has a telephone. So if you get sick you can call a doctor or Chef or Miss Courtney. And I'll be able to call you anytime, day or night.'

She had stared at him in astonishment. `You mean, you want to rent this flat – for *me*.'

`Not rent. I've bought it.'

`You *bought* it? No rent to pay?'

`No rent, no mortgage – *rien*. I paid in full and in cash and the deeds are in your name.'

`You paid in *cash*? How?'

`Well, by bank transfer, from my grandfather's trust fund. The money became mine two years ago, on my twenty-first birthday.'

`How much?'

'What? The flat or the trust fund?'

'The trust fund.'

'Half a million bucks.'

'Oh my God,' she had almost fainted, but then slowly it had made sense. How else could he have afforded the regular airfares from America, and places like the Savoy. Not on a lieutenant's salary. She had often wondered about it, and suspected he was getting the money from his parents.

'But why...' she asked, looking around the living-room, 'why did you do a crazy thing like this – buying this apartment without saying even a word to me?'

Marc shrugged. 'Because I knew that if I told you I wanted to buy you somewhere better to live, you would have said, "*Ohhhh no-oh*, thank you very much but I *caaahn't* let you do that. I can manage very well where I am, thank you."'

She had smiled, because that's *exactly* what she would have said, and he had mimicked her perfectly.

Four weeks later, the apartment was fully and beautifully furnished; a double bed in the main bedroom; nursery furniture and a white cot in the second bedroom; and she had received a letter from a firm of London solicitors to say the deeds of the apartment, registered in her name, were in their safekeeping.

'My own home,' she had said to Marc, looking around her in a daze of delight. 'Our own flat ... Do we really own it? ... I can't believe it.'

'It's only temporary, this flat,' Marc had warned her. 'Until after the baby is born. Then I'm going to *make* you marry me, whether you want to or not. Then, maybe, we can see about finding a nice house somewhere. Somewhere quiet and peaceful. Somewhere with a view of trees from the upstairs windows.'

'Here in England?'

'Yes. If British Immigration will allow me to live and work here.'

She stared at him in puzzlement. 'British Immigration ... you mean ... after the baby is born, if we married, you want to come and live *here* in England.'

Marc grinned. 'Why not? I've spent most of my life in New England. But now I think I'd like to come and live in the old one for a while. A fresh start. Clean break. A new life in another country.'

'Oh, Marc, that would be so *wonderful!*' '

But then she remembered, 'What about the Army?'

'I've already spoken to my commanding officer. It can be arranged. My leaving the Army.' His mouth tightened. 'But that's something, along with a few other things, that I can only sort out back in America.'

But now, ten days after the birth of their son, when Marc returned to the flat in Hampstead, Marian knew things had gone very badly for him in America.

The baby seemed to absorb all his attention, so she did not question him until later that evening, after their son was sleeping soundly in his new cot.

They were sitting together on the sofa. 'Just tell me the truth,' she said to him gently. And Marc did so, quietly and slowly.

'I think, perhaps, my mother *is* a little crazy,' he confessed. 'I think the horror and brutality of the war destroyed something in her. She was so young when it happened. Only sixteen when she took on the Nazis ... She's possessive, obsessive, and yet ... and yet ... I can't help feeling sorry for her.'

He looked at Marian with such distress and confusion in his eyes; Marian knew the battle was lost.

She felt a strange pain in her chest, as well as an awful sadness that had descended on her. But as she sat in silent thought, she remembered something Miss Courtney had once said to her, *'In life there is always a chance of a better tomorrow. Only the dead can lose the future.'*

And she realised this small battle was the only thing she had lost.

She still had Marc. They still had their son. And they still had the future.

Miss Courtney had also taught her the value of patience.

'It's only twenty months,' she said finally. 'It's not very long to wait.'

'To get officially married, maybe. But that doesn't stop us setting up home near the Base and living in America. I want you and Phil with me, Marian. I don't want to keep on being a once-a-month visitor.'

But she was shaking her head slowly, tears in her eyes. 'No, that is not how I want to start. In a strange country. Unacceptable to your parents, ignored by them, and refused admission inside your family home. Everyone would know it. I would be looked upon as a kept woman, someone less than a wife. I don't want to start our life together like that.'

She was hurt, very hurt, but she was also full of dignity. They must wait the twenty months and she would wait for him in England, she decided. And even though they talked all evening, nothing Marc could say would dissuade her.

'Okay,' he said finally in agitation. 'I'll break the promise. To hell with my mother. We'll get married straight away.'

'No,' Marian cried. 'No, let her have her twenty months, let her have her proof. Oh, Marc, don't you see? It's not only for us that I want everything to work out right – it's also for Phil. He has no one in the world, but you and me. No grandparents on my side. No uncles or aunts. No other family, except Miss Courtney. He is too young now. But in a few years time, when he is old enough to look around him and understand, I want him to know he has two loving grandparents. *See* them occasionally. I want them to spoil him, and buy him presents at Christmas, and all those other wonderful things that grandparents are supposed to do—' She dashed a hand across the tears in her eyes. 'But that can only happen if we wait.'

The baby started to cry. Marian looked surprised and alarmed. 'It's only half an hour since he was changed and fed.

So he can't be hungry again, can he?'

She jumped up and rushed to Phil's room, lifted him into her arms and whispered loving words while checking his nappy, which was still clean and dry. `And you *caaahn't* be hungry again,' she murmured anxiously.

Gently she laid his tiny head on her shoulder and walked slowly towards the window, patting him on his back and murmuring comforting words until he stopped whimpering and dozed off to sleep.

Still patting his back she turned round to the cot, and saw Marc leaning against the doorframe watching her, watching them both, a quiet desperateness in his eyes.

`You've got to come back to America with me, Marian. I can't leave you here alone.'

Gently she laid Phil down in his cot, and returned to the living room where she spoke very slowly and softly as she tried to make Marc understand.

`I have a newborn baby to take care of. And I still feel very nervous about it. And in America I would have no friends, no one to turn to while you are at work. But here – in this flat – I feel at home. The neighbours are all nice. And Miss Courtney is just a phone call away. So are Chef and Sofia. People who genuinely love me. People who would drop everything and come to my assistance if I needed it.'

She glanced down at her hands, her voice low and emotional. `With patience, Marc, I know we can get through this, because I know how much we love each other. I know it can still work out all right. Just twenty months, Marc. for the sake of our son. I can stand it if you can.'

And in the end, all Marc could do was accept it.

At the airport, Miss Courtney decided to take Phil off for a `little walk' while Marc and Marian stood hugging each other with a love they both knew would never end.

In the weeks following his return to America, Marc did not go near his parent's house, not even for lunch. All Jacqueline's telephone calls to Fort Devens failed to find him. All the messages she left for Marc to call her, piled up without reply.

Finally, swallowing her pride, she drove over to the Base and sought him out. His response to her was icily cold.

`How are you, Marc?'

`I'm counting the months,' he told her. `I hope you are too.'

`Marc, darling, please understand, all we are doing is waiting for time to tell us if this girl is right or wrong for you. That's all. Just waiting for time to tell.'

`That's what you may be waiting for. But me, I'm just serving my time and seeing it through. Then I'm getting married and moving to England.'

Driving back home, Jacqueline felt disappointed, but she also felt no fear. It was early days yet, and she knew she would win. And if nothing or no one else, at least she still had good old *Life* on her side. Because *Life*, as she had learned long ago, could always be relied upon to produce the unexpected – supply something or *someone* new to catch the interest when a person was least prepared.

She smiled confidently as her gaze moved over the New England countryside, bathed in golden sunshine.

Oh yes, life, beliefs, affections – all could change in a day. Especially for the young. And how flighty the young were! So often she had seen a young man's *One-and-Only* love cast aside when someone new and beautiful came on the scene. And Marc was very handsome. He would not find it easy to go through life unnoticed by women. Especially not here in America.

So why should she worry herself about counting months — almost two long years of them.

Eighteen

London
August –October 1964

_____/

Marc and Marian's love affair grew stronger every month. He phoned her every morning and every night, just to let her know he was thinking of her.

'As long as the day lasts, babe.'

Sometimes he was able to wangle or trade or buy extra leave and spend as many as five days a month in London. And whenever Marc was home, there was usually soul music playing on the stereo at night.

'Phil's becoming addicted to that music,' Marian told him. 'Won't go to sleep at night now, unless I put on some soul records.'

Marc grinned. 'My kind of guy.'

He adored his son, played with him for hours, even bought a huge new television for the living room so he and his son could watch the basketball in colour. But there was no basketball on English TV, nor any baseball games either.

'Ah hell,' Marc complained. 'What kind of country is this? No basketball or baseball. So what's a guy to do on a drizzly Saturday afternoon?'

'There's football,' Marian switched to the other channel. 'Or John Wayne in a cowboy film. Which do you want?'

'The football's in black and white, and our boy here wants to watch the colours, don't you, Phil?'

Phil, nearly four months old and propped on Marc's lap, stopped chewing a rubber toy and belched.

'There, you heard him!' Marc exclaimed. 'He wants to watch the cowboys. And he's one smart kid. Already he knows that's all those cowboys do – rustle cattle, ride horses, shoot guns, drink red-eye, and belch wind.'

Marian laughed. 'John Wayne always gets the girl,' she said, settling down beside him on the sofa.

'Wayne – the Duke - he's the biggest belcher of them all. Do you know why he talks like that? In that slow drawl?'

'Because that's just the way he talks?'

'No, no, it's because when he was starting out as an actor, he was real nervous about being interviewed by journalists. So Sam Goldwyn or one of those other movie moguls told him how to do it, how to answer journalists. He said, "Talk low, talk slow, and don't say too fucking much."'

Marc adjusted Phil on his lap. 'Only problem was, Wayne now talks like that all the time. And whenever any directors try to get him to speed it up, Wayne just looks at them and says real slow "The hell I will."'

Marian gave him a poke in the ribs and didn't believe him.

But ten minutes later, when John Wayne looked long and scornful at the sheriff of Tombstone and said, "The hell I will," they both erupted in laughter and gave Phil such a fright he began to cry.

'Ah, ah,' Marc lifted him up, 'what's this? Why the droopy lip? Don't you know you are your Mama's favourite child and your Daddy's favourite son?'

Phil looked back at him with watery dark eyes and a trembling lower lip, then suddenly grabbed at Marc's face and tried to suck the side of his chin.

'Ah no – he's going to send me back with love-bites all over my neck again. Here, Marian, take him, or all the guys will think I've been necking with a schoolgirl.'

'I think he's cutting his first tooth,' Marian said. 'I'm sure he is. He's like a little puppy, chew anything to ease the ache.'

At night, when the baby was asleep and they too went bed, they lost the friendly ease and lightness of daytime, and became lovers.

No matter what her mood, as soon as Marc drew her

towards him and began to make love to her, Marian felt as if her bones were melting like ice under a hot sun as he told her how precious she was, how beautiful she was, and as far as he was concerned they were already married.

He bought her a beautiful diamond ring, and put it on her wedding finger. And every month a large amount of money was transferred from his bank account to her bank account for the payment of all her bills, to ensure that she and the child had everything they needed.

Marian looked at him and smiled, and it touched him to the heart, because it was such a bitter-sweet little smile.

`All we really need is you.'

Nineteen

Massachusetts
October 1964
_____/

Alexander finally decided to search out his son and put things right between the two of them, once and for all.

The decision cheered him. He drove over to the Base with a hectic brightness, but by the time he entered the building, he was exhausted, his mood deflated, his eyes slightly glazed. He needed a drink.

But first ... first, he needed to get this demon off his back. It was time to tell Marc the truth, all of it.

Marc groaned when he heard who was waiting to see him.

Jimmy shrugged. `I think you should see him.'

`Why?'

`He's looking kinda spooky.'

`Spooky?' Marc was sitting at his desk, he looked up at Jimmy. `In what way?'

`Like he's been drinking disinfectant.'

Marc sighed: it had been months since he had last seen his father, and he didn't really care if he never saw him again.

`Ten minutes, Jimmy, ten minutes max. Then you come in and tell me that I'm wanted by the CO. And wanted *immediately*.'

Jimmy nodded. `Right.'

When Alexander entered the small office, Marc remained seated behind the desk and greeted him with a long frown, finally understanding Jimmy's impression of his father looking kinda spooky. His face looked unhealthily pale, dark circles under the eyes, his posture droopy and shrivelled.

Alexander sank down on a chair. `I'm not feeling so good.'

`Why?'

`Been on a hard bender, drinking for days, in Boston. Slept it off there too.' He sighed heavily. `Now I feel like I've been communing with the dead. Like I've just come out of a long dark séance.'

`So why are you here?'

Alexander sat for a moment staring emptily before him.

`To say I'm sorry, son. Truly and honestly sorry about all this. In Boston ... I tried to write you a letter ... but then, well, I decided to come here in person and do it myself, without being forced to do it. To apologise to you. For everything ... all the brain bashing about being a writer ... and maybe driving you into the Army.'

He looked at Marc like a sorrowful old Labrador, the same look he always wore after a drinking bout.

Marc averted his eyes, stared towards the window, and said nothing.

`I never realised ... never knew that was how you felt about me, never knew you hated me so much ... But then, you always were so calm about everything. Never answered me back. Never really seemed to care about my shouting. Just let it roll off your back ... and I used to think to myself, hell, ain't nothing going to touch this boy. He just doesn't give a damn about anything.'

Ironically, Alexander half-smiled. `Christ, was I wrong about you! I should've seen your emotions were all chained down, just waiting to break ... And that day, when you made me grovel like a dog and apologise to you, I knew then ... I knew no son would do that to his father unless he had years of hate in him. And you know what, Marc ... it almost killed me.'

Alexander looked at Marc desperately, but Marc was sat back staring fixedly at the window.

And it was then Alexander realised that Marc was just letting him have his say, but that was all. He didn't know if Marc was even listening. All he knew for sure was that the boy had stopped listening to him years ago, and now maybe it was all too late. Too late for even trying to make things right, too late to help him.

'Listen to me, Marc,' he pleaded, 'I know your mother's been brainwashing you with lies against me all these years. But that's what liars do – they make out it's the *other* person who is lying so that no one will believe them – not even when they are blatantly telling the truth.'

Marc remained silent.

'But just for once in your life, Marc, why don't you consider believing *me* for a change? Dammit – I want to help you! I want to get you out of this Army! I want you to break that promise! I want to tell you the truth about that blood-stained bible, the *truth* about your mother.'

Alexander's hands tightened into fists on his knees. 'You see, Marc, these pasts months I've come to realise something about your mother – she's not just off her rocker, she's *evil*.'

Marc stirred impatiently. 'This old bullshit. Is this what you really came here to lay on me? This same old crap, same old sick hatred. If you really do feel that way about my mother – why the hell don't you just up and leave her?'

'Because she's made sure I *can't* leave her. She's made me financially dependent upon her for every mouthful of food I eat, every cent I spend. And she deliberately set out to destroy any confidence I had in myself as a writer for that very purpose!'

Alexander swallowed. 'I know ... I know she told you lies about my book, claiming all the words were hers, that I was not a true writer. But I don't blame you for believing her. Even *I* started to believe her, shivering over my typewriter in the chill of self-doubt, then full-blown panic attacks. I haven't been able to write a decent paragraph in years. Even the *New York Times* finally let me go. Sent me a letter of sad farewell. And you know why she did it – ruined me as a writer – to keep me under her control and in her power, because she despises me as she despises most people.'

Alexander cleared his throat. 'And do you know *why* she despises me, keeps me in her power and under her control? Because I'm the only living soul that knows the truth, the awful truth about her father, Philippe Castineau.'

At last he had Marc's full attention.

'There's nothing you can tell me about Philippe,' Marc said positively. 'I know all there is to know.'

'Horseshit! All you know is what *she* told you, and what I wrote in my book – a load of goddamned fiction! All that crap about how bravely Philippe died at the hands of the Gestapo, how courageously he stood up to their torture? It's not true, Marc, I made it all up! Because she wouldn't *allow* me to write anything near the truth. Not about Philippe and the Gestapo. So all you know and all you've read is the best piece of fiction I've ever written – and let me tell you, I *deserved* that Pulitzer prize!'

The anger in Marc's eyes was blazing, but he kept his voice low. 'So now you have turned your venom on Philippe Castineau? A dead man. A hero of the Resistance. A credit to France. My grandfather was a good man and *nothing* you say will ever destroy my respect for him.'

Alexander was hurt and astonished. 'No, no,' he protested quickly, 'you've got me all wrong, Marc. I don't want to destroy your respect for Philippe! Chrissakes, that's not what I came to do—'

'*What* then?'

'I came to warn you, to help you, to try and give you a fair deal for a change ... I came to tell you the truth about that blood-stained bible. It's a demon I've had on my back since the day she made you swear on it—'

Alexander's voice was low with emotion. 'I stood in the hall and I heard what she said to you and I couldn't believe my ears. And that's when I knew she was evil, utterly and ruthlessly *evil*.'

Jimmy knocked and entered. 'Sorry to interrupt, Marc, but

the CO wants you to report to him in his office immediately.'

Marc jumped to his feet. 'Right.'

'Marc, wait—'

'Sorry, Dad, I've gotta go.'

Marc was halfway through the door when Alexander lunged after him, caught his arm, his voice desperate.

'She'll *never* let you be your own man! She'll make you live your life as *she* wants you to live it. Twenty months or twenty years – she'll *never* let you marry that English girl. She'll never let you marry *anyone*. That's why she's keeping you in the Army – to keep you in her power. To keep you close by. That's why I haven't told her about your kid. And I'm not going to tell her, because she'll destroy him as sure as ... Chrissakes, *Marc!*'

Jimmy stood looking embarrassed as Marc strode off. Guiltily he passed a hand over his blond crew-cut. 'I'm sorry, sir,' he murmured, 'but when our commanding officer says immediately, he really does mean ... immediately.'

Sunken and defeated, Alexander stared at Jimmy with wry bitterness. 'I saw your CO drive away from the Base as I was arriving. He's not even in the building. So go fuck yourself, soldier. And you can tell your buddy to do the same.'

Twenty

New York & Massachusetts
October 1964

_____ /

Jacqueline was in New York, lunching at Le Pavillon.

From the moment she had entered the maître d' had greeted her, and seated her, with eminent respect. She wore a navy coatdress which he knew had been designed especially for her by Chanel or Dior. Her gleaming black hair was drawn back from her face and coiled up into a chignon *soigné*. On each ear she wore a sparkling blue-fire solitaire diamond – simple and stunning. As always her taste was faultless.

He led her to a secluded table where her dining companion sat waiting for her.

`Jacqueline—'

Lewis Belfort beamed as she was seated; hardly able to believe he had her all to himself. He knew that Jacqueline was elusive and exclusive and she was courted by high society, but she chose her associates very carefully.

`How are you, Lewis?'

The smile she gave him was radiant. It would have weakened the knees of a less solid, less stable-minded man.

Lewis Belfort was not impressed by Jacqueline's beauty; he preferred the more homely attractions of his wife. He was more impressed by her intelligence and her amazing knowledge of business. At times he suspected she knew more about high finance than many accountants, and more about corporate law than many lawyers.

And he was her lawyer.

They started lunch with pleasantries, and then moved on to business, the subject Lewis enjoyed most. Finally, they sat back and relaxed as two waiters nimbly cleared the table and

194

another served them chilled champagne.

'How is Alexander?' Lewis asked. 'Still working on his novel?'

Jacqueline's brief smile was sardonic. 'He is still searching for a subject, still lost for a theme.'

Lewis was surprised. 'Jane Austen once said that all literature had only *two* great themes – love and money.'

'And Alexander, regrettably, has a limited comprehension of both.'

This unexpected revelation about her husband startled Lewis. Usually she was remote and enigmatic about her private life, and he had always respected her right to be so. But now he felt she had deliberately given him an opening. He sat silent, debating with himself, then hesitantly asked, 'Jacqueline, your marriage to Alexander, is it—'

'Like living in a barren room,' she admitted softly.

It was dark and raining when Jacqueline returned home the following evening. Alexander heard her come in, heard her pass his door, heard her speaking to Eddie, and heard her go upstairs.

The door of his study was open and all the lights were on, but she had not paused to pop her head inside to see if he was okay, say hello. Alexander was not surprised. She often went about her life as if he did not exist. Especially after a few days with her Manhattan friends.

Had she a lover? Had she *ever* had lovers, unknownst to him?

A suspicion that often niggled the back of his brain – ever since something Bill Simons had once said, a vague comment, a look in the eye, something that made Alexander almost fight with Bill, defending her honour, her good name.

But he and Bill had patched things up, too long good friends, and in the end Bill had admitted that no – unlike everyone else in Massachusetts – he did *not* like Jacqueline, no, didn't like her one bit ... `Something about her, Alex. Can't think what. Just something about her.`

Alexander knew what, but it was nothing to do with lovers.

He thought of the what, and the why, and he felt his anger build to rage. A rage that had been burning inside him for months about that bloodstained bible.

Only his rage gave him the courage to do it – rush out of the room and up the stairs until he reached her bedroom – opening the door without bothering to knock. The room was empty, but he could hear the sound of running water in her bathroom, sniffed the steamy scent of her bath oil, the one she always used – Parisian Roses.

He stood for a moment, uncertainly, his rage draining, his voice weakening as he felt his old obsession returning.

`Jacqueline?`

She appeared in the doorway of her steamy bathroom, sensuously beautiful in a flimsy robe of white satin, a long clingy thing that seemed to shimmer, tied loosely at the waist, revealing the curves of her breasts. A memory from long ago – satin sheets, smooth skin ... the scent of Parisian Roses – all working on his memory like a heady aphrodisiac.

As he gazed at her with longing, she leaned against the doorframe, looking at him darkly, silent and unmoving.

`Jacqueline, I want— ` He had to look away from her, keep his resolve. `I want ... I almost did ... I want to tell Marc the truth, about the Bible, about Philippe and the Gestapo.`

`But you won't,` she said simply.

`Why not?` He looked at her. `I have nothing to be afraid of.`

`You have me.`

She was standing calmly, studying him calmly, a stunningly beautiful woman, but her eyes were like dark winter – zero-cold.

`If you tell Marc the truth,` she said softly, `or if you even attempt to do so again, I will not divorce you, Alexander, I will kill you.`

For the first time she had put it into words what Alexander had always known. She wouldn't use a knife or a gun, nothing that obvious, but she would find a way.

Chilled he remembered how close he had come to telling Marc, unheeding of the consequences to himself, forgetting her cruelty, her sadism, her natural instinct for revenge against any enemy.

She closed the bathroom door quietly.

Alexander felt a sudden need to sit down. He moved over to the bed, sank down on the edge, heard the sound of her shower turning on, listened to the rush of the water, his mind not registering the fact that when he arrived, she had just filled a scented bath.

The hot scented bath, which Jacqueline had longed for, on the journey home was not what she needed now, but the cold cubicle of her shower. She stood with face raised to the torrent of freezing water crashing down on her, beating into her, numbing her mind and body.

But there was no relief, no cleansing, no baptism into a new life, just a drowning darkness back into the past, back to Paris in January 1944, back into the apartment on rue de Berri where a young French girl was softly singing a lullaby to her child ...

Allons, enfants de la patrie ...

Philippe Castineau was sitting in his chair reading. He glanced up with a wry smile at Alexander. 'Most mothers sing their child to sleep with a lullaby. But Jacqueline, she sings the *Marseillaise.*'

'Because it is so beautiful,' Jacqueline murmured. 'And look, Papa, see how he sleeps?' She turned her body to let him see Marc's face lolling unconscious on her shoulder. 'See how he loves the lullaby of our beautiful anthem. See, Alexander.'

'Yeah, your singing has done the trick,' Alexander said absently, then stopped scribbling in his notepad and looked over at Philippe. 'What are you reading?'

Philippe glanced down. 'I'm reading about David.'

'David who?'

'King David.'

Alexander looked more clearly towards the book in Philippe's hand. 'Oh, I see, you're reading the *Bible*—' Alexander smiled sheepishly. 'Sorry, Philippe, my mind was miles away, locked off in these scenes of mine.'

'Scenes for your book?'

'Yeah, for my book. I want to write as much of it as I can here in Paris, to ensure that the tone and *feel* of it is fresh.'

'And what you have just written,' asked Philippe, 'what scene is that?'

Alexander glanced down. 'An old one – June 23rd 1940 – Hitler's arrival in Paris. I'm just polishing it up a bit.'

'May I read it?'

'Read it?' Alexander stared at him with surprise. 'You know all the writing for my book is in shorthand.'

Philippe nodded apologetically. 'Oh yes, yes, for a moment I forgot.'

'I can't use longhand, you see, can't type it up – can't take the risk. Not while the Nazis are here. And maybe not even until I get back to America.' Alexander grinned nervously. 'Hell, if the Nazis could see what I've got written here, about their beloved Führer, they'd give me a bullet in the head.'

Jacqueline stopped humming. 'Then *you* read it to us, Alexander. If we are going to love this book as much as you say, and if you are truly going to dedicate it to the men and women of the French Resistance, then perhaps Papa and I can tell you if the men and women of the French Resistance will like it.'

'Read it aloud?' Embarrassment coloured Alexander's young face. 'Ah, Jacqueline, you know that's not my kind of thing ... And anyway, it's only rough—'

'Please!'

Philippe nodded. `Yes, Alexander, it would be very interesting to hear in what way you write of Hitler. Is he a demagogue? How do you describe him?'

`Well ... okay then,' Alexander still looked embarrassed, `I'll read it, but as I say, it's only rough, and—'

`Wait!' Jacqueline whispered. `Wait until I put Marc in his bed.'

She carried Marc into his room and gently laid him down with a kiss, then returned to the main salon with a hand resting on the pregnant-looking mound of her stomach. She had an array of dresses padded out to make her look as if she was in the growing stages of pregnancy. It was a brilliant disguise. No one could suspect a pregnant woman of doubling as a boy – a lesson she had learned when she was genuinely pregnant with Marc, and found herself *unable* to double as a boy.

She knelt down at Alexander's feet. `Now read, chéri. Read to us your description of Hitler in Paris.'

`Well, okay ...' Alexander looked at his shorthand pad, flicked back a few pages. `But if you don't like it ...'

`We will not be cruel,' Philippe assured him.

Alexander held up the pad, stared at the page, cleared his throat, and spoke quietly in the tone of an objective narrator.

`*He arrived in Paris on a Sunday morning, before dawn, before the city had awakened from the dull concussion ...*'

Jacqueline listened silently as Alexander described the awful reality of that morning. Of himself, the narrator, rapidly dressing and rushing out to see if it was true.

Grim-faced she listened as Alexander described so perfectly the indifferent way Hitler had looked at the city of Paris, its pride, its beauty, its architectural magnificence, strutting around like a tourist, gazing here, gazing there, but none of it touched him, not Adolf Hitler. He was standing in the art-capital of the world, but he was not an artist. He was a mass murderer.

`*Yet he looked as proud as Lucifer, unmoved by suffering mortality,*' *blessed in his own vanity ...*'

'You have captured him like a camera,' Philippe said softly when Alexander had concluded. 'Like a camera.'

'Yes,' Jacqueline nodded in agreement. 'Yes.'

'Well, like I said, it's still in rough,' Alexander murmured, 'still needs a lot of polishing–' He broke off at the sound of a car's engine outside. All three of them sat rigid. Only the Nazis had gasoline these days. Only the Nazis drove cars at night.

Philippe rose swiftly and hurried to the window, his hand moving the thick blackout curtain to peep down at the street. He quickly stepped back. 'Gestapo!'

Jacqueline jumped to her feet. 'Gestapo? Are you sure?'

'Yes, they always come in the night.'

'Coming here? Are you sure? Perhaps they are going to the Lancaster? To see the collaborator?'

Madame Poirey was an active resister, but the Nazis had no suspicion of her because she covered so well as a collaborator. '*The Maquis —those terrorists! All peasants!*' Madame would proclaim in disgust. '*Better to live with Germany than be ruled by the English.*' Then she would listen to them speaking in German as she poured more wine and collected glasses, finding out as much as she could to pass back to the Resistance.

'Yes,' Jacqueline whispered hopefully. 'Perhaps it is Madame Poirey they have come to see.'

But moments later the dreaded sound finally came – a loud banging on the door below.

'Admit them at once,' Philippe ordered.

'No!' Jacqueline gasped.

'Yes!' Philippe insisted. 'We must seem to have nothing to fear. Innocent Parisians living life as normally as possible. You know this, Jacqueline. So admit them now, and admit them politely.'

'Chrissakes – wait till I hide my shorthand pad!' Alexander jumped up and disappeared into the bedroom.

Philippe looked at his daughter, his face stern. 'Do as I say,

Jacqueline, open the door to them.'

Turning away, she heard her father quietly murmur a few words which she had often heard old Monsieur Haffel murmuring, words from a Psalm of David: `Hear my voice, O God, in my prayer; preserve my life from fear of the enemy.'

They came in twos, they always did. One spoke, the other remained silent. Jacqueline's step faltered only for a second as she led them into the main salon, rigidly straining to remain polite, a hand quietly fumbling over the padded bulge of her stomach.

The young German Intelligence officer was very polite. A stranger dressed in civilian clothes. But Philippe had known instantly – Gestapo.

`Herr Castineau,' he said softly, `forgive us for calling so late at night, but we have had a very busy day.'

Jacqueline knew him then – a stranger, yes, but they were all so alike. All had that hypocritical politeness, hypocritical smile. All were young, carefully selected and well trained for the Gestapo – sadists who knew every vile method of inquisition and torture – sadists who found no difficulty in smiling as they did their work.

`What is it you want?' Philippe asked.

`To question you.'

Philippe inclined his head in agreement, elegantly gestured to a chair. `Then please, do sit down.'

The young German smiled. `Thank you, but no. We think the time has come for you to be questioned at our headquarters in Avenue Foch.'

`Avenue Foch?'

Philippe did not flinch, but Jacqueline felt the blood swelling hotly in her brain. Everyone knew what happened inside the house numbered 84 in Avenue Foch – endless interrogation, sleep deprivation, vile torture. Sometimes, when they were certain the resister had the information they needed – code-names of resistance leaders, true identities, secret addresses –

the torture became horrific.

And if that did not work, the Gestapo became impatient–pushing the resister to his knees and holding him there while others viciously kicked him in the back until his spine was broken.

Then their questions would resume, while the resister lay in agony on the floor. That's what they had done to Etienne, before they had thrown him into a windowless van that took him away to die a lingering death in the prison at Fresnes.

No, no, she would *not* let her beloved father suffer that. He was a gentleman; he had the blood and genes of an aristocrat. How could he stand up against such torture? He would break. He would tell them all. And that would break his heart more painfully than a broken back – to know he had betrayed France and the Resistance. No, *no*, she would not let them do that to him!

Her hand moved down to the secret pocket in the padded bulge of her dress and touched the revolver – she would kill them first – *kill them now!*

Her father suddenly turned his head and looked sharply at her, his eyes blazing a warning, `No more murder in my home!' he had said furiously to her after the disposal of the two SS officers. `No more Nazi blood on my walls! No more nightmares for Marcel!'

`Herr Castineau, if you wish to travel with us in our car to Avenue Foch, you are very welcome to do so. But if you prefer—' the Nazi glanced a smile towards the window, `we can offer you the choice of alternative transport.'

Jacqueline wrenched her eyes from her father and stepped over to window, shoving aside the curtain and seeing what Philippe had not had time to see earlier: a black windowless van. The same type of van they had thrown Etienne into. Around it stood a guard of helmeted soldiers holding machine guns. *Too many to kill!*

Philippe did not even glance towards the window; he did

not need to be told about the van. He remained calm and dignified and turned only to lift his Bible, slip it into his pocket. Jacqueline knew what he was thinking: *Hear my voice, O God, in my prayer: preserve my life from fear of the enemy.*

'Courage,' Philippe whispered in her ear as he embraced her. 'Have courage, Jacqueline, and do not doubt mine. I shall not let them break me.'

But they *would* break him, she was sure they would. What they had done to Etienne and to others, they would do to Philippe Castineau. They would make him suffer and he would eventually tell all. She could not allow that.

Pale as death she watched her father turn and walk away from her. The two Gestapo politely stepped back to allow him to lead the way out of the room, and that's when she withdrew the gun and fired four bullets into her father's back – then another – and another – into the two Gestapo.

All done with the speed and accuracy of a professional killer. She threw the gun down. It was empty.

Only Alexander knew the truth.

Only Alexander who had stood hidden and unseen, but who had seen and heard it all, knew it was she who had shot and killed Philippe Castineau, not the Gestapo.

Only Alexander saved her from the soldiers who stormed into the salon seconds after the explosion of gunshots.

'The gun! The gun!' Alexander pointed to the gun on the floor, pointed to Philippe, but the soldiers did not comprehend. All they understood was what their eyes showed them – two officers of the Gestapo and a French national lying dead on the floor.

Madame Poirey pushed her way in, stared at Philippe's blood-soaked body in horror. Alexander did not hesitate, grabbing her arm so tightly she cried out in pain.

'Tell them,' Alexander ordered, his eyes blazing into her, 'Tell them what I say happened here!'

And Madame Poirey suddenly understood-rapidly translating into German everything Alexander told her ... and Alexander told the most convincing story any writer could.

... Philippe had already drunk far too much cognac and was argumentative and aggressive even before the Gestapo came, accusing his daughter of being a collaborator, accusing her of hating Jews and liking Nazis, accusing Alexander of being a disgrace to America, but Alexander had replied that no, he was just a writer, a reporter, and his policy was the same as Switzerland's – neutral.

Then when the Gestapo came Philippe just went crazy, the gun must have been in his pocket – in his hand in a second, shooting the two Gestapo, then threatening to shoot his daughter ... `threatened to shoot my pregnant wife, the mother of my son!'

Alexander continued desperately – `he had no choice but to wrestle with Philippe, get the gun ... shoot him once, then again, make him lie down for Christ's sake, but he kept getting up ... a crazy man, kept trying to stand up ... ' Alexander was panting for breath, his face as white as a sheet, but the more he talked, the more they believed him ...

Any lingering doubts they harboured were finally removed by their own collaborator. Madame Poirey spoke rapidly to them about Philippe, assuring them yes, lately poor Monsieur Castineau had started to drink excessively, slightly crazy ...

Jacqueline wanted to scream, but all she could do was keep staring at the body of her father, listening to the voices, listening and staring until there was only silence – only one dead body left lying on the floor – only two other people standing in the room.

Madame Poirey and Alexander.

`Why?' Madame Poirey rasped furiously. `*Why* did you do it, Jacqueline? Philippe was a true patriot. A proud Frenchman. A great leader of the Resistance. He would have preferred death from Gestapo torture than to be shot in the back by his own daughter. Why did you do it, Jacqueline?'

Jacqueline could barely answer, even her lips felt numb.

'It was for the best.'

'For the best?' Madame Poirey's furious eyes were like fire. 'You killed your own father – because it was *for the best!* Who are you to decide life and death? *Do you think you are God!*' The sudden slap across Jacqueline's face was so violent she stumbled back and hit her head against the wall.

When she regained consciousness, only Alexander was in the room, lifting her into a chair, stroking her face.

Only Alexander understood.

'You understand, don't you, Alexander?'

Alexander's face looked pale and drained. She knew how much he had loved Philippe. But still he nodded. 'Yes, Jacqueline, I understand.'

'And you forgive me?'

'Yes, Jacqueline, I forgive you.'

And that's when she had first started to hate him.

And that's when she knew she could never leave him, nor allow him to leave her. He would be her punishment, her penance for the past, and she would make him suffer too. For understanding so easily, and forgiving so easily ... the murder of Philippe Castineau.

Alexander was gone when she came out of the bathroom. She walked into the large, luxuriously furnished bedroom and sat down at her dressing table, her eyes resting on a framed photograph of Marc.

Only Marc made her feel closer to her father, bridging the death that separated them; and even, at times, making her believe that none of it had happened, that Philippe was still alive and well.

Philippe had been tall, and Marc was now tall, and each day from boyhood as Marc had grown older she had seen her father come back to life before her eyes – the wry smile, the gentle touch, the refined intelligence, the Castineau blood and genes emerging.

Not even her brother, now a priest out in the Belgian Congo, could remind her so much of her father. But then Jean-Michel didn't look like a Castineau, he was the son of his mother, brown-haired and blue-eyed. He looked nothing like Philippe, nothing like her, he looked like the youngest apostle, the one Jesus had loved ...'Mother, here is your son.'

Only with Marc could she identify, because he was a part of her as she was a part of him, and Philippe's blood ran in both their veins.

Only with Marc did she feel exciting bursts of love, and a wonderful sense of belonging.

So how could she allow some stupid English girl to take Marc away from her?

A common waitress. Some hard-headed sexpot who knew a good catch when she saw one. Knew the smell of money more sharply than the mixed aromas of the food she served in the restaurant where she worked.

In time, Marc would grow tired of her.

Jacqueline was sure of it.

And if Time proved her wrong, then...

She lifted a jar of moisturiser from her dressing table and began to smooth the cream into her face, slowly and moodily.

Twenty-One

London
November 1964

_____/

'**M**arc may *seem* impulsive,' said Marian, 'but really he isn't.'

Miss Courtney had observed a cushion out of place on the sofa. She straightened it with a murmur of satisfaction. 'Tidy room, tidy mind.'

'Like when he joined the Army, for example. It just *seemed* sudden to his parents because he had never once mentioned the Army to them, but he had been thinking about it for months.'

Marian was standing with her hand pressed against the glass of the window, staring out as if she was watching and waiting for someone. 'He studies all the advantages and disadvantages,' she went on. 'Even with people he likes to weigh up the good against the bad.'

'Marian,' said Miss Courtney, 'what day is today?'

'Saturday.'

'So why are you standing by the window, waiting and watching? Marc is not coming until Sunday, is he?'

Marian glanced back at Miss Courtney and smiled, a small guilty grin. 'He came a day early last month.'

'And he may come a day late this month. You really *will* have to calm this excitement of yours, dear. It's very unhealthy to be so up and down. One must always try to maintain an even keel if life is to run smoothly.'

Marian mused, 'No, he never comes late. Well, no more than a few hours, if the plane has to refuel in Ireland. But usually it doesn't. Most times it just flies straight across to London.'

'And it's raining.' Miss Courtney lifted her knitting. 'One should never stare through a window in winter when it's raining, so depressing. Oh, really – will you *please* sit down,

207

Marian. Standing there won't make Sunday come any quicker.'

Marian turned back into the room, and sighed, `Shall I make another pot of tea?'

`Oh yes, dear,' Miss Courtney smiled. `Now that *is* a good idea. A nice cup of tea always cheers me up when it's raining.'

In the kitchen, Marian unsealed a jar of strawberry jam and spread it between four buttered scones: Miss Courtney's favourite snack. When the tea was made she carried in the tray and set it on the coffee table. Miss Courtney sat with her knitting in her lap and her head drooped in sleep.

`Miss Courtney ... ' Marian whispered, but Miss Courtney dozed on. Marian gazed at her fondly, knowing how hard she worked at Barnardo's, and let her sleep.

Less than an hour later, Marian was sitting in an armchair feeding Phil at her breast when the doorbell rang.

Miss Courtney awoke with a start, saw Marian fumbling with the buttons of her blouse, and immediately jumped up and trotted out to the hall. `I'll see to it, dear.'

She undid the latch and opened the door. Marc stood with his collar turned up against the rain.

`Hi,' Marc grinned.

`Is it Sunday?' Miss Courtney blinked uncertainly. `Oh dear ... have I been asleep that long?'

`No, it's still only Friday,' Marc teased, then looked beyond her and smiled because Marian had come into the hall.

She thrust the baby into Miss Courtney's hands and in a flash she was in Marc's arms.

Miss Courtney took one look at the passionate way they kissed, and carried Phil back into the living room. `She *knew* he was coming today,' she muttered. `She knew!'

`No, I didn't,' Marian laughed later. `He only said he *might* be able to get here today, but I didn't know for certain. And I didn't want to disappoint you.'

Later that evening, after the delicious dinner Marian had cooked and served, Miss Courtney decided it was time to leave.

She refused to hear any talk of a taxi, not even if Marc paid.

`Such nonsense! Such *expense!*' She patted Marc's arm. `No, dear, it's quite unnecessary. A short bus-ride to the station, then onto the train, and I'll be home before I know it.'

In the end Marc gave in, and walked her to the bus stop.

When he returned to the flat he opened the door with his own key. The only time he never used the key, preferring to ring the doorbell, was on his arrival from America, a simple courtesy, in his opinion.

Music was playing on the stereo, Phil was in his cot, and Marian was washing up the dishes.

He stood leaning against the kitchen door. She glanced over her shoulder and smiled at him. `Do you want coffee?'

`No, I'm fine.'

`I was just about to make some.'

`Then go ahead, have some yourself if you want.'

`Me? No, no, I never drink coffee, you know that.' She switched off the kettle and put the percolator away.

Now they were alone, she was nervous: on his first night back she was always nervous, always slightly shy.

`I'll just put these plates away.'

He watched her as she moved to and fro, putting away plates, stacking cups and saucers. She ached for him to come closer, but he kept his distance.

`Did you get my letter?' she asked.

`Yes, I did. ' He hesitated. `Marian, something puzzling – why do you still write me letters, when we talk on the phone twice a day?'

`Oh, I don't know.' She gave a slight shrug and turned away. `I just find it easier to write the things I want to say.'

`Well, you know, in your letters, you say them beautifully ... all that poetry and passion ... like something out of Romeo and Juliet.'

He was smiling.

She was embarrassed. She couldn't stop herself from

blushing, feeling a sudden urge to flee from him, out of the kitchen, anywhere to hide her embarrassment.

`I-I'll just go and see if Phil's all right.'

As she moved to rush past him, his arm caught her, holding her back. `Phil's okay,' he said. `It's me that needs your tender care.'

`No, I-I,' she struggled slightly, still embarrassed. He bent his head and swiftly kissed her lips.

`The things you say in your letters, why can't you say them to my face?'

She shook her head. `Oh Marc, no ... no, I *couldn't* ...'

But he tried to make her, for the rest of the night and in bed he tried to make her, kissing her, loving her, thrilling her, until finally it was he who lay on her breast and spoke his love ... `I love you, Marian ...'

She couldn't help smiling as her arms encircled him.

Waking in daylight, Marc peered through eye slits at the rumpus going on beside him. It was Phil – lying in her space – kicking his legs in the air and gurgling slurping noises at the ceiling.

Marc slowly grinned. `Hi, little buddy.'

Caught off-guard, the boy stopped, turned his face and stared, then squealed with delight and continued thrashing his arms and legs up and down. Marc lifted him, sat him squarely on his chest, smiling and chucking him under the chin.

Marian came into the room carrying a glass of orange juice and a plate of granary toast. She was smiling as she placed it on the locker beside him, `Good morning, Lieutenant, it's a warm and sunny Sunday.'

`Marian, it's November, and this is England, so it can't be warm.'

`Well it is. A *lovely* day!'

Still in her pyjamas, she climbed over the bed and bundled under the covers beside him. `When do you have to go back home?'

`*This* is my home,' Marc murmured. `This flat, this girl, this boy—' Phil lunged forward and began to suck his face. `Aw, hell, here we go again.'

Phil was unceremoniously dumped into Marian's arms.

`He's hungry,' she defended.

`Then feed him, for God's sake.'

She opened her top and he saw a soft round breast and a hard rosy nipple. The child began to suck and Marc's eyelids lowered. He turned away and lifted a slice of toast from the plate on his locker, then turned back and held the toast before the boy's eyes. `Swap?'

Phil's mouth immediately detached from her breast and gurgled happily as he grabbed for the toast. Marc flopped back and laughed. `Oh boy, now there's innocence – I'll remind him of this one day.'

`And you'll embarrass him,' Marian murmured, comforting her confused son. `He's only a baby, a sweet and trustful little child.' She pulled the sheet closer around her and lay for a few moments in a silence of contented mothering. Then she looked up and smiled, a sweet, happy smile.

Marc touched her face. `When you smile like that, you look little more than a child yourself.'

`But I'm not a child, Marc,' she replied solemnly. `I'm nineteen. In less than two years I'll even be old enough to vote.'

The pride in her voice made Marc laugh again. He was still giggling frantically when she hit him.

The next three days flew by. They went out in daytime and in the evenings Marian cooked all his favourite dishes for dinner. Those nights of dining in the French restaurant were no longer possible without a babysitter, but she had a stack of French recipe books, which she had studied earnestly.

When they were in the flat their life was simple. They talked and read and played chess or played with Phil, or just stretched

211

out together on the sofa and watched television.

Every so often, when he was unaware, she watched Marc with curious eyes, but the life of domesticity which she feared he might loathe didn't seem to bother him at all. He even seemed to dread the moment when the time came to leave.

On his last night she placed two pale blue candles on the table. Blue was his favourite colour. She struck a match and lit the candles, her eyes watching their wavering lights until they flamed strongly, washing the cutlery and glasses in a bright, hallucinating glow.

Marc glanced at his watch and switched on the television.

She turned back to the kitchen. Behind her the TV news reported on the latest polls for the American Presidential election in two day's time.

`Oh God, Oh Christ ...' she heard Marc exclaim in disgust. `Oh Marian I've just seen something real mean and ugly ...'

`Where?'

`On the television.'

`What?'

`Lyndon Johnson's face.'

She smiled sympathetically, knowing how much he despised Lyndon Johnson – ever since Johnson had shocked the Democratic Convention by refusing to recommend Robert Kennedy as his running mate for Vice-President.

And Marc was not the only Democrat who had responded with stunned disbelief when, instead, Johnson had chosen JFK's old opponent, Hubert Humphries.

`He's jealous as sin of the Kennedys.' Marc had fumed. `Johnson knows he only got into the Oval Office over President Kennedy's dead body. But he's a fool if he thinks Robert Kennedy is prepared to be kept out of the cabinet. No way, not Bobby. He's determined to pursue his murdered brother's policies to the bitter end, civil rights, everything.'

His attention was riveted on the television when she returned to the living room. The telephone rang. He didn't even glance up, leaving her to answer it. When she did, she turned and looked at him with surprise.

`Marc ... it's Jimmy.

`Jimmy?' He looked as surprised as she was. `Why the hell is he ringing here? I told him this number is only for emergency.'

`He says it's urgent.'

Switching off the news, Marc picked up the receiver. `Jimmy, what's up? ... When? Tomorrow. I'm coming back tomorrow. ... Yeah, definitely! No I won't frigging promise! What? ... You're kidding me!'

Astounded, he looked at Marian. `He's only ringing to make sure I get back in time to register my vote, make sure Massachusetts stays with the Democrats.'

Marian was so relieved she began to laugh. After a breath, Marc also began to see the funny side. `Jimmy,' he said more patiently, `I thought I told you this number was only for an emergency.'

Marian sniffed something burning.

She rushed back into the kitchen and opened the oven. The coronation chicken was simmering fine its sauce, but the meringue on the top shelf was turning black. She grabbed her oven gloves and lifted the meringue out, stared at it glum-faced, then shrugged, oh well; they'd just have to make do with cheese for dessert.

When she returned to the living room Marc was placing the phone back on the hook.

`Is Jimmy all right?' she asked.

`No, he's all in a state because the latest polls predict that Keating will win New York, not Robert Kennedy.' Marc sighed. `But I've told him, Keating hasn't a chance. I don't care what the odds are – Bobby Kennedy *will* win in New York.'

And so it proved.

On the same night that Lyndon Johnson swept home with a landslide Presidential victory for the Democrats, Robert Kennedy was elected to the Senate by the State of New York, and Edward Kennedy re-elected by the State of Massachusetts.

To Marian's surprise, Marc was not very jubilant about it when he telephoned her the following evening.

'Only one thing could have bought that kind of victory for Lyndon Johnson,' he told her. 'Kennedy's assassination ticket. The people are still voting for JFK. Giving their vote to the Democrats because they feel they owe it to John Kennedy. I hope Lyndon Johnson knows that.'

Marian agreed. She never disagreed with Marc about American politics, because he obviously knew the situation so much better than she.

But later, after she had put down the telephone and turned on the television to hear British politicians give *their* opinion of the American election results, she heard a different view.

The majority view was that it was *Barry Goldwater*, the Republican candidate, who had won the White House for the Democrats: due to his anti-Communist campaign and his continuous calls for America to "defoliate North Vietnam".

Johnson had contemptuously dismissed such a proposal, declaring Goldwater to be a hotheaded extremist, hell-bent on a war with the Viet Cong.

Throughout – from start to finish – Lyndon Johnson had campaigned as the 'Peace' candidate. And *that* was why he had won.

A baby was crying ... real life intervened ... Marian quickly turned off the television and rushed to Phil's room. As soon as she lifted him out of the cot he stopped crying, his little feet kicking happily against her belly.

She sighed, gave him a naughty-child smile, then carried him into the living-room so they could play together for a while.

And as they cuddled and chuckled and played on the sofa, Lyndon Johnson and American politics faded very far away, like an American movie, not real life at all.

Gretta Curran Browne

Twenty-Two

Massachusetts & London
May to September 1965
_____/

In the spring of 1965, just a few months after being sworn in as an elected President in his own right, Lyndon Johnson ordered massive air attacks on North Vietnam and committed a huge build-up of American ground forces to be sent to South Vietnam.

`Vietnam?'

Jimmy didn't mind so much, but Marc was stunned.

`*Fucking Johnson!*' he exploded furiously, spinning round and thumping the wall with one fist. `How am I going to tell her this, Jimmy? How am I going to tell her?'

`I don't know,' Jimmy replied quietly. `But you can't think about it now, we've gotta go to a briefing.'

When Marc eventually arrived in London and told Marian, she stared at him in white shock.

`But where on earth ... I mean ... where in the world ...'

`Indochina.'

`And how long?'

`A twelve-month tour of duty.'

She stood stricken and silent, then she squeezed her eyes shut and groaned, `I can't do it, Marc! Not for a whole year. I-I can't live without seeing you for a whole year. It's hard enough now, seeing you for just a few days every month.'

`Marian—' He wrapped his arms around her and tried to comfort her. `I'm sorry, Marian, I'm sorry.

`But why ... why should America ...'

`It wouldn't be happening if John Kennedy was alive.' Marc was convinced. `He always said he would never allow America

215

to become involved in a full-scale war in South East Asia. "It's *their* war," Kennedy said. "It's *their* war and *they* must fight it." American aid would only be in small measure, military advisers to help the South Vietnamese resist the force of the Communist-backed North. But now Johnson—'

Marc looked at her helplessly. 'I go in ten days, Marian.'

For the next ten days they lived every second of life as intensely as they could. They were determined not to spoil it by sadness, to enjoy every minute together and not even think of the long separation that lay ahead.

But still there were moments when Marian couldn't help thinking about it.

'A whole year.'

'It won't be that long before we see each other again,' Marc revealed. 'Not as long as a year.'

'No?'

'Because now for the *good* news,' Marc smiled. 'After five or six months over there, we get a week's R & R out of country. Rest and Recreation. And officers, especially, are allowed to leave Nam and meet up with their wives or girlfriends in places like Singapore or Hong Kong.'

He looked at her thoughtfully. 'So as soon as I know my week's R & R is coming up, I could book you and Phil on a flight and meet you at a hotel in Hong Kong. What do you say?'

'Oh Marc, that would be *wonderful!*' Marian was almost bursting with joy. 'Five or six months?' It sounded so much closer than a whole year. 'Why didn't you tell me this before?'

'Well, the worst news first – then out with the rest and make it not so bad.'

'Hong Kong.' Marian giggled excitedly as she sat Phil in his high-chair and lifted a bowl to feed him. 'Do you want to go all that way to see your daddy, Phil? To Hong Kong? When he gets his R & R?'

Phil turned his head away from the spoon and continued

chewing his favourite rubber toy.

'It sounds like Rock and Roll,' Marian murmured as they got into bed that night. 'R&R. Rock and Roll.'

Marc rolled onto his side and grinned wickedly at her. 'You know, R & R is the official name for it – the week's rest and recreation. But most GI's call it I & I.'

'I and I?'

'Intercourse and Intoxication,' he whispered, his mouth moving down on hers.

And later, goaded into a struggle of white-hot passion, she heard her own cries as the world rocked to a wild rhythm, groaning, gripping, never letting go. Not even after the lingering end of her wail had finally silenced.

She finally opened her eyes slowly and saw Marc looking down at her. 'You're so nice,' he grinned, 'letting yourself go like that, making all that pleasureful noise. You weren't just faking it to make me feel good, were you? Cos if you were, let me tell you, I could stay in this bed faking with you forever.'

She pushed her long hair back from her face. 'I need a cup of tea, but I'm too tired to move.' She smiled pleadingly. 'Will you get up and make me some?'

'Tea?'

'Please? Just this once.'

'That's what you said last night. And now you're trying it again. Do I look like a man with unmanly habits?'

'Oh, *honestly*, what rubbish! Making tea is a good old English tradition. And not just for women. How do you think the British won two wars? And if *you* are going to come and live in England—'

She remembered he was not going to come and live in England; he was going to serve in Vietnam.

'Oh Marc—'

'Oh Marian,' he smiled, then realising her thoughts, his smile faded and he said in a voice low with emotion, 'Let's just fake again.'

She nodded tearfully. `I don't want any tea now.' Then she gave him the juiciest, sweetest, loveliest kiss that set him on a slow launch to heaven, all thoughts of Vietnam left far behind.

Over the next few days she was so affectionate she nearly drove him mad, kissing him all the time: on the street, in shops, during meals, even while he was trying to shave his face. `What are you trying to prove?' he finally asked. `That you love me?'

`Oh Marc, I do!'

`I'll give you,' he said, `the benefit of any doubt, if you'll just leave me alone while I shave.' Smiling, he chucked her under the chin. `Go kiss Phil instead. Give me a break.'

On the last day they took Phil to Regent's Park to see the chimps in the zoo, but he was more interested in the lions.

When they returned to the flat, Marc flopped down on the sofa, and as Marian walked in and out from the kitchen where she was cooking a meal, she saw Marc's amused smile as he watched his son playing on the carpet:

Phil was now a sturdy ten months old, and he was down on all fours, crawling around like a lion, making animal noises and trying to growl fiercely – chuckling happily when Marc suddenly leaned forward and lifted him up.

But a few seconds later the chuckling stopped.

Marian turned round in the sudden silence, saw Marc sitting with Phil clutched to his chest, his face buried against the boy's neck, and she knew Marc was crying.

`Marc ...'

She sat down beside him and put a hand on his shoulder, but the tears were falling so strongly down Marc's face, the grief in his eyes so painful, she knew that his cheerfulness of the last ten days had all been a pretence, and in truth his heart was breaking.

And so many times ... *so many times* ... in the questioning years that followed, Marian often wondered if Marc knew then – if not in his mind, but in the depths of his soul – that this time he would not be coming back.

Four months later, it was Alexander who first heard the roar of the motorcycle coming up the small country lane to the house in Massachusetts.

Alexander who stood at the window and stared whitely at the US flag flapping on the back of the bike.

Alexander to whom Mrs Edwards nervously handed the telegram.

Jacqueline was in New York.

Alexander fumblingly pulled open the buff envelope, his hands still shaky from all the drinking benders he was making a habit of.

'I don't need to read it,' he suddenly croaked. 'I know what it says ... It says that bitch killed her own father. And now ... forcing him to stay in the Army ... now she has killed my son.'

He suddenly pushed the envelope into the housekeeper's hands. 'You read it, Eddie. You tell me ... Oh Chrissakes, tell me I'm wrong!'

Mrs Edwards opened her mouth, and then closed it without saying a word. Slowly she took out and unfolded the long telegram.

Alexander was staring at her face as she silently read, and it must have been then he felt his heart falter, felt the pain and the life squeezing out of him as he uttered the most awful groan and collapsed on the floor.

Alexander died before Mrs Edwards could tell him anything.

Twenty-Three

London
September 1965

_____/

Marc had died in Vietnam, killed by a Viet Cong booby trap. And if it were not for Jimmy, no one would have bothered to let Marian know about it.

Miss Courtney was sitting on the carpet playing with Phil, helping him to draw with his new crayons, when the letter arrived on the second post. Marian jumped up like an excited child when she heard the flap of the letterbox.

'Three times a week I get a letter from him,' she told Miss Courtney, 'but sometimes, if he's out in the field, a whole week can go by without a word.'

As soon as Marian returned to the living-room and opened the letter, Miss Courtney knew something was wrong.

'Marian, what is it?'

'This letter ... it's not from Marc, it's from Jimmy ...' She took out a photograph which Jimmy had included with the letter – a photograph of Marc in green combat helmet, the chinstrap hanging down, his dark eyes grinning at the guy holding the camera, his hand raised towards the helmet in lazy salute.

Frowning, Marian unfolded the letter, and as she read it, Miss Courtney saw the girl's face beginning to convey trauma as she slowly read aloud in a disjointed way.

'... breaks my heart to have to write this ... hills around An Khe ... guys in his platoon said Marc kept firing to the end, but ... moving backwards ... Charlie's tripwire, hidden low on the ground and covered by leaves ... the Cong's favourite ... detonated a firebomb... '

'My God,' whispered Miss Courtney.

Two neighbours were outside the flat door, knocking on it loudly and ringing the bell, looking at each other in alarm. From inside the flat they could hear the terrible sounds of Marian's agonised screaming.

Miss Courtney finally opened the door, flustered and distressed, holding up her hand to stem any complaint.

`Yes, I know, I know, but she's just received news of Marc's death, his death in Vietnam ... the doctor is on his way.'

When the doctor inserted the needle of the syringe into Marian's arm, she was still sobbing uncontrollably, her eyes glazed and distant. `Oh Marc ... Oh my darling ... Oh, Marc ... Marc ... Marc...'

In the days that followed, lost in the darkness of her insanity, Marian wandered and stumbled around the rooms of the ground-floor flat like a drunk, her face tortured, her eyes wild, her lips pleading for someone to tell her it wasn't true.

`It's not true!' she howled. `Not Marc! Not dead! He's only twenty-four! No, no, *it's not true!*'

She began slapping her own face violently, banging her head against the wall, trying to wake herself up from the nightmare she was dreaming.

Miss Courtney sobbed as she watched her, fearing her poor girl would end up in a mental hospital and her child taken into the care of a Barnardo Home.

`Marian, please...' But then the sound of the baby crying made Miss Courtney turn and rush to the bedroom, and Marian was left stumbling around the living-room, her hands frantically touching everything Marc had touched.

She picked up every one of his framed photographs and sat with them piled in the lap of her nightgown, kissing each one, weeping over each one, touching his beloved face and feeling only cold glass ... `No, no,' she groaned. `No, no ... Not my darling ... my darling...'

Chef and Sofia came to console her. For a time Marian sat on the sofa and clung to the lovely big Italian woman and found comfort within Sofia's arms, only whimpering now and again as Sofia gently stroked and kissed her hair. `Cara ... Cara ...'

Chef sat down and held Marian then, but within minutes the terrible racking crying started again, and as all looked at the girl's wet hysterical face, they knew Marian just could not cope with her pain.

`Marian,' Chef said soothingly, `Marc would not want you to suffer like this.'

`No!' Marian cried. `Valentino! You always called him Valentino! Don't change that, Chef! Don't change that!'

Again the baby started to cry, but this time it was Sofia who rushed to comfort him while poor Miss Courtney rushed into the kitchen to make more tea.

In the hall, Sofia walked up and down, kissing and hushing the whimpering child, and calling on God and all her favourite Saints to send some help to their poor Marian.

`Dio!' Sofia rushed to the kitchen, the child still in her arms. `We must send for the doctor again,' she said to Miss Courtney. `Marian – she needs more help than our love.'

The doctor came, the same kind-eyed doctor who had come before. This time he did not give Marian an injection, but a very strong sedative, and a prescription for some strong tranquillisers.

At the door of the living-room, as he was about to leave, the doctor paused and looked back sadly at the weeping girl and sobbing child. `Lyndon Johnson should come and take a look at this!' he said to Chef, then marched out.

Hoarse and broken, the sedative beginning to take effect, Marian allowed Chef to lead her back to bed, then Chef sat beside the bed holding her hand until her eyes closed in a barbiturate sleep; while in the adjoining bedroom, Sofia rocked and sang the baby to sleep in her arms.

Sofia sat gazing at the boy's beautiful little face, and fell in love. `Angelo mio...' she whispered.

The tranquillisers helped Marian to cope a little better, but they did not help to cure the pain.

She got up from her bed in the middle of one night, her breath panting, her hands shaking as she opened a drawer and dug out Marc's home address in Massachusetts. He had given it to her a lifetime ago. And Jimmy had told her in his letter that the US military had flown Marc's body home to America.

So now, in the kitchen, with his address on the table before her, she sat down and wrote a letter to Marc's father, begging to be told where he was buried in Massachusetts, begging to be allowed to visit his grave, begging his father to let her have Marc's metal identification tag and Vietnamese Cross.

Jimmy had told her about the Vietnamese Cross, and she meant to say in the letter that she wanted it for Marc's son, but her mind was shrouded in such a fog, the tranquillisers she was taking so strong, she forgot to make any mention of Marc's son, and her writing was so scrawled and childish, it looked like it had been written by someone semi-literate.

She pulled on a pair of jeans under her knee-length nightgown, pulled on a coat and, despite Miss Courtney's protests, she went out in the middle of the night and posted the letter. The sooner it got there, the sooner she would get a reply.

Every day she waited, every day through long weeks lived in a barbiturate haze, through Christmas into January and February, but no reply came from America.

She wrote a second letter, more urgently scrawled, more desperate, more pleading: and after she had posted it, the silent staring waiting game continued.

One night she heard the telephone ring. She turned her head slowly and watched as Miss Courtney answered it, talked for a while, nodding her head occasionally, then replaced the receiver and looked at Marian with a tired smile.

'Just Chef,' she said. 'Every night he rings just to know how you are.'

Every night he rings ... A memory ... the ringing of the telephone, Chef glancing up at the clock, seeing it was almost eleven, a sigh and a nod, `Valentino.'

Miss Courtney was startled and flustered when Marian stood up and prepared to go out.

`Marian! Where are you going?'

To recapture the past, one had to go back. There was no other way.

`Marian! It's after nine o'clock!'

That's why she had to hurry – the call always came a few minutes before eleven o'clock. She put on her navy coat and woollen gloves although she had no idea what the weather was like, no idea what month it was, then she lifted her shoulder-bag and opened the hall door, unheeding and unhearing as Miss Courtney tried to ascertain where she was going, begging her not to go.

`Marian!'

The journey through dying dark streets and in rumbling underground-trains finally came to a halt outside Chef's brightly lit bistro. She opened the door and entered like a figure in a dream, surprised it was still so early, still so many customers sitting at the tables. Her gaze was like frozen blue crystal as she stared at them, seeing only indistinct shadowy forms, yet seeing so clearly where it all began ... *I'm also called Jimmy, by the way. And this guy here is my buddy Marc...*

`My dear girl!' exclaimed Chef as she entered the kitchen; but he too was just a hazy substance in a world she had once inhabited, long ago – a bulky white figure who slowly led her over to a chair, gently sat her down, but her eyes were on the clock: ten-thirty: almost half an hour to wait.

Chef was talking to her, then Peter, both talking together, both bending over her. Then, at last, silence ... a long silence from both of them. And that's when she heard the sound of Chef's radio, heard the music swelling in the silence, heard a man's voice singing so clearly ... `*Strangers in the night, exchanging glances...'*

The music and voice rolled on, seeming to get louder and louder as she sat in a frozen blue stare listening to each word: `*Lovers at first sight, in love forever...'*

Yes, that's how it had been, for both of them, from the very first moment, the very first night ... lovers at first sight.

`*...It turned out so right, for strangers in the ni—'*

When the radio was abruptly switched off mid-song, she blinked, reawakening. Slowly, she lifted her head to stare at Chef . . . and whispered through dry lips, `He's not going to phone me tonight, is he, Chef?'

`No, Marian.'

`Nor ever again.'

`No.'

`No,' Marian echoed, and stood up slowly, embarrassed by her foolishness. `It's the tablets, Chef, they help to numb the pain but confuse my mind.'

`Perhaps you should stop taking them now.'

`Yes, perhaps,' Marian murmured, looking down at her clasped gloved hands. Then, hesitantly: `The singer of that song, his voice sounded familiar, who was it?'

`Frank Sinatra.'

`Ah,' she nodded. And now she understood why the singer's voice had penetrated through her senses so clearly; it evoked a memory of another more familiar voice coming back to her from the distance of a green park ...

... They mix in a very rich set. Country club dinners. Weekends in New York at their suite in the Plaza. Shows on Broadway. Carnegie Hall at the personal invitation of Frank Sinatra, a few drinks with "Francis" afterwards ...I suppose the best way to explain it is my mother is a bigger snob than ...'.

It was then she realised that however many letters she wrote to America, however much she pleaded, her letters would never be answered.

Twenty-Four

London
1966-1968

_____/

A year had passed.

The neighbours still pitied her. Only twenty-one years old, she still physically looked only twenty-one-years old, still a beautiful young girl, but her eyes held a dark-blue sadness which even her smile could not hide.

Yet she was not depressing to be with. Her neighbours in the Hampstead block thought her a lovely person, always respectful, always polite, and her child was always turned out immaculately. But she had become very grown-up and serious, very mature in her manner – nothing at all like the laughing girl who had come in and gone out with the handsome American.

Even the little boy had changed, the neighbours noticed. He was the cutest little thing, with the most *beautiful* black eyes. But he never smiled! No, never. And such a bubbly little baby he had been, always chuckling with laughter. But now, whenever the two of them came in or went out, you could see him sitting in his buggy, as silent as a stone, looking at the world with the most sombre little face.

One day, one of the neighbours finally mentioned this to Marian. It gave her such a jolt – a red flush of guilt spread over her own face.

Inside the flat, as soon as she had closed the door behind her, Marian squatted down in front of the pushchair and looked into the face of her two-year old son. A face too young to understand sorrow or grief – he had probably forgotten his father: a year was a long time in a child's memory.

A terrible awareness came over her – he had picked up his

sombreness from her. He was learning from her the ways of life and behaviour, and so when she sat in sombre silence, so did he. Because he thought that was the natural way to behave.

Images from the past rushed into her mind and she saw again Marc playing games with Phil, always amusing him and trying to teach him something new – pretending to throw his favourite toy out of the window – causing the boy to scurry furiously across the carpet on his hands and knees ... Then Marc laughing as he held the boy on his shoulder, pretending to throw *him* out of the window instead ... Phil reacting with howls of laughter; sullen and disappointed when Marc stopped the game and put him safely down.

`This boy's a real daredevil,' Marc had said proudly.

But what would Marc say now? There was no fun in the boy's life anymore. He had forgotten how to laugh, forgotten how to play.'

`Oh, Phil,' she whispered, gazing into his serious face, `what have I done to you?'

She smiled at him.

He stared back at her silently, a puzzled expression in his eyes. She realised it was the first time in a year that he had seen her smile. He had probably forgotten that she had ever smiled.

She rolled her eyes and grinned at him clownishly, wagging her head from side to side, until, finally, he lost his puzzlement and began to smile at her antics.

A sudden pain flared in her, because it was Marc's smile, and he was Marc's son, and Marc would not have wanted her heartbreak to deprive their boy of some fun.

She lifted him out of the buggy and tickled him as she took off his coat, making him squirm and chuckle and try to tickle her back.

`Know what, babe,' she said, imitating Marc, `it's time for you and me to start living again. Time to push up the blinds and let in the sunlight. Time to do what Camus said, and make each day a celebration of life.'

227

In the kitchen, as she served fried potatoes onto their plates, she was still telling him, still imitating Marc's way of saying things:

'It's time for you and me to waken up to what's going on in the world, Phil. Time to lighten up. We're too young to be seeing life so dark. Too young not to be noticing the sun. Your daddy wouldn't want that. It would make him real sad to know his death was depriving you of fun. He was so full of fun himself.' She smiled softly. 'He was my kind of guy.'

Later that evening, when Miss Courtney let herself into the flat with her own key, she was startled to hear loud music coming from the living-room. She peeped her head around the door to see Marian and Phil dancing. Well, Marian was dancing – Phil was jumping up and down on the sofa as if he was on a trampoline.

'Marian, dear, what *are* you doing?'

Marian smiled. 'I'm teaching Phil how to rock 'n' roll. Or at least I *was* teaching him how to rock 'n' roll, until he decided to jump on the sofa and do his own thing.'

Miss Courtney looked up to heaven and thanked God for answering all her prayers. Marian was going to get well again. Marian was going to be all right.

The six o'clock news was on the television. Marian immediately turned the sound up, listening carefully to every word, every intonation of that New England accent. Robert Kennedy's voice always brought a shimmer of emotion to her eyes. He was Marc's hero, both were from Massachusetts, and the accent of the voice, almost identical.

'... *It's not my opinion, it's a fact,'* Bobby was saying to a reporter. '*A fact that people, with no income, are literally starving here in the Mississippi Delta. And when you consider that we are a nation that spends 75 billion dollars a year on armaments and weapons, and* three billion dollars *each year, in the US, on the care of our dogs ... well, then I think, yes, we could be doing more for our poor – especially our poor children.'*

The words 'poor children' made Marian think of her own problems. While Marc was alive, she and Phil had been generously provided for, but with his death everything had stopped. Even the monthly payments from his bank had stopped.

Those monthly payments had been so generous, so in excess of her needs, she had been able to live for a further two years on the surplus that had accumulated in her bank account. But although she had been very careful, very thrifty, now the money was all gone. And she had no income whatever.

'Would you not reconsider going to the Social Services for help?' Miss Courtney asked her a few days later.

'No!'

Marian was sitting in the kitchen sewing some of Phil's clothes; she stared at Miss Courtney, terrified.

'If I go to the Social Services looking for help, looking for money, they might take Phil away from me – put him in a Home for deprived kids. No, I'm not risking that!'

Miss Courtney sighed. 'Marian, this fear of yours is totally irrational—'

'No! He's my child. I'll decide.'

'Then let me help you,' Miss Courtney pleaded. 'Let me at least pay this electricity bill?'

'No, your own income is small enough. No, thank you, Miss Courtney, I can't let you do it.' She folded the small shirt and placed it on the ironing pile.

'Anyway,' she said, telling Miss Courtney the same lie she had told to Chef and Sofia, 'I still have some money saved from Marc's allowance, so we'll get by just fine, Phil and I ... we'll get by.'

The shopkeeper was busy dealing with a woman buying a stack of groceries.

Marian, fearful and hesitant, stood near the back of the shop watching the two of them. Then seeing the shopkeeper totally preoccupied, she took her chance and quickly slipped a packet of ham into her bag. A minute later, a Cadbury's chocolate cake also went in.

The shopkeeper glanced up as she made to leave the shop. `Can I help you, love?'

`No, I um ... forgot my wallet. I'll come back later.'

He nodded and smiled. He knew her well. A lovely girl.

Back at the flat, Marian stood in numbed silence as she watched Phil innocently tucking into the chocolate cake.

She went into the bathroom, stared at herself in the mirror, and didn't like what she saw. What a hypocrite she was! Too proud to take Miss Courtney's charity. Too nervous to go to the Social Services. But not too proud or too nervous to walk into a shop and steal.

But how was she to carry on? Phil was still too young to go to school, and she could not ask Miss Courtney to give up her job at Barnardo's to look after him. Neither was there any nursery day care available around here. None that was affordable. So how could she go back to work? How could she keep her boy respectably dressed? He was always immaculately clean, but of late, she noticed, his clothes were beginning to look a bit over- washed, and his little trousers too short.

Reluctantly, she looked down at the beautiful diamond ring on her left hand. The ring Marc had bought her. Her engagement ring. Could she ever bear to part with it?

The question was – and this is what she must think of – what would Marc prefer her to do? Wear his beautiful ring on her hand? Or allow their son to go hungry and become shabbily dressed?

Well, whatever she did, she knew she could not steal again. That one event had left her feeling too sick with guilt and self-disgust.

She took the ring to a jewellers in Hatton Garden.

The young man on the Front Counter answered her nervous little questions, and waited patiently while she hesitated. When he felt unable to endure the suspense of her indecision any longer, he finally suggested that she postpone making any decision, until they had given her a valuation of the ring.

She nodded. `Yes, a valuation, please.'

The young man smiled gently. He was well trained in situations like this. So many people brought in items of jewellery that they believed were valuable, priceless almost, then were extremely shocked and hurt when, in their expert's opinion, the item's second-hand value turned out to be less than twenty pounds.

He watched the girl slowly slip the ring off her wedding finger, and knew it was something she cherished. A love affair gone wrong? An engagement broken for another woman? One had to be so very careful – apply a particular style of good manners – in situations like this.

She handed him the ring reluctantly. He smiled as he took it. Unhurried, holding it carefully, as if he understood its sentimental value. He turned the ring around in his fingers, examining it, then looked at her again.

`You do realise that if we wish to purchase the ring, we could only give you a portion of its original value.'

`I want two hundred pounds for it,' she wanted to say, but the lump in her throat was choking her and she was unable to say anything.

She watched him silently as he took the ring to the back of the shop and disappeared through a green baize door to have it valued.

When he came back, he smiled at her again. `A few minutes, that's all.' He gestured towards a chair. `Would you like to take a seat while you wait?'

She nodded, and sat down. The young man moved down the counter to serve another customer.

It seemed an age before a much older man came out of the back of the shop, holding the ring in his hand.

She stood up quickly and hurried to the counter. His impersonal manner discouraged her, and his words dismayed her – almost a repetition of what the young man had said.

`Should you wish to sell the ring, I'm afraid we could only give you a small portion of its original value.'

`*I want two hundred pounds for it!*' she wanted to scream – because that was what she *needed*. And needed urgently. She had no rent or mortgage to pay, but for another six months, at least, she needed to buy food and clothes for Phil and to pay her electricity bills. She could do it on two hundred pounds, if she was very careful, very thrifty with every penny.

`How much?' she asked softly.

The jeweller pursed his lips, turned the ring back and forth under the light, and then shrugged. `Four thousand pounds.'

Marian stared at him, then stared at the ring in his hand, shocked and incredulous. The struggle of pain was threatening to overwhelm her. She should have known ... she should have *known!* Everything Marc had bought for her, whether it be furniture or champagne, had always been the best.

The jeweller looked slightly dismayed at her reaction. Again he turned the ring back and forth under the light, sighed, and shook his head. `Perhaps we could go as high as four thousand, five hundred ... but it really wouldn't profit us to pay any more than that.'

`Yes,' she said softly. `Yes, yes, I will accept that.'

At last, the jeweller smiled. `Will you also accept a cheque?'

Marian nodded, then added hastily, `Please, could I have five – no ten pounds – in cash?'

`Certainly,' the jeweller agreed, his eyes glistening behind his glasses. He turned to the young man who was smiling at Marian with genuine delight at her windfall. `Please give the lady ten pounds.'

She left the shop with the cheque, bill of sale, and ten pounds in cash safely in her purse. She walked along the street feeling giddy and very rich, and at the same time guilty and miserable.

Would Marc approve of what she had done? Selling his ring in such a mercenary way? Or would he be pleased that she had chosen to put the comfort and welfare of their child before the possession of a ring?

Yes, Marc would approve, she decided. He had loved his son, so he would be very pleased at her sacrifice.

She could not know that Marc would have been furious. Not with her, but the jeweller. The ring was a solitaire diamond, a flawless stone of ten carats, its quality currently worth four thousand pounds a carat, and the value of diamonds still rising rapidly as money devalued.

Years later, amongst Marc's possessions in Massachusetts, Phil found the receipt for the ring. It had cost $50,000 in 1964, and in 1967, even its second-hand value, in English sterling, would have been worth at least £30,000.

`Yes, love, what can I do for you?' asked the shopkeeper.

Marian took out the ten-pound note, but was unable to meet his eyes. `You ... um, forgot to charge me for two things when I was last in.'

`Did I?' The shopkeeper pitched his brows together. It was not like him to make a mistake like that. And this girl checked every item – would never let you make a mistake and overcharge her a penny. `Are you sure about that?'

`Oh yes,' Marian insisted. `When I got home and checked my bill to ensure I had not been mistakenly overcharged, I discovered two things were not on the receipt – a packet of Honey-roast ham, and a Cadbury's chocolate cake.'

The shopkeeper stood open-mouthed for a moment, and then shook his head in smiling amazement. `By Crikey, love, I wish everyone was as honest as you!'

Marian's face reddened with embarrassment; she stood hugging herself as if cold. She wanted only to pay up and be gone. Relieved her days of crime were over. Never again, dear God, never again.

In late 1967, Robert Kennedy finally broke publicly with Lyndon Johnson and spoke out against the Vietnam War.

Although, speaking on television before the Democratic Convention, he refused to allow Lyndon Johnson to take all the blame:

... In the last Administration, I was involved in the question of the struggle in Vietnam, and I'm sure President Kennedy made mistakes, of which I was personally involved. So if it's a question of the blame, or the responsibility, for the problems of Vietnam – then I think there is enough blame to go around for all of us.'

'But Johnson was the one who turned it into a full-scale war,' Marian said to the television screen.

She never missed the nightly news on television, because most of the foreign news came from America, a country constantly in turmoil. Not since the Civil War had America suffered such a traumatic decade as the 1960s.

Night after night, Marian watched the television as the turmoil went on. She saw Martin Luther King, in magnificent eloquence, stand up and ask the Government of America why it sent so many young black men out to Vietnam as soldiers – "*to guarantee liberties for the people of South East Asia, which they themselves do not have in Southwest Georgia.*"

On the night of April 4th 1968, Martin Luther King was shot and killed.

When the news came on the television, Marian clapped both hands to her face and could not believe it. Martin Luther King – that beautiful man – publicly assassinated, just like John Kennedy.

She watched in horror as the ghettos went ablaze, blacks rioting against whites, fury and mayhem running rampage at the news that Dr King – their Black Moses – had been removed from the world as easily as JFK had been – both taken out without mercy or warning.

Marian stared at the television transfixed, nodding her head in agreement as many American commentators voiced their opinion that `only one man now,' was capable of healing the racial divisions caused by Dr King's murder.

Robert Kennedy, many believed, was the last hope for America to turn away from the path of crazy violence it was speeding down, and lead the country in a more sane direction. The leaders of the Civil Rights Movement agreed. All was not lost.

`We've still got Bobby Kennedy!' they reminded their supporters. `We've still got Bobby!'

As soon as Robert Kennedy announced he was entering the Presidential race, Lyndon Johnson withdrew from the contest, leaving only Eugene McCarthy to oppose him in the Primaries.

McCarthy hadn't a hope. Everywhere Robert Kennedy went on the campaign trail he was mobbed like a rock star. He had two aims as President – an end to the war in Vietnam; and at home – more attention to the problems of the cities. He promised all races a New Deal and a Fair Deal and, like his brother, promised to take America on to a New Frontier.

Almost four years old, Phil sat at the table, lost in a world of colours and shapes as he painted pictures while his mother watched the television. He loved to draw, loved to paint, and showed little interest in the television. Too young for world affairs, he found the droning of politicians as boring as any child would. Only when Robert Kennedy was on the news, did he look up – because that's when his mother always turned the sound up.

Marian stared at the screen, mesmerised. `The war in Vietnam,' Robert Kennedy was angrily telling his colleagues in the Senate, `is not the responsibility of the people of America –but yours and mine! It is we who send our young men off to die!'

He demanded a halt to the war, which he was certain could be done by means of `a negotiated settlement.'

Was it possible?

The newscasters seemed to think it was.

Marian thought of all those young Americans still out there in Indochina – young men like Marc, like Jimmy – and breathed a sigh of relief at knowing the conflict might soon be over.

The whole of America seemed to sigh a breath of relief. Few parents wanted their sons drafted out to South East Asia. Few young men relished the idea of giving up their careers to go wading in a mine-filled jungle on the other side of the world.

Marian sat riveted to the television as the results of the Democratic primaries came in: `*Robert Kennedy elected in the State of Indiana ... Robert Kennedy elected in the State of Nebraska ...* ' It went on and on ... A Kennedy was ready to reclaim the White House.

Until, on the night of June 5th 1968, just hours after he had won the Democratic nomination in California, and only two months after the murder of Martin Luther King, a bullet from an assassin's gun also struck down Robert Kennedy. A stranger in the crowd who quickly did his deed, then vanished into the night.

Bobby was still alive – but few held out hope.

Phil tried to console his mother as she lay on the sofa and cried and cried – his little hands patting her head.

Seeing his bewildered distress, Marian sat up quickly and wiped her eyes. `I'm all right, babe, I'm not really crying.'

`You are.'

`No, not anymore.' She smiled. `See, look, I'm fine.' She pulled him onto her lap and smiled again. A forced, beaming smile.

`Are you happy now?'

`I'm happy,' she assured him, then hugged him close, and tried to hold back the tears as she stared over his shoulder at the television and heard again a replay of those awful words –

words like a chilling echo from the past.

`Today, June 6th, 1968, Senator Robert Francis Kennedy died at 1.44 a.m ...'

A Jordanian immigrant named Sirhan Sirhan was brought forward as the culprit. It was claimed that he was upset by Kennedy's support for Israel. Like Lee Harvey Oswald, he was a loner.

But it was just too much, one political murder too many, and many Americans were now doubting that this brutal slaughter was the work of lone assassins.

Marian no longer cared. After the murder of Robert Kennedy she switched the television off, and rarely watched the news again. All the good men were gone, Richard Nixon was elected President, and the Vietnam War went on.

Twenty-Five

London
September 1980

_____/

By the time he was sixteen Phil had developed two real passions – the constant physical practice of oriental martial arts, and the creative beauty of true art.

Two weeks after his sixteenth birthday he sat down at the easel in his bedroom and started sketching the line work of his first painting of his father, working from a photograph.

He worked for hours, unaware of time passing, the pencil in his hand moving in delicate feather-light touches

He always wore headphones and listened to rock or soul music while he painted or sketched, yet this did not interfere with the intense concentration he always gave to his work. Nothing existed for him but the music and the developing sketch on the canvas.

Tonight he was listening to Queen's `Bohemian Rhapsody' pounding through his headphones, so he did not hear the ring of the doorbell.

Only when a fist began to pound on the door did he stop and look round, then take off his headphones to listen.

He sighed, turned up his eyes, and stood up muttering to himself, `Forgot her key again!'

He went into the hall and opened the front door blithely, about to make some joking remark to her ... until he saw the two police officers, male and female.

After the first few sentences, he stared at them in some confusion, then as they entered the flat and talked on, quietly and carefully, he slowly began to shake his head in total disbelief. It was impossible.

What they were saying was not possible. He did not believe

them, and he told them so.

'You have made some kind of mistake. The wrong name, wrong address.' He smiled faintly at the absurdity of it. 'What you say can't be true ... It just can't.'

His attitude was positive and final.

The policewoman glanced apprehensively at her colleague. This was going to be even more difficult than she had anticipated.

At the hospital their footsteps were slow, but direct. The two police officers walked each side of him down a long corridor that looked very white and felt very cold, but all else was a blur.

Finally they stopped at a door on the left. The young policewoman caught his arm, holding him back while her male colleague went inside.

As they waited the policewoman spoke to him softly, but he did not reply, his stare fixed rigidly on the closed door. Still she regarded him with compassion. He wore blue jeans and a red sweatshirt and he was a very good-looking young lad, but his manner was as cold as ice.

He was frigid with terror.

The door opened. The policeman, silently and gravely, beckoned them both to come inside.

The policewoman gestured for him to go in first.

He stepped through the door, unprepared for the chilliness of the room. He shivered, suddenly and violently, and it broke his trance. A man dressed like a doctor was speaking to him, but he was not listening.

He was staring at the woman lying on a trolley bed in the centre of the room, her slim body covered to the shoulders by a white sheet. He walked forward slowly and looked at her, and he felt his last faint hope drain away.

They had tried to clean her up, make her presentable, but the blood was so thickly matted in her hair it was impossible to remove.

He slowly stretched out a trembling hand and let his fingertips touch her face in a helpless caress, and continued his silent gazing.

Her face looked so pale, and she looked so young. Younger than thirty-five. Too young to be dead.

The policeman spoke gently to him, hesitantly, asking the vital question.

`Is it...?'

`My mother,' he whispered.

He was still shivering violently. The policewoman attempted to put a blanket around his shoulders but he jerked away from her, taking a startled step back, staring at her as if she had struck him.

He did not want her comfort, did not want anyone's warm touch. The coldness inside him was like a protective shield, his only armour against the hatred building inside him, dense and dark and dangerous.

Her killer – nothing else stirred inside him now save thoughts of the man who had killed her.

The police had said his name – a name he had never heard before – a name he would never forget.

Find him, get him, destroy him.

He turned his head and looked at her face, her pale, lovely face; and in that moment he swore it.

Find him, get him, *annihilate* him. And he would – oh yes he would – somehow, some way some day.

Returning to Hampstead, the two police officers accompanied him inside the flat. `Phil, can you give us the name and address of someone who knows you?' one asked. ` Someone who can pop in and keep an eye on you. Someone in the other flats, perhaps?'

`No,' he said quietly, `I don't want to see anyone from the other flats. Not now, not yet ... not tonight.' But he knew from the glance they exchanged they were determined, and eventually he gave them Chef and Sofia's address.

The policeman nodded, putting his pen away, satisfied. `This Chef, is he a cook?'

His real name is Albert.'

When they finally left him alone, the sudden silence was eerie. He stood alone in the empty desolateness of the flat, so strange now, without her.

For a long time he stood unmoving in the vacuity of the silence, a tearful haze swimming over his eyes, pictures of her floating in his mind – just this morning, how *happy* she had been, excited, triumphant, like a perverse schoolgirl who had boldly defied the rules and proved everyone wrong.

She had done it. The night before. She had finished her book.

And there it was, on the desk by the window, a proudly stacked manuscript waiting for a padded envelope and a professional opinion.

He moved towards it … her book, her gift to Marc, her promise from a long-ago morning. The story of Marian, the story of Marc, the title: *Some Kind of Wonderful.*

Phil lifted the typed title page and turned it over, gazing at the poignant dedication she had written inside: *For Marc – still tender is the night.*

Outside the window the rain had started to pour, drowning the world in a filth of melancholy and blackness, its clattering uproar filling the silence.

He turned away from the window and slowly wandered around the living-room, emptied of her presence. But no matter where he looked, there was not a thing that did not remind him of her.

He paused by the left alcove; the shelves were lined with photographs of Marc, and of himself in various stages of childhood. But amidst the array of family pictures stood a brass-framed photograph of Marian sitting up in a hospital bed holding a newborn baby in her arms. Her eyes shone and looked deeply blue, and her face was the face of a very young girl, exuberant, joyous, excited ... *I was a child and she was a child, in this kingdom by the sea ...* He shook his head, squeezed his eyes, not wanting his readings of Edgar Allan Poe to intrude into his memories.

Memories?

Is that all he had left now?

Bewildered, he stared around him. How could it be? How could his happy home and his loving mother disappear in a day? A night? An hour? A bloody minute of violent destruction.

Violent destruction?

The coldness returned ... it crept over his heart and his mind and into his black eyes until all warm emotions had numbed. Only sixteen, he looked as dangerous as a young French girl in Paris had once looked, when she was sixteen. A foreign relation he had never met.

Again he was thinking of the man who had killed Marian. The police had said his name—

The doorbell rang.

He stood silent, waiting for whoever it was to go away, but the bell rang and rang and he remembered it was the middle of the night, and the two police officers had gone to tell Chef and Sofia.

As soon as he opened the door Sofia pounced on him, wrapping him in her arms and hugging him so tight he could barely breath. `*Angelo mio! Oh Dio! Oh God! Oh my baby, my bayyybeee!*'

Part Two

Phil

1984 — 1993

Gretta Curran Browne

244

Twenty-Six

Massachusetts
September 1984

_____/

A bright and warm New England September. Massachusetts in a noon-day sunlight.

It was the taxi that drew Jacqueline's attention, made her pause curiously by the bedroom window. A white *Harvard* taxi turning off the country road into the private lane that led up to the house, slowly winding its way through the gaps in the green trees until it finally came to a halt at the end of the landscaped garden.

A young man stepped out.

Jacqueline stared at him – and time stopped.

He was beautiful. The most strikingly beautiful young man she had ever seen. Tall and young and strong, with hair as black as jet.

Marc! Oh my darling, after all these years you've come back to me! You've come back, chéri!

Watching him undetected from her bedroom window, Jacqueline gazed down at him as he paused to speak to the taxi driver, the sunlight glancing off his leather jacket, his favourite black leather jacket.

Oh Marc! Everything I did was for you. All my love was for you. And now you know that. And you've come back.

She turned away from the window quickly, a hand to her cheek, her mind racing. She must look her best. After all this time – she must look her best!

She rushed into her dressing-room, flung open the doors of the closet and began searching through her dresses ... Chanel, Dior ... the very best money could buy ... She finally chose a Chanel dress in soft pearl-grey silk with matching grey

245

stilettos. Her black hair was swept up into a neat chignon. She removed the small gold earrings and replaced them with a pair of Japanese pearls.

Above the pounding of her excitement she heard the doorbell ring. With one shoe on and one shoe off she rushed out onto the landing and called down to her housekeeper.

`Eddie! It's Marc! He's come back! He's at the door!'

Mrs Edwards appeared at the bottom of the stairs and gaped up at her. `Marc?'

The doorbell rang again.

`Quickly!' Jacqueline urged. *`Ne le faites pas attendre!* Don't keep him waiting! Let him in. Tell him I will not be long.' A beaming smile. `Oh, Eddie! *It's Marc!* He's come back! I saw him with my own eyes.'

Mrs Edwards gaped until Jacqueline disappeared back into her bedroom, then she turned towards the front door, shaking her head with a sigh of deep despair. When would Jacqueline accept that Marc would *never* come back to her.

So here it was ... *the house in Massachusetts* ... the forbidden house. Large and elegant, a stately multi-level house of the old Colonial style with a half acre of green slope leading up to the front porch.

Phil stood outside the door waiting for his ring to be answered, waiting calmly, his manner cool and dispassionate. He did not intend to stay long. He had asked the taxi to wait.

A woman eventually opened the door – a sturdy grey-haired woman in her late sixties. From her dress and manner he knew she was some sort of housekeeper.

`May I see Mrs Gaines,' he asked politely.

The housekeeper stared at him oddly, her blue full-moon eyes blinking in strange puzzlement, like someone awakening from a deep sleep, wondering if they are still dreaming – or seeing a ghost.

She looked him up and down, taking in his blue jeans,

leather jacket and red T-shirt. But then her eyes settled on his black hair and dark eyes, and her own eyes began to blink rapidly.

Now twenty years old, Phil was no longer a boy but a young man. His years of dedication to the study of martial arts had made him lean, strong-limbed and fit. He was gentle-mannered, but had no fear of any adversary's muscular strength. He had studied a system of martial art that used speed and subtlety to overcome an opponent's natural advantages. By the time he was eighteen he could execute a flying kick at an angle of 180 degrees before a coin had dropped to the floor, followed by a swift strike to the face completed in 0.5 of a second. He had trained with a master, yet he rarely displayed any show of aggression to the world, always remaining respectful and polite – a natural trait he had inherited from his mother.

The housekeeper was still blinking at him dumbly.

'May I see Mrs Gaines,' he repeated. 'Is she home?'

'Who *are* you?' she said at last. 'What's your name?'

'Gaines,' he replied with slow deliberateness. 'Phil Gaines.'

Truly startled now, she took a step back. 'You're English.'

'Yes.'

'Holy Moses...' realisation of who he must be had dawned on her. Without saying another word she slowly opened the door wider, beckoning him to enter.

He followed her down the hall into a beautiful large drawing-room with cerise silk on the walls.

'Now,' she said shakily, as if short of breath, 'I'm going to tell Mrs Gaines that she has a visitor, but that's all I'm going to tell her.'

He looked at her curiously. 'Why?'

'Because you're English and, well, years ago, there was a whole lot of trouble in this house over an English girl—' She glared at him moon-like again. 'And if you are who I think you are, then I know there's going to be even more trouble – I can feel it in my bones.'

She didn't wait for his reply, turning and rushing out ... leaving him alone to gaze around the room.

The first thing that caught his eye was a photograph on a table by the window – a silver-framed photograph of Marc in full regimental uniform.

He walked over and lifted it; a sudden sadness sweeping over him as he gazed down at Marc's smiling face. A sudden yearning to be able to roll back time, bring back the past, and see that beloved face again – *in life* – not just in a photograph. He had lived too long with just photographs.

The curtain fluttered slightly in the breeze from the open window. A golden ray of sunlight shone directly onto his own face, making him turn his head slightly, to see he was not alone.

She was standing in the doorway, staring at him, her face a portrait of emotion.

He gazed at her silently. She was tall and slender and looked no more than forty-five, although he knew she was in her sixtieth year now, but she was still an incredibly beautiful woman. She wore a grey silk dress and grey stiletto shoes. She looked like a French aristocrat. He knew instantly that she was his grandmother.

She finally spoke to him, but her words were mixed up in a moan, half words that trickled away as he stepped towards her, out of the sunlight, and her vision cleared.

`You are not Marc,' she whispered.

`I'm Marc's son.'

She shrunk back in shock, her head shaking. `No, no,' she breathed, `how can that be?'

He knew her thoughts were swirling in disarray, but he continued to look at her with effortless detachment, a distance of twenty years and two deaths stood between them.

`Marc's son – how can that be?' she repeated.

He shrugged. `You were once a mother, so you must know the facts of life. And I'm one of them.'

She walked further into the room, smooth and graceful, but her black eyes were now burning with anger. 'I knew there was a girl in England, yes. But I did *not* know there was a child. How could your mother be so cruel as to keep this fact from me?'

'Cruel? *My* mother?' He smiled derisively. 'When it comes to cruel mothers, *you* should take a look in the mirror.'

'How can you say ... you do not understand, you do not know—'

'I do know,' Phil interrupted. 'I know she wrote two letters to this house, my mother, asking if she could have Marc's military identification tag and Vietnamese Cross, asking to know where Marc was buried, asking if she could visit his grave. Alexander couldn't answer, he was dead. But you ... you read those two letters, didn't you? And you didn't even have the decency to reply.'

She stood thoughtful, her mind churning back to the past, remembering the stupid English girl who didn't even know how to write an intelligent letter. She had thrown it away in disgust. Then a second letter that she did not bother to read but immediately tore up.

'I blamed her, you see. The English girl. I blamed *her* for Marc's death. Blamed her for causing such discord between us. But she may have treated Marc better than the American Army did. Oh yes, how wrong I was. I should never have trusted them. I gave them my son in full health and youth, and they gave me back a corpse. Oh, it was insupportable! The way they tried to console me with a bit of tin. A Vietnamese Cross – in exchange for my son.'

'In exchange for my father.'

Jacqueline stared at him, her face a study in pain, her hand touching her heart. 'Oh ... you are *so* like Marc. '

'I'm also like my mother.'

'But why...' Jacqueline asked, still bewildered. 'Why did Marc not tell me about you? Did he know? No—' she shook her head emphatically, `No, he could not have known! You must have been born *after* he went to Vietnam. How old are you?'

He removed a paper from his pocket and handed it to her. `Here, keep it as a gift, my birth certificate.'

Jacqueline took the certificate and stared at it. `Philippe Castineau Gaines ... Eighth of July 1964 ... A year before Marc's death ... yet no one told me about you ... why?'

`You tell me why? Your husband knew. Well, he was *told* about me, by Marc himself.'

Jacqueline had to sit down.

A voluptuous sofa covered in cerise velvet faced the fireplace. She sat down on it thoughtfully, as if wondering if this could be true.

`Alexander *knew* Marc had a son?'

`Yes, Alexander knew.'

Her eyes went very dark and still. Then, suddenly, a strange smile moved on her face, a smile that was acid and ugly. `So, Alexander had his revenge on me after all. He always vowed that he would.'

Slowly she lifted her head and looked at him, and the look on her face suddenly changed into a trembling, beautiful smile.

`May I call you Philippe?'

`I prefer Phil.'

`I prefer Philippe ... It was my father's name. He was a jeweller in Paris. Oh, many years ago. He was killed by the Gestapo.' While she spoke she turned a gold bracelet round on her wrist. `It must have been Marc who named you Philippe. '

`Yes, it was.'

`My own name is Jacqueline.' She pronounced the J with `zha' sound. `Zhacqueline.'

He did not repeat it, did not give voice to her name.

`To think— ' she said reflectively, `all these years I thought Marc had left me nothing. Nothing but the sound of his voice in my dreams. But he *did* leave me something. All these years I have had a grandson, and did not know. Marc's son—' Her eyes were beginning to sparkle.

`Marc's son—' she repeated, and suddenly she looked young and zestful, glowing with purpose and excitement.

`Have you come from England? Or do you now live in America?'

`From England.'

`To find me?' Her smile was radiant. `Yes, and I know why you did so. Because deep in your soul you know you are a Castineau. Just as Marc was. Just as I am. Just as your namesake and great-grandfather was. It was your *French* blood that brought you to Massachusetts. You could not stop yourself. You knew you *had* to come.'

She patted the sofa beside her. `Come, Philippe, sit beside me so we can talk. We have wasted many years, but now we must get to know each other.'

`Sit beside you?' His voice was cool and neutral. `Don't you know how sick I feel just being in the same *room* as you?'

His words hit her like bullets; all the blood seemed to drain from her face. She could only stare at him as he calmly fired again.

`Don't you realise how despicable I feel being in the same *house* as you. Especially *this* house – the one my mother was considered unfit to enter.'

`Then why ... why did you come here?'

`I came here four days ago. To New England. I've been to Fort Devens. I've been to St Teresa's cemetery in Harvard. I've even been to see Bill Simons over in Shirley. You remember him – Alexander's best friend – nice man, very hospitable, very talkative, especially when he realised I was Alexander's grandson.'

He was looking directly at her eyes.

`I've also read Alexander's book. And I've read my mother's book. Marc always told her everything – did you know that? So, those are some of the reasons why I came here. You're looking at a pilgrim. A son searching for his father, searching

251

for the truth. Now there's not much more I need to know. Now I can get on with my holiday in America, away from Massachusetts.'

`But before you went,' Jacqueline realised, `you had to come and meet me—'

`You? No, no, I had no particular ambition to meet you, except as a means to an end. I've come here to get from you what is rightfully mine. I've come for Marc's military identification tag, the one he was wearing around his neck when he died.'

Jacqueline was stunned. `Rightfully.... yours?'

`You can keep the Vietnamese Cross. As you say, it's just a bit of tin. Marc never even saw it.'

`Rightfully yours?' Jacqueline repeated. `Why should you think anything of Marc's is rightfully *yours?*'

`Because what belongs to the father, passeth to the son. And I am Marc's son.'

`His *illegitimate* son!' Jacqueline flashed.

Phil smiled a little. `Very well, his illegitimate son. And that's why I'm not asking for much, nothing except this one small thing—Marc's military identification tag.'

`No!' Jacqueline refused. `No! I am his true next of kin. All that I had was taken from me, my father, my son, taken from me by war! But I will not give up that. I will not give up anything belonging to Marc. Not even his military identification tag. Not even to you. '

`Then you are the meanest of women.'

Jacqueline's face hardened into viciousness. `You want it for *her*, don't you? That English girl. I remember now – she wrote in her letter that she wanted it. It was *she* who poisoned Marc against me, just as she has poisoned you against me. Why else should you feel sick to be in the same room as me – when you don't even know me?' Her eyes darkened murderously. `It was *she* who sent you here, wasn't it?'

`No.'

Without another word, without a backward glance, he turned and walked out of the room and out of the house.

Moments later Jacqueline heard the sound of the taxi's engine, and sat back. She was shaking, full of anger and agony—a raging agony she had not felt in years. And it was a glorious—because for the first time in years she felt *alive*. Not half-dead, not half-living, but raging with passion for the challenge before her, the new chance Life had given her.

She had seen the condescension and contempt in his eyes, seen a glimpse of the coldness and the cruelty he was capable of, but she did not mind, because all of those things were in her too.

'He's gone then?' Mrs Edwards entered nervously. 'He didn't stay long. Doesn't seem like he intended to either, seeing as how he kept the taxi-cab waiting outside.'

Jacqueline was slowly coming out of her shock, realising the enormity of what had just happened, a hand moving slowly up to her face.

'Oh, Eddie ... did you see him?'

'He's Marc son all right. No doubt about that.'

'Oh Eddie, *Eddie* – did you see the blackness of his eyes? Did you see the way he walked, the way he stood, so dignified, just like my father, just like Marc. And the way his eyes looked at me, how *beautiful* he was! Oh, Eddie, my grandson, he's a true Castineau!'

Mrs Edwards was gaping moon-like again, because tears were spilling down Jacqueline's cheeks, big child-like tears.

'He hates me, Eddie. Oh, how he hates me. But I can't let him go. I can't just forget him. Not now I've seen him. Not now I know he exists!'

She was stammering almost piteously. 'He behaved like a stranger to me. But he is *not* a stranger, he is *Marc's* son ... my darling Marc ... he would not want this; he would not want his son to hate me. He would want his son to love me as much as he always loved me. You know how much Marc adored me! That's why he named his son Philippe Castineau — in honour of me, in honour of my father.'

`But if he hates you, and he's gone—'

Jacqueline sprang to her feet in agitation. `I don't want any of your arguments, Eddie! Not about this. I will not allow it. People like you stare at life and see only the obvious, only defeat, that's why your lives are so tedious, and your characters so simple. But me – I have fought *the Nazis!* I have never considered defeat.' Her slender hands clenched into angry fists. She turned her dark eyes to Mrs Edwards.

`I can bring him back, Eddie.' She nodded emphatically. `Oh yes, I can. He thinks he hates me now, but I can change that. He lied to me, I'm sure of it. His mother – that English girl – she *did* send him here. She *did* poison him against me. But I can change that. I can make her see how stupid she has been. How wrong she is about me. Oh *why* did I not keep her letters? All I know is her name.' She stopped suddenly. `But ... the bank will know ... if they still have the records, they will at least know where she banks in London ... '

`But if she—'

`She will be no problem, Eddie, believe me. I know how to handle someone like her. A simple waitress, not very intelligent, what is someone like that compared to me? And he will see it too—Philippe—my grandson. He will see his mother and I together and he will realise that he is more like me than her. He will see that he and I have the same blood, the same genes, the same ancestors, and the same name. Eventually, all that will count.'

Mrs Edwards was shaking her head worriedly. `Well, if you ask me—'

`Did you see way he was dressed, Eddie? Casual, yes, but utterly clean and perfectly groomed, with that certain *chic* so natural to the French. He reminded me so much of my father, so much of Marc—'

She stood up quickly, brisk and young again, full of excitement, snapping out orders like the young commando she had once been.

'We need a plan. But the first step is to find him, find out where he came from, and where he has now gone. For that we will need expert help ... we have a fight on our hands, but we will win, we always do.'

Eddie sighed, filled with compassion and despair. She knew that Jacqueline was sick, knew she needed the help of a psychiatrist. But who would dare to suggest it? Even her lawyer was terrified of her. Jacqueline was still a powerful antagonist, as her lawyer once called her. Few dared to cross her.

Eddie shrugged. 'Well,' she said, 'do what you must, Mrs Gaines. All I can say is good luck.'

Jacqueline turned a beaming, beautiful smile on her housekeeper. 'I don't need luck, Eddie. I never have. I have always relied on my own resources. And I will win my grandson over to my side in the end. I *will* win, you know. I always do.'

'Yes.' Eddie nodded, and suddenly she felt great pity for Marc's son. He hadn't a chance in hell of walking away from this.

The following morning Jacqueline was in the library sitting at her desk, speaking into the telephone. ' ... You are certain of that? He was on the seven o'clock flight from Logan to New York? Then you know what you must do ... Yes, of course I understand. I don't care if you have to search every hotel in New York to find him. I don't care if you have to search every address in England to find his mother. I'm paying you and your investigators good money, more than you have ever been paid. So I want no arguments. And I don't care what it costs. I just want you to *find him!*'

Twenty-Seven

New York
September 1984

_____/

It took Phil only three days to find Jimmy, thanks to the help of the Vietnam Veterans' Association. The address, a seedy apartment house in the Bowery.

The paint-peeling front door was wide open, there was nothing to indicate who lived in which room, and the dank stairway had the sour and musty smell of a house rotting with decay.

Phil stood in the hall, unable to believe that Jimmy lived in a place like this. And which room?

He knocked on the first door.

`Yeah? Who is it?'

Phil didn't know what to say, so he knocked again. Seconds later the door was opened by a bullish bald-headed old man with an unlit cigarette in his mouth.

`Yeah?'

`I'm looking for Jimmy Overman.'

`Who?'

`Jimmy Overman.'

`What's he look like?'

Phil remembered Marian's description of Jimmy. `Tall, about six-one. Thin. Blond hair. Used to be a soldier.'

`Oh, the weirdo! Two flights up, then second door. But yuh betta bang loud. If he's out he won't hear yuh, but if he's in his TV'll be blasting.'

`Thank you,' Phil replied, but the door had already slammed in his face.

Two flights up, then second door, Phil knocked. He could hear the sound of a television but it was not blasting, normal sound level. He knocked again.

The door opened, but the man who stood there was not Jimmy. Not the Jimmy of his mental image. This guy was mid-forties. He had more grey hair than blond, shaved close in a crew-cut. His blue eyes looked slightly vacant. A jagged scar puckered up one eyebrow into a quizzical expression. He was also missing an arm.

`Jimmy Overman?'

`Lord Almighty!'

He disappeared, and moments later Phil heard the clink of a bottle rattling against a glass.

Phil slowly pushed the door open wider and stepped into the room. Its cleanliness surprised him. The bed was neatly made, everything in its place. Army training, he supposed. Few soldiers lost the habit. The colour television was on, an armchair positioned in front of it. By the window were a small table and two chairs, and it was there Jimmy stood, gurgling down a shot of bourbon.

`I'm sorry to disturb you,' Phil apologised.

`Jesus Christ!' Jimmy put down the glass and wiped his mouth with the back of his hand. `For a minute there I thought you were an old buddy of mine.'

`No.'

`No, I can see that now,' Jimmy said slowly. `You ain't him. Not my buddy. But this country is full of ghosts, you know? Oh, sure! I see them all the time. Even in daylight. Turn a corner and there they are, all my old buddies, laughing and jostling each other, then I come up and *phit* – they're gone.'

A wary, confused expression was forming on Jimmy's hard-lined face. The puckered eyebrow rose higher. `You ain't Marc. You ain't a ghost. So who the hell are you?'

`I'm Marc's son.'

`Lord Almighty!'

Trapped silent for a time, Jimmy stared, as motionless as a still life while his mind searched back down the avenue of a long yesterday.

Phil moved forward and held out his hand. `My name's Phil. I just wanted to meet you, Jimmy.'

Jimmy's one hand came out and grasped Phil's hand in a clasp as strong as a vice. `I remember now ... the little kid in London ... with Marian ... kept climbing onto my knee. Was that you?'

Phil smiled. `I can't remember, but Marian told me you came to see her once in London, after your first tour in Vietnam' ... `*He was so nice,*' Marian had said sadly. `*He had lost his boyish Elvis Presley leer and he looked a thousand years old, but he was so nice, so kind...*'

`Then in 1975,' Phil said, `when the war was over, you sent her a card from New York.'

`Yeah, so I did, on the tenth anniversary of his death ... I wanted to remember it somehow, let her know that I still remembered, still cared about what happened in 1965—'

Jimmy stared through the window, but he was not seeing the street below, only shadows under an orange sun.

`1965,' he said softly, `when the world was young ... the year the Los Angeles Dodgers beat the Minnesota Twins in the World Series ... it seemed to matter then, baseball, our transistors constantly tuned to Armed Forces Vietnam who were beaming it live to us boys in Tigerland ... even out on patrol most GI's had their transistors plugged into their ear. Yeah, it seems funny now, but it still mattered then. We still cared who won at baseball...'

He turned suddenly. `Thanks for coming, Phil, searching me out. It was a nice thing to do. Just what I'd expect from Marc's son.' Tears were pushing, but Jimmy blinked them back. `But aiyyyy – listen, I'm not being very polite. Sit down, will you? Have a drink?'

Phil hesitated. `I was hoping I could take you out somewhere—to a restaurant or a bar. Wherever you like?'

`Nah!' Jimmy shook his head. `Thanks, but I don't care much

for the outside world these days. Guess it's because it's so long since I played a part in it all. No, I'm happiest here in my room with my television. Do you like television?'

Phil nodded. `Sometimes.'

`Then stay awhile, will you?'

They sat talking until three o'clock the following morning. And during that time Jimmy told Phil things that brought tears to both their eyes. A casualty of the Vietnam war, Jimmy's real disability was not his missing arm, but an illness which the Vietnam Veteran's Association had fought to get officially recognised – Post Traumatic Stress Disorder – guilt at being a survivor, a sense of alienation from the normal world, constant depression, and a high rate of suicide.

`So you see, I'm not doing so bad,' Jimmy smiled, easing himself into the armchair. `Some vets are so fucked up after their experiences in Nam, they can't adapt to normal civilian life and have to live out in the wilds. They're the ones who are *really* paying the price – those poor guys alone with their ghosts. But me, well, as long as I'm left in peace here in my room, with the television on all the time...'

`Why do you like the television so much?'

`Stops me thinking,' Jimmy admitted truthfully. `Helps me to forget.'

`Do you have a family?'

Jimmy's face changed. `Yeah ... I used to have a family, once. A father and a sister, as I recall. Nearly drove me nuts. Both of them. Always talking about how wrong the war was. How wrong America was. When I came back after my third tour in 1970, there was no homecoming welcome, not for any of us. We vets were an embarrassment to all decent people in the United States.'

He poured another drink.

`God! I *still* get mad when I think of the treatment handed out to soldiers returning from Nam, especially the draftees. To me, those guys weren't villains but victims – young men, some only kids, drafted out to fight a war they didn't understand in a sweating jungle that nearly drove them insane ... and after surviving the hell of it, after spending months in muddy bunkers living on tinned ham and lima beans, and after seeing their buddies maimed or blown to pieces by Charlie's trip wires and booby-traps – what happens then? They fly home to be greeted at the airport by crowds of unwashed hippies shouting, *'How's it going, baby killers? How many children did you kill at My Lai? How many villages and women did you bomb?'*

Jimmy clenched his one fist furiously. 'No matter that most GIs were innocent. No matter that the North Vietnamese were also aggressors, backed to the hilt by the Chinese and Soviets. No matter, no matter, no matter ... No wonder so many vets prefer to live alone in the wild.'

Phil was bewildered. 'If it was such hell, why did you keep going back?'

Jimmy shrugged. 'I honestly don't know ... but after Marc's death, after my first tour, things back home didn't seem the same anymore. I couldn't get excited about having enough money to buy a new car, stupid things like that ... not while I knew there were guys getting their blood blown out through their ears in Nam.'

'How did you lose your arm?' Phil asked.

'Same way I lost my leg from the knee down.' Jimmy grinned and pulled up his trouser leg, knocking on what looked like a plastic leg. 'I was on short time, only two weeks to go before my DEROS, and Charlie decided it was about time I had some punishment. It still hurts, you know, my lost leg. When it stops hurting, I'll know I'm dead.'

Jimmy sat back and sighed. 'Couldn't manage the false arm, though. No matter how I tried, it just kept sticking out in front of me like I was continually pointing at something. Gave up in the end. Took the damn thing off. Use it now to bash cockroaches.' He chuckled. 'Lord Almighty, between my lost leg and my lost arm and the near-miss of a bullet taking away a piece of my eyebrow, I don't know why I'm still alive!'

Despite his disabilities, Jimmy insisted on getting up from his chair and frying them some supper: fried eggs and bread and strong steaming coffee. And no, he wanted no help.

Jimmy suddenly frowned. 'Know something, Marc, this is the first time we've talked so long in years.'

Phil looked at him steadily. 'Jimmy ... I'm not Marc. I'm Phil.'

Jimmy frowned again, then smiled with bemused uncertainty. 'Well, you know, you're a helluva lot like my buddy Marc. He was a good listener too.'

Phil grinned. 'I can believe that. He once said you talked so much he had to beg you to let him share the air.'

Jimmy laughed. 'Yeah, Marc said that all the time.' He shook his head, puzzled. 'But how do *you* know that?'

'I'm his son, Jimmy. I've read all his letters.'

'No kidding!' Jimmy was struck with amazement. 'You're Marc's kid? Well, whaddaya know!' He held out his hand to shake, beaming with delight at this discovery, and Phil realised that Jimmy's grip on reality was slipping.

Whether it was due to the weariness of long hours of talking, when he was normally used to spending his time sitting silent before the glare of the television screen, Phil didn't know why, but he decided to persuade Jimmy to go to bed.

Phil saw a lot of Jimmy in the following week. And by some change of heart, Jimmy even agreed to go outside with him.

They went to Manhattan, the Village, and other places Phil wanted to see around New York – anywhere outside the Bowery – a place that Phil could not feel relaxed in, faced with so much human degradation and defeat.

Twice he had been forced to step over a drunk lying comatose on the pavement, a third he was sure was a corpse, but all his efforts to get someone to phone for an ambulance had met with a waving hand of disinterest. 'That drunk? Nah, he'll wake up soon enough – soon as his gut wants feeding from a bottle.'

'Why do you live in a place like the Bowery?' Phil asked Jimmy.

Jimmy paused, a rain-cloud passing over his eyes. 'I didn't always live in the Bowery, you know. I lived in other places, nice places, but the people weren't nice. No, sir. Treated me like they thought I was crazy or something. Always sniggering at me.' He shrugged. 'Can't think why.'

He looked around him in bewilderment, like a saddened stranger who no longer felt welcome anywhere in America.

'But the Bowery, well, it's not Washington or Boston, but it's a place where I can come and go and nobody gives me a second look. Nothing odd about a one-armed man amongst a load of no-hope zombies. But now, listen—' he asked curiously, 'do you think it's because I've got only one arm and this here puckered-up eyebrow – do you think that's why those people kept sniggering at me?'

Phil looked at him. 'The nice people who lived in the nice places?'

'Yeah.'

'No,' Phil shook his head. 'They sniggered because they couldn't see past their own eyeballs, Jimmy. Because they were born with mean little souls.'

'A lot of nice people in nice places are like that,' agreed Jimmy, 'mean as monkeys underneath.'

'What about money?' Phil asked. 'Are you okay for money?'

'Yeah, I've got my pension, you know, so I'm not too badly off,' Jimmy explained. 'And I don't spend much. Don't go out much neither. I get all the entertainment I want from my television. Usually I only like coming out for my groceries and the occasional bottle of bourbon.'

Jimmy suddenly stopped. 'What about you? Are you okay for money?'

Phil nodded, but did not explain that when the flat in

Hampstead had been sold, all the money had come to him – fifty thousand pounds of it. A posthumous gift from Marc, from Marian, his future was secure.

'I'm fine, Jimmy.'

'Are you sure? Because if you need any money I could—'

'No, Jimmy, not a cent. I've got all I need.'

Jimmy held out his one hand, palm up. 'Now give me your promise? Tell me no lie.'

Phil grinned and slapped Jimmy's hand with his own. 'Swear to God.'

'Good.' Jimmy nodded with satisfaction, and walked on. 'Nice to know we're both doing okay.'

'You'd never know you had a fake leg,' Phil observed. 'You don't even limp.'

'Practice, boy, practice.'

They ate in cafes and small restaurants and sometimes stopped for a few drinks in a bar, and Phil tried not to look embarrassed when Jimmy would suddenly switch off from reality and stop to have a conversation with one of his ghosts, talking cheerfully to an empty space in the street, or to the empty barstool beside him.

He also kept confusing Phil with Marc, and Phil decided the kindest thing to do was play along. In a bar, after one such conversation with an empty barstool, Jimmy turned back to Phil and grinned, looking pleased as punch.

'You know who that was – McKenna! You remember him, don't you? The lippiest grunt in my platoon. From the Bronx. Used to make you laugh because of what he had painted in black on the front of his green helmet – *Izzat an order?* – You remember?'

Phil laughed. 'Sure I remember.'

Others were laughing too, at Jimmy, behind his back. Sitting at tables and looking at the crazy guy at the bar as if he should be locked up. What else could he be but crazy – having a conversation with an empty barstool?

Like Phil, they had been unable to see the ghost of Michael McKenna, a young lad from the Bronx who had died saving Jimmy's life.

'Out there in Nam,' Jimmy said, his voice croaky, 'we weren't fighting for any great ideal. In the end, we weren't even fighting for America, we were fighting for each other – for our buddies – for the guys in our platoon. It was us or Charlie. All the way. Us or the Cong.'

Not ten feet away, a smart-faced bucko in a snazzy suit was sitting at a table with two blondes, continually looking at Jimmy then making snide comments which made the three of them howl with laughter.

Jimmy seemed unaware of them.

He suddenly turned to Phil, the lucidity back in his eyes, and more amazement. 'I can't believe it, you know. Me sitting here with Marc's kid, all grown up now. What happened to the years in between?'

Another howl of laughter from the table behind.

'They just drift by, Jimmy, the years. That's why we've got to make the most of them while we can.'

'Drift by? Hell no – they speed past you while you're not looking. Least, that's how it seems to me. And the older you get the faster they go.'

He smiled at Phil, a sad smile. 'Not that I care much. Damned if I do. My only fear is that when my time comes, I'll die out here on the streets, flat on the sidewalk, like some tramp.' He shivered slightly. 'That's one of the reasons why I don't like to go out much these days. Why I prefer to stay at home with my television.'

Another howl of laughter from the table behind.

Phil glanced towards it and saw the smart-mouthed bucko in the snazzy suit getting up and walking towards the men's room.

Phil stood up. 'You stay right here, Jimmy, I'll be back in a minute.' He gestured to the bartender to give Jimmy another bourbon.

In the men's room, Bucko was standing by the sink looking at himself in the mirror when Phil walked in. He didn't even glance round, taking out a comb and raising it towards his hair.

`Hey,' Phil said to him quietly, `you know that tall thin guy sitting at the bar?'

Bucko turned, curious. `You mean, the one-armed guy? The loon?'

`Yeah, the one you've been making fun of all night, entertaining your two women, and none of you being too quiet about it either.'

Bucko's expression changed. `Say, what *is* this?'

`This?' The sudden strike to the face broke Bucko's nose, a guaranteed eye-opener, blood spurting like a tap onto his snazzy suit. Before he could even react, Phil grabbed him by the shoulders and bounced him hard against the wall.

`Next time you decide to entertain your women by making fun of a harmless, mixed-up, disabled man, make sure he's not the owner of a Purple Heart, Bronze Star, and Vietnamese Cross for gallantry.'

Phil left him slumped over the sink, and showed no sign of any disturbance when he sat down again beside Jimmy and smiled. `You okay?'

Jimmy nodded. `Yeah, I was just talking to the bartender there. Did you see *Kojak* on TV the other night?'

`No, I didn't.'

Jimmy gritted his teeth. `Makes me mad. You can bet your last dollar that whenever there's a psychopath roaming the streets in cop shows or soap operas these days, he's always a Vietnam Veteran. A walking time bomb. A dope-head. Hell, these people who write these shows, they don't know shit. Never been near Vietnam.' He knocked back his bourbon. `Well, I'm not gonna watch *Kojak* no more.'

Phil grinned. `They're not all portrayed as bad guys. What about *The A-Team*?'

265

Jimmy's eyes brightened. 'Sonofagun! I forgot *The A-Team*. Yeah, they're all supposed to have fought in Nam, aren't they? And then there's this new guy *Magnum*. He's a Vietnam Vet who's not so bad and almost sane – which is more than I can say for that *English* guy in the show – the one with the snooty voice and dinky little moustache. Now if *he* ain't crazy, I'm Clint Eastwood!'

Phil was waiting for Bucko to come out of the men's room and show his bloody nose to his two women, give them another howl of laughter, but still no sign of him.

'Come on, Jimmy, let's go.'

Phil called on Jimmy the following afternoon. The television was on as always. Jimmy smiled his boyish smile, looking real pleased to see him.

'Coffee?'

'Thanks.'

Jimmy chuckled. 'You know who was on TV today? Phil Silvers. You always loved that show, didn't you? That rascal Bilko. Do you remember how we used to sit in front of the television at Devens and howl? Course, Bilko'd never get away with any of that stuff in a *real* army.'

There was a lump in Phil's throat, a terrible sadness in his heart as he watched and listened to this man who had been his father's best friend. '*Jimmy? – nicest guy in the world.*'

And look at him now, a broken man, a misfit, his mind trapped in a time warp from which he couldn't escape.

But Phil was going back to England the following morning, and he was worried. Very worried about Jimmy.

When the coffee was poured, he sat down at the table with Jimmy, and took a deep breath.

'Jimmy, I'm not going to be able to come around again. Not for a while. Tomorrow morning I fly back to England.'

Jimmy looked sad. 'To Marian?'

'No, to Cambridge University. I start my first year there next week. But before I go, I want to know—' He paused, and looked directly into Jimmy's eyes. 'What are you going to do with the rest of your life, Jimmy?'

Jimmy seemed taken aback, his lips moved, but he didn't speak. He sat back in his chair, turned his face towards the window, and went into an endless stare, tears slowly trickling down his cheeks.

'Don't cry, Jimmy. I was just wondering, that's all.'

'No, grown men don't cry,' Jimmy's throat rumbled, then he croaked. 'To tell you the truth, I suppose I'm just hanging around waiting to die.'

Phil brought back to mind all the symptoms he had looked up in the past few days about Post Traumatic Stress Disorder, suffered by forty percent of Vietnam veterans.

'Do you ever feel guilty about being a survivor?'

'Sometimes, yeah, sometimes.'

'Have you ever contemplated suicide?'

'Suicide? Hell, no! I've seen too many GIs wounded, in pain and covered in blood, maybe even a limb blown off, some with their chests hanging open, but *all* were desperate to survive, desperate to live ... young GIs, some no more than kids, crying out for life, even if it meant life as a cripple ... crying out for life.'

Tears were pushing again, but Jimmy blinked. 'So those times when I *have* thought of suicide ... I think of those boys crying out for life, and I know I couldn't do it. It would be like some kind of insult to their memory.'

A minute later Jimmy had switched back and was cheerful again. 'My buddy Marc, you know, he loved Saigon when he first saw it. Know why? Because it looked so French, reminded him in ways of Paris. But then Vietnam was once part of the old colonial French empire, wasn't it?'

He chuckled. 'I remember one day, just a few days after we'd arrived in Saigon...'

Phil had stopped listening. It was all just memories – the sum of Jimmy's life. A reject of society, a man suspended in time and trapped in the past. A lonely, lonely man, with no real purpose in life except surviving from one television show to the next.

Not exactly out of the blue – because Phil had already decided his own future career – he had an idea.

`Before you lost your arm, Jimmy, which hand did you write with?'

`The one I've got left – my right hand.'

`So would you do something for me, Jimmy? When I get back to England, would you write to me there, say, every few weeks or so?'

Jimmy smiled. `Sure I will. I always liked writing letters. These days, though, I got no one to write to.' He frowned. `Ain't got much to say either.'

`That's okay, because what I want you to write to me about, Jimmy, is Vietnam. All your memories, all your buddies, what happened to them, and what happened to you. All the little details you can remember, funny and sad. Just a few pages every week. Would you do that for me, Jimmy?'

Jimmy's face beamed, as if there was nothing he would enjoy doing more, not even watching television.

`Write about Vietnam? Sure I will, Marc. Anything for a buddy.'

Twenty-Eight

New York
September 1984

_____/

`Gotcha!'

Phil had just returned to his hotel on the corner of West 63rd and Columbus, had just entered the foyer, when he heard the voice behind him. He turned to the young brown-haired man who had obviously mistaken him for someone else.

`Just kidding.' The young man grinned. `I've always wanted to say that to someone. Hope I didn't scare you?'

Phil assessed him quickly: he wore a three-piece tailored suit which must have cost a fortune, blue silk tie, and looked like he had come straight from a business meeting in Wall Street. Either he was a resident of the hotel just trying to be friendly, or an off-the-street diner heading for the restaurant.

`My name is Tom Kennett,' he said. `I'm a detective for a firm of private investigators. Let me give you my firm's card.' Like a magician he produced a card through his fingers. `And you, I have been reliably informed, are Mr Phil Gaines.'

Phil frowned. `So?'

`Now I do understand this must be something of a surprise for you,' said Tom Kennett with solicitude. `And it's also very difficult for me. So can we just step aside here for a minute and talk.'

`About what?' Even as he asked Phil knew about what.

`The fact is, Mr Gaines, I have two of my colleagues waiting in a car outside, and the three of us are in a grim predicament. We really do need your help. We have a job to do for our firm, an important job, but we are running out of time. Only you can help us out of the jam we're in.'

Phil stared, amazed at this performance of charming

audacity.

`You see, this is our problem – we were ordered by our firm to find out where you were staying in New York, which we did, yesterday afternoon. And now we have been ordered to escort you to the suite of Mrs Jacqueline Gaines at the Plaza Hotel before you leave for England, which, according to our investigations, is tomorrow morning on a British Airways flight at 8.15 from Kennedy.'

Tom Kennett sighed apologetically. `So now you understand why we would be very grateful if you would come with us this evening. To the Plaza Hotel.'

`And if I refuse to go?'

Kennett screwed up his lips and looked thoughtful. `Well, we can't strong-arm you out of the hotel. That wouldn't be very polite. And we have been ordered not to use violence. Not that we ever do. Violence is not our style.'

`I'm very relieved to hear that.'

`So, if you refuse to come with us tonight, ' Kennett continued in an amiable, conversational tone, `I suppose we could always arrest you in the morning before you board your plane at Kennedy. Show the airline staff a fake warrant for your arrest. Tell them we are FBI and you are responsible for two murders in two states and the cops have been looking for you everywhere –haven't they been watching their televisions, for God's sake?' Kennett grinned. `Works every time. Especially when you mention the word television. Makes it more real.'

Despite everything, Phil couldn't help liking Kennett. The man was either extremely clever or an absolute clown.

`So you see, Mr Gaines, it would be much easier all round if you just came along with us now.'

Phil stared off towards the centre of the hotel lobby as if pondering the consequences of his decision. He finally made it, and looked at Kennett. `Okay, let's get it over with. Let's go to the Plaza.'

`Now you're talking! Look, son,' said Kennett, who was no

more than thirty. 'I know this is all very inconvenient for you, but where's the harm? She's just a little old lady after all, your grandmother. A poor old lady just wanting to find her grandson.'

'A little old lady?' Phil almost laughed. 'Evidently, you have never met her.'

'No, but I believe in karma. And helping old ladies is good for my karma.'

Outside the hotel the two colleagues were standing by a silver-grey BMW, attempting to placate the doorman who was shouting furiously at them to move their car.

'It's *against the law* for any car to park inside these yellow lines! The space between these yellow lines is for taxicabs and limos delivering and collecting guests from the hotel! And it's *against the law* for any other vehicle to park here!'

Kennett flickered a glance at Phil. 'I told you we were in a jam.'

As soon as the two investigators saw Phil and Kennett coming out together, they pointed. 'And that's just what we're doing –collecting a guest. Look.'

The doorman turned, looked at Phil with recognition, then turned back to the car. 'I see one guest, and I see three men to collect him. Know what that means to me? It means that this here vehicle is no taxicab and no hired limo. So it's *against the law* for it to be parked here!'

'Aw, shove it up your ass,' said Kennett, opening the back door of the car for Phil to get inside. 'We can park where we damn well like. We pay our taxes to the City, which is more than any of your guests do. Know what you are – a *toady* to foreigners. A disgrace to your parents!'

As the car moved off into the early-evening traffic, Phil looked wryly at Kennett sitting next to him. 'Being civil to hotel doormen – not good for your karma?'

Kennett laughed. 'Well, you know, there is one huge difference between your sweet grandmother and that blowhard

271

doorman. Your grandmother is paying us a jumbo rate with a sizable bonus on top. And for that we don't take no interference from some ten-cent tip-technician.'

He sat back and relaxed. `Now let me introduce you to my two esteemed colleagues here in the front, Mr Tony Martinez and Mr Stephen Ward. The three of us always work as a team and we always get results.' He pointed to each of the two in turn. `He's the balls of the outfit, and he's the brains.'

`And what are you?' Phil asked Kennett.

`He's the biggest prick in the State of New York,' said the driver, grinning at the guy in the passenger seat. `That right, Stevie?'

`Yep.'

`I am the *negotiator*,' said Kennett with authority. `I know how to handle people without any unpleasantness. Right, Stevie?'

`Right, Tom.'

`Did you phone the Plaza?'

By the time they reached the Plaza Hotel, Phil decided he had been hoisted by the Marx Brothers, three well-dressed clowns. As he got out of the car the driver shook his hand firmly. `Adios, amigo.'

Stevie stretched and did likewise. `Hey, Phil,' he grinned, `don't let us down when you get inside. Don't strangle your grandmother. We'd feel responsible. So keep the peace now.'

Only Kennett escorted him into the hotel, after putting on a pair of dark glasses.

`Now this really *is* getting theatrical,' Phil murmured.

After stopping at the main desk, and while waiting for the elevator, Kennett took the dark glasses off.

`Maybe you're right,' he murmured. `They're not exactly a natural requirement for wandering around the Plaza. It was just a final little touch to impress your grandmother. Little old ladies always expect you to look the part. Get real disappointed if you don't. Comes from watching too much television. All of

America watches too much television. It's the nation's God and all the presenters are hallowed apostles.' He nodded his head slightly, and Phil continued to look amused.

'But these shades are valuable tools of our trade, you know,' Kennett went on. 'For instance, if we had been forced to arrest you at Kennedy, pretending we were FBI, all *three* of us would have been wearing shades. Know why? No one would believe we were FBI without them.'

'I still can't believe any of you are private detectives,' said Phil. 'If you want the truth – not one of you look the part. Or is that the idea?'

'You got it – that's the idea.' Kennett grinned, pleased. 'But tell me, just out of interest, why, in your opinion do we *not* look like private detectives?'

'Well, three young guys, all dressed like Wall Street yuppies—silk ties, Gucci shoes and Rolex watches—'

'You *noticed* all that?' Kennett looked impressed, then looked at his watch, and down at his shoes.

'Wouldn't wear anything else,' he said, and laughed. 'So what did you expect? Tough guys with snap-brim hats like Philip Marlowe or Mike Hammer? Nah – that's *old* time! Old Fifties and Sixties Hollywood stuff! And this is the Eighties, friend, the *Eighties*.'

The sitting-room of the suite was yellow and white, and mirror bright. Jacqueline smiled her brilliant smile.

'So, Philippe, we meet again.'

Phil looked at her silently, certain that Kennett was still standing outside the door, stunned. The little old lady he had expected was tall and slender and black-haired, wearing a close-fitting beige jersey dress, designed to show her mature but still lovely figure to perfect advantage. Her style, her sophistication, her charm – the way her dark eyes had glowed as she had clasped Kennett's hand in both of hers with a delighted smile – all made her look a much younger woman than she actually was, and implied a sensuous energy and attractiveness that would never age.

Kennett had stood, open-mouthed, even as Jacqueline dismissed him by closing the door in his face.

`This is all a waste of time,' Phil said. `I don't know what you hope to achieve.'

A waiter had wheeled in a trolley of silvered-covered dishes. Jacqueline gestured for him to take it over to the dining table by the window. The table was dressed in a lace cloth, lighted candles and gold-rimmed white china, and already set for two. A second waiter carried in a bottle of champagne in an ice bucket.

Jacqueline said, `I thought it might be nice if we dined as we talked, Philippe. It's not yet seven, so I presume you have not dined?'

`I'm not hungry.'

`Nevertheless, you will at least have a glass of Roederer's Cristal with me, won't you? It was Marc's favourite, you know. I'm sure he would like you to try it, and would consider it very ungracious of you to refuse.'

`Nevertheless, no, thank you,' Phil said. `I see no point—' a waiter was holding out a chair for him, the other was pouring him a glass of the champagne – `in causing a scene,' he finished with a sigh.

As soon as he had sat down opposite her at the table, Jacqueline gave a slow easy smile. `Roederer's Cristal, as Marc used to say, is the champagne of champagnes. The late Tsars of Russia drank nothing else.'

She lifted her glass, letting the glow from the candlelight illuminate its sparkle. `All I want, Philippe, is a little time for us to talk together without accusations or anger. And after all my trouble in finding you, surely you will allow me that?'

`I would find all this easier,' he said evenly, `if you would stop calling me Philippe. It's not a name I am used to, or feel comfortable with.'

`Then I shall call you Phil,' she said agreeably, and nodded for him to taste his champagne, smiling in triumph when he did so and she saw his instant appreciation of its cool and soothing seduction.

`I knew you would like it,' she said. `All the French have a natural appreciation for good wine and perfect champagne.'

`Yet I am English,' he said curiously, eyebrows raised. `So it seems we English know a good champagne when we taste it too.'

She smiled almost teasingly. `You are half-French. Your father was a Parisian, born in Paris.'

`My father,' he said quietly, `was an American soldier, the son of an American. He paid for his American citizenship with his blood.'

`And that is all you know of him,' Jacqueline said softly, `because that is all he left you, the American legacy of Vietnam. But there is so much more you need to know, things that only I can tell you. Things about Marc, about Alexander, about Paris, about my father, Philippe Castineau. Things about your *paternal* family. Things that your mother does not know. Will you not let me tell you some of those things, before you make a final judgement about me? Will you not at least hear my side of it? It would be a fair thing to do, I think. And I'm sure Marc would agree.'

`Very well,' he said, `I'll listen.' Then he looked up inquiringly at the two waiters who had finished serving food onto their plates.

Jacqueline read his expression and instantly dismissed the two waiters with a wave of her hand. She did this with a grace that was not offensive, simply expedient and not unexpected.

When the waiters had retired from the room, leaving them to continue their conversation in privacy, Jacqueline smiled, looking at ease and appreciative, and then spoke softly as if shyly venturing a confession.

275

'Not everything I have done has been right. But then, you must understand...'

He sat back and let her talk without interruption, and without touching a morsel of the food on his plate, finally turning his eyes away to gaze out of the window at the figure of Abundance atop the Pulitzer Fountain.

But throughout he continued listening as she told him of her life in Paris, her work for the Resistance, her father's murder by the Gestapo, her early years in America, her disastrous marriage, her complete devastation at Alexander's betrayal, writing down every word she had said to him in confidence, using *her* words to win himself a Pulitzer prize ...

He glanced at her face and saw the faraway look in her eyes as she spoke – as absorbed as a small child lost in the telling of an enthralling story in which she was the heroine.

Then the tone and story changed.

'But, oh! ... how can I tell you my love for my son? How can I explain to you the love between a mother and her only son.'

He didn't need her to explain the love between a mother and her only son. He had experienced sixteen years of it.

But she told him anyway, occasionally waving her hands as though trying to describe with her hands what she could not articulate, occasionally speaking in French and not realising it, an unstoppable monologue, explaining everything in the only way she knew how – from her own point of view.

When she had finally finished speaking, her eyes drifted from the window across the table to him. Her eyes, so dark, illuminated by the candlelight, were glistening with tears.

He sat there, saying nothing, looking at her intently.

She whispered, 'Well, Philippe?'

'Well,' he said, pushing back his chair and standing up. 'Thank you for dinner, Mrs Gaines. But now I must leave. I have an early start in the morning.'

'But you said—'

'I said nothing. You manoeuvred me into agreeing that you

should be allowed to talk about yourself without suffering any accusations or anger from me, and I have complied.'

`But ... did nothing I say mean anything to you?'

`It might have meant more, if you had once – just once – mentioned my mother. Made even the smallest inquiry about her. But she was never of any interest to you, was she?'

He stared at her coldly, then suddenly changed his mind and sat down again. `Well, Madame, whether you like it or not, I am going to tell you about that English girl named Marian Barnard.' `Oh, *please*, please do!' Jacqueline gushed. `I want to know *everything* about her. Marc told me so little. And now I so much want to meet her. I so much want to talk with her about Marc. I want to make her understand how wrong she is about me. I was hoping you *would* – tonight – tell me about her.'

A long silence.

`She was not like you,' Phil said finally. `She would not have considered herself brave or daring or reckless. She didn't know about such things. She hated hurting others, and often feared for her own courage. But she was the sun and rain and earth to me. She was kind and loving and as ordinary in her ways as ... as a childhood morning full of bowls of cornflakes and fresh milk. An ordinary mother, watching over my boyhood, helping me to put the pieces of a jigsaw into place, her fingers leaving a timeless imprint on my life, never to be erased, no matter how long I live. Do you understand?'

`Oh, yes,' she agreed. `I understand so well. That is how I think of my father.'

`But to Marc ... Marian was someone else,' Phil went on. `Someone quite different to the person I knew. To Marc she was a beautiful girl, the love of his life, constantly crossing sky and ocean just to be with her. He wanted to give her the world, marry her, and bring her to America. He wanted you, as his mother, to welcome her.'

`Yes,' Jacqueline agreed, moving restlessly. `But you see—'

`To you, though, she was someone else again. To you she

was not good enough. An unintelligent waitress. An immoral slut. My mother.'

`I was wrong, so *wrong*,' Jacqueline said penitently.

`And you do regret it now, don't you? The way you insulted her. The way you hurt both of them. Marian and Marc. My parents.'

`Yes,' Jacqueline nodded. `So much I regret it now.'

`Now that you know they had a son?'

Her hand reached out to him. `Will you forgive me?'

`No.'

Jacqueline fought off her panic – an unprepared moment of terrible alarm – that quickly gave way to a feeling of exasperated anger.

Oh, how *foolish* young men were. How stubborn. How naïve. Did he really believe she would take `No' for an answer? She would *not* take `No' for an answer, and she was a good fighter when it came to getting what she wanted. She had learned early in the Resistance, and instructed others with the same duty: *Whatever the obstacle, the mission must be accomplished.*

Marc had also said `No' to her, at first, but she had quickly found a way to persuade him. And as bitterly as she now regretted forcing that promise from Marc – now that she had met his son – she was ready to use the same tactics again. Except this time she would not use a Bible. This time she was better prepared.

`Wait, please!' she begged as Phil turned to leave. `I have something for you!'

`Marc's military identification tag?'

`No, something much better.'

He had called her the meanest of women, but she would prove him wrong. She rushed over to the escritoire and took a slip of paper from a drawer. He was almost at the door when she rushed over and handed it to him.

`For you.'

He stared at it, and thought at first it was some kind of joke.

He shook his head to clear it, and stared again, but there it was, filled out in black ink – a cheque from the Chase Manhattan Bank payable to Philippe Gaines, and signed by Jacqueline Gaines – $1,000,000. One million dollars.

He looked at her and smiled. 'Very funny,' he said, and handed the cheque back to her. But she pushed it back in his hand, deadly serious.

'You must allow me to make amends,' she insisted. 'You must understand how important this is to me. I lost my son, but now I have found my grandson. You must allow me to give you a fatted calf.'

'A million bucks is one hell of a fatted calf.'

'So?' She made a careless gesture with her hand; diamonds flashed before his eyes. 'You are my grandson. My brother died out in the Congo, and now you are my only living relative. So who else should I give it to?'

She smiled at him, almost flirtatiously, knowing that money was the greatest persuader in the world.

'Do you not know how wealthy I am, Philippe? When I married my husband I did not marry a rich man. He married a wealthy woman. Did I not tell you that my father was a Parisian gentleman, a jeweller, a man who dealt in gold and diamonds? The Gestapo got his life but not his wealth. No-n-no, we Castineaus were far too clever for that.'

Phil looked at her smiling face, and thought of his mother, penny-pinching all her life; selling the only diamond she had been lucky enough to possess.

Jacqueline sighed, 'You should have had this years ago. Your mother should have had some too. But I shall make amends to her. I shall see she has every luxury. Really, it's too bad, my grandson growing up without the Castineau wealth to support him.'

'My mother wants nothing from you,' he said softly. 'And neither do I.'

279

He tore up the cheque.

Jacqueline stared at him, incredulous. It was impossible! No young man would tear up a cheque for a million dollars.

'Nothing,' he reiterated, letting the torn pieces fall before her eyes. 'Not a cent. Not from you.'

She stepped back, stung, as if it was salt being thrown in her eyes. She quickly turned away, her hands gripping the back of the sofa, her voice beginning to shake.

'Why ... *why?*' she moaned. 'Why do you hate me so? Has it always been?'

'No, not always. Until a week ago you were just a stranger who lived in a house in Massachusetts. All I ever wanted from you was my father's military identification tag. But when I went to see Bill Simons and was told – what Jimmy forgot to tell Marian all those years ago when he visited her in London – that Marc's father had died upon news of Marc's death, I realised then that the vindictive tyrant of the family was not Alexander, but *you*. Because it was *you*, wasn't it, who ordered the bank to stop the monthly payments to Marian Barnard?'

'Yes, yes, but I didn't know there was a child! If I had—'

'Oh, so it was only *her* you wanted to punish – the waitress. The girl you knew Marc was deeply in love with. And so despite his instructions that she be supported from his *own* money – from his *own* trust fund – even in the event of his death, you brought in your clever lawyers and had Marc's instructions rescinded.'

'But please, you *must* understand – after Marc's death I was so tortured with grief ... I was deranged.'

'No!' Phil snapped savagely. 'You were deranged *before* Marc's death. Long before. And don't give me all that sob stuff about how you suffered in the war. How you were *forced* to kill Nazis. You loved the violence. It was the only time you felt passion! When you were killing, destroying, getting your revenge. You revelled in it! The war, to you, was nothing to do with good and evil – it was all about *power*. The power you felt every time you killed, every time you gave an order, every time someone knuckled under to you.'

She was staring at him, eyes wide, without voice, only words in her ears, words scourging her with remorseless intent.

'Especially Marc. You revelled in emasculating Marc even more than you delighted in humiliating Alexander. So don't try and use the war, or Marc's death, or anything else as an excuse for your badness.'

'B-Badness?'

'All I know is that you treated my mother with as much contempt and malevolence as any Nazi treated a Jew – so it doesn't wash with me, Saint Joan. You're a selfish, malicious, evil bitch. And it's about time somebody told you so.'

He paused at the door and smiled at her unkindly. 'I can't tell you how pleased I am that it was me who did.'

Jacqueline sprang out of her shock, lunging forward, grabbing him fiercely, her hands holding onto the lapels of his jacket, her eyes manic with rage. 'It was *her*, wasn't it? The English girl! Your mother! It was *she* who sent you here to torment me!'

He caught her hands in his own, removed them from his jacket, and viciously pushed her away.

'My mother is dead! If you had been listening when I spoke about her, you would have realised that immediately. Everything I said about her was in the *past* tense. Strange you didn't notice that – a woman who claims to have been the true literary voice behind her husband's prize-winning novel.'

He gave her one last disgusted look. 'Poor Alexander.'

Jacqueline was unable to utter a sound. Not even when the door slammed behind him.

The suite had two bedrooms.

Mrs Edwards, standing in her own bedroom with her ear pressed to the door, had heard it all. She opened the door slowly but did not enter the sitting-room, just stood and stared in disbelief at Jacqueline's motionless figure. On the carpet, near her feet, were the scattered pieces of the torn-up cheque.

Eddie shook her head. After all these years living with Jacqueline, she would not have believed it possible. Poor Alexander had not been able to stand up to her, nor Marc, nor any single person that Jacqueline had ever come in contact with. She was possessed by a ruthless conviction in her own power, and in any battle of will, she always won.

But yes, tonight it had actually happened. Jacqueline had finally met her match, and lost.

Eddie closed the door quietly and turned back into the bedroom. But would she give up? Eddie wondered. Even now, would Jacqueline give up?

When Phil returned to his hotel room, he immediately opened the small drinks cabinet and poured himself a shot of bourbon. Since his mother's death he had a particular detestation of strong drink, and rarely drank anything stronger than wine – but it was not every day he was given a chance to tear up a cheque for a million dollars.

Was he crazy?

He knocked back a slug of bourbon. Shuddered. Threw the rest down the sink.

A million dollars.

Maybe he was as crazy as her?

No, only a sleaze would forgive for money.

Slowly, the terrible tenseness that had gripped and held him, began to leave him. His muscles relaxing, his mind clearing. He thought over all Jacqueline had told him about her reckless and violent teenage life, and wondered what kind of woman she might have become, if the Nazis had never invaded her beloved Paris.

Would she still have become a psychopath? Or would she have put her intelligence and talents to better use?

Strangely, he found himself, at last, feeling some compassion for her.

Not much, but some.

In her suite at the Plaza, Jacqueline sat listlessly on the sofa, staring into nothingness. Eddie tried to comfort her.

`Aw, he'll come round! Now he's had his vengeance, he'll start thinking about that million dollars and wonder if it was worth it.'

`No,' Jacqueline said quietly. `There will be no forgiveness. Not from him. I know that now. I thought he was like my son. My beautiful son who died in Vietnam. I thought he was like my father. My wonderful father who died for France. But he is not like either of them – he is like *me*.'

Eddie didn't know whether to agree or disagree.

`I knew it that first day I met him,' Jacqueline continued. `When I saw the way he looked at me. Dear God, my heart – in that moment I saw a memory of myself as I had been when I was young. So proud, so aloof, so heartless! Like me, as I was then, he is beautiful, but cold and immovable. Like me, he will never allow anyone to stand in his way. And like me – he will *never* forgive an enemy.'

`An enemy? Aw, you're no *enemy*. And what's there to forgive? Okay, so you stopped Marc from marrying his mother. But that's all in the past. And anyway – his mother is dead now.'

Jacqueline winced, and bit her lip. Such lack of subtlety still appalled her.

`If only his mother was *not* dead,' she said a few moments later. `If only his mother was still alive – then there would be some hope, some chance of a reconciliation, some way to win him back. But now it is too late.'

`Oh, come on, it's never too late.'

`You do not understand him, as I do,' Jacqueline said softly. `In France there is a saying: Hurt the mother, and you make a lifelong enemy of the son.'

She closed her eyes. `And I hurt them both. His mother *and* his father. And now both are dead. No, no, he will never forgive me, I see that now.'

The following morning, three hours after Phil had caught his flight and left New York behind him, Jacqueline visited her lawyer.

`I have come about my grandson.'

Lewis Belfort's eyes widened. `Your grandson? I didn't know—'

`Yes. He gave me his birth certificate as a gift.' She threw it across the desk.

Belfort picked it up, read it carefully, noted the legal stamps and signatures, and then looked at her in amazement. `So ... Marc had a son?'

`As you can see.'

Belfort nodded, and thought he understood her problem. `And now he has come to you looking for money, has he?' Belfort smiled confidently. `Well let me put your mind at rest immediately, Jacqueline. The child was born out of wedlock. He is illegitimate—'

`He is magnificent!' Jacqueline cut him short. `I gave him a cheque for a million dollars and he tore it up in my presence.'

Belfort swallowed. `A ... million dollars?'

Jacqueline smiled. `Oh, Lewis, he would have been *superb* in the Resistance. He would not have been bribed. My father would have been proud of him.'

Lewis Belfort was losing track, flummoxed by Jacqueline's reaction, and unsure what she wanted from him now.

`I want him legitimised. As Marc's son. And my grandson. You have his birth certificate there before you. And as you can see, it bears Marc's signature.'

Belfort looked again at the certificate. `Yes, Marc must have been present when the birth was registered.'

`Yes,' Jacqueline echoed, her dark eyes transparent with

pain. 'My darling Marc was present when the birth of his son was registered. But he never told me...'

And as Jacqueline sat staring back into the past, all the mistakes of her own making came back to haunt her, taunt her – blades of bitter sorrow shooting through her for the lives that had been wasted, her own life, and her son's. The baby grandson she could have loved.

Oh, regret was bitter indeed when she looked back on what she had not known, yet could have known, if only ... if only...

'Jacqueline?' Lewis Belfort touched her shoulder. She looked up at him and he saw her suffering, her despair.

'How was I to know Marc would be sent to Vietnam?' she groaned. 'How was I to know...?'

She dropped her head and finally told Lewis Belfort the full story of Marc and the English girl and the action she had taken to prevent their marriage.

'But I didn't *know*, Lewis, I didn't know they had a child ... I didn't know ... the girl ... I didn't know she would remain faithful to Marc, remain unmarried...'

Lewis Belfort looked into the black desolation of Jacqueline's eyes and pitied her, as he had never done before. He had never seen her so vulnerable, and wanted to comfort her.

'And now their son—' she whispered. 'Oh, how he hates me, Lewis.'

'I'm sure,' Lewis said, 'that in time, some sort of understanding will be reached between the two of you. Perhaps if you were to—'

'No, no,' Jacqueline shook her head hopelessly, and repeated to Lewis Belfort the same words she had said to Eddie. 'Hurt the mother, and you make a lifelong enemy of the son.'

The plane was somewhere above the mid-Atlantic, Phil reckoned, but he was too wide-awake to sleep, and too restless to read. He thought of all the places he had been, and all the people he had seen, during his time in America.

The only person he did not think of was Jacqueline. Nor would he allow himself to think of her ever again. She belonged to the past, and now he was concerned only with the future.

He knew exactly what his goals were, and he knew nothing would stop him, no matter how long he was forced to wait. He would personally publish his mother's book, and he would personally destroy the man who had killed her.

Twenty-Nine

Cambridge
1984-1987

_____/

It was a thirty-page letter written on lined foolscap in close neat words, so neat in fact, Phil suspected Jimmy had written it at his own disjointed pace, then had painstakingly copied it all out again, neatly, to make it more readable.

An act of true decency and true nice-guy consideration – from a man with only one hand.

Yet every word was powerful with authenticity: the nuts and bolts of everyday life of soldiers in Vietnam – the long scorching days out on patrol in tiger-striped camouflage; the jungle with its blood-sucking leeches; the dark nights of silvers stars watched by young men in green helmets who smoked Cambodian Red and dreamed bamboo dreams, all wishing and wondering and counting the days until they could go home again – back to the place they called `The World.'

The sheer guts and truth of Jimmy's storytelling surprised Phil, although he had known that Jimmy would be incapable of writing anything other than the truth about Vietnam. No ballyhoo or baloney, no fake sentimentality – all of it was as real as the skin on your face. But much of it was mixed up, out of order, and out of shape.

After reading it carefully three times, Phil took out his own foolscap pad of paper and began rewriting Jimmy's pages, not taking away or adding anything, but giving it form, chronology, removing a paragraph from page twenty-two and using it as the opening paragraph:

In the beginning, every American soldier in Vietnam was sure of one thing – `Ho Chì Minh ain't gonna win'. That was in the beginning...

287

Phil worked for hours, oblivious of time passing, committed to the task before him, lost in the images and words, some of it written in Namspeak, the regular language of the US soldiers out in the field – `Give 'em some rock 'n' roll!'` (automatic fire). `An Angel hovering above.'` (A helicopter coming in to pick up the wounded) `Men, I want you to welcome our latest FNG.'` (Fucking New Guy). `On short-time.'` (Less than 30 days left in Vietnam) .

The door of his room suddenly flew open – Phil looked up in vague disorientation, snapping back to the conscious present, to his surroundings – his room at Cambridge – and saw that his visitor looked even more disorientated.

`I'm sorry,' David Gallagher muttered. `Oh God, I'm sorry, I've walked into the wrong room.'

He appeared to be almost weeping with rage. Phil looked at him curiously.

`Something wrong, David?'

`Oh God, yes ... It's Coles. Bloody Mr Coles! This time he's really upset me, that's why I walked into your room instead of my own.'

`That's okay.'

Now he was in Phil's room, David Gallagher seemed reluctant to leave it, hovering indecisively in the silence.

Phil sighed patiently. `Do you want to talk about it?'

`Yes, oh yes, God, I can't tell you how much I hate Coles. From the first day I got here he's been making snide comments about my looks...' Tears glistening in his eyes, David sat down in the armchair and blurted it all out.

David Gallagher was the same age as Phil, both were reading English at King's, and both had rooms on the same staircase. But there the similarity ended. Whereas Phil was dark and undoubtedly masculine, David had the golden hair and fresh-faced looks of a choirboy. Sensitive and poetic and intellectual, he was unable to cope with the constant jibing of Stephen Coles, a man of extreme arrogance and intimidating wit, who seemed to have chosen David Gallagher as an easy prey for his predatory humour.

`All my life I've been called a pretty boy, and I've *always* hated it,' David Blurted. `Sometimes I wish I could have a real bad car accident and get my face all smashed up, *then* maybe creeps like Coles will leave me alone.'

Then David felt like a blubbering fool, and said so. `I'm sorry, I've no right to come in here burdening you with my problem.'

Phil shrugged. `I can't see the problem myself. You don't look that pretty to me. But then people usually only see what they want to see.'

`What do you mean?'

`Coles – I think *he's* the one with the problem.'

`You do?' David looked at him earnestly. `In what way?'

`Well, you know, some of these overtly macho guys ... it's all a front. A cover-up for their own weaknesses.'

David looked down at his clenched hands for a long moment. When he spoke again, his voice was very quiet. `I understand what you're saying. But I don't know what I can do about it. All I know for certain ... is that I have suffered this kind of thing before, and I can't go through it again. Not with a man like Coles, and *definitely* not for the next three years.'

Phil sat looking at David in that dark thoughtful way of his. `Why don't you just tell Coles to bugger off and go fuck himself?'

David blinked. `Charming, of course. But I didn't come all the way to Cambridge to start using language like that. Don't you know that men such as Tennyson, Wordsworth and Byron all studied here? So did Prince Charles.'

Phil shrugged. `Well I can't speak for Charlie, but I doubt that a man like Byron would have taken any personal crap from a lecturer.'

`No—' David said thoughtfully, `No ... not Byron. And come to think of it ... judging by his portraits ... Byron's face was somewhat on the pretty side too – don't you think so?'

'I know his tongue was as smooth as a razor – cut an opponent dead with just one sentence, perfectly phrased.'

'Yes, yes, every time.' David nodded. His eyes suddenly filled with a quickened, reverent light. 'No man ever succeeded when trying to intimidate Byron.'

Phil smiled. 'So, go act like your hero, David. Tell Coles what he needs to be told, and put a stop to this thing now. Fight back and make it clear you're taking no more crap. Coles is out of order here, and it's up to you to tell him so. And tell him straight.'

'Right, that's just what I will do, and right away.' David jumped to his feet determinedly and headed for the door.'

Phil turned his eyes and attention back to the pages of Jimmy's letter. Back to the world of soldiers in Vietnam.

The following day David Gallagher was still feeling exhilarated and immensely relieved as he walked beside Phil across the grounds. 'I still can't believe I stood up to him, strong on every point, and afterwards, God, I felt bloody marvellous!'

Phil laughed. 'So there's hope for you yet, David. You may even make it all the way through the next three years to your degree.'

David felt so good, he accompanied Phil all the way into town and into an art shop. The young girl behind the counter had a perfect heart-shaped face, long chestnut hair, and was very attractive.

'Now *that's* what I call a pretty face,' Phil whispered to David with a grin.

He bought an easel and a number of canvases. David helped him to carry them, still looking somewhat surprised.

'Do you paint?' David asked curiously. 'I mean, *seriously* paint?'

Phil turned his head with a wry smile. 'No, David, I'm buying this easel to hang my ties on. And these canvases, well, I thought they might be useful for blocking out the beautiful view from my window. Of course I bloody paint!'

`And my God – you have talent!' David said a few days later, coming up behind Phil unexpectedly and staring at the canvas on the easel. *You really do have talent!'*

Phil glanced round at David, then at the open door of his room. `Don't you ever knock, Gallagher?'

`I'm sorry,' David apologised, `I did knock, but you obviously didn't hear me. Must be the headphones.'

Phil, as usual, was wearing headphones and listening to soul music while he painted. `And looking at this—' David exclaimed, staring at the painting of a young dark-haired girl with soulful sapphire-blue eyes – `makes me wonder why on earth you chose to study literature instead of art?'

Phil ignored the question and delicately dipped his brush into black paint. `So what do you want?' he asked.

David racked his brains to remember what, then smiled vaguely. `Do you know, I've completely forgotten.'

Phil sighed, and continued to paint.

David sat silently for a long time, just watching, while Phil ignored him.

David didn't mind being ignored. As long as Phil did not object, David would have been happy to sit there all day long. This room was the only place in the world he wanted to be. It had an attraction for him that was hard to describe. Even more than his own room, sitting here in a high-back chair, legs stretched out, he felt safe and content.

And in the weeks and months and years that followed, David Gallagher ventured towards Phil's room as often as possible, on any pretext, although he did not understand why he did so.

Friendship, David finally concluded – that was the reason he was constantly lured like a magnet towards Phil's company. Happy, invigorating, genuine friendship. Something David had known very little of in his boyhood years.

Phil, in contrast, seemed to have no need of anything or

anyone. And so he had lots of friends.

Sitting in his usual chair, looking over at him, David realised how impossible it was to summarise Phil Gaines, to rubber-stamp him into any category. An enigma in many ways, Phil did not reveal himself to others, refusing to be drawn into any personal revelations about himself, often with a smile of gentle mockery in his eyes.

It was true that Phil did not reveal himself to others, not because he was in any way sepulchral about his privacy, but simply because he felt no need to do so, and saw no reason why he should.

Not even when he received the life-changing telephone call from New York did he trouble himself telling others.

The call came in May, 1987, at eleven o'clock at night, but still early evening in New York.

Phil's first thought, when Lewis Belfort introduced himself over the telephone, was to wonder how Jacqueline's lawyer knew where to contact him.

`Don't ask me how, Mr Gaines, but your grandmother seems to have been kept well informed of all your activities since she last saw you ... or perhaps I should say, since she last *spoke* to you.'

Was there a difference? Phil instantly knew there was. It made him shudder to think he might have been unaware of hidden eyes watching him.

`Spoke and saw? Where's the difference? I know when I last *spoke* to her – three years ago. So when was it that she last *saw* me?'

`The last time? Oh, that was a few months ago. When you came to New York to see Jimmy Overman. She always came to New York whenever she knew you were over from England on a visit. But as I say, I can't tell you how she knew.'

Again Phil shuddered. So for the past three years, Jacqueline had been keeping tabs on him.

`Has she been to Cambridge?'

`Yes, I believe she has. Three or four times, as I recall. It was her greatest hope, I must tell you, to go to Cambridge for your graduation ceremony. She had no doubts about you securing your degree. She even predicted honours.'

Was, had, did – all words belonging to the *past* tense.

`Your grandmother is dead, I regret to say, Mr Gaines. Less than a month ago she was informed she was suffering from cancer. Her death following so quickly was quite unexpected.'

It didn't take many seconds of thought for Phil to work it out. A woman like Jacqueline Castineau would never allow herself to descend into fragility or a sick dependence upon others. So, an efficient sorting out of her affairs, then a self-administered drug to end it all with dignity.

`She killed herself, didn't she?'

Lewis Belfort's voice sounded appalled at such a suggestion. `Most certainly not! As I have told you, Mr Gaines, your grandmother died of cancer.'

Phil was not convinced.

`It was for the best – and end to her suffering,' Belfort murmured.

`When did she die?'

`Three days ago. Her funeral was held this morning at Saint Teresa's Catholic Church in Harvard, Massachusetts. I have just flown back from there. There was quite a crowd, I can tell you. Friends from all over America. Even a wreath from Ted Kennedy. He's the State Senator of Massachusetts, you know. Your grandmother was always a great supporter of the Democrats—'

`Well, thank you for letting me know,' Phil cut him short, not caring to hear all the details of the funeral.

`If you will just give me a few minutes longer, Mr Gaines, I promise to be brief.'

`About what?'

`About your grandmother's will. She has left her estate in its entirety to you.'

`I don't want it,' Phil replied immediately. `I told her when she was alive, and I'm telling you now – I don't want anything from her. She was Marc's mother but she was nothing to my own mother or me.'

Lewis Belfort sighed. `She expected this to be your reaction. She warned me that you would be difficult. That's why she instructed me not to inform you of her death until after she was buried. She knew you would probably refuse to attend her funeral. But, Mr Gaines, I must stress ... your grandmother spent the last three years of her life living in bitter regret. And she really *did* want to make amends. Not only to you, but also to Marc. Especially to Marc.'

`Marc?'

`In her will, your grandmother wishes it to be made clear to you, that the legacy of the Gaines estate in its entirety comes to you, posthumously, from her son Marc, your father. What should have been Marc's shall now be yours. She pleads with you to accept it on Marc's behalf, and with her apologies.'

After a long pause, Phil said, `The Gaines estate in its entirety? What exactly are we talking about?'

`Oh ... the country house in Harvard, the townhouse in Boston, the apartment in Paris; stocks and shares, bank accounts, various other assets ... Your grandmother was a very astute business woman, Mr Gaines, so apart from the two houses and apartment in Paris, we are talking about a total of approximately thirty-three million dollars. And all of it now belongs to you.'

`And Marc's military identification tag? Do I get that too?'

`Oh yes, that too. Absolutely everything.'

An hour later Phil was sitting on the window seat in his room looking down on the garden below, still thinking about everything Lewis Belfort had said to him.

Jacqueline ... here in Cambridge ... hidden and unseen ...

watching him, keeping tabs on him, knew his every move. She even knew when he was over in New York visiting Jimmy – `Don't ask me how, Mr Gaines, but your grandmother seems to have been kept informed of all your activities since...'

Kept informed?

Under normal circumstances this realisation would have made him sick to the pit of his stomach, but now it was over and so it didn't matter. Now he was considering Jacqueline's actions from a detached perspective, analytically ... Only one thing could have bought that kind of surveillance. Big money. Lots of BIG MONEY.

He thought of Tom Kennett in New York. Even then Jacqueline had used private investigators, no expense spared.

He thought of the millions he had just inherited. Enough BIG MONEY to hire his own investigators.

He thought of the man who had killed his mother – and all at once, as if scenes from a film were running across his eyes, he was sixteen again, sitting at the back of a courtroom ...

Close-up:	The defendant, James Duncan, a businessman in his forties, described as a `successful publisher'.
Close-up:	The witness-box, a police officer reading from his notes, then stepping down – his place taken by an old man, a witness – `Yes, sir, he just stood there, watching her bleed to death on the road, just stood there, smoking a cigar.'
Close-up:	The defence lawyer, pleading mitigating circumstances on behalf of his client. A skilled and eloquent lawyer – a bastard liar.
Scene:	Same courtroom, afternoon of same day, the verdict: the sentence statute, a fine of £150 plus a three-year ban.

Close-up:	James Duncan, laughing with relief and shaking his lawyer's hand in gratitude and congratulation.

He had got away with it. He had killed a thirty-five year old woman and he had not been made to pay for it. No more than £150.

And amidst all the joyous handshaking, Phil saw not a hint of remorse as James Duncan, with a blonde bimbo on his arm, sailed past him full of smiles, unaware of the presence in court of his victim's son.

Scene:	The street outside the court, James Duncan, exuberant, lighting a cigar, laughing, hugging the blonde, waving down a taxi.
Close-up:	The Blonde, fluttering on her stilettos toward the taxi with excited gaspings `... *champagne, darling, champagne, what else?*'

FADE-OUT.

A film without an end, a long tunnel without an exit, a hatred without respite, a vendetta without retribution, the good die young and the iniquitous go unpunished ... until now.

Phil stood up suddenly and went in search of his old wallet, found it in a drawer, flicked through all the bits and pieces and found Tom Kennett's card – now why had he kept it? It didn't matter why. What mattered was now and how.

Jacqueline, God bless her sick soul, had not only given him the idea, she had also given him the money to pay for it.

Again he looked at Tom Kennett's card, but he forced his mind to shift down a gear and thought, No, not yet, time enough. First, he had to get his graduation over.

Then he would move on and meet his opponent on the same pitch, beat him at his own game, and find some perfect but truly risk-free way of destroying him.

Again he heard a voice in his head from the past: Bill Simons in Shirley, Alexander's best friend from boyhood: `...*Alexander was convinced of it, he kept saying it, every time he got drunk he would say it – she won't use a gun or a knife, nothing so obvious, but she'll find a way...*'

Phil smiled a little.

And he too would find a way. But first, his graduation. Then the pitch and the game. If an unconscionable swine named James Duncan could become a successful publisher, then a multi-millionaire named Phil Gaines could also, and easier.

Thirty

Cambridge
June 1987

_____/

It was a day to remember, that Friday in June 1987.

With three thousand graduates about to collect their degrees, and twenty thousand guests present to see them do so, Cambridge was alive with excitement as tourists lined the streets to see the procession.

At nine-fifteen the undergraduates of King's College were the first to proceed through the streets in a long procession of fours, en-route to the Senate House, followed by undergraduates from Trinity and St. Johns, until the graduates of all thirty-one colleges had been awarded their degrees in a ceremony that would last two days.

Phil Gaines and David Gallagher had both achieved their B.A. with Honours. And as both had a surname beginning with `G' they walked side by side, both dressed in white tie and white neckbands and black graduate gowns.

Chef and Sofia, who had taken Phil into their home and had been his surrogate parents from the age of sixteen, watched Phil with pride. He was a man now. Tall and dark and handsome. A graduate of Cambridge.

`Marian would be so proud,' Chef whispered.

Sofia was too emotional to speak.

Miss Courtney was fidgeting anxiously with her broad-brimmed cream hat, convinced it was far too flamboyant for a lady of her age. She should never have allowed an Italian to choose her outfit for such a special occasion.

`Are you *sure* my hat is not just a bit too flashy?' she whispered to Sofia.

`*Bellissimo*,' Sofia sighed, but her eyes were on Phil, not the hat. `*Angelo mio.*'

After the presentation ceremony, the graduates from King's returned to the grounds of King's with their families where refreshments of strawberries and cream and white wine were served.

`My dear boy,' Chef said, smiling. `I am proud of you. You know that.'

`Yes, Chef, I know that.'

`And now?' Chef asked. `What are you going to do now?'

Phil was going to do what he had always intended to do. Only now he would be able to achieve his ultimate goal five years earlier than planned.

`I'm going to work in a publishing house in London to gain some ground experience, before I open my own house in a few years' time.'

Chef was startled for a second. `Your own publishing house? Your own business?' He gave Phil a cautionary look.

`It takes a lot of money to open your own business, Phil. And huge loans from the banks. Not a good idea. Not with borrowing being so expensive these days. Look at me – still struggling in my restaurant. Still worrying about costs and receipts and bills. And no pension for the self-employed. Only the small State handout of a pension, and who can live on that? So I must work on.'

`But, you see--'

Chef shook his head positively. `Don't listen to all that claptrap from Mrs Thatcher, Phil. Too many people are falling for it. Too many people deciding they want to be employers instead of employed. Even Peter is planning to open his own restaurant now. Huge loans from the bank, his house put up as security, and now his wife and children's future is dependent upon market forces.'

`I won't need to borrow money from any bank,' Phil said quietly, and finally told Chef about the call from Lewis Belfort a month earlier.

Chef almost fainted. `I knew Valentino was not poor. He always had enough money to fly over from America, and he bought Marian the flat ... but I never realised ... thirty-three million!' He reached for another glass of wine and downed it in two gulps.

Phil smiled. `I think it's time for you to retire from slaving in that restaurant of yours, Chef. Time to start thinking about la *dolce vita.*'

`Me?' Chef just stared at him. `Me, retire? You mean—'

`*Alberto!*'

Sofia and Miss Courtney returned from wherever they had disappeared to. Sofia was smiling happily at everyone she passed, loving every minute of the occasion, but Phil noticed that Miss Courtney was still looking anxious.

`What's wrong, Missy?' Phil asked her.

`This hat – it's far too ostentatious,' she muttered self-consciously. `And matching cream coat and shoes! I feel like the Queen Mother.'

`You look *wonnnnnderful!*' Sofia assured her. `Sophia Loren wore a hat just like that when she married Carlo Ponti. Or was it Gina Lollobrigida when she married – who?'

Sofia turned to Chef. `Alberto, who did Gina marry? Was it Roberto Rossellini? No, now I remember, it was Ingrid Bergman who fell in love with Roberto Rossellini—'

`But Sofia,' protested Miss Courtney, `all those women may have got married in this hat, but I am *not* getting married, am I?'

Sofia sucked a strawberry and eyed Miss Courtney speculatively. `Do you *want* to get married?'

Miss Courtney sighed and reached for another strawberry; she'd always been childish about strawberries, just the taste of them made her feel young again.

`Sofia,' she said, `you are the kindest person in the whole world and we all love you dearly, but at times you would try the patience of a saint.'   Miss Courtney chuckled. `Married! Me? My dear, I know you are an incurable romantic, but don't you know that I am seventy-four years old.'

`So? Marry a man seventy-four years old,' Sofia said simply. `Hold hands and smell the flowers together. Days of wine and roses – who says when they should begin? Who says when they should end? Now look at me, I'm fifty-eight,' Sofia said, subtracting five years from her age, `and I still hold hands with Alberto.'

Chef impatiently caught Phil's arm and turned him aside from the women, spoke in a low voice. `Let's get back to you, Phil – why publishing?'

`Does it really surprise you?'

`No,' said Chef after a moment. `No, nothing you do surprises me anymore. You're too much like Valentino. He once flew all the way from America just to take Marian for a walk in the park. Did you know that?'

Phil nodded. `I know everything, Chef. It's all in my mother's manuscript.'

`My dear boy—' Chef was smiling in amazement. `So that's why you locked her script away and refused to let anyone see it. I often wondered why. And why you chose English instead of Art ... you know you *should* have studied Art, Phil, it's what you do best, you know that ... but Marian's book means that much to you?'

`It's more than a book, Chef. It's everything she worked towards. All the days studying for her A-levels in English. All the nights writing her book, struggling over sentences, determined to get it right. It was, in effect, her life's work. I can't let it all go to waste.'

`*You* were her life's work,' said Chef. `But yes, you're right. Once Marian saw you were growing up, out every night learning your Kung Fu or studying art with Mr Hughes, that book of hers became her dream. Did it never occur to you, though, to just send it to a publisher?'

301

`It occurred to me, yes. It's what I thought I would do one day, later on, when I felt more reasonable about her death. But then one day—'

Phil sighed. `Chef, publishers bring out hundreds of books every year. Only a few get special attention. Promotion and Advertising. The rest have their fifteen minutes of fame then disappear into oblivion. So the only way I can ensure that Marian's book gets the attention it deserves, is to publish it myself.'

`And now you have the money to do it. Thirty-three million!' Chef shook his head again and reached out to a passing tray for more wine. `You know, I think Sofia is right about you. The gods may have been cruel in the past, but now you seem to have all the angels on your side.'

Phil smiled as he looked beyond Chef's shoulder. `And here comes a guy that loves books almost as much as my mother did.'

`Phil, may I introduce you to my father?'

David Gallagher was deliberately full of false bravado to cover his nervousness as he introduced Phil to his father, a stern, broad-shouldered man from the green belt of Surrey.

`I was beginning to despair of ever meeting you in the flesh,' Simon Gallagher said, eyeing Phil genially. `Apparently we keep missing each other. But here we are at last, face to face. My son tells me you are his best friend.'

`A friend,' David put in quickly, clearly embarrassed by his father's use of such an adolescent term. `Phil has many friends.'

`We both do,' Phil rejoined. `Cambridge is a very friendly place.' He then introduced David's father to Albert and Sofia and Miss Courtney.

`Ah! This is the lady!' said David's father, clasping Miss Courtney's hand. `Do you know, my dear, in that outfit you look exactly like the Queen Mother.'

`Oh gracious....' Miss Courtney's face turned a dull red colour.

Thirty-One

London
September 1987

_____/

Phil's new home was a three-bedroomed flat in a new block on Prince Albert Road in St John's Wood, directly overlooking Regent's Park. It had a large south-facing terrace, video-Entryphone, twenty-four-hour porterage, and was furnished for his every need. He had looked at other properties, but had finally chosen this flat because it provided him with all the advantages of Central London living.

As well as the tranquil green view of the park.

One night, as September came to a close, he glanced at his watch and saw it was eight-thirty – so only three-thirty in New York. Time to take the next step.

A minute later, with Tom Kennett's card beside the telephone, he was dialling the area code for New York.

`I'm so sorry, but Mr Kennett no longer works for this firm,' chirped the telephonist. `He has his own firm now. I can give you the number.'

Two telephone calls later, Phil was still trying to contact Tom Kennett, but now, at last, Tony Martinez had given him the number of Tom's cell phone.

As the line started to ring, Phil suddenly heard a voice in his head from the past, the voice of his Wing Chun master ... _Others may seek only to grasp the bird's tail, or play with the monkey, but you must face the tiger—_.'

`Yeah, hello? ...' Tom Kennett sounded like he was chewing a burger. The connection was loud and clear.

Three minutes later Kennett gave a chuckle, which expanded into laughter. `Yeah, I remember you too. Mr Phil Gaines. The guy with the grandmother.' He laughed again. `Some

303

grandmother! Did I feel a schmuck! Even my *sister* didn't look that good.'

`But seriously,' said Phil, and went on to explain very carefully what he wanted from Kennett.

`What d'you mean?' Kennett sounded hurt. `*We* are the best!'

`In New York.'

`You bet! Listen, you don't get into my tax bracket unless you keep getting results. And we always do. Because we are the best. We've even got our own firm now, but you won't find us in the *Yellow Pages*. No, sir. It's all word-of-mouth recommendations.'

`And that's why I'm ringing you, for a word-of-mouth recommendation, to give me a start ...'

Five minutes later Kennett was chuckling again. `Boy, you must be just like your grandmother.'

`Was it you she hired to tail me whenever I was in New York during the past three years?'

`Ah, now, listen—' Kennett sounded disappointed, `why did you have to go and spoil things by asking me a question like that?'

`Because I'd like to know the answer.'

`Which is confidential. Everything we do is confidential. So I'm not saying we did, and I'm not saying we didn't. Anyway, it was the old firm your grandmother employed – we left there nearly a year ago.'

`Do you know she died?'

`Yeah, I heard. I also heard she left you a huge heap of dough. So we did you a favour picking you up that night, didn't we? Though none of us could ever figure out why you kept turning your back on her. I mean—' he chuckled again, `if *my* grandmother was that loaded, I wouldn't care if she—'

`But seriously,' Phil interrupted again.

`Okay, let's get serious. Let's see if we can give you what you want. Well ... okay, now listen....'

Kennett mumbled something. Then he mumbled something

else. When Phil asked him to speak more clearly, he said, `The number ... I'm just looking here for the number of a particular firm over there in London that we've used a few times ... a real high-class team. And like us, you won't find them in the *Yellow Pages*. No, sir. Word-of-mouth recommendations only....'

`Is it the same firm that was employed to keep an eye on me in Cambridge?'

`I couldn't say, couldn't tell you, not even now. I told you – everything in this business is confidential. Or it *should* be. How else is a client gonna trust us? Who wants to pay good money to a team of private investigators who gossip like actors ... okay, here we go, I've found the number...'

Phil wrote down the number. `Are you sure they're good?'

`In England – they're the best! Real neat and very elite. Like I said, top-class.'

Phil grinned. `That's what I want.'

`And listen,' added Kennett, `if you *really* want the best, then go straight to the top man there. He's ex-CID, an ex-cop who retired at fifty and started up his own firm. If you say I recommended you, he'll see you get the best. Hang on, I'll give you his name....'

From the second-floor window of his office near Baker Street, Joseph Irving watched the driver of a black Mercedes as he stood pressing coins into the parking meter on the opposite side of the road.

A tall young man with black hair and a charming look of *savoire faire* about him. He wore a perfectly tailored dark blue suit, pale blue shirt, and dark blue tie. The meter fed, he walked across the road toward the building and Irving noticed his black shoes were perfectly polished.

Irving sighed appreciatively. Sloppiness of dress was something he had always despised, especially in plain-clothes police officers.

Joseph Julius Irving was fifty-nine years old and looked a

personification of the perfect English gentleman. Always impeccably dressed in Savile Row suits and Jermyn Street shirts, he was as British in every way as the Houses of Parliament. English dignity oozed from his every pore. So it was no surprise that few people ever successfully guessed his true occupation.

Phil stood outside the front door of the black-railinged Victorian terraced house, and smiled a little. If Joseph Irving himself had not given him instructions, he would wonder if he was at the right address. There was no outward indication of the business that went on here. The brass plate on the front wall bore the names of a firm of chartered accountants: *Jones, Lipzburgh, Trippett & Associates*.

He pressed the bell. A female voice spoke through the Entryphone. As soon as he gave his name and the time of his appointment, the door was buzzed open.

He passed through a glass vestibule and was met in the hall by a grey-haired woman who looked as prim as a civil servant. But she greeted him graciously, and invited him to follow her upstairs.

As they moved down the hall and up the staircase to the second floor, Phil noticed that all the doors of the other rooms were closed, but he was given no time to think about it, because his escort chatted to him all the way up from the bottom step.

She was Mr Irving's PA, she informed him, but she did not provide her surname. 'Oh, just call me Anna,' she said brightly. 'Everyone else does. Even my mother.' Her laugh made him smile, because her personality was obviously nothing as prim as her looks.

'Here we are,' she said, knocking on a door and opening it.

Joseph Irving was still standing by the window when Phil entered the large office which appeared ideal for a senior accountant – right down to the dark green walls, white marble fireplace, genuine Regency desk and armchairs, and a number of eighteenth-century oils on the walls. All of it elegant and old money.

'Mr Gaines, how very nice to meet you.' Joseph Irving smiled genially, shook hands firmly, then moved to his desk and invited Phil to sit opposite him.

Anna asked if either gentleman would care for some refreshment. 'Some tea or coffee?'

Phil shook his head. 'Thank you, nothing.'

When she had left the room, Joseph Irving clasped his hands together on the desk and looked paternal. 'Now, how may I help you?'

'I need information, as much of it as possible,' Phil withdrew a folded white paper from his pocket, opened it and placed it on the desk, 'on this man, James Duncan.'

Irving picked up a pair of spectacles from his desk and put them on, showing no reaction as he read while Phil said, 'As you can see, in 1980 he lived at that address in Berkshire, and he's still living there.'

'You've telephoned occasionally to make sure,' Irving guessed.

'Yes, and apologised for dialling a wrong number. He lives there with his wife, a blonde woman named Joanne Duncan. I don't know if they have any children. I don't think they do.'

'You've been there,' Irving guessed again. 'You've looked at the house and the people who live inside it?'

'Yes, in 1980, but not since then. Neither of them are people I enjoy looking at.'

'His occupation?' Irving's eyes moved down the page.

'As you can see, in 1980 he worked for a publishing house, Garland Press. Yesterday afternoon he was still working there, which is not surprising as Garland's is a family-run firm owned by his father. From what I have been able to ascertain, Garland's has a somewhat distinguished name for publishing good literature. But beyond that—' Phil shrugged, 'that's all I know.'

Joseph Irving gave him a long thoughtful gaze, observing

again how totally relaxed he appeared to be, despite the reason for his being here. Unlike other clients he did not twitch or cough or finger his tie repeatedly. Neither did he look guilty about his desire to seek unusual methods in obtaining what he desired. Nor did he betray the slightest hint of being riskily emotional or overtly vengeful. He was, it appeared, a most suitable client to do business with.

'So,' Irving asked, 'what exactly do you want us to do?'

'Why not tell me exactly what you *can* do?'

Irving's expression did not flicker. 'I thought Mr Kennett had already informed you of the services our firm provides. There is little we cannot do. All our staff are highly skilled professionals. All ex-police operatives. We can provide twenty-four undercover surveillance, electronic surveillance, executive and diplomatic protection, personal investigation ... just about everything. However, we are *very* expensive.'

Joseph Irving smiled apologetically at the young millionaire. 'But then you *did* say you wanted only the best.'

'Yes, and I don't care what it costs.'

'Nevertheless, we will not cheat you nor overcharge you. On that you can rely.'

Irving placed Phil's written information about James Duncan to one side. He picked up a pen in readiness to make notes. 'Now, I would like to know a little more about you,' he murmured. 'Just a few relevant details.'

Phil smiled. 'Oh, I think you know quite a lot about me already, Mr Irving. I suspect you could even supply the name of every girl I slept with in Cambridge.'

Joseph Irving lifted his head slowly and gave him a wonderfully innocent stare. 'Cambridge? Mr Gaines, I have never set eyes on you before today.'

'Not you personally, no. Just as you, personally, will not set eyes on James Duncan. It will be left to your operatives. But you knew who I was as soon I contacted you. As soon as I mentioned my name. As soon as I mentioned Tom Kennett.

And *I* knew – as soon as you said, "Ahhh yesss."'

Irving continued to look splendidly baffled ... His operatives –skilled men of experience – treated him like a king. Yet instinctively he knew that this young man regarded him with no awe at all ... and he was astute and straight to the point ... just like his grandmother.

He sighed, removed his glasses, rubbed an eye, and allowed himself a second to remember that particular French lady, and not without some delight. The dinner they had shared together at the Grosvenor had lasted four hours, and her charm had not only inspired him, but utterly captivated him.

And now, here before him, was her grandson and heir. However pragmatists may deplore it, it seemed to him like another of those little touches of ironic melodrama that often occur in life. Or as the French say, *C'est la vie.*

He replaced his glasses and said sternly, `You seem very sure, but you are quite mistaken. However, let us move on. Let us deal with the facts of the matter before us ... Now, may I ask you the situation behind all this? The reason why you want to obtain as much information as possible on this man?'

Irving looked at Phil questioningly, and when Phil made no immediate reply, Irving explained, `I always find it helps me to assess the needs of a client more clearly if I know the situation. I cannot give orders empirically. I cannot operate on theory. I need to have valid information in order to know if the client's motives are within our boundaries. And we *do* have boundaries. We are not interested in helping petty criminals, for instance.' He looked a little apologetic. `Not, I hasten to add, that you in any way appear to be of that type.'

Phil considered, his eyes dark and thoughtful. `Very well,' he said at last. `I'll tell you my reason.' Then, unflinching, he took his time as he told Joseph Irving in a quiet voice the precise details of the situation.

When he had concluded, Joseph Irving did not speak for some seconds, but there was condolence and understanding in his eyes.

Condolence for a young boy having to identify his dead mother, then having to watch the perpetrator and his wife laughing gleefully as they headed off for a champagne celebration.

And understanding of the son's determination to execute some sort of revenge. The practice of *vendetta* was as prevalent in Corsica and parts of France as it was in Sicily, the unspoken law that allows the family of a murdered person to seek vengeance on the killer.

But not in England. The English had always been far more subtle and less violent in their methods of retribution, but just as effective, nevertheless.

'I would like to help you,' he said sincerely. 'But you must understand, we do not operate outside the law. Nor would we want to help *you* to break the law as a result of our investigations on your behalf. I must have your assurance on that. You intend to do nothing illegal?'

'No, nothing like that, nothing illegal.' Phil looked at Irving with the clearest honesty. 'I simply want to see James Duncan get what he deserves. I want to see him ruined. Utterly destroyed. No hope for him, no help, nothing. He's fifty-two years old so his father must be over seventy and ready to either die or retire. After which, if James Duncan takes over, I want to see his business decimated, and rapidly so. I want to see him bankrupt and paupered, unable to afford champagne. I want to wipe the smirk off his face for ever. I want to make him pay a lot more than a fine of £150 for the crime of killing my mother.'

Joseph Irving sat back in his chair, and looked grave. 'So what you really want,' he said quietly, 'is to kill the man.'

Phil's dark eyes moved to the wall above Irving's head, as if pondering. 'Yes,' he admitted, and his voice was very calm. 'In 1980 the law denied me justice. In 1980 I would have settled for a jail sentence for James Duncan, but when I saw him walk away from the court laughing, then I wanted his life. And it would have been easy to kill him. Very easy. One winter night in 1980, I stood in his garden in Berkshire, I watched his car pull into the drive, watched him step out, watched him bend over to get his briefcase. One swift move and I could have had a knife in his back. One of Chef's carving knives. I knew the exact spot to make the thrust. But just as I was about to make my move, that's when I saw my mistake – Chef's carving knife.'

Joseph Irving was studying him intently. 'Why?'

'Marian ... all the years she had worked in Chef's restaurant. From before I was born, and then after I started school. All the years she had struggled to bring me up well ... to be decent and respectable and as well behaved as anyone else's son. That had always meant a lot to her. In a way, her whole life was one long prayer that I should turn out well. That I should be a credit to Marc, and prove that, if nothing else, she was a good mother ... and then James Duncan was gone, walking into his house ... and I knew I had missed my chance ... I had let it go.'

A silence had fallen on the room. Joseph Irving sighed, 'I'm glad you held back. But I do know how you feel.'

'No, you don't. Only I know how I feel.'

Phil shrugged. 'But that's all in the past, The mad demented dreams of boyhood. Now I have grown up, more mature, more reasonable. Now I merely want to ruin him. And I will.'

Joseph Irving sat silent and watching, and the eyes of the two men met, and for a long time neither spoke

Then Joseph Irving smiled, a small enigmatic smile, and at last Phil knew that Irving understood and agreed and was on his side.

'So, to begin,' Phil said, his tone calm and practical, 'I need to find out his weaknesses and his strengths. How successful he really is, or is not. How financially stable his father's firm is, or is not. The names of the most *financially* successful authors on their list – which are not, by the way, necessarily the most prestigious or famous. I would also be interested to know....' Irving made notes of everything he said.

Half an hour later, when the meeting concluded, the two men rose and Joseph Irving inquired, `How soon do you want this information?'

Phil considered. `I've waited a long time, and I'm prepared to wait a while longer. Just as long as it takes.'

`Good.' Joseph Irving smiled as he escorted him to the door. `One does hate to be rushed.'

As they shook hands, Irving suddenly patted Phil's arm paternally. `Now remember, we do nothing illegal. And neither must you.'

Five nights later, the offices of Garland Press were broken into without the alarm going off. Two of Irving's operatives went about their business calmly and efficiently and without turning on a light. Both wore a small torch strapped to their foreheads and both wore light surgical gloves. Everything was done without haste or mistake. Although it all would have been done a lot swifter if Garland's accounts had been on computer. Everything about the place was old-fashioned, even the old manual typewriters. The only machine that was activated was the photocopier.

Four hours later, after all the files and documents had been carefully replaced in cabinets and drawers, the counter on the photocopier was returned to its original setting, the paper tray refilled. Even a used coffee mug, which someone had left on top of the machine, was placed back in the exact spot it had been found.

When the staff arrived for work the following morning, there was nothing to indicate that a break-in had taken place, or that anything had been disturbed. The two operatives were, as Tom Kennett had promised, top-class professionals.

A third operative, who had been detailed to take care of the house in Berkshire, cruised behind Joanne Duncan's Alpha Romeo as she drove to her hairdressers in the High Street.

He watched her go inside, then followed her in and looked around the salon, looking for his wife. He smiled a sheepish apology to the receptionist. 'Sorry, wrong hairdressers. It's the one further up.'

Although only a few seconds, it had been long enough to see Mrs Duncan being led to one of the sinks, confirming she would be away from the house for at least an hour.

When she returned two hours later, tripping into the hall on ridiculously high stilettos, her blonde hair wildly glamorous and lacquered as hard as cement – there was nothing to make her pause and wonder, nothing to indicate that anything in the house had been disturbed.

Even the drawers of the desk in the study, where James Duncan kept all his private papers, remained securely locked and apparently untouched.

Yet the following morning Joseph Irving was handed a report containing specific figures from James Duncan's credit card and private bank statements.

Thirty-Two

London
October 1987

_____/

Phil stood in Joseph Irving's office and could not help smiling as he stared at the thick file of photocopied documents containing all the inside information he needed on Garland Press and James Duncan.

He looked across the desk at Joseph Irving with approval, wondering if it would be imprudent to ask questions. He said, 'Thank you.'

Irving smiled. 'My pleasure.'

'I thought you did nothing illegal.'

Irving's expression did not flicker as he affected deafness. 'I'm sorry, I didn't hear that.'

Phil was unable to hide his amusement. 'Mr Irving,' he said sincerely, 'you are not only a perfect gentleman, you are also the most serene crook I have ever met, and I admire you enormously.'

'And I like you too,' Irving replied smoothly. 'Because despite your present activity I don't believe you are really a scoundrel. You are simply a young man living in a Heaven-or-Hell world where the good must be applauded and the wicked must pay. In time you will find the middle ground, as most people eventually do.'

'I'm sure I will,' said Phil, and smiled again. 'I'm not too old and not too young, so anything is possible.'

But this time Irving did not smile, his eyes were fixed on the thick file of papers and he looked a little grave.

'In this case, I'm afraid we _were_ forced to circumvent the law slightly. But then in this case we were prepared to do that, because the law can be rather ambiguous at times, can't it?

Sometimes it just doesn't even up.'

`No,' Phil said, and knew that Joseph Irving was referring to a particular law which, in 1980, had allowed a man to walk away laughing, even though he had killed a thirty-five year old woman.

`Ask any police officer,' Irving sighed. `They do their job, often at great risk to their own lives, and succeed in getting the criminals to court. Then they have to listen to two lawyers disagreeing about the law. Arguing endlessly about what is strictly legal, and what is not. In the end it's left to a judge or jury to decide, and they don't always get it right.'

Phil said nothing.

`Much of our work, believe it or not, is for the police,' Irving continued. `Only in special cases, of course. And only when a certain line has to be crossed. But then most private investigators have to work close to the edge, or how else could they be investigators. How else are they to flush out the real criminals? No drug baron is going to open up his books and show the police a list of the firms he is currently using to launder money from narcotic sales.'

They talked for a further fifteen minutes, then Phil stood up and lifted the thick file of papers. `Well, I am very grateful to you, Mr Irving. And as for these—' he tapped the file, `whatever I do in the future, I won't do anything downright criminal, I promise you.'

`Good.' Irving smiled in a paternal way, and spoke as if to a beloved young relative. `I would be very disappointed if you did.'

Joseph Irving watched him from the window as he left the building and walked over to his car.

Anna knocked and entered carrying a tray of freshly percolated coffee. `Oh, has he gone? I've just made him the coffee he requested!'

Joseph Irving did not answer or glance round. She laid down

the tray and joined him at the window, and she too watched Phil unlock the boot of his car and place the thick file of papers inside.

Irving sighed. 'Down there, Anna, is a young man who will not be content until just one other man in this world knows how dangerous he is. Yet that other man doesn't even know of his existence.'

'Hmm ... now that *is* interesting.' Anna narrowed her eyes. 'And will he be back?'

'Oh yes, he'll be back. In his own good time. This is just the beginning for him. He has a long way to go, and other things to do. But meanwhile, as he is willing to pay whatever it costs, we shall continue to work on his behalf.'

'Meanwhile?' Anna was surprised. 'In what way?'

'Garland Press,' Irving said. 'From their personnel records it seems they are presently seeking a new secretary. The pay is so bad they are not having much luck. Now which of our female operatives would enjoy a nice, cushy job for a change?'

'Quite a few, I'm sure.'

'Will you see to it?'

'Certainly.'

Irving looked at her and smiled sweetly. 'I knew you would.'

Thirty-Three

London
1988 –1990
_____/

Phil and some of his closest friends from Cambridge had entered the world of publishing. All worked in different firms and different departments – sales and marketing, editorial, production and design, foreign rights – and all learned as much as they could, because they knew their present positions were temporary.

In the two years that followed their first meeting, Phil and Joseph Irving kept in regular contact. Even though Irving's fees were high, they made hardly a dent in the huge income that Phil was earning from his grandmother's legacy.

Phil had been stunned to discover the extent of Jacqueline's investments. She owned shares in three lavish hotels in New York, a newspaper in Paris, properties in Boston, Washington and Los Angeles. Endless investments, enormous sums of money in various banks. All of which now belonged to him. Without lifting a finger or doing a day's work, his personal income, after tax, was in excess of £1,000,000 a year from interest payments alone.

In August 1988, James Duncan's father died, but James Duncan did not – as he had hoped – inherit the company.

`He was so distraught about his father's will, he made everyone's life a misery for weeks,' Joseph Irving reported to Phil. `But he has calmed down somewhat, and seems to have reluctantly resigned himself to the situation. Garland Press is now owned in three equal parts by James Duncan and his two sisters, Helen and Felicity. It's common knowledge within Garland's that Duncan utterly despises his two sisters – neither of whom are involved in any way with the business.

317

Nevertheless, Garland Press is now a limited company and they own two-thirds of the shares, so James Duncan has been denied the sole autonomy he desired.'

Phil considered. 'The two sisters?'

'Both were devoted to their father, unlike the son. The eldest sister, Helen, visited her brother's office a week ago and loudly accused him of—' Irving looked down at his report — 'being an avaricious bastard who had spent the past ten years wishing their father dead so he could move into his office and chair.'

'Ah, so there's a degree of animosity there.'

Joseph Irving was highly amused by the understatement. 'Possibly, Phil, quite possibly.'

'Good,' said Phil, and smiled grimly.

In December 1989 Joseph Irving said to Phil, 'I think this will interest you. It seems our man at Garland Press does not possess the talents of his father. He has made severe cuts to all advertising budgets and is in danger of losing his two most lucrative authors.'

'Howard and MacAllister?'

'Yes. He insists he won't lose them, of course, and seems quite confident of their loyalty.'

'Then he's a fool,' Phil said contemptuously, 'because he *will* lose them, and soon.'

Joseph Irving folded his hands on the his desk, his eyes bright with mirth and curiosity. 'How soon?'

Phil smiled. 'Everything is more or less set up, offices found, equipment bought. So, all being well, we should be able to open in about three months.'

Thirty-Four

London
1990 –1993

_____/

In April 1990, it all started with the poster.

A poster of a beautiful painting — a head-and-shoulders portrait of a dark-haired young girl with sapphire-blue eyes gazing soulfully at the viewer; the background surrounding her was a cloudy mixture of various shades of blue and silver. And the book the poster advertised – *Some Kind of Wonderful* – by Marian Barnard.

David Gallagher, the Editorial Director of the newly opened Gaines Publishing Ltd, could not believe there was still a month to go to the official publication date: orders were rolling in. But then, with such a massive advertising campaign backing it, most bookshops wanted to have at least a few copies of the book in stock when it was eventually published.

In their offices on Shaftesbury Avenue, Phil grinned at David. `As Sidney Sheldon once said— "If you want to win, you have to know how to play the game."'

`Not exactly,' David corrected, a stickler for accuracy when it came to quotes, `"If you want to win, you have to learn to be a *master* of the game."'

`Well, one eventually leads to the other,' Phil replied. `And anyway—' his secretary interrupted him: a telephone call from the distributors.

He returned to his own office and left David Gallagher wondering if he could keep up with Phil's inexhaustible energy. No other book in the world was as important as this launch book for Gaines Publishing – not in Phil's view. In the months leading up to its publication, he had left no call unanswered, no contact unmade, and no minute left spare in his determination to see it succeed.

By May the poster for the book was displayed at airports, underground stations, bookshops – almost everywhere. Every national paper and women's magazines carried a full-page advert to coincide with publication.

And so, naturally, curious book-readers were interested, and seeing the book there in front of them, they picked it up, looked at the cover, read the blurb on the back, liked the quotes from the favourable pre-publication reviews, and bought it.

`A customer cannot buy something the shop doesn't stock,' Phil had said when instructing his reps. `So I want to see this book in as many shops as possible.'

Some Kind of Wonderful entered *The Times* bestseller list at Number 9.

A week later it was Number 6.

All the staff at Gaines Publishing – which consisted of eight in Editorial and twelve in Sales and Marketing – were buzzing with excitement. Then a telephone call from *Bookwatch* informed them it had moved up to Number 3.

Miranda Alvin, the Sales Manager, was discussing the proofs of a jacket for a cookery book with the art manager, Ben Anderson, when David Gallagher popped his head around the door of her office and grinned, `*Wonderful* – it's number 3.'

`What!'

Miranda stared at David, and then at Ben – then threw down the proofs and did an excited little victory dance on the spot. `Oh, bloody bloody bloody *brilliant!*'

The art manager stared at her in wide-eyed amazement, and scratched his dyed-blond short hair. Miranda Alvin was a woman of mystery to Ben, and usually she terrified him. She was a Cambridge Honours graduate who had read English at King's with Phil and David. She had long wavy Titian red hair, dairy-fresh skin, red glossy lips, dressed in St Laurent, and had a reputation for being cool, composed, and insanely intelligent.

But look at her now!

She stopped jigging and grinned at David. `What's Phil's reaction?'

David shrugged. `Oh, you know Phil—'

Phil was showing no outward reaction, covering his excitement with breathtaking skill as he followed the progression of Marian Barnard's book up the bestseller list. It consumed him, obsessed him, but no one in Gaines Publishing knew why. No one – not even David Gallagher – knew that the author, Marian Barnard, was Phil's mother.

Just publishing the book was not enough – not enough! From the time of publication he had been tense and restless and barely able to sleep at night as he realised how close he was to fulfilling the greatest dream of his life. His gift to his mother, her gift to Marc ... From Day One he had been on the phone to *Bookwatch* tracking its progress ... tracking it ... tracking it ... every move up.

Until, finally, four weeks after publication, the great day came, the one he had been so desperately waiting and praying for. As soon as Phil heard, he slammed down the phone and sprinted down the corridor into David Gallagher's office. Miranda Alvin was already in there.

`We've done it! – *numero uno!*'

David Gallagher let out a whoop and within minutes all hell broke loose as the news was spread by Phil's secretary. Phones were put down, conversations halted, computers deserted.

`*Wonderful*—' David Gallagher told them. `It's reached the top —*number one.*' Everyone cheered. Number One! Jackpot first time! It was all heady stuff.

`Wow, look at that!' Miranda was so excited Phil had lifted her up and swung her around. He was so happy there were tears in his eyes.

`Come on, everyone,' Phil announced. `Time to celebrate! Time to close up and have a party. '

`What – another one?' David Gallagher had only just recovered from the launch party, but he went along with the mood and asked, `Where? Here? Shall I send out for champagne?'

`You have to be joking!' Phil laughed. `No—' he had already decided where, already chosen the place where he wanted to celebrate the success of Marian and Marc's love story – `The American Bar, at the Savoy.'

Three months after Marian's book, Gaines Publishing brought out a second major book that had every male reviewer raving about it – *Tigerland: A Cry for Life*, by Jimmy Overman.

`Not since Oliver Stone wrote his script for *Platoon* has a story about Vietnam been told with such power and authenticity by a Vietnam Veteran,' said *The Times*. `The book is perfectly structured, the writing superb, and Jimmy Overman tells his spirited and occasionally tear-blurring story as if it all happened only yesterday. Once I started reading *Tigerland* I could not put it down...'

All the reviews were excellent, which made David Gallagher push even harder to get Phil to change his mind about bringing the author over to England for interviews, television. But Phil would not be persuaded.

`No, no, he's a private man, very closed in on himself. I don't think he'd be able to cope with interviews.'

`Why? Because he's disabled? Because he's missing an arm and walking around on a plastic leg? Don't you see? That would only *increase* his interest value. Everyone loves a wounded soldier.'

But a wounded soldier who suddenly stopped in the middle of an interview to have a conversation with an empty space? Talking cheerfully to a ghost only he could see? No, Phil shook his head, he would not take the risk of anyone laughing at Jimmy.

Jimmy was crying as he read the reviews. `Lord Almighty ... if I'd've known way back when you asked me to write ... that you were going to turn my letters into a book! ... I still can't believe it, you know?'

He wiped his hand over his eyes. `See here now ... this guy in the *Daily Mail*, he says ... 'Read this book and you'll never sit through another preposterous *Rambo* film again without howling in derision.' Jimmy's puckered eyebrow rose higher. `Who's Rambo?'

Phil shrugged. `It's a film, Jimmy, about an ex-Green Beret who went back to Nam and destroyed most of the Viet Cong single-handed.'

Jimmy laughed. `Nah, that was John Wayne who did that. In 1968. Did you see that film, *The Green Berets*? Wayne in a toupee, defying all the odds. Biggest error in that film was a shot of the sun going down in the East – in all my life I've never seen the sun setting in the East, not even in a mixed-up place like Vietnam. And you know, when *The Green Berets* was shown to the troops in Nam, they laughed for days.'

Phil opened his black leather briefcase again, surprised by his own excitement, now the moment had come. Although Jimmy had seen a copy-edited manuscript six months earlier, and had sat answering all Phil's technical queries with patience, Jimmy had seemed bemused and unimpressed by the pile of typed pages, as if he could not comprehend the reality of them ever being turned into a *real* book.

So Phil had not sent him a proof copy nor an advance copy, but had waited until he could present Jimmy with copies of the published book.

`Here's the book, Jimmy.'

Jimmy stared at the glossy hardback book that Phil took out of his briefcase and laid on the table. He just stared and stared, then his eyes moved down the cover to the name of the author, *Jimmy Overman*. His eyes were like two pools of iced water.

Jimmy blinked, and at last his eyes finally saw the image that had been faintly superimposed over the jungle green background of the cover.

'It's the photo!' Jimmy exclaimed. 'The one I took of Marc in his green helmet and cammies, the one I sent to Marian all those years ago.'

'You agreed I could use it, Jimmy. The designer gave it the hazed-over look to get the effect we wanted. A misted photograph of a young American soldier in combat helmet and jungle fatigues.'

'Yeah, I know I said you could use it. It's just ... you know, *seeing* it again, after all these years, it takes me back...' The tears were spilling fast, Jimmy searched his pocket, drew out a hankie and mopped his eyes.

Then in a snap, his expression changed and he was grinning like a delighted boy. 'But aiyyyy – lookit that! The photo I took of Marc on the cover of a book by Jimmy Overman. Didn't I tell him we would always be buddies? Didn't I?'

Phil smiled. 'You did, Jimmy.'

'But you know what I wish sometimes,' Jimmy said wistfully, 'I wish that Marc had lived to see the Bob Hope show. Ah, it was great! Every Christmas, from 1966 to 1970, Bob Hope came over and did a show for us guys in Nam. We all loved it. Did I put that in my letters? About Bob Hope?'

'Yep,' Phil replied, tapping the book that was four hundred pages long. 'He's in there, large as life. Bob Hope. Some of his jokes too. And Ann-Margaret in her mini-skirt.'

'Ann-Margaret!' Jimmy sat for a moment in ecstatic stillness. 'Boy, was she something. None of us were listening to her sing. Couldn't take our eyes off her legs – long and golden as a summer's day in Oklahoma.'

Phil turned over the book so Jimmy could see the back cover – a full page black-and- white photograph of Jimmy which Phil had taken six months earlier.

'Hey, that's me!' Jimmy sat smiling at the photograph of himself in a kind of childish awe. 'Good-looking guy, ain't I?'

After a silence, he raised his eyes. 'Say, listen. Any chance my book could get published here in America?'

Phil nodded. `We've got eight New York publishers bidding for it right now. That's one of the reasons I'm over here.'

Jimmy's face restyled into shocked disbelief. `Eight publishers? You're kidding me!'

`No.' Phil took a deep breath, and attempted once again to succeed in his ambition to get Jimmy out of the Bowery.

`The thing is, Jimmy, this book is going to make you a hell of a lot of money.'

`More money? You've already paid me a bundle!'

`That was an advance, Jimmy, an advance against royalties. But I know for a fact that one New York publisher has already offered $300,000 for the American rights to your book, and it could be a lot more by the time the auction is finished.'

`Lord Almighty!'

`So you see, Jimmy, it wouldn't be charity. You wouldn't have to take any money from me. You could pay your own way ... if you went to that place in Connecticut.'

Jimmy eyed him suspiciously. `You sure it's not a loony bin? I don't want you to start acting like my doctor now, wanting to put me away. Because let me tell you something – I am *saner* than most people walking the streets of New York.'

`I know that, Jimmy, I know that,' Phil assured him, hand raised. `You're the sanest guy I know. That's why I visit you so regularly. Because you're such good company, and because you were my father's best friend.'

`Yeah, that's what I thought ... I thought you and me were buddies.'

More tears were burning in Jimmy's eyes, and it truly worried Phil. More and more, lately, Jimmy seemed to be on the edge of tears; the least little thing could trigger him off. Except when he had spent his days writing about Vietnam. Then he had been as perky and full of life as a twenty-five year old.

`I got a job to do!' Jimmy would say in those days, sometimes abruptly leaving Phil in the middle of a meal in a restaurant to rush home and write a letter to him.

But now Jimmy had written as much as he could remember, the book was completed, and as his only friend, Phil felt he had to do something to ensure Jimmy didn't end up dead in the Bowery.

`You see, this book of yours, Jimmy, it's going to grab America by the heart—'

`You think so?' Jimmy looked disappointed. `I was hoping it would grab America by the balls.'

`There too. But once it's published, and it hits the bestsellers, with your name on the front and your picture on the back, all these druggies and drunks around here are going to know you've got money. A lot more than your disability pension. It's not going to be a safe place to be.'

Jimmy turned his face toward the window and went into one of his endless stares: a common trait amongst long-timers in Vietnam – a look in the eyes known to Vets as `the thousand-yard-stare.'

After a lengthy silence, Phil said, `Well?'

Jimmy shrugged. `I dunno.'

`Will you at least think about it?'

`If I'm gonna be rich,' Jimmy said petulantly, `why can't I just move to Park Avenue?'

`Wherever you move to, Jimmy, you're still going to be alone. Unless of course you meet a woman and decide to get married. Any chance of that?'

Jimmy chuckled. `Are you kidding? With only one arm and one leg, what woman would have me? Anyway, I'm too tired for women these days . . . There was a woman there a while back, name was Ruth, kept coming up here saying she wanted to keep me company, wanted to cook me a nice meal. Not a bad cook either. But hell, it wasn't worth it. The damn woman kept talking non-stop through my television programmes.'

Jimmy sat back and frowned.

`And when she wasn't flapping her yap through my

television programmes, she was sitting there shelling pistachio nuts, cracking them with her teeth – all the way through a re-run of *Columbo* – cracking pistachio nuts with her teeth. I felt like strangling her. Couldn't do it, though. Not with only one hand. So in the end I picked up my old plastic arm there, the one I use to bash cockroaches, and then I told her I had a leg just like it. Asked her if she wanted to see the way I took my leg off every night before going to bed.' He chuckled. 'Never saw her again. And boy, was I glad!'

'But you still feel very lonely at times,' Phil persisted. 'You said you did. But this place in Connecticut ... you'd have the privacy of your own room when you wanted it – even room service for your meals when you didn't feel like mixing. But plenty of company nearby if you did.'

Jimmy sighed. 'Okay. This place. Tell me some more about it. What kind of people live there?'

'All are ex-officers of one rank or another. Vietnam Vets suffering from PTSD in varying degrees. Most, like you, are in their late forties or early fifties. Men who just can't take the noise and confusion of civilian life anymore. All they want is a haven of peace. Green lawns and green trees and comfortable rooms where they can watch their televisions in peace or, alternatively, mix with the other guys for a game of pool, a beer, a few hours conversation.'

'All Vietnam Vets?'

'Every one.'

Jimmy's growing interest was evident. 'Well, I suppose, being Vets, it would give us something—' he sighed, almost plaintively, 'something interesting to talk about.'

'And if you moved there, and then decided you didn't like it, you can leave whenever you choose. It's just like a hotel.'

'I could do that? Leave whenever I choose?'

'Sure.'

'And no cockroaches?'

'No cockroaches.'

`No stinking smells?'

`Shoes shined every day. Laundry laundered twice a week. Good food.'

`Sounds good.'

`Why don't you let me drive you out there tomorrow, just to take a look at the place. See what you think of it.'

Jimmy smiled. `Reckon I might.'

Phil would always remember that drive in his hired BMW along the wide freeway and then through the countryside of Connecticut. For a while he and Jimmy talked about everything and anything – good, sane, intelligent and entertaining conversation with quite a few laughs. Then with startling suddenness, Jimmy turned and commenced a conversation with an invisible guy in the back seat.

Phil listened, hands firm and steady on the wheel, eyes noting the passing scenery as if there was nothing unusual going on, nothing strange about Jimmy giving a lecture to a young black GI named Brig, who was obviously an FNG.

` ... so you'd better listen to me, Brig?' Jimmy said sternly. `I don't care how much you felt the draft back there in Motown. Out here in Nam there is no Mason-Dixon line. No black or white. No rednecks or blue-collars. Just American soldiers. This is an army that sees only two colours – mean green and olive drab. You got that?'

Phil turned off the main road and within minutes they were driving through woodland. Jimmy came out of his own inner cosmos and looked around him. `Say, this place has got a nice mosey feel to it. Wouldn't mind taking a walk around here. Nice and peaceful. Can we stop awhile?'

`We're almost there.'

Jimmy's expression became sharp as Phil turned the car into a leafy driveway, then along a long gravel path flanked by sweeping green lawns and tall pine trees in the near distance. The house was a mansion of grey stone and many wide windows; lazy green ivy clung leisurely to one of the walls.

`What's this place called again?' Jimmy asked.

`Silver Waters.'

`Silver Waters – why's that?'

`There's a beautiful lake only a short stroll away.'

Phil stopped the car in front of the main entrance. He turned and looked at Jimmy. `Do you like the look of it?'

`Looks the sort of place a millionaire might own.'

`But do you like it?'

`My God, yes.'

`Okay.' Phil opened his car door. `Let's take a closer look.'

As they started up the stone steps, the front door opened and a broad-shouldered man came out to greet them, standing on the top step and grinning.

`So it *is* you!'

Jimmy paused, looked up, and locked a startled gaze on the man. `Sonofagun! Lewis! What the hell are you doing here?'

`Came out to meet our new FNG.' Captain Lewis pointed his thumb at Phil. `You know, when Phil here told me he was bringing out Jimmy Overman, I didn't believe it could be the same Jimmy Overman I knew. Thought you were dead. We all did.'

`Dead? Me? Are you crazy? I'm about to be famous!' Then Jimmy's mind clicked. `You mean, there's other guys here I know?'

`Two or three. Come on, we're all out the back having a game of baseball. Wait a minute – where's your other arm?'

Jimmy shrugged. `Left it in Nam.'

Phil was completely forgotten. He spent most of the afternoon wandering around, talking to the staff, watching Jimmy sitting on the back patio in the sunshine with a group of men, drinking beer and talking with his old animation, as well as listening and revelling in the conversation of some of the others.

`Christ, remember ol' Kingpin? That guy was such a sadist,

such a vicious sonofabitch, no wonder his men fragged him ... No, I'm not kidding! I tell you – he was fragged by his own men. The skirmish with Charlie was all to the front, yet when the chopper brought Kingpin back to base, he had more holes in his back than anywhere else. His own men did it, had enough of him, so they wasted him out in the field and blamed it on Charlie...'

An hour later Jimmy was in the pool room, cursing Charlie for depriving him of his arm. 'I'd give anything for a game, but it can't be done. Even the dumbest sucker knows you've gotta have *two* hands to play pool.'

'You could still mark the board,' one of the players suggested.

'Yeah, I could, couldn't I?' Jimmy agreed cheerfully, and then became as engrossed in the game as a referee, walking over after each player's miss to score the board.

Phil had never seen Jimmy looking so happy, but he finally dragged him away to take a look at one of the rooms.

'Lord Almighty!' Jimmy exclaimed, his eyes on the colour television in the corner, 'This place is as swish as the Waldorf.' He looked at Phil. 'Is a stay here very expensive?'

'It's not cheap, Jimmy, but you can afford it now. The money you make from the book will keep you living comfortably for the rest of your life. Because, believe me, we intend to exploit all the rights.'

'All the rights? What does that mean?'

'Well, after America, there'll be foreign rights, translations. We hope to sell the book to at least twenty-two countries before we're done. Maybe even a film deal. So, believe me, you can *well* afford to live in a place like this.'

'And you'd be amongst friends,' Captain Lewis said. 'Guys who know what you're talking about when you tune into Namspeak.'

Jimmy looked thoughtful, went into one of his endless stares. Then he turned his head and looked at his old buddy. 'Lewis,' he said 'what exactly do the men do around here? You know, when they're not playing pool or baseball or whatever. What else do they do?'

Captain Lewis shrugged. 'Oh, you know, just lazin' and gazin'. Eating ice cream and watching television. Most of the time it's pretty quiet around here, very easy. The men have had enough conflict to last a lifetime. So here, well, it's all downtime, rest and recreation.'

'Sounds good,' Jimmy said quietly. 'Sounds real good.'

'So? Phil asked him. 'Do you think you might like to leave your room in the Bowery and come and live here, Jimmy?

Jimmy smiled. 'Reckon I might.'

Two days later Jimmy was back at Silver Waters, to take up residence. Having seen the car approach, Captain Lewis and two others came down the steps to greet Jimmy voicing expressions of welcome and smiles of genuine pleasure.

While the two others helped carry Jimmy's suitcases up the steps, Phil drew Captain Lewis aside and spoke to him quietly, almost apologetically.

'You know I told you that Jimmy sometimes has mind blocks, flicks off from reality, forgets where he is. Well, he's not crazy. I want you to know that. His mind just goes off-centre now and again. He's—'

'He's one of us,' Captain Lewis said gently. 'He's a Vietnam Veteran. A maimed survivor. That's all that matters here. And if Jimmy wants to talk a little crazy now and again, well, as far as we're concerned, he's got a Purple Heart, Bronze Star, and Vietnamese Cross that says he's entitled to do that.'

Phil smiled, reassured. 'That's okay, then.'

'Hot damn!' Jimmy said emotionally, when the time came for Phil to leave. 'What did I ever do to deserve you, son? You've turned my whole life around.'

'I'll keep in touch,' Phil assured him, and seconds later he pressed down on the accelerator as the car swished round on the gravel path and headed back to New York.

The following morning Phil caught a Pan American flight back to London, with a final and accepted offer of $750,000 for the American rights to Jimmy's book safe in his briefcase. Fifteen per-cent of that would go back into Gaines Publishing, the rest would go to Jimmy.

From the moment the plane took off, Phil sat reading a script which David Gallagher had taken from the firm's unsolicited pile a week before: a thriller, by an unpublished Irish writer named John Houlihan.

David had said the script was better than good, and so it proved to be, keeping Phil engrossed and page-turning while ignoring the stewardess who hovered round him more than was necessary, offering him drinks and pillows and `anything at all' he might need.

Finally, he looked up at her.

`I'd like a cup of coffee.'

She looked sassily into his dark eyes. `How would you like it?'

`In peace,' he smiled.

Ten months later John Houlihan found his script converted into a book, and Phil Gaines was earning a reputation as a very shrewd publisher. In fact, although Lewis Belfort was the only mortal who knew it, Phil possessed the same natural astuteness for business as his late French grandmother.

And also, just like Jacqueline, he was not afraid to take risks, and never wilted in the face of potential danger.

Within two years the firm's staff had increased from twenty to thirty-five, excluding the reps on the road. It was a young firm and a happy one, even if the boss did work twice as hard as anyone else.

`I think you really like this business,' David Gallagher said to Phil one day. `All the deal making and so on. What is it the

Americans call it? Being a player?'

'Russian roulette, publishing style,' Phil grinned. 'Hit or miss. Waiting to see which book is going blow up in your face and leave you badly burned.'

'Not me,' said David with a sniff, 'I prefer to do my job expertly and methodically and take as few risks as possible.'

'And that is why you are so indispensable, David.'

'Indispensable?' David thought about that for a moment, and then nodded. 'You're right. A little praise *does* go a long way. The conundrum is – do you ever mean it?'

The phone on Phil's desk rang. He gave David an amused glance. 'Saved by the bell.'

The flat in Mayfair belonged to one of London's leading literary agents. From the entrance hall a gilded lift carried all visitors up three floors to a mirrored and carpeted private landing, vibrant with lights, and noisy with the burr and buzz of cheerful voices coming from an open doorway. There was a party going on.

Although why the party was being held, Phil could not remember. All he knew was that it was a party for publishers and authors and anyone else who might be useful in the buying and selling world of London's literati, and his own presence here tonight was all in the line of business.

He was greeted by the literary agent himself, Martin Pellmann, a tough straight-talking American who had made London his own, as well as making a fortune for both himself and his authors.

'Phil!' Martin greeted him with a big smile and a hand thrust forward. 'Glad you could make it.'

Phil grinned as they shook hands. 'My pleasure.'

'There's a few people here tonight I want you to meet,' Martin said, putting a hand on Phil's shoulder and leading him into the buzz of the crowded living-room. 'But first, how about a long cool drink?'

The flat was huge, high-ceilinged and mainly white in carpet and upholstery, with a splash of rich deep colours here and there.

Only ten minutes or so after his arrival at the party, Phil saw them ... two people walking into the room ... a man and a woman. For a moment he thought he must be imagining it, but there they were, the two of them, in the flesh, but it was the *man* his eyes were fixed upon.

A tall, silver-haired man in his fifties, built as square and as solid as a brick outhouse. His head looked as solid as the rest of him, firmly planted on a thick bull neck. He stood tall and self-assured and peacock-proud.

Phil stared at him, and felt a deep and murderous hatred flaming back to life, still hardly able to believe that *there* – just a few yards away – was the man who had killed his mother.

David Gallagher had always known that he would never become Phil's confidante in any aspect other than business. But he also knew that Phil's reservations did not apply only to him. Phil never let *anyone* get too close – never discussed his own feelings, and never explained his reasons for doing anything.

So David could only wonder what had happened to Phil at Martin Pellmann's party. In the two weeks that had passed since then, Phil had upset everybody by attacking life and work as if making up for lost time.

He had upset David by ignoring all his protests and immediately entering into long lunch negotiations with the agents of John Howard and Ken McAllister, offering advances that he knew Garland Press could not match, let alone top. It was blatant bribery and worse – it made no sense to David.

`Apart from anything else,' he said to Phil, `it was bad business, because neither author is worth a *third* of what you paid.'

Phil glanced up at him sharply, then slightly smiled. `They are worth it, David. Every penny.'

`You should have left them picking up peanuts at Garland's,' David fumed on. `Because both are over the hill, out of time and out of touch, and they are certainly not right for *us*.'

`Then we'll *make* them right for us!' Phil snapped. `Both are good writers, and hardly over the hill in their fifties. They've just been neglected, let slide, when was the last time either of them got any promotion from Garland's? And without promotion even the *best* writers can fade from the public interest. Look at Agatha Christie – her sales had tailed away to library level until Collins put new and exciting covers on all her books and pushed her back into the public eye. Within a year her sales had risen by 40% and now most of them have been bought for television.'

`And you think we can do the same for Howard and MacAllister?'

Phil gave David a slow, enigmatic smile. `I think it's a challenge we might enjoy.'

David was not convinced.

`And James Duncan is going to be absolutely furious when he finds out,' David added. `Both those authors have been with his house for years.'

`And James Duncan has profited a lot more from the association than they ever did. They owe him nothing. Not even loyalty.'

`He's still going to be very upset at the loss. Especially as you bought up all their backlists. I know they were out of print, but Garland's have their own contracts, their own clauses, have never signed the MTA, and he still may call in his lawyers.'

`Life's no legal bargain,' said Phil in a voice of contempt. `As James Duncan will one day find out.'

Part Three

Rena

1993

Thirty-Five

Stockholm
June 1993

_____/

A warm late-June day in 1993. Opening his eyes onto a strange and unfamiliar place. His eyelids felt heavy but he forced them open and looked around the room. Scandinavianly white and gleaming. A hospital room. He wondered how he came to be here and tried to remember, but against his will his eyes closed again and he drifted back to sleep.

Seconds, minutes, maybe even hours later, he felt soft wisps of air passing over him; a soft unhurried sound very near. Then a touch: a soft hand gently placed on his brow, his wrist being lifted, his pulse being counted; still his eyes did not open. In the far distance somewhere, someone or something was playing music ... a radio?

Another touch, warm fingers smoothing up his left arm, as tender as the fingers of a lover ...

Something cold and rubbery was being wrapped around his upper arm.

His eyes slowly opened, and he saw her, bending over him – a girl, very blonde, very beautiful, dressed crisply in white – a nurse.

She spoke to him gently, in beautifully accented English. `You are awake now? You can understand when I speak to you?'

She had the bluest eyes he had ever seen. Scandinavian blue.

`Where am I?' he whispered.

`In hospital. You have had an appendectomy.'

`A what?'

`The surgical removal of your appendix.'

`Oh.'

Slowly, it came back to him: he had come to Stockholm on a flying visit to Bonniers for the Swedish publication of Jimmy Overman's book, because everything to do with Jimmy's book, even foreign rights, was handled personally by him.

He had not stayed long, preferring to retire to a nearby restaurant with the Rights Director to discuss other titles Bonnier might be interested in. The restaurant was cool and relaxing and the food looked excellent, but he was unable to do more than occasionally taste it. A pain in the lower right side of his body that had been nagging him on and off for weeks, suddenly became acute. No matter how much he tried to pretend there was nothing wrong, the charming man seated opposite him looked more and more worried.

It was only when they stood up to leave, and the agonising pain suddenly doubled him over, Kris Schneider immediately took charge of the situation, ordering the staff to phone for an ambulance.

'I am going now to take your blood pressure,' the nurse told him, and her voice was soft and unhurried and soothing on his awakening mind.

He watched her as she pumped the sphyg and studied the rising mercury, his eyes taking in every detail of her face: the Scandinavian blue eyes, the smooth line of her jaw, full pink lips, the long Swedish-blonde hair tied back for work, but which he could imagine all floating in the evening. Her freshness, the light gold of her skin, her sheer cleanliness, as if she had just bathed in a fountain of sparkling Perrier water. Everything about her was ultra feminine, exquisitely beautiful.

'The *doktor* will come to see you very soon,' she said, unwrapping the band from his arm. 'But I can now bring you a drink, something light to eat – would you like that?'

She was smiling down at him, bending towards him slightly, and the scent of her reached his senses.

He tried to sit up and ask her a question. She immediately pressed his shoulders back down on to the pillows.

`Rest,' she said gently.

Her name was Rena Olsson, she was twenty-three, but that was all she seemed prepared to let him know about her. An ambiguous angel, she was beauty and perfection, his dream girl, and whenever she came into his room and lifted his wrist to take his pulse or put a hand on his brow while he dozed, he pretended to dream while losing himself in the closeness of her.

In the days that followed when she was absent, or off-duty, he spoke to the other nurses, finding out small things about her.

He wondered if his incredible attraction to her was due simply to her being a nurse, all those tender little touches. But when other nurses came in and performed the same duties for him, he felt nothing at all. Only when she appeared did his heart begin thumping in the way it always did when he saw her.

She was on duty and in his room when Kris Schneider walked in. Kris looked at her and lost his step, almost tripping over a chair. She turned and left the room.

Phil grinned at the expression on Kris's face and suggested, `To borrow a phrase from Jack Kerouac – "the only word is wow"'

Kris nodded, his lips silently forming the word as he sat down. Phil handed him a basket of fruit. `Here, have a grape.'

Later that evening, while Rena was placing an Interflora bouquet of flowers from England into a vase, Phil asked her if she would kind enough to give him her home telephone number.

`In case, you know, I feel ill in the night.'

`So you ring for one of the nurses on duty.'

`Ah yes, but they don't speak English as well as you, Rena. That's why I thought your home telephone number would be very useful, in case of some verbal emergency.'

`No, I cannot give you my home telephone number.'

`Why not?'

She glanced at him over her shoulder. 'Perhaps I am married.'

'Are you?'

'No.'

'Neither am I.'

She looked at him with her ice-blue eyes and gave him a shadow of a smile as she lifted the card attached to the flowers. It read: *Missing you, darling, hurry home. Love Katie.*

'So who is Katie?' she asked.

'A friend, just a friend.'

Rena looked disbelieving. 'Do all your friends call you darling?'

He shrugged. 'It's an English thing, Rena. It means nothing.'

She gave him a small cynical smile, and walked out of the room.

For the rest of the day, all her responses to him were ice-calm and uninterested.

Lying in bed that night, Rena found that sleep would not come, her mind continually going off on a spin, thinking about the Englishman. The last few days seemed to have moved with a faster pulse, more funny and more exciting. Yet all this was new and strange to her, and she did not like it. It interfered with her efficiency, causing her moods to swing from excited and happy to pensive and confused.

It was not possible that she was attracted to him? No – she was incapable of becoming romantically attracted to any man. For four years, since her nineteenth birthday she had been suffering from a sickness which she kept a close secret from everyone in her life. She could not bear any man to touch her.

But the Englishman – she had been unprepared for him. Unprepared for the lightning flash of spontaneous attraction she had felt in those first few moments of speaking to him ... But that was all, just a lightning flash, before she retreated back into her own isolation and refused to succumb to his flirtation.

Yet when she arrived for work the following day and discovered he had left the hospital earlier that morning, her predominant emotion as she stood at the open door of his empty room, was crushing disappointment.

She was barely back outside the door when she was told there was a telephone call for her.

She was hesitant as she put the receiver to her ear, hoping yes, hoping no.

'Hej?'

'Rena?'

'Yes, Phil?'

'Ah, you recognised my voice.' He sounded amused. 'So you noticed then – that I'd checked out?'

'Yes, I noticed.'

'Oh well, that's something for me to remember.'

'You are at the airport?' she asked. 'You have ringed to say goodbye?'

'No, I am at my hotel, and I have ringed to ask you out to dinner tonight.'

'Do you not have to go back to England?'

'Not if you say yes.'

Rena's first sight of Phil outside the hospital environment caught her completely by surprise. He looked vital and full of energy and he was dressed in a black suit, as black as his hair, and his handsomeness almost took her breath away.

She looked around the lobby of the SAS Strand hotel. 'Are we going to dine here?'

'No.'

He took her to *Mälardrottningen*, a hotel of 59 cabins on what had formerly been the yacht of the American heiress, Barbara Hutton – a beautiful yacht now permanently berthed in its own lovely setting at Riddarholmen. They dined in the restaurant on the bridge.

'Why did you choose here?' she asked him.

`I rang a friend at Bonniers; he recommended it. Do you like it?'

`I like it very much,' she smiled, and gazed around the restaurant. `It's the first time I have dined on a yacht.'

The wine steward arrived. She had no particular preference, so Phil ordered a white burgundy. Chassagne-Montrachet.

She was the most exquisite girl Phil had ever dated. Gone was the cool crisp cotton whiteness of the nurse in the hospital. Tonight his dream girl was wearing a black dress that hugged her slender figure like a second skin. Her blonde hair was loosened from its regular plait and seemed even longer and glossier than he had imagined, like waves of cream silk.

`You're very beautiful,' he said.

She looked away.

Something was wrong.

He could see she was very tense and nervous, even when she smiled, but he knew it was not because of the unfamiliarity of her surroundings; she was a worldly woman in every sense, perfectly capable, assured and intelligent, with no pretence of simpering naivety or gaucheness. So why did she seem so nervous?

He said softly, `Rena, what are you afraid of?'

She turned her eyes to him, ice-blue and surprised. `Afraid? Why should I be afraid?'

He smiled. `No reason at all.'

`It was a strange thing to ask.'

`Forget it, please.'

After two glasses of wine she began to relax, her smile genuine, her conversation more free and natural. He watched her face as she spoke, fascinated by the changing expression in her eyes.

`Did you always want to be a nurse?'

`Oh no,' she replied seriously. `For a long time I wanted to be a mermaid.'

Rena was enjoying herself.

Much more than she had anticipated, and most especially because as the night wore on she found she could talk to Phil, very easily. He knew when to listen, when to offer his own point of view, and even when they disagreed, she enjoyed the disagreement.

Usually she found men not worth quarrelling with.

She thought back to the last man she had dined with – a year ago – a disaster. Lars had done nothing but talk about his work, his ambitions – himself.

Phil was different: his theme did not keep returning to the main subject of himself. In fact, that seemed to be his only taboo subject – himself. He shrugged her questions aside as if all the details of his life were no more interesting than slight trivialities, deftly bringing the subject back to her.

She liked him, and suddenly wished she didn't, not only because he was going back to England, but also because she knew he would not understand.

When the evening was over, she looked at him uncertainly. `Phil, would you mind if I returned home in a taxi, alone?'

Phil, who had been beckoning to the waiter, gave her a quick glance, quizzical. `Why?'

`I prefer it so.'

`Isn't this all rather strange, Rena?' He handed the plate containing bill and cheque to the waiter, then turned back to her.

`First, you had to go home to change out of uniform, you said, but refused to allow me to collect you there in a taxi, insisting we meet in the lobby of my hotel. And now you want me to allow you to travel home alone late at night. It's not a very gentlemanly thing for me to do, is it?'

`Sweden is not like England or America. We do not have such high crime rates.'

`You're not married,' he continued. `So what is it? Are you living with a man? Some guy who doesn't know you're out

344

with someone else tonight?'

`No, Phil,' she said, lowering her eyes wearily. `I live only with my parents.'

`Your parents?'

`But even if I was married, or living with a man,' Rena added softly, `what would it matter? Today on the telephone you agreed that we would meet tonight as friends – just friends.'

`Okay, just friends, so why can't I escort you home?'

`Because there is no need for you to come all the way out to my home. A taxi will take me there just as safely.'

Phil studied her for a moment, then decided to let her play this out in her own time, her own way, at her own pace. `Okay,' he acceded, `if that's what you want, I'll ask them to call you a taxi.'

When the taxi arrived, he walked with her down the brightly lit steps of the yacht and opened the taxi door for her.

`I wish you wouldn't be so afraid,' he said quietly, `because there's nothing to be afraid about.'

`I am afraid,' she admitted. `The way you see me ... `I'm not like you think I am.'

`I think you're gorgeous.' He smiled. `Are you going to allow me to kiss you goodnight?'

He saw the stark stricken look on her face as she drew back in sudden panic. `No, please, you agreed, we would be friends – just friends.'

He barely caught her whispered farewell as she disappeared inside the taxi, slamming the door shut behind her. Seconds later she was gone.

He stared after the receding taxi like a man who had been struck. Her hesitations he could understand, her stark horror he could not.

He was still baffled when he got back to his hotel.

What now? sang Plato's ghost. *What now?*

At this doubtful hour, Phil hadn't a clue. He looked at his watch: 12:16.am. Already she belonged to yesterday.

Thirty-Six

London
July 1993

_____/

It was almost two weeks since Phil had returned from Stockholm. He had tried unsuccessfully to forget Rena Olsson, put her out of his mind, but every now and then something reminded him of her: a question from David Gallagher about Bonniers, a girl in a restaurant with pale blonde hair.

The anodyne was work. Throughout the past eleven days he had worked as if making up for lost time, immersing himself in it totally until he had no time to think. The phone on his desk rang: he picked it up and felt his heart sink when he heard John Houlihan's cheerful Irish voice.

`Phil, I've been trying to get you all morning.'

`Sorry, John, I was in a meeting.'

`Did you read my new script?'

`No,' Phil lied. `Not yet.'

`Oh...' Houlihan managed to convey a huge tidal wave of disappointment into that one small word. `Oh...' he said again. `So when – when did you think you'll get round to reading it?'

`Today. I'll start reading it today.'

`Today?' Houlihan chuckled and was instantly joyful. `You'll love it, Phil. It's fabulous. It's the book I was born to write. Even Nancy says so. It's my _magnum opus_. And d'you know what?'

Five minutes later Phil replaced the telephone in its sleek cradle slowly. After a pause, he leaned forward and pressed down an intercom button.

`David...'

When David Gallagher walked into Phil's office, he looked baffled. `John Houlihan? Why did he phone you?'

`To know if I'd read his new script.'

David's face stiffened. `I didn't know he had sent in a new

346

script.'

Phil pointed to a cabinet on which there was a large box. 'It's over there. Came last week. Sent as always direct to me at my flat – marked *Personal*. I should never have given him my home address.'

David moved over to the cabinet and lifted the lid of the box, then closed it again without touching the contents, his anger consuming him.

'The spiteful sod ... sending it direct to you ... *I* was the one who discovered him and worked my back off to make him a success.'

Phil sat back in his chair. 'I know that David.'

David tried to push away his anger, but he couldn't. After all, *he* had discovered John Houlihan. Lifted his script from the slush-pile and taken it home to glance through over the weekend, expecting nothing much, then finding himself awake half the night, unable to put down one of the best thrillers he had ever read. *Foreign Relations*, a fast-moving story about the IRA and Loyalists in Ulster.

That had been the beginning for John Houlihan. Success had come fast and Houlihan had loved it. It charged up his batteries and oiled his ego until he was writing at a furious pace, turning out two books a year. *The Final Demand*, quickly followed by *The Death of Napoleon Smith*. By the time he had started his fourth, his books were sitting on bookshop shelves alongside John Grisham and Scott Turow.

And all thanks to David Gallagher, who had discovered him, edited him, and worked his back off for him.

'I put his books on shelves in every bookshop from here to Japan,' David said. 'But even now, *even now*, Houlihan is still sending his scripts direct to you.'

'Why don't you ask him why?'

'I did ask him once.'

David would never forget the night he had asked John Houlihan why. The night of the launch party for John

Houlihan's third book.

'*Why*? You're asking me *why* I send my scripts to Phil?'

Houlihan had looked at David for the longest time, slightly boozy-eyed, a man now in his late forties, physically going to seed, but still showing signs of the fairly handsome young man he must once have been.

Then a slow smile had finally come on Houlihan's face. 'Well now,' he said, 'I'll tell you just why. I'm a man's writer. I write books mainly for men. And I send my scripts to Phil there—' he pointed, 'because, like myself, Phil is ... well, a *real* man.'

Shocked, and deeply hurt – because the insinuation simply wasn't true – David had never forgiven Houlihan for that. In fact, from that night on he had despised him. But he was too intelligent to allow personal feelings to interfere with business. The discovery of John Houlihan had helped to establish David's name in the publishing world, and that had meant a lot to him, because – unlike Phil, who now seemed to care only about the business side of publishing – David loved books, and loved reading good writers.

And Houlihan had been a cracking good writer, until he had started his really serious affair with the bottle.

'So what did Houlihan say?' Phil asked. 'When you asked him why?'

David shrugged. 'He just answered with a load of rubbish. A pile of nonsense. He was drunk. It was just before he disappeared to write his fourth.'

'And now he's back, stone-cold sober, with a script that stinks like a dead dog.'

'Stinks?' David stared at him, mystified. 'You're not serious? Listen, I may hate the man, but Houlihan *is* a cracking writer.'

'Houlihan *was* a cracking writer,' Phil corrected. 'When he drank nothing but the best and not too much of it. But now he's cold sober— ' He shook his head ruefully. 'I mean, who the hell wants to read a thriller that takes twelve pages of gloomy introspection to reach every point? Not Joe Public. He has enough gloomy introspection of his own to cope with.'

David's gaze was a study in disbelief. 'Is it that bad?'

Phil nodded. 'It's awful, I promise you. Most pretentious load of garbage I've ever read. No story that I could find. And the writing itself is as soggy as a swamp. Chapter after chapter of overladen prose. Houlihan sets out to write a short racy thriller about the IRA, but ends up – well, at times it was so dense, so congested with obscure words and jabberwocky, so devoid of any clear narrative, I thought I was reading *Finnegan's Wake.*'

David looked wounded, as if Houlihan had not only failed him, but also betrayed him in a very grievous way.

'It will sell, of course,' Phil continued, 'if we publish it. But it will ruin Houlihan's reputation irrevocably. And damage ours into the bargain. At best it's the work of a mocking bird. Houlihan trying to imitate Joyce. But Houlihan is a man looking at himself through a cracked mirror. He may be an excellent writer in the thriller genre, but another James Joyce he ain't.'

David removed the lid of the large box and stared agog when he saw the box was filled to the brim with typed pages.

Phil grinned. 'Twelve hundred and eighty-eight pages, to be exact. Some short, racy thriller, eh?'

David immediately returned the lid. 'Well, there's only one thing to be done with it,' he said determinedly, lifting the box and walking towards the door.

'Hey!' Phil exclaimed. 'What are you going to do with it?'

David paused. 'I'm going to do what I always do with Houlihan's scripts. I'm going to *read* it.'

'Okay,' Phil held up both hands, 'don't take my word for it. Read it yourself and make your own judgement.'

Later that afternoon, David appeared in the doorway of Phil's office, bleary-eyed. 'Well, I've read the first two hundred pages.'

Phil smiled. 'Of Houlihan's *magnum opus?* That's what he called it. Said it was going to launch him among the greats.'

'An egotist *par excellence.*'

'So?' Phil asked. 'What did you think?'

'Immensely interesting, it is not. A Promethean feat of the intellect, it is not. But it does contain a certain—'

'Cut the crap, David. Give it straight.'

David blinked his bleary eyes. 'I was so impressed I fell asleep.'

The following day, Friday, Miranda Alvin arrived at Phil's office to collect him for their lunch meeting. They always went out together for a working lunch on Fridays. The office was empty. Miranda looked at her watch – she was on time. So where was he?

Liz Walters, Phil's secretary, rushed down the corridor a few seconds later and informed her, 'Sorry, Miranda, I forgot – Phil said to give you his apologies and tell you he can't make it for lunch today. He's had to dash off to a meeting.'

'A meeting.' Miranda frowned. 'Who with?'

Liz hesitated. 'I don't know. He just said he'll be back on Monday.'

'*Monday?*' Miranda smiled, astonished. 'So where the bloody hell is this meeting – New York?'

'No,' Liz replied, as curious as Miranda. 'In Stockholm.'

Thirty-Seven

Stockholm
July 1993

_____/

Swedish clocks were one hour ahead of England, but Phil made it to the hospital just in time.

He entered the lobby only a few seconds before the elevator door opened and the most beautiful girl in the world stepped out.

She was out of uniform but dressed very simply in flat white nursing shoes, a sleeveless vest that looked whiter than white against her golden arms, a red summer skirt, and a bag hanging from her shoulder.

His heart was already beating fast from the fear of missing her, but now as he looked at her, she made his heart beat even faster, because despite the simplicity of her clothes, she looked startlingly, physically, sexually, stunning.

She didn't see him until he walked over to her and touched her arm. 'Hello,' he said politely. 'Remember me?'

She stared at him, her ice-blue eyes full of shock. 'Phil!'

'Rena, I must talk to you,' he said, and was surprised when instantly she nodded.

'I want to tell you something else too,' she replied.

Puzzled, he smiled, and put it down to a mix-up in her English. 'Can we go somewhere for a drink?'

'No, I have only a few minutes, then I must go.' She took his arm and drew him over to a quiet corner of the lobby. 'Have you been in Stockholm again for business?' she asked.

He ignored her question and asked, 'Why are you in such a rush? Have you got a date tonight?'

Choosing her words carefully, she said, 'I want to tell you something else . After our dinner at Riddarholmen ... I

351

telephoned your hotel the next day to tell you, but you had gone back to England.'

'Tell me what?'

She was embarrassed, her face flushed. 'After our dinner at Riddarholmen ...' she began again, 'when the taxi came, and I rushed away, I didn't mean to hurt you. I know I did, and I'm sorry.'

'You didn't hurt me.'

'It's true, I did.'

He was smiling. 'So you've been thinking about me then? These past two weeks. You've missed me?'

She sighed impatiently. 'No, I have *not* missed you. I only wanted to apologise to you. I wanted you to know that I so much enjoyed my evening with you, and I didn't mean to be so rude at the end and spoil it for you.'

'Nothing is spoiled, Rena, not for me. Not if you'll allow me to take you out again. That's why I've come to Stockholm.'

She was puzzled. 'You are not here on business? You are not going away from Sweden now? Back to England?'

'No.' He grinned. 'I've only just arrived! I managed to throw my things into the hotel before getting back into the taxi and coming straight here. I remembered you didn't work at weekends. But I don't know where you live.'

It was her turn to be flustered. 'So you have come only ... to see me?'

'Yes.'

After a long pause, she said, quietly, 'Phil, I like you very much. I would be happy to spend time with you. But I can only be friends with you – platonic friends.'

'Platonic?' Phil could not help smiling – she had to be crazy. His eyes moved down to the lush ripeness of her breasts under the close-fitting white vest – her sexual attraction was ravishing. Few men would be capable of having a platonic relationship with her.

She had seen the look in his eyes, and immediately her own

eyes were bright with anger.

'I was foolish to think it possible, even with you. You English men – you think all Swedish girls are promiscuous.' She pushed past him angrily, and then she was gone.

He immediately chased after her, catching up with her just a few yards away from the hospital. 'All right, all right,' he exclaimed, 'platonic friends, whatever you say, anything you say.'

'No, you don't mean it.' She tried to move past him but he prevented her. Her eyes looked up at him, but now there was a film of tears over their blueness.

'Rena,' he said quietly, 'all I'm asking for is a chance.'

'A chance for what?'

'A chance ... to be platonic friends.' He could lie as well as any man. 'Just tell me one thing,' he said. 'Just tell me you're not a lesbian. I could cope with anything but that.'

'No, I am not a lesbian!' she cried, and her voice was choked with tears as she said, 'But I hate men, all men, even you.'

It was the 'even you' which made Phil realise that she did feel something for him. 'Look,' he said, 'let's go somewhere and sit down and calm down. Do you have a date tonight?'

'No.'

'Then why the rush?'

'I want to go home. I'm very tired. The hospital has been very busy all day, and I have been working without a break since eight o'clock this morning.'

'Well, then,' he suggested, 'we could go somewhere relaxing and have something to eat, a few drinks, just talk for a while, a short while, and then we could go to bed early.'

The last evoked a look from her that made him add quickly, 'Separately, of course. You to your home, and me to my hotel.'

She turned up her eyes like a persecuted schoolgirl. 'You will not give up, will you?'

'No,' said Phil, and smiled.

She hesitated, looking quickly at her at her plain T-shirt and skirt. 'We could not go anywhere special, I'm too tired to go home and change.'

'We'll go anywhere you want.'

And since restaurants were such an important part of Stockholm's social life, they had an extensive choice.

They met again on Saturday morning. Rena stared in amused amazement when she saw that Phil had hired a motorcycle. He was wearing a leather jacket and jeans and he was gazing over the Harley Davidson with sighs of admiration.

'Now I know why you told me to wear jeans,' Rena said.

'More comfortable.' Phil agreed.

'But why a motorbike?' she asked him. 'Can you not drive a car?'

'Rena, I drive a car every day. This is more fun.' He smiled. 'Come on, climb aboard. They gave me two helmets.'

It was years since she had ridden pillion on a motorcycle, not since she was sixteen, and she felt both thrilled and frightened at the prospect.

'This is crazy,' she said, climbing behind him. 'Drive carefully.'

'I always drive carefully.'

Then his foot went down and as the engine roared Rena's arms gripped his body tighter. Phil grinned to himself as they zoomed away: always more than one way to skin a cat, make a deal, or get the girl's arms around you.

The city and the suburbs were left far behind. Thick lines of green pine trees occasionally obscured the beautiful Swedish landscape.

Now, Rena thought suspiciously, now he will take me to some secluded place and try to seduce me. She had experienced it all before, all the tricks men played, though never on a motorbike.

They stopped for lunch, they later stopped by the cool blue

waters of a beautiful lake, but in the early evening he brought her back to the city, untouched.

Rena was smiling as she climbed off the bike. 'That was very entertaining.' She removed her helmet and let her hair tumble around her. 'I felt young again.'

'You *are* young,' Phil reminded her. 'Only twenty-three.'

'Yes,' Rena nodded, as if it was something she had forgotten. 'What now?'

'Well, let's see ... how about we get something to eat and then go on to a movie?' he suggested.

'I'd like that,' she agreed. Throughout the day they had agreed and disagreed on a number of things, but they both loved the cinema – they had agreed on that. And American and British films dominated in Sweden, so again they had plenty of choice.

Phil disappeared inside the garage to return the keys of the bike. Later, as they walked through the city, he stopped to buy an English newspaper which Rena insisted on glancing at in the restaurant. Her puzzled confusion over certain words kept him busy explaining their meaning.

'I can speak English better than I can read it,' she confessed.

'You're better than me, I can't understand a word of Swedish, let alone read it.'

'Would you like me to teach you?'

'That sounds promising.'

'What?'

'You offering to teach me hurdi-gurdi. Does that mean you want me to come back to Stockholm again?'

She responded with her uncertain smile. 'Do you *like* Stockholm?'

'Me? Oh, I just like Rena OIsson. But then you know that, don't you?'

She gave him a cool Scandinavian look. 'Let's go to the cinema now.'

'Which reminds me,' he said as they walked along. 'Bonniers

have just published a book by Vibeke Olsson. Is she any relation to you?'

`No, no relation. Olsson is a very common name in Sweden. Even some of my friends are called Olsson.'

`Your friends?' He smiled at her. `Are they all *platonic* friends? Like me?'

`Oh, shut up!'

In the cinema, in the darkness, she worried if this might be where he would try to touch her, get *too* friendly. Many men brought girls to cinemas simply for the darkness. But apart from the normal whispered exchange of comments at the beginning, she sat through the film warm and comfortable and completely engrossed, and left the cinema untouched.

`Tomorrow?' he asked, as they waited for her taxi. `Can we meet again tomorrow?'

`Yes,' she smiled. `Tomorrow. What time is your flight?'

`Not till the evening. Seven o'clock.'

`Then we will have most of the day. Would you like to see more of Stockholm? We could go under the bridges.'

`And what would we see under there?'

She laughed at his puzzled expression. `It's a boat trip, a two-hour cruise called "Under the Bridges of Stockholm". It takes you out to where Lake Mälaren reaches the Baltic.'

`Okay,' he agreed as her taxi drew up to the kerb. `What time?'

`Very early. I'll meet you on the waterfront. Outside the Grand Hotel at seven-thirty.'

`*Seven* – oh for God's sake, Rena, this cruise of yours better be worth it.'

`*Ja*,' she nodded, `it will be.' She looked at him and smiled. `And *I* will buy the tickets this time. I will show you Stockholm from the water, and prove to you that it is the most beautiful city in the world.'

And she did.

As the boat reached Lake Mälaren under the morning sun,

they leaned on the rail and looked down at the shimmering blue fresh water, under a cloudless sky.

'Now you understand why I wanted to be a mermaid,' she murmured, gazing longingly at the water's blue depths. 'I can swim like a fish, you know? I won medals in school.'

Their arms on the rail were only inches apart. He watched her face, and knew he had never wanted anyone so much in his life. She was so close, he wanted to reach out and take her in his arms and hold her tightly, but he didn't dare. He suspected there was something deeply traumatic behind her sexual frigidity, and knew it would be a mistake to even touch her.

As the boat veered back toward the salt water of the Baltic, he was confirmed in his decision. He had to let her play this out in her own way and in her own time, until they finally reached the end or the beginning. And amongst all his flaws he knew he possessed one definite virtue – extreme patience.

By Sunday evening, all Rena's fears were swept away. At last she had found a man who would make no physical demands upon her.

Gretta Curran Browne

Thirty-Eight

London
August 1993

David Gallagher was in Phil's office discussing a typescript when one of the phones on Phil's desk rang.

Phil picked it up. `Yes? ... No wait – no, don't put him through yet...' He looked at David. `It's John Houlihan.'

`Houlihan!' David's perseverance had reached its limit. `*The sod!* I've already spoken to him three times today! I've already told him the script hasn't a hope. And now here he is, taking not a blind bit of notice and going over my head to you!'

Phil spoke into the receiver. `Put him through.'

David listened with fury as Phil was patience itself with John Houlihan.

`Yes, John? ... Oh, pretty good. And you?'

A long silence from Phil followed, the only sound in the room being Houlihan's voice crackling louder and louder through the receiver that Phil held a few inches away from his ear.

Finally, Phil spoke. `Sure I can hear you, John. I'm not deaf.'

David nodded wearily. Houlihan always shouted down a phone.

`You're speaking to the wrong man, John. The man you should be speaking to is David Gallagher. You know everything to do with your scripts is down to him, and always has been. If he says the book is good enough, we publish. If he gives it the thumbs down, we don't. Simple as that ... Why? Because he's the Editorial Director here! I don't have time to read scripts. I run a business.'

Houlihan's voice raged on through the receiver.

Phil sighed. `I'm sorry, John, but as far as your scripts are

358

concerned, I rely implicitly on David Gallagher's impeccable judgement. Your previous books have all done well because they have always been under David's super supervision ... Yes I *have* read this latest script, but only as a courtesy to David Gallagher who wanted a second opinion.'

David grinned – now here was a man making a point. A point that even Houlihan might grasp.

David's secretary appeared at the door, beckoning him to come to his own phone.   For an instant David debated whether he should ask her to tell whoever it was to call back; but then, reluctantly, he stood up and left the room – *before* he had the satisfaction of hearing Phil giving Houlihan his own verdict on the script – the one Houlihan intended to launch him amongst the greats of literature.

Silence reigned for a few moments in Phil's office as he listened to John Houlihan, then – suddenly – the expression on Phil's face changed, as if he could not believe what he had just heard.

'No,' he said to Houlihan. 'No, I don't know what you're talking about.'

In his own study, John Houlihan sat back in his chair and did a slow swivel, spoke with aggrieved slowness.

'Phil, you know what I'm saying, ... I don't care what David Gallagher says about my book, because what does he know? He may understand all the managerial moves in a book's process. He may even understand all the creative components that make a good story. But what the hell does he know about what goes on between a man and a woman? And *this* book – *Rage Of The Soul* – is, as you know, a painfully *intimate* story of a man and a woman. So how can someone like Gallagher possibly evaluate its worth?'

When Phil did not reply, Houlihan continued, more cajolingly. 'How can you allow yourself to accept his decision? Feck's sake, Phil, you *know* what I'm saying. I *know* you do. You see, David Gallagher ... well, what you have there is a very nicely spoken pretty boy who looks as pure as a monk. True, he's intelligent, very bookish, very serious, and personally I think he should have become a professor at some university instead of a businessman. But at the end of the day, we both know what he is. So come on, Phil, let's talk about this, man to man.'

`Man to man? If you were here in this office, Houlihan, you know what I'd do man to man – I'd bounce you off the fucking wall!'

Houlihan reared up in his chair. `*What* was that you said?'

`You heard me, Houlihan! What makes you think you can get off with that kind of talk about one of my staff?'

`Hey, wait a minute! Now hold on, hold on there, Phil! All I was saying is that Gallagher ... well, he's shy ... doesn't talk, you know, like a man. Doesn't seem to know much about the sex thing—'

`The *sex* thing? So who are you? Some modern-day Casanova? Well you'd never guess it from your latest script. For three pages I thought I was reading about the Rain Forest in Brazil – turns out you're not describing the Rain Forest at all, but some woman's pubic hair. But you're right, Houlihan, you're *dead* right. David Gallagher might not have realised the difference.'

`Now, hold on there, Phil, just *hold on* a minute ... Look, let me explain something to you. I understand about people like David Gallagher. I understand why you're annoyed. You're his pal, so I understand. Deep down I feel the same myself. I feel very sorry for those people. They can't help it. Those people—'

`*What* people? I'm talking to you about David Gallagher. I'm telling you to mind your own damned business. I'm telling you that the private life of anyone employed here is nothing to do with you. Listen, Houlihan – No! Just shut the fuck up and listen! This is a *business*. A business concerned solely with *books*. Nothing to do with anyone's private life. Not even yours! The truth is, Houlihan – we wouldn't care if you spent your nights shacked up with a kangaroo, just so long as you turned in a good script.'

At the other end of the line, Houlihan suddenly grinned – a stupid grin for a stupid reason. 'Well, you've got plenty of spunk in you anyway, bejasus!' He slapped his hand down on the desk. 'You're all right, Phil. You're all right. Straight as a die! But now ... you said you've read the script? So let's talk about it. If you think it needs some rewriting, then I'll do some rewriting ... but let's not get sidetracked anymore by all this David Gallagher business.'

'You're the one who sidetracked, Houlihan. You're the one who was bloody insulting about my Editorial Director.'

'Yeah, sorry...sorry about that, Phil. Only I'm just a bit, you know, upset...' Houlihan passed and hand over his eyes. 'Phil, I'm *suicidal* here ... Can we *please* talk about the script?'

After a very long pause, Phil said in a quiet voice. 'Okay, let's talk about the script.'

When David Gallagher returned to the room, Phil was putting the phone down.

'Well?' David asked. 'What did you say to him? Did you tell him the script was no good?'

'I told him he had made a mistake. Taken a wrong turning down a dead end,' Phil replied quietly. 'I also told him that if he ever wanted to reverse back down the road to where he had started – back with an explosive script about Mafioso entrepreneurs or an IRA hit-man with eyes as steely as a pair of gun barrels – we'll still be here for him.'

'But you rejected his script?'

'Yes.'

'Did he give you any trouble?'

'No.' Phil picked up the phone and began tapping out numbers. 'No trouble at all.'

'Typical,' David muttered sullenly.

In his study in Islington, John Houlihan was sitting in his chair in a daze.

His wife, Nancy, a comforting and homely woman, also in her late forties, came into the room and looked at him anxiously. Houlihan turned his head and stared at her.

`Did you hear what he said, Nancy? That Phil Gaines. Did you hear?'

`No, pet, he was speaking to you on the telephone.'

`He said – that Phil Gaines – he said, "Why all this mania to be a ghost of Joyce when you have enough real live talent of your own?"'

`There now. Wasn't that a nice thing for him to say?'

Houlihan pressed his shoulders back against the chair and sat for a second squinting resentfully at the wall.

`Then he said to me – that Phil Gaines – he said, "Why don't you accept that you're a truly skilled *thriller* writer, who just took a wrong turning here."'

`Wrong turning? Well maybe he's right, Johnny.'

`"And when a new John Houlihan hits the shelves," he said, "that's what your readers expect – a thriller. Not a dark Irish lament as long as *War and Peace*."'

Nancy sighed. `He doesn't know our history or our heroes, Johnny. He's an Englishman.'

`He's a bloody basket case! That's what he is! Rejected my script. Said it was no good. Not even a rewrite would save it. Said it was ridiculous from start to end. Not only was it too long, it had no plot, no action, no excitement, *no balls!*'

`No what?'

`No kidding, Nancy, that's what he said. Came straight out and said it was no good. Anyway, what the hell does he know? He's only a publisher. If he knows so much about how to write a book, why doesn't he sit down and write one. But no. Can't do it. Got to rely on people like me to do it for him.'

`But he must know *something* about books,' Nancy ventured thoughtfully. `Because what he said to you, you know, about you being a good writer in the thriller style, but not so good in the *literary* style ... Well, isn't that what Mr Brennan, the schoolteacher who lived next door to us in Dublin, isn't that just what he told you? He did now, Johnny. I heard him myself. You must be fair.'

`Ah, fair me arse. What did Mr Brennan know about anything other than Greek and Latin? It might have served him better to have learned a bit of English.'

`Merciful God, isn't that a terrible way to talk about a dear man who set you on the road to making a name for yourself. If it wasn't for Mr Brennan, God rest his soul, we'd still be living in a four-roomed corporation house in Dublin now. Not this grand big house in Islington.'

`Yeah but ... Yeah but ... Yeah, you're right, Nancy. I shouldn't say anything bad about Mr Brennan. He was always very kind to me. But you see, Nancy—' He looked at her in a supplicating plea for understanding.

`I honestly don't think Mr Brennan was right in his evaluation of my work. You must remember, Nancy, it was over twenty years ago when he said that, and my writing then wasn't fully developed. I was a young man out working all day and coming home at night to a house of noisy kids.'

He angrily swished his arm through the air, taking a few imaginary swipes at those noisy kids of the past gathered round his chair, then he sat back and stared like a martyr at the wall.

`Dear God – it was a hard life for a budding genius to suffer! The only place I could get some peace to do my writing was sitting in the bath with a blanket under me and wearing my overcoat. So of course my writing wasn't *literary*. I was too damned cold to feel literary. So I made my stories fast and hot. Exciting stuff that got my adrenalin pumping and warmed me up. And why not? What the hell? A few quid is all I was after in those days. A quick sale to a magazine. *Ireland's Own* loved my short stories. Never rejected one. A cheque for twenty quid straight back to me in the post. Got me started. Kept me going. Enough to treat myself to the odd glass of whiskey now and again.'

The mention of whiskey made Nancy nervous. Johnny had been teetotal for almost a year now, during which time he had not seemed to give even a thought to whiskey, so busy was he writing his literary masterpiece. But look at him now – his poor martyred face!

`I'm still madly in love with you, Johnny.'

Houlihan slowly turned his head and stared at her. `Did you *have* to tell me that? Just at this minute?'

`The thing is, Johnny, I don't think Phil Gaines meant anything personal by it ... you know ... turning down your book.'

`Phil Gaines? That basket case!' Houlihan was furious again. `And what's more – he's a bloody *rude* basket case too! Did you *hear* the way he spoke to me, Nancy? Threatened to bounce me off the bollicking wall! Just because I spoke the truth about his pal Gallagher – that blondey Angel Gabriel.'

`Ah, sure you know Phil probably didn't mean it,' Nancy comforted. `He's always been very nice to you in the past. And he's always been very nice to me as well.'

`Well that just goes to show you what a bloody hypocrite he is, Nancy. Because d'you know what he said about you? He said you were a kangaroo!'

Thirty-Nine

Stockholm
August – September 1993

_____/

Phil seemed to have fallen in love with Stockholm, surprising Rena by coming back to it again and again – telephoning her as soon as he arrived at his hotel, then whisking her off to dine, followed by an early meeting the following day.

Every weekend, though, he found it hard to adjust to the climate in Sweden. He loved the long summer days, which were sunny and dry, but the summer nights – hardly any darkness at all. Sometimes the sun was still red in the sky at one o'clock in the morning.

'This is the land of the Midnight Sun and the Northern Lights,' Rena reminded him. 'We have bright warm summers and dark cold winters.'

Rena had to admit to herself that she enjoyed every minute in his company, yet whenever he tried to get close to her, even to just hold her hand, a chilly reserve came over her – as cold as snow-clad Stockholm in winter.

During the weeks, when they were apart, he phoned every night from London. She would always answer the phone coolly, pretending astonishment that he had called again, giving not a hint that she had been waiting restlessly for his call.

They would sometimes talk for more than an hour, late into the night, about everything and anything; the content did not matter. He had phoned just to hear her voice, and she had waited to hear his.

Was she falling in love with him? At times it felt so. His general compliance to her request for a non-sexual friendship bewildered her. With other men, there had been no middle ground. They gave her only two choices: lover or implacable

365

adversary.

The latter was usually the result.

With Phil it was different, and she was helpless to understand it. Often when he was not looking she would sit with her eyes upon him, trying to puzzle him out, trying to understand the mystery behind his relaxed attitude. He had taught her to laugh again and she had not known that so much laughter was left in her. He always gave her a wonderful time, but she gave him nothing in return, except her company.

Even so, he spoiled her shamelessly. He sent her flowers several times a week, delivered to the hospital. She would leave some behind and take the rest home; but before long her bedroom was filled with them, the entire *house* was filled with them.

`Who sends them?' her mother asked one night when she arrived home with more flowers and more Swiss chocolates. `The Englishman on the telephone?'

`Yes,' Rena replied quietly, `the Englishman.'

`What is wrong with him? Has he more money than sense? And why does he always send them to the hospital and not here?'

`I have not yet given him my address.'

`Why not?'

Rena didn't reply, just looked at her mother silently.

`What is wrong with him, Rena? That he does not wonder why you do not give him the address of your home?'

Rena sighed. `Yes, he wonders. But he has English good manners and he does not push the question.'

When they entered the living-room, her mother continued. `Why has he come to Stockholm seven, eight times now? And when he comes, why do you need to stay out with him all day, every weekend?'

`At least she does not stay out with him all night,' her father said, but not on her behalf, only in satisfaction.

Even during dinner, her mother would not let the subject

drop. 'Who is this Englishman, Rena? Why do you not bring him home for us to meet with him? Is he married?'

'No, Mamma, he is not married. He is a publisher. He comes to Stockholm to see business people.'

'At weekends?' Her father looked disbelieving. 'No businessman in Sweden works at weekends. Only shopkeepers.'

Her mother persisted. 'This Englishman—'

'At least he's not American,' her father interrupted. 'There is too much of America here in Sweden. All the young, dressing always like Americans, buying their clothes from Marc O'Polo and Gul & Bla on Hamngatan – shops that seem to be more rich and American than America itself'.

Her mother nodded in agreement with him. To them, the Swedish youth appeared to be obsessed with all things American, but they were devoted only to Sweden. Both were history teachers in the same school, and both knew every detail of the preserved chronicles of the Vikings. There was not a thing they did not know and love about Sweden, from the arrival of King Gustav Vasa who had fought to free the Swedish people from the rule of Denmark, to King Gustavus Adolphus who had made Stockholm the capital and heart of the Swedish nation.

'This Englishman, Rena....'

When the questions continued, Rena was unable to take any more, 'I feel unwell ... I think I must lie down.'

In her room she threw herself down on the bed and wished that Minna had not got married.

Six months earlier she had finally escaped from home, to share an apartment in the city with her friend Minna. But only weeks later, after a whirlwind romance, Minna had married and her new husband, an actor, had moved into the apartment with them.

So Rena had moved out, back home. Back to catching the train to and from work. Her parents had looked satisfied.

She had left once before, and once again after that, but always her parents found a way of bringing her back.

When the phone rang later that night, her father did not call her. She knew it was Phil. She leapt off the bed and ran downstairs to see her father putting the phone down.

'I thought you were asleep,' he said, but she knew he was lying. 'It was the Englishman. I told him you had gone to bed.'

'Did he leave a message?'

He nodded stiffly. 'He will be in Stockholm tomorrow night. He will telephone you when he reaches his hotel.'

She felt instant relief. 'But Rena...' her father said reprovingly, causing her to halt on the stairs and look back at him.

'Tomorrow night is Friday night, Rena. He is not coming to Stockholm for business. Do not tell me that. He is coming only to see you. So you must bring him home for us to meet with him.'

Rena's heart sank at such a prospect. 'Perhaps you would prefer me to tell him goodbye,' she said quietly.

'Perhaps that would be best,' he agreed gently. 'There are many good men here in Sweden, Rena. You do not need to settle for a foreigner.'

The late-September weather was warm in England, but brisk in Stockholm. The wind from the sea had an icy bite to it. Phil was glad he had brought some reasonably warm clothes along.

'*Hej!*' The young bellhop at the SAS Strand greeted him as if he was an old friend. Five minutes later he was in his regular room and as always it was stocked with fresh flowers in silver vases.

Before he had a chance to telephone Rena, there was a knock on the door. He opened it and stared in surprise to see her standing there. She looked very serious and didn't smile.

'Hello, Phil.'

Instantly he knew something was wrong. She had never

come near his hotel before. And the fact that she was here now, told him they had finally reached the end or the beginning. She had made a decision.

Judging by her clothes, it was the end. She had dressed as if for a funeral: black coat, black stockings and black high-heeled shoes. Even her blonde hair was tied back as if she didn't want it interfering with her thoughts.

`What's wrong?' he asked.

`Everything.'

She walked into the room and sat down on the side of the double bed, her hands clasped in her lap as if she was sitting in church.

`I want to speak with you,' she said quietly. `I want to tell you something else.'

`Would you like a drink?'

`No.'

`Do you want to take off your coat?'

`No.'

She looked up at him and he saw that she was very nervous. `I want to know if you are in love with me?'

He looked at her for a long time. `You know I am.'

`This is not just a Swedish affair?'

He half smiled. `This is not any kind of affair. Last I heard it was a platonic friendship.'

She nodded, and looked down at her hands. `Yes, and I want to tell you why—' She did not speak again until he sat down beside her.

Even then she found it difficult, drawing a breath as if to speak, then letting it out unused, her hands clenching and unclenching on her lap.

`I had a bad experience ... ' she said awkwardly. `It was horrible, disgusting. Since then just the thought of sex with a man— ' She shook her head, then suddenly looked towards the door and stood up again, as if to leave. `No, no, I should not have come, you are a man so you will not understand, you will

369

think it is nothing.'

He leapt up, put his hands on her shoulders, and pushed her back down. For the first time ever he lost patience with her.

'Rena, whatever is wrong with you, you'd better tell me. Maybe I'll understand, and maybe I won't. But since we're speaking the truth, I want to tell you truly that I am tired of playing your devoted eunuch – so unless you give me some kind of explanation now, you can stand up, say goodbye, walk out that door, and you'll never hear from me again, I promise you.'

She stared up at him, her ice-blue eyes flooding with tears. 'I don't want to say goodbye.'

He sighed, and sat down beside her again, reached out and took her hand. 'This man, the bad experience, the one who made you hate men, who was he?'

She bowed her head. 'His mouth ... that's all I really remember. His lips ... cold and wet and disgusting.'

'You must remember more than that,' he said gently.

'Yes,' she agreed. 'He was five years older than me...' And she could remember far more than his lips. But worst of all was her own shame, her own guilt. Even during the greedy assault of his mouth, even before the rough pain of the penetration into her body, she had an uneasy feeling that there was more in the room than met the eye. In cold terror she had struggled, and then she had seen them – his friends at the door, watching ... They had been watching from the beginning. And from the smirk on his face, she knew he had arranged it so.

Even when she had struggled free, mouse-like she had cringed, unable to speak, unable to do anything more than stare at their shameless faces, their insolent eyes, listen to their upper-class voices. Then she heard a sound, which made them all alert – a car outside. The front door closing, voices raised cheerfully – his parents had come back. They all quickly disappeared.

She was left alone, left to button up her dress with trembling hands and pull down the skirt – left to stand and stare at herself in the mirror and see another person there. Never had she felt such hatred. Never had she felt so ugly. Never again.

Don't you see?' she said, tears spilling from her eyes. `They just used me as a sex object. One to do it and the others to watch. They must have planned it. Because the house seemed empty when I arrived, but they must have been already there, hiding and waiting. And if his parents had not come back ... maybe I would have been raped by all of them.'

`How old were you?'

`It was my nineteenth birthday. I thought he was in love with me. But that day ... he turned into somebody else before my eyes ... they all did ... all men.'

For months afterwards she had gone through life on the verge of tears. `Everywhere I went I could feel eyes looking at me. Men's eyes, everywhere, looking at me. I thought I was going to go mad.'

Then, she explained, something strange happened, a mental click in her head. She had actually felt it – a mental click – and she had frozen. Clinically clean, emotionally sterile, sexually frigid. A perfect nurse.

Phil felt sick with disgust and rage as he thought of the scumbags who had abused her – especially the watchers, abusing her with their eyes – a mental gang-bang by a bunch of filthy cowards.

He was looking intently at her face, the nurse's face that had first awakened him in the hospital. He remembered the girl he had first seen. Poised, dignified, correct – going about her duties with a quiet manner and ice-calm control.

Not so now. She looked terribly young now, out of control, with tear-filled eyes. Desperately he wanted to take her in his arms, to comfort and reassure her and love her beyond words, but he held himself back.

He lifted the hotel's box of tissues from the side table and handed them to her. She began to dry her eyes.

'I told my father,' she whispered. 'He was the only one I told. He wanted to go and kill them. But I stopped him, I begged him to keep safe my dignity. He agreed, but he drank and drank and stayed drunk for a week, which was shaming for him, because he is a strict Lutheran. Since then he has tried to keep me away from all men. Always he is afraid for me. And now he is very afraid of you.'

Phil was still holding her hand, holding it tightly.

He said, 'Rena, are you afraid of me?'

'No ... I—' she shook her head and sighed helplessly. 'Phil ... oh, I can't explain, the words won't come ... but I know how I feel about you ... and I want you to know how I feel about you...'

She looked down at her hands. '*Jag älskar dig*,' she whispered.

His eyes were puzzled. 'I don't understand what you are saying.'

'I don't want to say it in English,' she said, unable to meet his eyes. 'Only in Swedish.'

'Then say it again.'

'*Jag älskar dig*.'

He stood up and lifted the phone on the side table. When the telephonist answered, he asked her, '*Jag älskar dig* – what does it mean in English?'

A chuckle, then her reply: 'I love you.'

'Thank you.'

He put down the phone, but did not speak immediately, tilting his head sideways to look at her.

'It's true, I do,' she whispered.

He moved towards her and caught both her arms, pulling her up from the bed so quickly she was not even aware it had happened. He wrapped his arms around her and held her so tightly she could feel his heart beating. She lifted her mouth to his and kissed him with the tenderest hunger. A moment later he was kissing her with all the intensity and passion of a lover.

It was the beginning.

In bed, her lips opened under his lovingly. Her body was very warm and soft with love, and he entered it with a slow sigh of ecstasy.

It took them hours to come to their senses. Long, wild, luscious hours of limitless love when he had lavished kisses of fire all over her body. Now he knew every inch of her, every line of her limbs, and she was even more beautiful than he had imagined.

'I just *knew* you would be exquisite,' he whispered, and she smiled dreamily and whispered back, 'You too.'

By the time the midnight sun had vanished into the darkness, he was more in love with her than ever.

He reached for the telephone and rang Room Service and ordered champagne on ice. Twenty minutes later she lay back on the pillows, her smile full of mischief and delight as he fed her small delicacies from a smorgasbord of light food.

He grinned. 'Makes a change, the patient looking after the nurse.'

Ten minutes after that, she wanted to make love again. He sighed, 'Rena, you're not frigid – you're the sexiest woman in the world.'

She smiled. 'I've been saving myself for you.'

'I'm beginning to believe it.'

She stayed with him at the SAS Strand for the entire weekend. They scarcely left the room and slept only fleetingly. The hotel provided 24-hour Room Service and they used it for breakfast and lunch. In the afternoon they lay in bed and sleepily watched a movie on TV. They had no desire to be in the company of others. The hotel was quiet, as most hotels are in the afternoon. No loud voices. No sounds of rushing feet as guests hurried back to dress for dinner.

In the evening they showered and then dined in the hotel's *Piazza* restaurant. Afterwards they took a stroll along the waterfront, walking as they had never walked before, as lovers, his arm around her shoulder, and her arm around his waist.

Under the evening shadows the water was dark and dancing. Clouds flitted across the moon. The lights all along the waterfront took on a more luminous brilliance. The air was as fresh as it must have been on the first day on earth. They felt as if they were the only lovers on earth. They stood in the breeze and kissed and forgot the world. Isolated in love and tenderness. Devastated by sexual passion. Every moment of the walk back to the hotel became more exciting. They glanced at each other and smiled in sweet expectation of another wild and wonderful night together.

As they reached the main doors of the hotel, he paused to tell her something. `I love you, Rena,' he said. `You do know that?'

She nodded. `*Ja,* I do.'

He smiled. `You're my own beautiful swede-heart.'

She laughed and pulled him inside.

Forty

London
October 1993

Wednesday Evening Blues.

John Houlihan had always hated Wednesdays. It was the worse day of all when you really thought about it. Not the beginning of the week nor the end. Not one thing or the other. He remembered hearing somewhere that Jews never attempted doing anything new on a Wednesday. Or was it Friday? Well, anyway, he hated Wednesdays! Really *hated* the fuckers! And this particular Wednesday was going to be the most memorable of his whole life – because he intended to commit suicide.

'Whiskey!' he demanded, peering round the liquor store. 'Have you got Jamesons? Right, then. Three bottles.'

'Ah, Johnny!' cried Nancy in alarm when he arrived home and opened one of the bottles. 'Don't be touching that stuff. You know it does funny things to your brain, and you've gone so long without it.'

'Too long, Nancy, too bloody long. And I'm entitled to the comfort of a small drink of the barley malt while I sit back and peruse the waste of my life.'

'Waste of your life? ... Ah, Johnny, you've done wonderful things with your life, so you have! And you're a lovely man under all that fierce bawdiness. A lovely man! And I'm not the only one who knows it.'

Houlihan managed to smile at his wife. After all these years he still loved her with a fierce tenderness that surfaced even now amidst the insensate rage that throbbed inside him. They had been married for so long, and had grown so close, Nancy was more like an extension of himself, than another human being. They were inseparable. She was the better half, and he was the lucky half.

So why was he thinking of suicide?

`Christ, Nancy—' he said quietly, running a hand through his extravagant head of hair, `what would I do without you, girl? As the song says – you're the best thing that ever happened to me.'

`It went badly, then?' Nancy realised. `The meeting with the publisher?' She sat back in disappointment. It was the fourth publisher he had sent *Rage Of The Soul* to, but none of them wanted to publish his masterpiece. And Johnny always made it worse by going to see them personally and demanding to know why.

`It went worse than badly.' Houlihan poured a large shot of Jameson's into a glass and gave a sad sigh. `The whole world has turned against me, Nancy.'

`Not me, Johnny. You've still got me.'

`They all think I'm finished. But, Jesus, whether I am or not, when I stood in that office today I'd had enough, and I wasn't going to let that priggish little worm of an editor call my work utter drivel. So I bashed him, Nancy. Gave him one good hard clobber in the chops.'

`Oh, for God's sake, Johnny, please tell me you did no such thing!'

`I mean...' Houlihan exclaimed, feeling furious again, `whatever I write it might be bad or not good enough, but it's never *drivel*. And even Phil Gaines wasn't that rude about my work – and *he's* a hot-headed, straight-talking, bloody basket case!'

`Would you not reconsider getting an agent?' Nancy asked.

`An agent—' Houlihan glared at her. `Now you know the word "agent" is the one word in the dictionary that I cannot abide, Nancy! Ever since that agent sent my script back with a sarcastic letter telling me not to even consider taking up writing as a career. Two months later David Gallagher bought my script and turned it into a bestseller! And then my second – and my third – all bestsellers! Now what does that tell you about literary agents, Nancy? It tells you they can't tell a good script from a dog's dinner.'

`Maybe you just sent the first one to the wrong agent.'

`Ah, stop annoying me about agents, Nancy. I'm having enough problems dealing with publishers.'

Houlihan knocked back a slug of whiskey, waiting for the golden medicine to tranquillise him.

Three glasses later he felt calm and philosophical. He sat back in his armchair and gave a profound sigh.

`Do you know what, Nancy? People in general are basically rotten. They're all "pal-of-mine" when you succeed. But when you fail – they *love* it! Makes them feel better, gives their rotten old jealousy a rest.'

He dropped back his head and gazed up at the ceiling ... `Beware of wily sycophants and false flattery. It's mere folly to prefer the acclaim of false witnesses, when the bitter truth of genuine criticism will help you to write much better.'

He sighed. `Oh, how right you were, dear Christy Brown, how right. But it's still painful, nevertheless.'

`Johnny, would you not prefer a nice cup of tea instead that whiskey,' Nancy asked pleadingly. `And a lovely steak dinner?'

She loved him more than her own life, and she didn't know what else to say to console him on this, his day of reckoning.

He ignored her question, but looked at her thoughtfully. `Did I ever tell you about my mother and Christy Brown's mother in the Iveagh Market in Dublin'

`You did, Johnny, you did. Many times.'

`Well sit back and I'll tell you again, because it just goes to show how *rotten* some people can be. Eaten up with jealousy when some poor mother's son gets a bit of success and they don't ... I mean there was that poor woman, Bridie Brown, and she with a regiment of children to rear. And one day, Bridie Brown was in the Iveagh Market, you know that big warehouse place up by the Liberties. Years ago it was. I was just a nipper at the time – 1954 or 1955 – I can't remember which. But it was not too long after Christy had got his first book published.'

He sipped his whiskey and thought back.

'So there she was, Bridie Brown, walking round all the dealer's stalls searching through the piles of second-hand clothes, when my mother bumped into her and stopped to pass a chat with her. They were hard times for most families in Dublin in those days, and we were also wearing the second-hand clothes.'

'"How're you doing, Bridie?" says my mother. "What size is that boy's jacket you've just thrown down?"

"It's no good," says Bridie. "It's got a hole in the elbow and a tear on the cuff. Doesn't it make you wonder about whoever first owned it? Merciful Jesus, wouldn't you think they'd have had the decency to throw it in the dustbin, instead of expecting some other person to buy it."

'And so on and so on, until my mother and Christy's mother went their separate ways, each in search of a few bargains. Then a short while later, my mother was standing holding this cardboard box containing about six geranium plants. She always had a passion for geraniums. But only the red ones. Couldn't abide pink. Said they were only pale imitations. And while she's standing there, deciding whether to buy this box of geraniums, my mother hears this group of women talking behind her.

'"Would you look over there," says one. "Isn't that Bridie Brown? Isn't that disgusting! Coming here buying the second-hand clothes when her son is a writer. Those Browns are loaded now, you know? Oh, indeed! The cripple got a fortune when his book was published. So she must be rolling in it. Wouldn't you think she'd go and buy what she needs in Arnott's like the rest of the rich. Her that was not too shy to go swanking into the Gresham Hotel like Lady Muck holding her bunch of flowers, just because she's the mother of a famous son. And all Dublin knows it wasn't the cripple who wrote that book at all.

It was one of his brothers. Of course it was! *My left foot*, my eye! Do they think we're fools altogether? Expecting us to believe that. Sure that Christy Brown—"

`And my mother could listen to no more. She turned and toppled the box of geraniums all over the women, brown soil and all.

`"You bitches!" she told them. "You dirty bad-mouthed bitches! If Bridie Brown got millions of pounds it could never compensate for the suffering of her son with cerebral palsy. Go on now! Go home and get ready for Sunday Mass tomorrow and when you get there, tell God what lovely Christian women you are. You never know. There might be a miracle. Jesus himself may come down from the Cross and slap the faces off the lot of you!"'

`Oh indeed,' said Nancy, `she had a fierce temper, your mother. And it's from her that you inherited your own temper, Johnny.'

`My mother hated injustice,' Houlihan said quietly.

`She did that,' Nancy agreed. `But Johnny, where is all this talk of the past leading you? If no one wants to publish your book, what are you going to do now?'

Houlihan sat for a time in silent reflection; then he spoke, not with anger or despair, but with renewed determination.

`Well, where it all leads to is this, Nancy ... whatever you do in life, never give a damn what other people say about you, good or bad. Just carry on, doing what you do best. And whether you fail or succeed, never stop trying to do better.'

Forty-One

Rome & Stockholm
October – November 1993

_____/

Sofia was ecstatic when Phil brought Rena for a long weekend in Rome.

`Capitale del Mondo1' Sofia exclaimed proudly. `Roma is the head of the world! The city of *La Dolce Vita*.' She lifted Rena's hand and kissed it. `You agree, *cara*?'

Rena agreed with most things Sofia said – because she understood less than half of it. But she delighted in the lovely big Italian woman who had taken charge of her from the moment they had met, two days earlier.

`He has brought you to Roma to meet his darling Sofia and beloved Alberto,' Sofia whispered to her secretly. `So you are very special to him, very special.'

Rena already knew that, but it pleased her to hear someone like Sofia say it with such certainty.

`The Agony and the Ecstasy. Michaelangelo's Eternal City.' Phil smiled at Rena. They were sitting drinking cappuccino in the lovely square of Campo dei Fiori with Chef and Sofia.

The only sadness of this meeting was that Miss Courtney could not be there to meet Rena, because she was no longer alive.

`In her sleep,' Sofia whispered to Rena. `A year ago. Said her prayers, went to bed, and died peacefully. I blame her dog.'

`Her dog?'

Sofia nodded. `When Marian died – Phil has told you about Marian?'

Rena nodded. `Yes, he has told me.'

Rena knew she would always remember the night Phil had told her about Marian. He had known such sadness in his life.

Both parents killed violently. Too much sadness for one person to suffer. They had talked for hours that night, all their private thoughts, sharing everything and sparing nothing.

`... and so the flat in Hampstead was sold,' Sofia was saying, `but the money from the sale could not be given to Phil until he was eighteen years old. So he came to live with his darling Sofia and his beloved Alberto. And when he was eighteen, they sent him the money, the solicitors who held the trust. Fifty-thousand pounds! A lot of money. He tried to give us some money but Alberto said no. He was our son now. We wanted no money. He must save it for his future. But Phil gave some to Miss Courtney. And Phil bought her the dog.'

`The dog you blame?'

`*Si*.' Sofia sighed. `Poor Missy. When Marian died, poor Missy her heart was too broke. So she stopped work, stopped everything, and never went outside the door. Phil was so worried about her. Then he bought her the dog, and Missy was happy again, looking after Barney like he was her child, out walking with him every day, walk, walk, walk, her and Barney.'

`How old was she?'

`Old when she died. Her dog was old too. Twelve years. Old in dog life. And last year, when Barney got a tumour in his stomach and the vet said to Missy that he would have to give Barney an injection and send him to sleep, Miss Courtney said, "Very well," and was not upset on the telephone when she spoke to me about it. But two weeks later – Missy did the same as Barney – went to sleep and woke up in Heaven.'

Rena looked thoughtful. `Do dogs go to Heaven?'

`*Si!*' Sofia nodded her head emphatically. `Why should dogs not go to Heaven? Many are better behaved than humans!'

And Rena, who had often noticed this herself, found it impossible to disagree.

Chef and Sofia had moved to Rome at the end of 1987. In their youth they had met in the Eternal City and it had always been their dream to retire there. They loved the noise and the vital, throbbing life of Italy's capital. And during the long and tiring everyday existence of their life in London, they had often daydreamed about the long afternoon siestas in the heat of an Italian summer.

`Some dream,' Chef used to say, looking glumly at his till receipts.

But then Phil had inherited thirty-three million dollars, and a few months after his graduation he had bought Chef and Sofia a beautiful townhouse in the residential, but central, Prati district of Rome. He had also bought them a small villa in the cool greenery of Tuscany for when life in the busy capital got just *too* hot in July and August.

Chef had protested vehemently, but Phil would entertain no arguments. `It's little enough, Chef, because I'll never be able to repay all you did for Marian. And for me.'

And Chef had sighed, because he knew that Phil was a man who believed in giving back as good or as bad as he got. An angel to his friends, but merciless to his enemies.

So the restaurant in London had been sold, and now Chef and Sofia were living without labour in Rome, enjoying, at last – *la dolce vita* – the good life.

Sadly childless, but always possessing a natural love for children, Sofia's greatest pleasure was that she now lived so close to her younger sisters and brothers and their children, a crowd of nieces and nephews of whom many now had their own children, and despite their general Catholicism, every one of Sofia's relatives loved Alberto, even though he was neither Catholic nor Italian.

`What I love about Italians,' Chef said to Phil, `is the way they excel in the art of *nonmifreghismo* – not giving a damn.'

In the crowded square of Campo dei Fiori, a young man strumming a merry guitar strolled past their table in a world of his own, singing about the Girl from Ipanema.

'And most Italians adore music and dancing!' Chef added, his shoes beginning to tap to the music.

Later that evening, in the courtyard garden of Chef and Sofia's house, Phil and Rena joined Sofia's crowd of relatives for a party. The night glowed with coloured lanterns and music and dancing and laughter.

'I didn't realise that Italians, on the whole, were such good-looking people,' Rena commented to Sofia, causing the older woman to clap her hands in delight. 'Now look at me, I'm sixty-four,' said Sofia, subtracting five years from her age, 'but I am still beautiful! And still in love with my Alberto!'

And five minutes later Chef and Sofia were dancing happily together to the lively music, both grey-haired and larger than life, both refusing to grow old, glorying in the ease of their retirement.

'Whoever has nothing else left in life, should come and live in Rome.' Phil smiled at Rena. 'Perhaps Chateaubriand was right.'

'Look, Alberto...' Sofia whispered to Chef. 'Look – see how in love they are?'

Chef looked over his shoulder to where Phil and Rena had retired from the noisy family throng to a small wooden bench in a shadowy corner of the courtyard scented with overhanging baskets of trailing vine, red geraniums, bougainvillea and white jasmine. They were talking quietly together.

'See, Alberto, see how she looks at him, how she adores him, how she worships him— '

Chef turned back and continued to dance like Zorba the Greek. 'You approve of her. Oh, that *is* a relief.'

Sofia suddenly flung her plump arms around Chef's broad shoulders, forcing him to slow down into a waltz, her chin tucked into his neck – not for any romantic reasons of her own, but because she wanted to pretend to be dancing while keeping her eyes on the young couple in the corner.

'See, Alberto, how beautiful she is ... so young and

feminine...'

Phil and Rena had their heads bowed, touching each other's fingers and speaking quietly. Phil was saying, ` ... I want you to know what you mean to me. I love you, and I love you in my heart. And from now on, wherever I go, whatever I do, none of it will mean anything without you.'

They were married in Stockholm a month later.

Phil experienced some difficulty during the ceremony, because everything was said first in Swedish, and then in English.

Apart from the language it was a simple wedding, no fuss, no flash. Rena wore a long-sleeved white satin dress, and Phil thought she had to be the most beautiful bride who ever stood before an altar. She looked like an angel, her blue eyes sparkling, her silvery-golden hair crowned by a circular headpiece and hanging down in loose curls. And whether it was the custom in Sweden or not, he was unable to resist leaning forward and kissing her on the lips.

It was the happiest day of Rena's life. And even her parents looked happy. They had liked Phil from the moment they had finally met him. And, they reasoned, Rena might be marrying an Englishman, but at least she was marrying him in Sweden. And *he* had even agreed to marry her in a Lutheran church.

And she would come back to them. Rena had promised. At least once a month she would come back from England to see them. And every night she would telephone and speak with them. She had promised. And Rena never broke a promise.

Rena slipped her arm through Phil's as they turned from the altar, smiling radiantly at Minna, and David Gallagher, and Miranda Alvin, and all the other intimate friends who had gathered in Stockholm for this special day.

Sofia was dabbing the tears from her eyes with a lace handkerchief, her extravagant hat taking up half the church.

But when Phil looked at Chef – and an unspoken message

passed over Chef's face – Phil grinned at the older man and almost laughed.

Rena whispered to him. `Phil, what is so funny?'

`Oh, just one of Chef's old Jewish sayings: "A wife, a life."'

Part Four

James Duncan

1994

Forty-Two

London
May 1994

_____/

James Duncan was studying himself in the bathroom mirror as he slicked the comb through his hair – completely grey now.

Pity about that. If he had taken Vitamin E in his prime it would have prevented his hair from turning grey – according to Joanne – who had just found it out from her nutritionist. But he hadn't taken any vitamins then. Not one from A to Z. So now he had to content himself having his hair rinsed a distinguished silver.

He gazed at his reflection with admiring satisfaction. He was fifty-seven, as tall and straight as an officer, but elegant, very elegant, and still a very attractive man. The fact that he thought this himself made it no less valid, he decided. It was simply true.

He returned to the bedroom where Joanne was sitting in front of her dressing table putting the finishing touches to her make-up. At forty, she was seventeen years younger than him, but she never admitted to being over thirty-five. Always expensively dressed, she prided herself on being a `mirror of fashion'. Her bouffant of blonde hair was swept up into a chignon – à la Ivana Trump.

`Well,' said James determinedly, `no rich ruthless whiz-kid of a publisher is going to push me around.'

`Don't be silly, darling. All Phil Gaines has done is to invite you to a party at his home this afternoon. Is that pushing you around?'

James Duncan sighed heavily. `I'm not going to get annoyed, Joannie, I'm not even going to bother to explain, because let's face it, you are fundamentally a very stupid woman.'

Joanne dabbed a tissue to her lipstick. 'What's there to explain?'

'You think our invitation to this garden party today is something social?' James shook his head. 'You've got no idea how business deals are made, have you?'

'Be a darling, James, and stop grumbling. You are *spoiling* my party mood.'

James eyed her coolly as she stood up and did a fluttery walk over to her wardrobe and began to slip into the skirt of a white suit.

At times like this, James felt deeply aggrieved.

He had not realised Joanne was so stupid when he married her, but at the time he had not been overly concerned with her cerebral fitness. She had been a great looker in those days, a great body, and all he had been able to think of then was how to secure her as his regular companion in bed. Marriage – that's what she had demanded. Claiming to be an old-fashioned girl of high morals, she would settle for nothing less.

After only one week of living with her in marital bliss, he had discovered Joanne's one tragic flaw – she was an airhead. Didn't have the brains of a gnat. Sometimes she was so stupid, so dumb, so deficient in ordinary common-sense intelligence, he often found himself wondering if she had truly been born on this planet? Her parents were dead, so he only had her word for it.

But despite all that – he stood for a moment basking in self-congratulation – he was *still* married to her, after twenty years, which proved what a truly *decent* man he was. Reliable, dignified, a man who knew how to shoulder his responsibilities. Still, someone had to look after the stupid cow.

'Come on, Joannie ... It's a long drive from Berkshire to Hampstead. I don't want to be caught in the Saturday afternoon traffic.'

Joanne slipped her arms into the jacket of her suit and smiled at her reflection as she fastened the buttons. The white jacket had a deep 'V' neck and all she wore underneath it was a half-cup bra and the tan from her sunbed. But then, Joanne had always enjoyed giving men a good eyeful.

Finally, perusing herself in the wardrobe's full-length mirror, her eyes travelling down from the sexy jacket to the slim-line skirt cut just above the knee, Joanne murmured demurely, 'How do I look, James?'

James was still watching his wife, the vainest woman in town, his eyes on the low 'V' of her jacket which revealed the deep cleavage of her breasts. 'That suit is new!' he challenged, his eyes like flints. 'How much did that cost?'

'Oh, pouf, pouf, pouf!' Joanne waved a hand dismissively. 'It's only money, James. And you don't want me to look *cheap* do you?'

James half opened his mouth to reply, changed his mind, turned and stormed out of the room.

He thumped heavily down the stairs, thinking to himself that if it weren't for the fact that she was always so commodious in bed and happy to indulge all his sexual idiosyncrasies, he would take her out to some lonely field and strangle her. Not only did she have the intellect of a paralysed flea, she was also a spend-happy catastrophe.

'If you're not down in one minute,' he shouted up to her, 'I'm going without you.'

And he would, too. The old bastard! Joanne rushed over to her dressing table in a flurry and clipped her earrings on ... she would simply *die* if she missed seeing Phil Gaines again. That man was just so *appallingly* good-looking. She would wrangle a lunch-date out of him if it killed her.

She smiled sexily at herself in the mirror – yes, what man could resist such a seductive smile? She lifted her perfume bottle and shot another spray down her cleavage, then grabbed up her purse and did a fluttery run out of the room and down the stairs to hear James starting up the car's engine.

'I'll poison him one day,' she muttered angrily. 'I'll put

weed-killer in his coffee in small doses, and then I'll weep tears of joy at his funeral.'

In December of the previous year, after their honeymoon in Bali, Phil had bought Rena a beautiful Georgian house near Hampstead Heath.

Although the deeds of the house were in both their names, it was his special wedding gift to her, because down in the basement there was a thirty-foot indoor heated swimming pool, which the previous owner had installed.

The marble floor of the pool was deep blue and the overhead lights were as golden as the sun, and it was to be her own little Lake Mälaren whenever she yearned to leave the world and become a mermaid. A compensation for leaving her beloved Sweden and coming to live with him in England.

But now, on this warm Saturday afternoon in May, the basement was locked because the house was filled with people enjoying a party, and Rena did not want any strangers frolicking in nor invading the privacy of her pool.

The party was turning out to be a spectacular success. The huge drawing-room was buzzing with conversation. Outside in the sun-streaked back garden more guests relaxed in clusters while waiters moved around dispensing champagne and hors d'oeuvres of beluga caviar.

There were more than a hundred guests gathered to celebrate the fourth anniversary of Gaines Publishing Limited, now one of the most successful independent houses in London. Since the publication of its first book by Marian Barnard four years earlier, Gaines Publishing had continued to publish a stream of exciting new writers, defying the recession and regularly reaching the bestseller list, regularly increasing their profits.

At thirty years of age, Phil Gaines still had the relentless energy he had when he first entered publishing, and everyone knew he was the driving force behind the firm's meteoric expansion and profitability. No one knew from where he had got his business acumen. Rumour still had it that he was already a millionaire before he entered publishing – and indeed he must have been – because no matter how successful, few independent publishers could afford to live in a house whispered to have cost three million pounds.

At first he had been branded as 'lucky' and a 'gambler' but now he was considered to be an innovator and regarded with respect. If he had simply been some rich dilettante dabbling in publishing he would have moved on by now, investing his money in films or television companies or some other equally exciting game.

But no, he had made the publishing world his world and was making it very clear that he intended to stay.

James Duncan wandered around the lower rooms of the house, sucking on his cigar and sighing at the monstrous injustice of it all.

Three years of the worst recession the publishing world had ever known, yet Phil Gaines was still rolling in it, and still making even more. According to the published figures, *Gaines Publishing* results for 1993 showed pretax profit up 46%. That hurt. That really hurt. *Garland's* figure for the same period showed a loss.

James reassured himself that one thing Garland's had *not* lost was its reputation. Quality literature. That's what Garland's published. Nothing but. And *nothing* in the world would ever persuade him to publish the type of mass-market crap that Gaines published ...Yet everyone admired Phil Gaines, insisted the man had *style*, for God's sake! A man who blatantly *poached* another publisher's authors!

James was still furious over the loss of Howard and McAllister, but he wasn't going to let anyone see that he cared. At the time he had publicly laughed it off, wished the two ungrateful buggers to hell, but privately he had seethed at the way Phil Gaines had pulled two profitable rugs from under him.

It made you wonder just what the hell was happening to the publishing world! It was turning into a group of lunatic asylums for money-mad careerists. Slips of girls and arrogant young men all ruthlessly chasing the next bestseller. There was no *goodwill* left in publishing any more. No *gentlemen* left.

Well, there were still a *few* gentlemen left, including himself, but on the whole the entire publishing business was rapidly going downhill. And it was upstarts like Phil Gaines who were helping to accelerate the process.

Joanne Duncan usually adopted the air of being slightly superior to her surroundings, but this house in Hampstead truly met with her approval.

Fascinated, she even crept upstairs to take a peek, and there, down the long landing, she found bedrooms beautiful and silent, fresh and lemony – not smelling of lavender bags as most spare bedrooms do.

The most exquisite room of all was the matrimonial bedroom, radiant and romantic in the rays of the afternoon sun – a peaceful oasis of muted blues and cream; the bed a luxurious affair covered in blue silk.

Apart from personal oddments, the only colour that differed from the room's overall blue and cream colour scheme was the television – square and black and as big as a small cinema screen. Beside it stood a huge library of video films. Her eyes scanned the videos: every sort of film imaginable; she rummaged quickly through the shelves, but no – not one porno movie amongst them. She tutted her tongue in disappointment.

Two doors – one at each side of the bedroom – led to a His and Hers bathroom, with a dressing-room adjacent to each one. Now *this* house, she decided, was a house she would *kill* for!

Moving back into the bedroom, her eyes rested once more on

the romantic-looking bed and wondered at the mystery of it, wondered just how much activity went on there. She stood, pondering on the unknown, her heart beginning to beat with the thrill of secret desires – and wondered whether his wife occasionally went away?

Surely the girl popped back to Sweden every so often? To see her family? Oh surely she did!

Well, whether she did or not, it made no difference. It would take time of course, he was very aloof, but Joannie always got her man in the end.

On the floor below, James Duncan was still wandering around the house trying to estimate its cost, his ears sticking out like two question marks.

He went into the dining room. The French doors were opened onto the patio and garden. Guests were wandering in to refill their plates from a long table covered in dishes and attended by two waiters who seemed to be there solely for the purpose of ensuring that no dish descended below the half-full level. As soon as it did they rushed away to the kitchen and returned with a full one.

`Good evening, M'sieur,' said one of the waiters, offering James a large gleaming china plate and gesturing an elegant hand over the table of food.

James decided he might as well tuck in, and found himself listening to some of the conversations in the room as he moved down the table filling his plate.

As usual, the talk was all about the ups and downs of publishing.

`... believe me, it's quite true! W. H. Allen really did make the mistake of rejecting a script by an unknown writer called James Joyce.'

`God, I hope *I* never make such a terrible mistake. If I did, David Gallagher would fire me on the spot. He's a lot tougher than he looks—'

James Duncan sucked his teeth in contempt. David Gallagher—another low-life whiz-kid posing as an intellectual.

By the time Duncan had reached the end of the table, a familiar voice caught his ear, the voice of a young woman. He glanced over his shoulder and saw that yes, it was her – Miranda Alvin. He had met her for the first time a few years ago and thought her very attractive and refreshingly intelligent.

Now he despised her.

She had turned down his offer of a job at Garland Press without even pausing to think about it.

She had also responded to his invitation to join him on a weekend trip to Paris with a condescending look that went from his face right down to his shoes and slowly came back up again.

`Certainly not,' she had said dismissively. `You are married, Mr Duncan, and I am a feminist who firmly believes in the sisterhood code of never betraying other women. So, why don't you take your wife instead.'

Bitch! As if any sane man would waste a weekend in Paris on his wife!

She had a rich, upper-crust voice, and a propensity for using the word 'bloody' whenever she wanted to emphasise a point, just as she was doing now.

`When we published Marian Barnard's book four years ago,' Miranda was saying, `we promoted it and backed it all the way because we knew we were giving the readers something they expect all publishers to give them – a bloody *good* story. Written by a bloody *good* writer. And at the end of it all – bloody *good* value in return for their money.'

James Duncan picked up a silver fork and napkin and carried his plate out of the dining-room into the garden, unwilling to listen to another word from Miranda Alvin. Such arrogance! Such smuggery! What that toffee-nosed bitch deserved was a good slap. And God knows – he'd like to be the man to give it to her. Right across the face. Miss Alvin — *slap!*

take that with your afternoon tea. *Slap!* – and that – and that – and that!

Just thinking about it made him feel slightly aroused. Anger always went straight to his scrotum.

Joanne stood in the doorway of the drawing-room, her eyes frantically searching out her host until she saw him. He was sitting sideways on an oyster-coloured long sofa, his shoulder turned away from the door, leaning his head back in very relaxed fashion as he listened engrossed to the conversation of an angelic-looking, auburn-haired girl.

Joanne smiled as she weaved her way towards them. The girl was no rival – she was no more than seven years old.

Joanne sat down on the sofa quietly, her presence unnoticed as the child continued chattering ... 'It was at her wedding. My mummy and Charlotte are friends you see, and that's why we were invited to the wedding.'

'And that's where Richard Attenborough kissed you on the cheek.' Phil looked hugely impressed. 'At his daughter's wedding.'

'*And* he called me darling.'

'Did you like that?'

'Welllll—' she put a finger to her lip as if deeply pondering the question. 'Mummy *always* calls me darling,' she chuckled. 'So I didn't *really* mind. I've met a lot of famous actors too. Do you want me to tell you their names?'

'Famous actors? Oh yes, tell me who?'

She suddenly giggled and pointed past him. 'That lady is listening to us.'

Phil turned and looked.

Joanne's stomach did a delicious flip when their eyes met.

'Such a darling child,' she said sweetly, although she hated all children, 'but isn't she rather young to be at a party for adults?'

'Her mother couldn't get a babysitter,' Phil replied, his face expressionless. He turned back to the child and smiled. `Mrs Duncan is without a drink, Agatha. Do you want to come with me while I get her one?'

Agatha scrambled off the sofa. `All right, if you want me to. ' She looked earnestly at Joanne. `Do you want lemonade or coke?'

`Neither, thank you,' Joanne replied, put out by this desertion. Still, early days. She turned her most seductive smile on Phil. `I'll have champagne or Pimms,' she said in a whispery warm voice. `Either, I really don't mind.'

Joanne sat back po-faced as they walked away. Oh well, she thought, cheering up, he'll be back in a few minutes with my drink, then, like the child, I'll get him into a nice little tête-a-tête.

`Why don't you like her?' Agatha asked Phil once they had left the room.

Startled, Phil laughed at the child's perception. `What makes you say that, Agatha?'

She shrugged. `I don't know. But I can always tell when someone doesn't like somebody else.' She looked up at him earnestly. `*Do* you like her?'

`I can't say, because I don't really know her,' Phil replied evasively. Which was a total untruth.

Although Joanne Duncan was unaware of it, he knew everything about her. Everything he needed to know. She was feckless and stupid and for years she had been cheating on her husband and having short-lived affairs with a succession of young men, mostly young waiters, foreign and penniless. For a woman like Joanne, they were as easy to pick up as a cup of coffee.

Agatha returned to the drawing-room alone, carrying a small tray in both hands on which stood two glasses. She smiled sweetly at Joanne. `We couldn't decide which – champagne or

Pimms – so we got you both.'

Joanne glared at her. `Where's Phil?' she snapped.

The child's face paled nervously in response to Joanne's harsh voice. `He ... he had to take a phone call ... in his study ... from America.'

`That you, Marc?'

Phil smiled. `Hi, Jimmy.'

`Can you hear me?'

`Sure, Jimmy, I can hear you loud and clear.'

`Only I've got a real bad cold, a real stand-down. Hang on a minute while I get out my hanky, I need to blow my honker.'

A few seconds later Jimmy came back on the line. The nose-blow seemed to have cleared his mind.

`That you, Phil?'

`Yes, it's me, Jimmy. How did you get the cold?'

`Aw hell, it was just a bit of fun. Me and some of the guys decided to try a bit of fishing in the lake. Middle of the night. Damn well started to rain. Thunder and lightning. All I caught was a cold.'

`Any particular reason for phoning, Jimmy?'

`Yeah. Listen, son, I got something to tell you, something to show you, so jump in your car and rattle up here quick as you can. Can you drive up today?'

Phil rolled his eyes. `I'm in London, Jimmy. You're calling me in London.'

`Am I? Damn, I meant to ring your number at the Pierre. Thought you were still in New York? When did you go back to London?'

`A few days ago.'

`Ah, that's a pity.'

`Jimmy, what is it? This thing you want to tell me?'

`Last time you were up here – you remember that book you gave to me to read? *Some Kind of Wonderful*? The one written by Marian? The book about her and Marc ... 'cept for the names

399

being changed?'

`Yes.'

`Started to read it last night, went to bed early with my cold, and you know what, it made me remember. Can't think how I forgot ... Lord Almighty, son, *where have all the years gone?'*

Washed away by the tide, like all sandcastles, Phil wanted to say, but he knew Jimmy was referring to the gaps in his own memory.

`What did you forget, Jimmy?'

`You see, son, I never meant to hold anything back from you. I guess I just locked them away with the rest of my souvenirs and tried to pretend they didn't exist. Only explanation I can think of. But last night, while I was reading Marian's book ... well, I began to wonder if maybe I was only dreaming ... So I got up, put my leg back on, searched through that big ol' brown suitcase of mine, and sure enough – there they were!'

Phil said patiently, `What was there, Jimmy?'

`Marc's diaries. Five of them. Five thick books. Covering the years from 1960 to 1965. All his thoughts written down in them. All about Kennedy and Khrushchev. All about Marian. All about you.'

`*What?'*

`Yeah, well, these diaries, I've had them since he died in Nam. Don't know why I took them. Guess I didn't want the army guys reading through Marc's personal stuff before sending it back home with his body. There's some photographs inside, a few of Marc with Marian, and a few of Marc carrying you ... looks like he's walking around some zoo. There's an unfinished letter too. A letter to Marian.'

Jimmy went on talking ... unaware of what Phil was going through, a possibility beyond all his imaginings, being able to read Marc's diaries – Marc's *own* private thoughts and words about that time out of time. Words that would reveal and give Phil a greater knowledge and deeper insight into the young man who had been his father.

After he had put down the phone, it was twenty minutes before Phil could leave his study and return to the party.

And a house like this was not the only thing that stacks of money bought you, James Duncan was thinking. It also bought you something like *that*.

He stared at the Swedish girl standing in the garden, sipping wine as she spoke with David Gallagher.

God, she was sexy! She looked as cool as dew, but was probably panting hot underneath. An experienced man could always tell. And a wonderful figure! He had noticed that earlier when he had caressed her breasts with his eyeballs.

He sighed, sucked harder on his cigar, envying Phil Gaines for having a woman like that fall into his hand.

But of course, the reason why was obvious – money. Women like that, young and sexy and beautiful, women like that were only happy with men who kept them happy with lots of money. And looking around this place, every room a masterpiece by some interior designer, she was clearly getting as much money as she needed from Gaines.

A waiter paused before him, holding out a silver tray of glasses of champagne.

`M'sieur?'

James shrugged, dumped his empty glass on the tray and scooped up a fresh one. He might as well make the most of this shindig while he was here. But as soon as the chilled smoothness of the excellent champagne rolled over his tongue, it only gave him greater cause to feel umbrage.

The smile faded from Rena's face when she saw James Duncan standing by the French doors, watching her. Every now and again throughout the day she had noticed him watching her in a way that made her feel uneasy – the same way a hungry fox stares at a chicken.

`Who is that man?' she asked David Gallagher.

David glanced over his shoulder at the man standing alone sipping champagne, then turned back to Rena in surprise.

'You know who he is. You met him earlier. James Duncan.'

'Yes, I know his name, but who *is* he?' Rena asked. 'Phil has never mentioned him before. Yet all day he has been walking around the house like an estate agent doing a valuation.'

'He's a publisher,' David said. 'A business associate of Phil's. It's strange, though, now you mention it. Phil always gave me the impression that he thoroughly disliked James Duncan. But now it's all turned around and—'

At that moment James Duncan approached them and the conversation changed.

Simply because he was Phil's guest, Rena did her best to be pleasant and polite to the man who was so rudely ogling her breasts while he talked, but before long she was blushing and squirming in embarrassment.

She secretly squeezed David's arm in a silent plea to rescue her.

David immediately did so, with a quick and polite 'Excuse us a moment,' to James Duncan.

Joanne had swiftly eaten a plate of delicious food, gulped down two glasses of champagne, and had returned to sit on the sofa where, she decided, Phil could easily find her when he returned from his telephone call.

A very *long* telephone call, as it was turning out.

But 'America' the child had said. The phone call was from America, so what could one expect? Those Americans never stopped talking. Once, in the late seventies, she had sat next to an American woman on a plane, and the woman had talked so much, never pausing for breath, she finally fainted in mid-sentence, then later blamed it on the Russians.

'The Russians?' Joanne had exclaimed, and immediately regretted asking the question because she would be forced to listen to the woman's answer.

'Interfering with the oxygen, honey, that's what they're doing. All this hullabaloo about their space programme. All a front, all a blind. The Ruskies don't give a damn about space. It's the world they want. America. Trying to make us weak by sending up their space probes and interfering with the oxygen. That's why I fainted. Not enough oxygen in this airplane. Never used to be like that. Always plenty of good oxygen in airplanes before the Russians started interfering.'

Joanne had avoided Americans ever since.

So, that had been the plan – to return to the sofa and sit waiting in a nice, attractive pose, long slim legs in good view ...

Moments later, Joanne jumped up with a burst of excitement. God, what a ninny she was! Why hadn't she thought of it before? If the man was alone in his study taking a telephone call, then that was the place to waylay him – in private!

Phil was coming out of his study, closing the door behind him when Joanne breathlessly rushed up to him. 'Oh, Phil!' she gushed in a whispery voice. 'May I *please* have a few words with you?'

He stood looking at her silently for a few moments, and her stomach did another flip ... Oh, *those eyes*, those *sexy* dark eyes.

'Certainly,' he said, in a way that pleased her. 'Go ahead.'

She glanced towards the closed study door, then looked at him appealingly. 'May we go in there? It *is* rather private.'

'I can't imagine what it is,' he said, watching the way her bosom heaved seductively, 'we hardly know each other. If it's something personal, something so private, then I'm hardly the person—'

'No!' she said quickly, having hastily sketched a plan. 'It's about a book! I'm writing a book.'

'*You* – are writing a book?' Phil's eyes widened in what Joanne was certain was interest.

'Well, not exactly, I mean, I haven't actually written it yet, but I have this wonderful idea for an absolutely *wonderful* book.

If we could just talk about it—' Again she glanced at the closed study door.

Phil appeared perplexed. 'But, Mrs Duncan, why talk about it to me, when your husband is a publisher?'

'Oh, *please*, call me Joanne.'

'Very well, Joanne, if you have an idea for a book, why don't you discuss it with your husband?'

'Because he simply *refuses* to take me seriously,' she whispered conspiratorially. 'Simply *refuses* to believe that his own wife is capable of being a writer. But, believe me—' her voice pulsated with a subtle passion, 'I am *very* capable. Some of my short stories have reduced my friends to tears.'

Joanne had never written a story in her life, but she roused her bosom into another seductive heave, and waited for his response.

'This book?' Phil said. 'Your idea for it. Can you give me the gist in a few sentences?'

'Yes, well, some years ago, I met this beautiful Italian girl, and became very friendly with her. And, eventually, she told me her life story, which I think would make a *wonderful* book.'

Phil thought she had paused for breath, but when the pause became prolonged, he looked at her questioningly. 'An Italian girl—life story— what?'

'Well, her name was Isabella ... and she was distantly related to Mussolini...'

Joanne couldn't think what to say next, but covered it up quickly. 'But really, you're absolutely right – it's very unfair of me to ask you to discuss business during your party. So why don't you allow me to take you out to lunch one day, and we can discuss my book then? How about Monday? Lunch at Claridges?'

Phil looked at her thoughtfully – at the blonde who had been in court and laughed with delight when her husband got away with killing Marian Barnard. Another self-centred egotist who didn't have the decency to remember the dead woman's name –

not even when it was on the front cover of the book which, she had gushingly told him at Martin Pellmann's party, she had read *three* times.

Intrigued, more than anything else, during the past few minutes he had allowed Joanne to play her hand, and now she had laid her cards on the table. Lunch on Monday at Claridges. Lunch with *her*.

He would rather eat dirt.

His inner feelings did not show on his face. He even allowed himself to smile apologetically. `I already have a lunch appointment on Monday.'

`Tuesday then? Well just about *any* day next week would suit me.' She heaved another sigh, the `V' of her jacket opening wider. `I have simply *nothing* on ... 'she purred, looking at him with a kitten-like innocence. `Not next week.'

`Joannie!'

James Duncan was walking down the hall. `Wondered where you were!' he grunted. `It's time we were going.'

`What – so soon!' *The old bastard! Trust him to come along at the wrong moment.*

`It's a long drive to Berkshire.' Duncan looked at Phil. `Thanks for the invitation to the party, Gaines. Can't say I enjoyed it much. Too much self-congratulation and backslapping going on for my liking. Especially from some of your sales staff. But still, it was interesting. However, we must be off.'

Now it was Phil's turn to ask for - `... a few words? In private?'

James Duncan chuckled sarcastically. `Thought you might ask that. I knew your reason for inviting me here today wasn't solely social. Always time for business, eh? Even during a party. Very well, let's get it over.'

And seconds later Joanne saw her irascible husband succeeding where she had failed – disappearing into the study with Phil the door closing behind them.

What *is* it about men and business?' she screamed inside herself, mincing away furiously in search of a drink.

Damn James! If he hadn't come along when he did, she would have her lunch date with Phil Gaines all arranged by now.

'Now that is a question to which I can give you an answer here and now.' James Duncan sat back in his chair and smiled at Phil with pleasant malice. 'No. Not now. Not next month. Not ever.'

Phil stood in front of his desk, slightly leaning against the edge, his arms folded, his eyes considering his shoes. 'Why don't you take some time to think about it,' he suggested quietly.

'I don't need to think about it. You see, Gaines, you're not as clever as you think. I've been one step ahead of you for months now. But the only way it's going to happen is over my dead body!'

Phil looked up from his shoes and fixed his dark eyes on Duncan's face until the silence became uncomfortable.

'Well?' said Duncan. 'You've had my answer. Anything else?'

'But I think we *should* merge,' Phil said quietly. 'It would serve both our interests in the long run.'

'Not mine! No sell-out will serve my interests. My father started that firm, built it up from scratch, turned it into one of the most *respectable* publishing houses in London. And I've kept it going. So why should I hand it over to you?'

'A merger is not a hand over.'

Phil turned and lifted a book from his desk. He held it square in front of Duncan. It was *Some Kind of Wonderful*, by Marian Barnard.

'This book, by Marian Barnard...' As Duncan looked blandly at the book, Phil saw not a glimmer of recognition. 'This book, so far, in worldwide sales, has earned us four million. And that's just one book. Jimmy Overman's book is still backlisting at thirty thousand paperbacks a year. And that's just in the British territories. Others – all doing well. Our titles this year number over two hundred. So a merger with us could only prove profitable.'

James Duncan sat back in his chair, big and solid in a silver-grey suit and silver-grey tie, both the same colour as his hair. Even his eyes were silver-grey, smiling now as he took a pack of cigars out of an inner pocket of his jacket.

'Mind if I smoke?'

Joanne was upset. But James seemed unconcerned as he turned the ignition key and started up the car's engine. 'You've had enough champagne for one day. And I've got to be up early tomorrow morning to play a round of golf.'

'But, James, it's because of all the champagne that I desperately need to use the bathroom. And it's such a *long* drive to Berkshire. Please, darling, *please* let me go back inside?'

'Sometimes, Joannie,' he said with a sigh, 'I think the only person you are capable of having any consideration for is yourself.'

'That is just *not true*, James. You know how much I worship you.'

'Oh, all right,' he relented, 'go back inside, but be quick.'

'Bless you, darling – you really are the sweetest man in the world,' Joanne murmured as she opened the car door and swung her legs out.

Crabby old bastard! she fumed, doing a fluttery run on her stilettos back up the drive. *Weed-killer in his coffee is too kind. I think I'll just stab him in his sleep.*

As Joanne rushed inside the open door of the house, it was not the bathroom she was frantically seeking. And as she rushed along the hall – *Hallelujah* – she saw Phil standing at the foot of the staircase talking to the child Agatha and her very attractive mother – an actress in her thirties who was called Mary

407

something.

'*Daaaahling!*' Joanne gushed apologetically to the child. 'I almost forgot to say goodbye to you. And you were *so* kind, bringing me drinks. And you, Mary, it was *sssso* nice meeting you.'

Mary, who was usually nice to most people, found herself being kissed affectionately on the cheek, then Joanne bent and kissed Agatha affectionately on the cheek, 'Such a *beautiful* child,' then she grabbed Phil's arm and drew him aside.

'Phil, about my book...'

By midnight, only David Gallagher remained.

He was standing in the dining-room, by the French doors, staring out at the dark garden, turning round when Phil came into the room.

'Everyone gone?'

Phil nodded. 'Everyone except you.'

'It was a good party.'

'Yes, I think so.' Phil poured himself a scotch and soda, an unusual drink for him.

'What was wrong with Rena?' David's eyes were studying Phil intently. 'Why did she leave the party so early and not come back?

'She felt unwell, slightly dizzy. The noise and the crowd. I made her go to bed.'

'Oh, I see,' said David quietly. 'Only we spent most of the afternoon together. Rena seemed to be enjoying herself ... apart from one disagreeable incident—' David decided not to elaborate further. 'Yes, she seemed to be really enjoying herself. But then suddenly, she was gone. She *is* all right, isn't she?'

Phil smiled at his friend. David and Rena were two people who just couldn't help liking each other.

'She was exhausted, David. She was called in to do an emergency shift at the hospital last night, then refused to go to bed when she came home this morning, insisting on overseeing all the arrangements for the party. So she's had no sleep since Thursday night.'

`Thursday night? My God, she *must* have been exhausted. But I never would have guessed. And she didn't mention it.'

Phil sighed. `Well, that's Rena, a true nurse. Keeps her own problems hidden while she attends to the job in hand.'

Phil slumped down in a chair by the table, sat back and loosened the knot of his tie, changing the subject. `Did you have any talk with James Duncan?'

`Yes, I did.' David nodded gloomily. `He seems to be the sort of man who would sell his grandmother if he thought she would fetch a good price.'

`His grandmother, yes. But not his firm.'

David looked sharply at him `He said no?'

`He said "Never".'

`Well thank God for that!' David exclaimed in relief, his face breaking into a sudden boyish grin.

`It's all for the best,' David said a moment later. `Phil – that Duncan! Him and us? It wouldn't work. He belongs in a world of antiquated typewriters. Even his literary gossip is from another time. He was telling me what Kingsley Amis said about Graham Greene, and what Graham Greene said about Evelyn Waugh. Not – you'll note – what James Patterson said about John Grisham, or what Dean Koontz said about Stephen King. No, no, I don't think Duncan's even *heard* of them!'

David shrugged. `To be honest, I can't understand why you even considered a merger with Garland's in the first place. It's not a house for young men or big profit, it's covered in dust.'

He poured himself a glass of red wine. `Even now, the whole thing is still a mystery to me. No matter which way I look at it, none of it makes sense. Point one: business goes from strength to strength, so who needs a sinking ship like Garland's?'

He looked questioningly at Phil but, getting no comment, he went on, `Point two: it can't be that you want to *rescue* the man. Help him out of his financial difficulties. It can't be that, because you truly *dislike* the pompous old sod. I know you do. So why?'

Phil was silently considering. 'Well,' he said, 'I tried to be merciful – tried to do it the civilised way, with a merger, to save his face – but now James Duncan has left me no choice but to return to my original plan.' He shrugged indifferently. 'Either way, the end result will be the same.'

'Original plan?' David stared at him, confusion and exasperation returning. '*What* original plan?'

Phil took a drink of his scotch, shuddered. 'David,' he said, 'what you don't know, won't hurt you.'

Forty-Three

Berkshire
May 1994
_____/

`A *feather in his cap! That's what Phil Gaines is after, Joannie. Another feather in his cap!'*

Joanne ignored her husband's voice from their en-suite bathroom, adjusted the clock-radio, and slipped into bed with her *Hello!* magazine.

Wearing navy pyjamas, James returned to the bedroom, sat down heavily on the edge of the bed, flicked open a box on his side-table, removed a cigar, and began to light it.

`James, *must* you smoke those things in the bedroom!'

James always smoked a cigar in the bedroom, every night, and had done so for more than twenty years. It was his last ritual to unwind before sleep. Just as it was his ritual to ignore his wife when she complained.

He smoked contemplatively on his cigar; his eyes fixed upon the dressing-table where, tilted at a perfect angle, the mirror gave him a full reflection of his image.

His eyes narrowed, he puffed a cloud of smoke in the air, and made a sharp tutting sound.

`A bastard, Joannie, that's what he is. An arrogant bastard.'

`True,' Joanne said amicably, thinking how much she simply *adored* arrogant bastards. Had she not married one?

She shot a sharp look at her husband's back – although she didn't think much of *him* anymore – he was a brute! To the outside world James's face was usually arranged in an expression of gentlemanly humour, but he had a cruel streak in his nature and possessed a need to dominate everyone around him. And he sometimes took great pleasure in inflicting pain and humiliation on those who displeased him – even her.

411

Of course, there was a time, years ago, when she had seriously considered leaving James. But, well, she was not trained for any role but that of a wife, had no real skills, other than a passable hand at typing. And being forced – as she once had been – to sit in a stultifying office all day! Just the thought of having to *work* for a living left her feeling quite ill.

Marriage to James at least kept her free from all that. Free all day and every day to do what she wished. It also provided her with a pleasant home, a generous allowance on her credit cards, and – *best of all* – with James she had never needed to worry about being saddled with tiresome children.

Poor man – because of some boyhood illness, James had discovered very early on that he would be unable to father children. A fact which had dismayed him somewhat. But to her it was simply an *exquisite* relief, and one of the reasons why she had married him.'

`Gaines – who is he?' Duncan said with narrowed eyes to his reflection. `Where did he come from in the first place?'

Phil Gaines.... Joanne's eyes illuminated with a lusty glow. She had rubbed one earlier and smudged her mascara. Her hair was unpinned from its chignon and hung around her face like a yellow halo of steel wool.

Phil Gaines ... Joanne wriggled her toes, a hot sexy demon licking up her legs to her thighs. She simply could not *think* of that gorgeous munchie man without wondering what he would be like in bed?

But then, these days she was unable to look at any attractive young man without wondering what he would be like in bed.

She had thought by the time she reached forty she would have eased up on sexual attraction, but no, life went on same as ever. The only difference was that now she was attracted to younger men, not older.

But Phil Gaines ... `Call me at the office,' he had said when she had gone back to ask him about her book. `At the office,' he had repeated, taking her arm and escorting her to the front door – and Joanne knew from experience what *that* meant. No married man liked 'the other woman' calling him at home.

'Don't worry, Phil,' she had whispered seductively in her husky warm voice. 'I'm *very* discreet ... And the ideas I have for my book will *certainly* give you something to sleep on.'

Then James – the impatient bastard – had banged the horn of his car and she was forced to leave, glancing back over her shoulder with a seductive little murmur of 'Ciao.'

Well, a little of the lingo gave her suggestion for a book about an Italian heroine a bit more authenticity.

So, she would do as he asked, and phone him at office, on Monday afternoon, and arrange a lunch-date with him for later in the week – Claridges, of course. A nice hotel full of bedrooms above the restaurant. She hunched up her shoulders and smiled deliciously – she *always* got her man into bed in the end. Never yet failed. Not once!

'Gaines, you see, we know so little about him.' James chewed on his cigar. 'We know all about his business life, his relentless success, his skill in making money, but when it comes to the man himself, knowing what makes him tick, what drives him, he's as deep as hell.'

Joanne sighed dreamily.

'Deep as hell!' Duncan glared at his reflection in the mirror. 'I'd give anything to find out how he managed to get the world rights to Marian Barnard's book. A dead author. An unpublished manuscript. No hungry agent baying for a bigger advance. I mean, just how *lucky* can one man get?'

He glanced over his shoulder at Joanne. 'Makes you sick, doesn't it?'

'What?' Joanne snapped out of her erotic fantasy and glared at him sourly. *What* makes you sick?'

'Gaines getting the *world* rights to Marian Barnard's book. Total control. No bloody agent. A book that made his firm a fortune.'

'It could have been David Gallagher,' Joanne suggested.

`He's the Editorial Director there. And from what I heard that Miranda woman saying, David Gallagher has – what did she say? –"unerring talent for finding good scripts." She seems to respect him enormously, but I think she respects Phil Gaines even more.'

`It makes me puke! The way everyone treats Gaines like Mr Wonderful. But what does anyone really know about him?'

James drew on his cigar, sitting thoughtful while his lips manufactured a smoke ring. `I still say there's *something* strange about him. I've known it since that first day I met him. At Pellmann's party. I was introduced to Gaines and I'd been told beforehand that he was a very polite young man, very likable. So when we were introduced, I reached out to shake hands with him, very pleasantly, welcome to the club young man, all that kind of thing – but he just ignored my hand!'

Duncan looked over his shoulder at Joanne and nodded, as if he still could not believe it. `Would you believe it?'

Joanne merely shrugged, bored, utterly bored. She had listened to this tale at least a hundred times before. And even more galling was the fact that she had *been there* when it happened.

But could she stop James from telling the story over and over again? Could a fly hold back a steamroller?

`Just ignored my hand!' Duncan turned back to glare indignantly at his image in the mirror. He chewed furiously on his cigar, then spat. `Gaines stood there with one hand in his jacket pocket, and the other holding a glass of wine, and merely inclined his head in acknowledgement – leaving me standing there with my hand held out like a fool!'

`And you *looked* like one too,' Joanne thought happily.

James ruminated for a minute as he considered the ash on his cigar, then repeated the incident to her yet again.

`Now, it was Martin Pellmann who introduced us, and he looked as embarrassed as I felt, although he covered it up with conversation, and a short while later he took Gaines off to

414

introduce him to someone else. But before that, never once while we stood talking did Phil Gaines acknowledge anything I said. His conversation was solely for Pellmann and one of Pellmann's authors. Disregarded me as if I wasn't there. Cut me dead.'

Joanne opened her *Hello!* magazine.

'I couldn't understand it. I'd never before met the man. He was a total stranger. But still, whenever I joined in the conversation, Gaines just stared past my shoulder at other people in the room as if he was bored to death. You get the picture?

Joanne's head was lowered over her magazine.

'So finally I thought, Oh, for Christ's sake, this upstart doesn't know who I am. And later Pellmann assured me that was the case, that Gaines had not realised I was the head of Garland Press.'

Duncan sat for a moment fuming. 'But I've always hated Gaines since then, always despised him. Not that I've seen very much of him. And then the bastard goes and poaches two of my most reliable authors! No – not *poached*, he did more than that, Joannie – he deliberately *seduced* them away from Garland's with big money and promises of big promotions. Well, I tell you, Joannie, the sheer *arrogance* of that man takes some believing.'

Duncan sat frowning, still baffled.

'But now, these past few months, I've been wined and dined by his accountants and lawyers and every other puppet he's got dangling on his string. All sucking up to me for a merger. And then comes a call from Gaines himself, inviting us to a party at his home. Of course I knew straight away what he was after, but that's not what he got!'

Duncan tapped the ash off his cigar.

'You see, Joannie, when I make my strike against a man, I strike hard. And the only reason I accepted the invitation in the first place, was because I wanted to put that arrogant bastard to the trouble of waiting on me hand and foot, pouring out my wine and so on. But he never did. I should have known there'd be people on hand to do all that for him ... Never even shook my hand. It was his wife and David Gallagher who greeted us. Did you notice that? Yet later on I saw it was Gaines himself who greeted and smiled and shook hands with others.'

Duncan mused. 'Now what's his game? I thought. What's his bloody game? For months he's been leading me on some cat-and-mouse dance trying to get me up his own garden path – and when I get there, he's not even there to greet me! So what's his bloody game?'

He shrugged. 'I mean, if you want to persuade a man to go into business with you, *that's* not how you do it. I thought I was going to be the guest of honour. I didn't expect the host to leave my welcome to his wife and one of his staff. Christ, *that's* not the way you do it.'

He sighed. 'You know what it made me realise, Joannie? It made me realise that Gaines doesn't know as much about business dealing and wheeling as he *thinks* he does.'

Joanne suddenly looked up from her magazine, thoughtful. 'Do you think they're having an affair?'

'Who?'

'David Gallagher and the Swede. I didn't like her one bit. Cold as ice. She hardly said two words to me all afternoon.'

'Yeh, just like that Miranda Alvin – a real stuck-up bitch. Did you hear the way Alvin was slapping herself and all the other members of Gaines staff on the back? Made me sick. These upstarts – they publish crap and crow about it! They're destroying the publishing world, Joannie. These upstarts. Especially the women. If I had my way, I'd erase them all from the face of the earth with a blow-torch.'

'Yes—' Joanne was looking thoughtful. 'I was watching them, James, and well ... they certainly seem very *fond* of each other. Do you think they are having an affair?'

'Who?'

'David Gallagher and the Swede.'

'How the hell should I know?'

He suddenly swerved his attention in her direction. 'By the way, what were you and Gaines talking about?'

Joanne blinked, an alarmed crimson colouring her cheeks. 'When? Where?'

'When and where I saw you. Outside his study.'

'Oh, *that*?' Joanne shrugged. 'We were talking about books. All very boring, I assure you.' Joanne patted back a yawn. 'He was interested in my choice of literature.'

'Literature – you?' James chuckled sarcastically. 'The nearest you've ever got to a piece of real literature was a quick thumb-through *Lady Chatterley's Lover*.'

Joanne gave him a clowning smile, stuck out her tongue, then rested her head back against the headboard and closed her eyes as if sleepy. *What a stinker! What a pig! What was the best way to kill him without being found out?*

Duncan turned back to the mirror and continued the conversation with his reflection, rehearsing how he would tell it to his friends at the Golf Club tomorrow.

'But once Gaines and I were alone in his study, that's when I gave it to him. That's when I got my own back. "You know, Gaines," I said, smoking my cigar. "You *do* surprise me. You really do. Did you *honestly* think I would consider merging a respectable house like mine with one that published mass-market crap?"'

'James – you didn't!' Joanne sat up, eyes glaring.

'I did!' James heaved in silent laughter for a moment. 'You should have seen his face, seen his eyes, mad as hell, mad as Caligula. Of course, he's a good actor. Managed to cover it up. Calm as calm can be.'

'But James— Joanne was in a state of panic. 'What did he say? When you said what you said?'

'Well, as I said, he's a good actor, he covered it well, calm as calm, never even raised his voice, but I knew he was furious. I

417

knew I had paid him back—'

`What did he *say?*

`He said: "You've had your chance, Duncan. It won't come round again. And now the party's over. So I suggest you gather up your cigars and your wife and get the fuck out of my house."'

`Oh my God!' Joanne's hand was over her mouth.

`Oh, it's a true fact, Joannie, these upstarts are quite happy to sell crap, but they don't like it when you rub their faces in it.' Duncan chuckled. `Makes them curse!'

`But he has *money*, James,' Joanne argued, thinking desperately of her lunch-date and the Cartier watch she had set her heart on. `Absolutely *oooodles* of it! And you said yourself that you *need* all the money you can get just to keep Garland's afloat.'

James shot her an unfriendly look.

`I don't need it *that* badly. Not *Gaines's* money!' He stubbed out his cigar. `Do you think I'd seriously consider going into business with a man like Phil Gaines? Do you seriously believe after all my years as a Gentleman Publisher that I'd allow myself to end up in the sewer with the rats. With the very people who are destroying the respectable world of publishing!'

`But James, what about the bank? '

`Come on, Joannie.' Duncan was  tired of the subject. `Come on, Joannie, I've finished my cigar. And I'm in the mood ... a bad mood, so I need cheering up.' He turned and smiled at her, a long bilious leer, which turned her blood to ice.

`Come on, Joannie, let's play Master and Maid.'

An hour later, Joanne's backside was so sore from all the hard smacking the 'Master' had given her, she staggered into the bathroom and searched for her sleeping pills. She leaned against the sink and swallowed one with a sip of water.
Slowly she raised her head and looked at her reflection in the mirror on the wall. Her tears had streaked two sludges of

mascara down her cheeks.

He'd better keep his promise and buy me the Cartier watch in return for this. He'd bloody well better!

Forty-Four

London
May 1994

_____/

The morning looked anaemic, a hazy grey light filtering into the bedroom. Phil slowly opened his eyes and seconds later he realised that Rena was not in bed.

A flowery scent drifted out from her bathroom and the open doorway was steamy. No doubt, she had just taken a hot shower.

She came into the bedroom a few minutes later wrapped in a large white towel around her body and a smaller towel turbaned around her head. She caught his eye and smiled.

'You should be well rested,' said Phil. 'You were asleep by ten o'clock last night.'

She removed the towel from her head and loosened her long pale hair. 'I know, and I know it was rude of me to leave our guests so early, but I was so *tired* after my night shift at the hospital.'

'I don't know why you do it. You don't need to work.'

She sat on the bed and bent over to give him a toothpaste-flavoured kiss. 'I *do* need to work.'

'Not night shifts. You never said anything to me about doing night shifts.'

'It was only a one-time.'

'A one-off.'

She looked puzzled. 'Is that how you say it? One off? But it was the only once I have been on duty at night. So shouldn't it be a one-*on*?

He smiled and ran a finger down her cheek. 'No more night shifts. Promise?'

'*Ja*, I promise.'

From the earliest days of their marriage, Rena had refused to be nothing more than the idle wife of a rich man. She did not *care*, she had told Phil, how much money he had. She could not just sit around all day. What was she to do? Read magazines and arrange flowers?

Nursing – that's what she wanted to do. She was trained for nothing else, and it was what she loved best – nursing.

Nothing Phil could say would dissuade her.

Despite being married to a British citizen, she had endured weeks of red tape, but had finally been employed by a private hospital in central London. And from the first day she had loved it there. Her biggest surprise was the friendliness of the other nurses. None had the English stiff upper lip she had been warned about. All were welcoming and helpful, and within days she had felt accepted as one of the team.

So she was disinclined to refuse when the hospital had telephoned her on Friday evening to ask if she could cover for a nurse who was away sick.

She bent and gave Phil another toothpaste-flavoured kiss, holding the top of the towel over her breasts with one hand. 'Do you want me to cook breakfast now?'

'No,' he sighed, 'I don't want you to cook breakfast. I want to know what you've got on under that towel?'

She smiled. 'What do you think?'

He breathed deeply but said nothing. They had not made love for two nights running and for them that was an age.

'I've missed you,' she said softly.

He tugged at the towel and it opened under his hands. He slowly skimmed her breasts with his palms. Her blue eyes clouded with arousal. She leaned forward and kissed his lips, her tongue darting into his mouth in quick tantalising movements of erotic enticement. He groaned and grabbed her, and seconds later she was sliding down in the warm bed beside him.

From then on it was all sensation and ecstasy and Rena

421

naked. He could feel the heat of her urgent young body consuming him, passionately, deliciously, and his mind zoomed ecstatically to the centre of a blinding rainbow.

Later, she gave him her happy and contented morning-after smile, then looked down at her naked body, shiny with sweat.

`I need another shower.'

He circled his palm over her damp stomach. `So do I. Nice and cool.'

`Then breakfast,' she decided. She was an excellent cook and she asked him, `How would you like some crêpes with bacon and cheese, croissants with apricot jam, and some delicious hot roasted coffee?'

`Sounds just perfect,' he said. `Just like you.'

`I'm not perfect.'

`Maybe not in your eyes.' He sighed. `But to me, Rena, you're the eighth wonder of the world.'

Forty-Five

London
May 1994

_____/

On Monday, Phil's lunch appointment was at the Grosvenor House Hotel on Park Lane.

As soon as he entered the Red Room bar, he saw Joseph Irving sitting alone at a table reading a newspaper. Whenever he and Irving met here at the Grosvenor, they usually had a drink in the bar before going in to lunch.

As he approached, Joseph Irving looked up from his newspaper and smiled.

'Ah, Phil, on time as usual. So, how are you, dear boy?'

'Fine, Joseph. And you?'

'Oh, tip-top as always. Now, I'm going to start with my usual straight malt,' Irving said, beckoning to a waiter. 'What about you?'

'Club soda, nothing else.'

Irving gave the order to the waiter, then sat back and looked at Phil with a shrewd expression in his eyes.

'I think I know why you wanted this meeting today. You are becoming somewhat irritated by the tedious photographs we continue to send you.'

'That's right,' Phil agreed. 'Every delivery is just more of the same. Waiters, gym instructors, more waiters. The photographs all say the one thing – the lady obviously likes her playmates young, the younger the better.'

'Indeed.' Irving's tone was as dismissive as flicking dust off his sleeve. 'She is clearly nothing but a cheap tart in expensive clothes.'

The waiter arrived with the drinks. Irving sipped his malt and regarded Phil intently. 'I take it that the lady and her sordid little sexual dalliances are of no further interest to you?'

`No. Forget her. Now I want you to concentrate solely on the man himself, James Duncan.'

Irving sighed deeply. Phil's hatred of James Duncan had not abated over the years, but then Irving had not expected it to abate. And as the years had passed Irving knew that Phil had never once lost sight of his hated enemy, slowly and quietly pursuing him, nibbling and biting at the edges, irritating and annoying him, waiting for the day when he could finally make his real attack.

He asked curiously, `What exactly do you mean, Phil, when you say, "concentrate solely on the man himself"?'

`I want you to put someone back inside Garland Press,' Phil said. `I want Duncan put under twenty-four hour surveillance. Night as well as day. I want you to dig up everything you can on his two sisters, his present relationship with both of them. I want to know everything there is to know about James Duncan himself, every detail, no matter how small, how trivial, I want your people to find it out for me.'

Joseph Irving said thoughtfully, `The two sisters, yes, we know very little about them, so perhaps we can help you. But James Duncan...' Irving leaned closer, `Phil, there is very little that you don't know about him now. So what *are* you looking for?'

Phil frowned. `I don't know, Joseph, I don't know ... I just feel there's got to be *something*—'

He hesitated, not sure how to explain it. `It's his eyes, Joseph, there's something about Duncan's grey eyes ... up close, looking at his eyes, there's something not right, something about the man that's not, well – not *right*.'

Joseph Irving merely waited.

`I just feel certain,' Phil continued, `that if we watch him close enough, and for long enough, we'll turn up something. Everyone's got something to hide, and a man like Duncan is so basically selfish, so innately *unpleasant*, the way he treats his staff, his authors, his wife ... I'm sure there must be something lurking in the shadows that I'll be able to use against him.'

'Very well,' Irving agreed simply. 'We'll see what we can find.'

Forty-Six

London
June 1994

_____/

Phil slowly manoeuvred his Mercedes through the evening traffic in St John's Wood, heading up towards Swiss Cottage, the music of Queen's *'Bohemian Rhapsody'* thumping through the back speakers.

Since his meeting at the Grosvenor with Joseph Irving three weeks ago, the reports on James Duncan had been sent to him at regular weekly intervals, always in a plain manila envelope, marked `Private and Confidential,' and always delivered by hand through his home letter box.

Much of what the reports told him, he already knew – Garland Press was doing so badly that if James Duncan did not find some good writers soon, he would have to find some *very good* accountants.

He smiled grimly as he cleared the lights at Swiss Cottage and accelerated up the long hill of Fitzjohn's Avenue towards Hampstead.

James Duncan seemed impatient and preoccupied as he ate his dinner that evening.

He placed a forkful of fish inside his mouth, muttered a few astonished words to himself, `... *adapt to circumstances ... Helen and Felicity ...!*' and swallowed the fish with an expression of acute irritation.

Joanne laid down her fork. `James, are you *listening* to me? Have you heard even one word I've said?'

Duncan's eyes darted up from his food to Joanne's face. `What? *What?*'

`Oh, really, this is all becoming very tedious, James. What on earth is wrong with you tonight?'

He scowled at her. 'Nothing that a bit of silence from you wouldn't cure!'

'Darling, that is *so* nasty! And doubly nasty because I have done and said absolutely *nothing* to upset you.'

'How dare you say that? When you do *nothing* but upset me! You and Helen and Felicity! A bunch of greedy cows bent on destroying me!'

Joanne's hand drooped towards her wine glass. There was really no point in arguing with James when he was like this. At times like this, she had long ago learned, it was simply best to butter him up until he was back in a good mood.

'Well, yes, Helen *is* very tiresome,' she agreed. 'All those aggressive telephone calls – I do believe that if she telephoned the Speaking Clock she would disagree and argue with it. And as for Felicity, well, I can hardly believe that such a *timid* creature is truly your sister, James. All that cringing cowardice whenever Helen lays down the law. But now, I wouldn't say poor Felicity is a greedy cow ... no, she is more, let me see ... more *porcine* I would say ... a bit like that sweet old sow we saw last year at the farm in—'

'Joannie – shut up!'

Joanne glanced beneath the table as she slipped a slender foot back inside its shoe. 'James dear,' she said patiently, 'we really can't go through the entire evening having you feeling so unhappy, now can we?'

She stood up in her high heels and minced over to the drinks cabinet. 'What you need is a nice scotch. A nice smooth malt. We'll have one together, shall we?' She lifted down two glasses and poured two shots of Glenmorangie.

She minced back and handed one to James. 'Go on,' she said. 'Ease up. Knock it back. It will calm you better than any heart pill.' She raised her glass. 'Cheers!'

James looked from her face to the scotch in his hand. 'Cheers,' he said, and emptied his glass in one gulp.

'I've already had two nifedipine tablets today,' he said miserably. 'My angina seems to be getting worse.

'And understandably so,' Joanne soothed. 'Lunching with Helen and Felicity – both at the same time – is enough to distress anyone's poor heart.' She tapped his glass. 'Another?'

'James nodded. 'Why not.'

She took his glass and turned on a swivel back to the cabinet. 'I tell you what, why don't we just take the bottle and go and relax in the sitting-room and have a nice long talk.' She scooped up the bottle and swivelled again. 'Come along, James, come with Joannie...'

James fixed his eyes on the neat roundness of her rear as she minced away, and found himself following her. His mind was agitated, his stomach was nervous, and his angina was getting worse. But no matter which way you looked at it – Joannie still had the cutest backside in Berkshire.

'After all, James,' Joanne said, when he was seated comfortably in his favourite chair in the sitting-room, 'I really *dooo* need to talk to you about money.' She pressed a fresh glass of scotch into his hand, at least four shots full.

'My dear, your husband is not rolling in money like the rat pack,' he said impatiently, reaching for a cigar. 'Your husband, Joannie, has problems. Serious money problems.'

'But, *Jaymesee*,' she said, unfolding herself languidly onto the settee. 'A little gold Cartier watch won't make much difference, will it? It's one of the cheapest in their range. An absolute *snip* at twelve hundred pounds.' She pouted perfectly. 'And you did promise—'

'No, Joannie. I can't do it. And if you think I can, then you're a stupid bitch barking up the wrong tree!' He stared at her. 'Don't you realise how bad things are for me? For Garland's! Don't you realise that for almost a year now I've been forced – on occasion – to fund the firm with my own money! Joannie, the situation is becoming desperate! The bank is on my neck every week. But there, that's banks for you!'

He sucked viciously on his cigar. 'Oh, I hate banks. I despise them. When you're doing well and the money's rolling in, the bastards are grovelling at your feet like coolies. But come the problems, come the shortage of cash flow, and the bastards are snapping at your neck like vampires.'

Joanne sipped her scotch and looked back at him sympathetically while wishing she could strangle such a miserable, mean specimen of a provider. What was twelve hundred pounds? Compared to the villa in Portugal that Emma Friedman's husband had just bought for her. Well, bought for them both, but still...

Joanne sat in stark jealousy and suddenly felt like being very nasty.

'But, James,' she cooed, 'why don't you get some new authors? Some *exciting* authors for a change! Half the stuff you publish goes straight to the libraries and nowhere else. And when was the last time you did any decent advertising or promotion? No wonder all the *good* authors take their second books elsewhere.'

'What?' James stared at her, furious. 'What do *you* know about the business of publishing? What do you know about anything?' He sat forward and stabbed the cigar in her direction. 'All *you* know about the publishing business is the amount of money you've been able to scrounge from it all these years.'

Joanne realised she had worked him out of his bad mood into a temper, but she didn't care. She unfolded her legs gracefully, and reached for the whisky bottle. 'I know more than you think I do, James. A lot more.' She nodded her head, and poured a good measure of scotch into her glass.

'That afternoon I went to the Romantic Novelists Association with Sylvia, I was in the ladies, in a cubicle, and I heard some of the authors talking around the sinks. "Oh for God's sake," one said, "whatever you do, *don't* send your book to Garland's. They'll pay you peanuts and your book won't get any further than the libraries.'

James attempted to laugh it off. 'Listen, Joannie, surely you know by now that authors are the biggest load of whingers ever born.'

He puffed a cloud of smoke in her direction. 'But as for that bunch of bitchy cows you overheard, I can tell you this – not one of them would be *good* enough to be published by Garland's.'

He took a slug of scotch, his eyes suddenly jumping with fiery malignancy. 'No, if it's crap they want published, then they will have to go to Gaines.'

'Well, ye-es, that's *exactly* what those authors said – if you want a decent deal, why not go to one of the big conglomerates, or even one of the smaller but more modern independent's like Gaines.'

Livid, he stared at her. 'You stupid cow!' He slapped his knee furiously. 'Don't you realise that it's those big conglomerate whales and *sharks* like Phil Gaines that have me in the mess I'm in. They just go around, those greedy fishes, swallowing up all the stalwarts. But here's one die-hard that will *never* merge, and *never* sell!'

'Then don't sell,' Joanne sulked. 'Do what you like. I don't care. All I know is that Phil Gaines offered to merge with you, and I thought that was a very nice, and very *friendly* thing to do.'

'Well *you* would, wouldn't you? But I'm no fool. I know his game. The only reason he wants to merge and take away my independence, is because he wants the respectability of Garland's name to add weight to his own. But afterwards I would be left exposed and scarred with my own failure.'

James sighed and wondered again at the monstrous injustice of it all. What had he done to deserve such bad luck? He sat back, stretched his feet out, and stared up at the ceiling with a sad dog gaze.

'Even if I had married someone with a little intelligence,' he

430

said with a sigh, 'I would now have someone to give me comfort and support in my hour of need. Instead of that I married you, Joannie. You, of all people. If I'd known how it was all going to turn out, I would have thrown myself in the Thames the day before I met you.'

'Ha-bloody-ha.'

'It's the truth, my dear. I should have married for money or brains. Only a fool would marry for shapely legs and a nicely rounded bottom.'

'Oh, stop pitying yourself. You were madly in love with me then, and you still are now.'

'I don't think I am, Joannie. I don't think I ever was. The fantasy is always much better than the reality. As most married men discover.'

'Most married women too.'

James's chin sank onto his chest. 'Why do I have to get older year by year? Life was so much better in the old days. Even *you* were much better in the old days.'

'You sound like a Dinosaur, James. Come to think of it, you probably *are* a Dinosaur. That's why you like eating fish so much.'

'You were my dream girl in those days, Joannie. The prop for all my sexual fantasies. I used to dream about you every night. In those days, Joannie, my life was one long lustful fantasy – but then you gave me plenty of provocation, didn't you?'

He sighed again. 'Now you provoke me so much I often dream about throttling you dead and stuffing you under the floorboards.'

'Oh enough of this marital bickering.' Joanne shrugged irritably. 'And you're not so perfect either, James. There was a time when you used to be fun. But now all you do is moan, moan, moan. And *always* about money. And you *hate* everybody. You *despise* everybody. These days you're always so hot with rage against somebody, I often wonder why you don't

431

just blow up. Explode like a bomb. What do they call it – internal combustion? It happens quite frequently apparently. One minute the person is just sitting there having a cup of tea, and the next minute they explode into pieces. An arm here, a leg there, bits of body all over the place.'

`Joannie – shut up!'

It was too much for James. All he had to suffer. Not only from his wife, but his two sisters. He put his glass down with a thump, stood up in fury, and levelled a vicious scowl at his reflection in the mirror above the fireplace.

`Helen and Felicity want me to sell,' he said darkly. `The bitches actually want me to sell! Told me out straight. They want me to take the money and run. Or as Helen put it, *sell* – but make them give you a seat on the board."'

As James launched into a word-by-word recitation of the lunch meeting with his two sisters, Joanne lifted her legs and reclined back languorously on the sofa, her head resting on the sofa-arm, a hand draped above her expensively bleached hair. All this talk of publishing had made her feel bored, utterly bored with the subject. Not that it was a very exciting subject at the best of times.

`Yes,' said James, `that was the biggest mistake my father made, giving those two bitches equal shares in the firm. And Felicity parrots everything Helen says. If Helen says "Frog" Felicity jumps. If Helen has a cold, Felicity sneezes. And Helen wants me to sell.'

James took a slug of his scotch and grimaced. `But, just like you, Joannie, Helen doesn't seem to realise there is more to a man's life than money. There's his life's achievement to consider. His self-respect. His standing in the community. His reputation amongst his peers ... Oh, I hate that bitch, I despise her—'

Joanne stretched out fully on the sofa and gazed wistfully at the ceiling. It was *such* a long time since she had had any decent *amour*. Well, not since that young Spanish waiter more than a month ago – such an attractive young darling, so adorably *sweet*, but a mere boy ... Oh, how she longed for a *real* love-affair, full of warmth and passion, but most of all ... lots of *tenderness*.

James had turned and was staring at her. She smiled dreamily at him, not seeing him at all.

James stood looking at her with eyes that were narrowed. He knew that look – Joannie was in the mood. And, by God, so was he!

`Well, Joannie,' he said, consulting his watch. `It's nine o'clock. A bit early I know, but how about it?'

`What?' She snapped out of her dreams and frowned at him quizzically. `How about what?'

`Hitting the stairs and heading up for a roll on the old mattress.'

He shrugged. `You're right, enough of this marital bickering. And let's forget all about business. I'm sick to death of it. Come on, Joannie, let's forget about everything and play.'

`What?' Her eyes focused on him, and instantly she knew what he had in mind.

`Would you like to give me a nice hot bath with soapy hands?' he asked. `Or shall I tie you up? Yes, let's play the game where I tie you up and you plead for mercy?"

Oh no! She couldn't bear to even think of it – let alone endure it. Not tonight. She was not feeling at all robust or up to persevering with the old bully tonight.

`No, James,' she said, scrambling off the sofa and grabbing her handbag from the coffee table, snatching out a bottle of sleeping pills. `Not tonight.'

Then remembering that James was, after all, her bread and butter and credit cards and, hopefully, her new Cartier watch, she attempted to cajole him.

`*Jaymesee*, you know I think you're absolutely wonderful and I hardly know how I can resist you—' She tumbled a few pills onto her palm, `but I really feel so *queasy* after that fish, I think

I'll just take one of my little sleeping pills and have a nice warm bath.' She popped a pill in her mouth and gulped at her scotch.

`Come on, Joannie, do your duty. Play your part. Be a good girl. Or I'll have to put you over my knee and smack your bottom.'

`No-no-no!' she almost screamed, frantically popping another pill into her mouth and gulping down more scotch.

`As much as I'd love to, James, it's really not possible.' She patted her stomach and looked at him apologetically. `I really do feel a bit sick.'

He looked at her suspiciously, sure she was lying, but what could he do?

`Well, this has been one hell of a hairy day!' he said furiously. `First those two bitches of sisters. And now you.'

He lifted the bottle, poured himself another measure of scotch, and walked out of the room muttering to himself. `May as well go to bed anyway.'

As soon as he entered the bedroom, his eyes went straight to his bedside cabinet and he let out a furious groan.

`I've no cigars!' he shouted as he came back down the stairs. `Not one upstairs and none left down here. Now how the hell am I going to unwind before sleep without a cigar!'

`Look in the study,' Joanne suggested.

`There's none in the study,' he announced two minutes later, standing in the doorway and staring at Joanne with such naked malevolence that she unconsciously took a step back from him.

She knew that look in his eyes, and feared it.

`Not one bloody cigar in the whole house!' he hissed. `Did you forget to buy some *again!* You lazy-arsed bitch! Just what the hell do you *do* all day?'

`D-darling,' she stuttered nervously, `let me see if there are any in the kitchen.' But his eyes blazed at her with such contempt, such malice, she took another step back, as if fearing a physical blow.

And she was right to fear him, because he wanted to grab

her and slap her violently, leave her black and blue for a week. He had done it before, and she was asking for it again. He suddenly understood why husbands committed murder. Why the clever found life impossible with the stupid. His rage – how could he restrain it? Or release it?

'J-James,' she whispered meekly, shrinking under the gleam of violence in his eyes, 'I really do feel unwell ...'

He stood for a moment glaring at her.

'Bitch!' he hissed, then abruptly turned and left the room.

Hundreds of rapid heartbeats later, Joanne heard the front door slam and the car engine starting up. She gave a huge sigh of relief, knowing where he had gone – driving off to the lat-night supermarket or pub to get some cigars.

But now she must act fast if she wanted a peaceful night. So a quick bath, and with two sleeping pills inside her, she would be in bed and zonked unconscious by the time he got back.

Still incensed, still feeling like a bear in a trap, he came out of the supermarket having bought his cigars. He unwrapped one and lit up immediately, standing in the glow of the store window.

He sucked deeply on the smoke, and slowly exhaled. Dismally he looked at his watch: nine-thirty. He didn't feel like going back to bed and sleep. He felt like committing murder.

He gazed around him and mentally pleaded his case ... I was driven to it, Your Lordship. My patience and indulgence, which had lasted for twenty years, finally ran out. The woman conned me with endless glasses of scotch and flattery. She purred and pecked and kissed me and told me she wanted to be my slave. And I, Your Lordship, infantile in my love for her, believed her and married her. Then she turned into a mad vain bitch with a brain in her head that only a slug would envy.

But all that – all that I could have coped with, Your Lordship, if it wasn't for her constant craving for money. Every week something else, something new. I should have known the first time she invited me to lunch at Claridges – then left me to pay the bill. Oh no, your Lordship, divorce was out of the question because I couldn't *afford* it! The money-mad bitch would have stripped me clean, tried to get everything her lawyers could grab for her! That's the only reason I stuck with her so long, Your Lordship, because I couldn't afford to dump her.

He walked slowly back to his car, sat behind the wheel for some minutes, smoking his cigar, looking thoughtful. What was he to do now? He didn't want to go back, didn't want to go home, didn't want to be driven to murder. But there was still rage in his brain and he needed to release it.

An idea occurred him. He played it around his mind for a while. Then he smiled nastily and started up the engine.

As James Duncan drove away, another car which had been parked a few yards behind, driven by one of Joseph Irving's operatives, followed him.

Forty-Seven

New York & London
July 1994

_____/

Phil held one of Marc's diaries in his hands.

`Can't think how I forgot them for so long,' Jimmy said quietly. `I guess I must've just wanted to forget. Pretend they didn't exist. Moseying through life deluding myself that Marc didn't end up dead. That he was still alive somewhere.' Jimmy turned away, distressed. `Hell, son, I honestly didn't *mean* to keep these books from you!'

`I know you didn't, Jimmy, I know.'

And Phil did know. He had talked to enough Vietnam Veterans to know that many found release and peace in amnesia, convincing themselves that what happened to their friends was only nightmare, not memory ... GI Joe, that great guy, naw, he didn't fry in a VC firebomb ... No, he was back home somewhere in America...

A psychological symptom of combat trauma. So many wanted to forget the past, not remember it.

`I'm grateful to you, Jimmy,' Phil said, `for keeping them safe for so long. It's the best thing you could have done for me.'

Jimmy turned and looked at him. `Are you going to turn Marc's diaries into a book?'

Phil shook his head. `No. They're all I have left of him. And they're mine. Mine alone.'

Jimmy smiled, pleased. `You're just going to keep them safe. Same as I did.'

`I'm going to treasure them, Jimmy. A private family legacy to pass on to my own children. Someday.'

Three weeks after returning from America, Phil was back at

Heathrow Airport again. This time to see Rena off on a flight to Sweden.

It was her paternal grandmother's seventieth birthday, and the whole family were going down to her home in Malmö to celebrate it with her.

'I wish you were coming with me,' Rena said.

'So do I,' Phil lied.

He had already met Rena's grandmother in Malmö, and was convinced the woman was mad. Like most Scandinavians she was bilingual and spoke good English, but whenever she got Phil alone, all she spoke to him about was Nordic myths and legends and the powers of the supernatural, always beginning with the words, *'Many full moons ago...'*

It was for that same reason that Rena cherished her paternal grandmother. As a child she had loved spending summers with her in Malmö, loved smelling the lilac hedge around her house, and the Swedishly-clean rooms that always had the tangy perfume of dried herbs.

And unlike her parents, who were not physically demonstrative about their affections, Rena's grandmother was very loving, allowing the child to climb into her wooden bed at night, telling her wonderful stories about the angels, and the occasional flight of the soul during sleep, and the power of dreams and wishes, always beginning with the words, *'Many full moons ago...'*

Rena adored her, and was excitedly looking forward to seeing her again.

'Do you think she will like my present?' Phil asked.

Rena smiled. 'She'll love it.'

Phil had bought the present at Cartier. In miniature – an exquisitely made gold angel with sapphires for eyes and outstretched wings poised for flight. On the same day he had bought Rena a similar miniature, but hers was of a mermaid.

They were calling her plane for the last time. At the departure gate Phil hugged her so hard it took her breath away.

Then he gave her a last quick kiss and she went to catch her plane, waving to him over her shoulder, then turning again and calling back:

`*Jag älskar dig!*'

He nodded and smiled and watched her until she had disappeared from view.

The sun was dazzling as Phil drove out of the car park at Heathrow. He opened the glove compartment, took out a pair of sunglasses and slipped them on. Ten minutes later he received a call on his car phone. He put the phone on speaker and concentrated on the road. `Hello?'

`Phil, dear boy, I've been trying to reach you for hours.' The voice belonged to Joseph Irving.

Phil instantly became alert. He flicked a glance to the overhead mirror, then signalled a move from the fast to the middle lane.

`Yes, Joseph, what is it?'

`Something I thought you might like to know as soon as possible. About the subject under surveillance. We have at last come up with something.'

`Something good?'

`Something bad.'

Phil smiled grimly as he moved into the slow lane. He had *known* there would be something.

`So tell me about it.'

`No, dear boy. Not on the telephone.'

`When?'

`It has to be tonight. My time is fully booked for a week otherwise. Are you free tonight?'

`Very free. My wife's just gone away for a week.'

`Then I'll see you tonight in the Grosvenor at seven.' Irving slammed down the phone with his usual abruptness.

Phil smiled. For an ex CID cop like Irving, some habits were hard to break.

Forty-Eight

London
July 1994

_____/

Joseph Irving took his first sip of malt.

'So,' Phil asked, eager to get to the point, 'what's this something you've turned up on Duncan?

'Sad, really sad. Incidentally, I was very surprised to learn that our man suffers from angina, and has a regular prescription of nifedipine as well as a nitrolingual spray.'

'So? Why so surprised?'

'Because, dear boy, if he is suffering from angina, the silly man should not smoke cigars. What is the point of his doctor providing him with relief if he continues to agitate his condition by puffing Havanas?'

Joseph Irving sat back and frowned, as if such foolishness really annoyed him. 'Angina is not a condition to treat lightly. And I should know. My wife suffered from angina for years before she died.'

'I'm sorry,' Phil said.

'No need to be.' Irving shrugged. 'It was a long time ago. Her heart had never been good. But obviously our man's condition is nothing as serious. Still, he should be more careful and give up those damned cigars.'

'Okay, so the reports say Duncan has angina. But what's this "something" you've turned up?'

'He's a cruiser,' Irving said tersely.

'A what?'

'A kerb crawler.'

Phil was speechless. He had come up with at least five possible things that Irving's investigators could have turned up on Duncan. But *this* he had not expected.

`You mean—'

Irving nodded, a faint grimace of disgust on his face, as if all this was quite beneath him. He took a pair of spectacles from his breast pocket and put them on, then removed a folded paper from an inner pocket, unfolded it, and sat for a moment surveying it sternly through his glasses.

`Three weeks ago, on the night of Tuesday the fourteenth of June, at exactly 9.20 p.m., the subject left his house and drove to a nearby supermarket where he bought a packet of cigars. He unwrapped and lit one immediately, and sat for approximately two minutes in his car smoking the cigar. After which, still smoking, he drove off.

`But instead of returning home, he headed towards the M4 motorway. Then drove non-stop to London at a recklessly dangerous speed of 96 miles an hour. When he reached London, he then drove to the red-light area of King's Cross. It was there he kerb-crawled and solicited a prostitute from the window of his car. A quick pick-up. A quick drive to a nearby railway goods yard. Then the subject drove back and dropped the prostitute off near to where he had found her. She appeared to have blood on her face, but my operative could not be certain. After which, the subject drove straight home.'

Irving looked up. `Kerb-crawling is against the law.'

Phil stared back at him, puzzled. `But what made Duncan do it?'

`Oh, it's not the first time. After the incident we did a check through police records and discovered that, three years ago, in the area of Paddington, he was caught in the act of soliciting a female from a motor vehicle for the purposes of prostitution. He was taken to Paddington Green Police Station where he was cautioned, advised, and let off with a warning. Usual procedure for first offences of this nature. But his name still goes in the records. It may not have been his first offence, of course, but the first and only time he's been caught.'

Phil was still thinking, still slightly shocked.

'Being cautioned by the police usually frightens them off for life,' said Irving. 'Our man, however, has obviously forgotten the fear as well as the warning. At any rate, he obviously decided it was worth the risk.'

'Do you think he will do it again?'

Irving looked down at his report.

'Six days later, on the night of Monday the twentieth of June, the subject made another trip to King's Cross. Then again on Wednesday the twenty-ninth. On this third occasion, my operative got a clear look at the prostitute when she was dropped off – a young girl of no more than sixteen. Her face was very badly bruised and she was holding a bloodstained handkerchief to her nose. The subject drove off at speed.'

'My God ... the bastard ... going out to beat up young girls.' Phil was feeling sick in his stomach.

'It's a risk all prostitutes take.'

'Yes – but a kid of no more than sixteen! I'm sure she didn't *agree* to get beaten up.'

'I suspect,' said Irving, 'that our man is suffering severe stress in his business and personal life.'

'And that's not all he's going to suffer,' Phil said. 'If he does it again I want photographs. Large twelve-by-tens of the prostitute bending down to his car. Then another shot of her getting into his car.'

He looked steadfastly at Irving. 'That's what I want, Joseph. And I'm prepared to pay whatever is necessary to get them. Photographs. And once I've got them, that will be the end of Duncan's whoring.'

'We already have photographs,' Irving replied, without a change of tone or expression. He looked down at the report in his hand.

'The young detective who supplied this report is an ex-police operative who never fails to do a perfect job. As soon as the subject first approached that particular area of King's Cross, he knew what was on. As it was dark he used high-speed film,

1600 ASA, and secured clear shots on each occasion of the subject soliciting the prostitute from the window of his car, the prostitute entering the car, and numerous other shots until the prostitute was finally dropped off. But, most importantly, in *every* shot, the car's registration number is clearly visible.'

`How soon can you get the photographs to me?'

`Within the next twenty-four hours. Delivered by hand, of course.'

Phil nodded, and smiled grimly. `This is it, Joseph. This is what I've been waiting years for. My time with James Duncan has finally come – time to make the payback.'

Forty-Nine

London
July 1994

_____/

At two minutes before six, on the following Thursday evening, one of the telephones on James Duncan's desk began to ring.

Duncan ignored it at first, rubbing his temples with both hands and mumbling to himself as he studied the firm's accounts. Last year had been a disaster. This year looked as if it was going to be even worse.

He urgently reached for his nitrolingual spray and took the cap off and gave himself two shots under the tongue. Instant relief.

The telephone kept on ringing. Duncan glanced at it irritably, then saw it was his private line. It must be Joannie, wanting to know what time he was leaving – wanting to know if he intended to ruin her casserole *again*. Nagging old cow.

He grabbed the phone and opened his mouth to bark.

`Duncan?'

James Duncan sat speechless. He knew that voice. He had only spoken to Phil Gaines on the phone once before, but he knew that voice – smooth and cool as a mentholated cigarette.

`What do you want, Gaines?'

`I think it's time we had a business consultation.'

`A *business* consultation?' Duncan sat forward on his seat. `Listen, Gaines, I've got no business with you, so there's nothing to consult about.' He slammed down the phone.

The silence seemed to blast the room.

Duncan sat staring at the phone, furious. Gaines! The sheer *nerve* of that man took some believing. A *business* consultation! So Gaines was still after a merger, was he? Well, he could wait till Hell froze.

His attention swerved back to the accounts on his desk, looking at them with glittering eyes. Gaines – the man with the money! As fast as he was losing it, Gaines was making it. How did the bastard do it? Of course, Gaines had stacks of money to begin with, and that was always a help.

The telephone rang, his private line again.

Duncan consulted his watch, and sprang forward. This time it was definitely Joannie ringing for a rant. Best to just mollify her.

'Hello?' he said smoothly.

'Duncan?'

'No! Listen, Gaines, I know what you're after, but you're not going to get it! Not now or ever! No merger!'

'I'm not after a merger, Duncan ... Not now or ever.'

Duncan blinked, then his lips curled suspiciously. 'Then why ask for a *business* consultation? I've only got one business. *Respectable* publishing.'

'I've got some valuable information for you, Duncan. Something you should know as soon as possible. Someone's trying to cripple you. Someone's trying to close down that respectable little firm you're so proud of ... I just thought you should know.'

'Close me down?' Duncan searched for his nitrolingual spray. 'Why should I believe you, Gaines?'

'Because I'm telling you the truth. A lot of dirty business has been going on behind your back. And as one independent publisher to another, I think it's only fair that you should be told about it.'

'So tell me about it.'

'Not on the phone. Listen, Duncan, I'm being straight with you here. Personally I don't like you at all. I never have. You know that. But this business that's been going on behind your back – well, it's just too *dirty* to believe. And I think it should be stopped as soon as possible.'

Duncan had managed to get the top off his nitrolingual

spray; he gave himself another shot under the tongue.

'Gaines, listen, if what you say is true – if one of those conglomerate whales has been trying to nobble me – this is very serious.'

'It is, yes. The problem is ... you've made it very clear that you won't sell to anyone, haven't you? And the piranhas don't like that. They don't like the small fish clogging up their waters. If they can't buy you out, they'll chase you out. And when you've got nowhere else to go, they'll snap you up cheap.'

Duncan jerked upright in alarm. 'Who?' he demanded. 'Listen, Gaines, just tell me who?'

'Not on the phone.'

'Where then?'

'Well, let's see ... Can you come to Hampstead tonight?'

Duncan hesitated, the suspicious look back on his face. 'But why you, Gaines? Why should you want to warn me – unless it *is* a merger you're after. Is that it? Is this some kind of scheming ploy to get what you want? You and me standing together against the congloms?'

'You can go to hell, Duncan. I don't really care what you do. I've done my best to warn you, but I'm already tired of this conversation. My wife just happens to like your wife and that's the *only* reason I've agreed to warn you. But now my good deed is done for the year. My boy scout's badge is honoured. I'm hanging up now, Duncan.'

'No, wait, *wait*! Listen, Gaines, tell me – do you have an documental evidence to prove what you're saying?'

'Yes ... copies of letters ... with the name of the publisher who's already contacted your two sisters and secured their *willing* agreement to each sell their third share in the firm ... even if you cannot be persuaded to sell yours.'

'The dirty underhanded bitches!'

'If you want to know more, Duncan. If you want to see the evidence, then be at my house at eight o'clock tonight. If you haven't shown by then, I'll be out.'

`Yes ... all right, eight o'clock, I'll be there.'

Five minutes later the telephone rang in David Gallagher's flat. David could hear it ringing as he turned the key in the door. He rushed to answer it.

`Hello.'

`David?'

`No, this is Prince Charles.' David grinned. `Who else would it be, Phil? You know I live alone.'

`So what are you doing tonight?'

`Nothing.'

`Then will you do me a favour, David?'

`Depends on what it is.'

`I had a call from Rena, on my answering machine. She's not supposed to be coming back from Sweden until Saturday afternoon, but she's decided to surprise me and booked herself on a plane this evening. Could you go to Heathrow to meet her for me?'

`Okay.'

`I wouldn't ask you, David, you know I wouldn't. But Rena's call has put me in a tight corner and some business I planned to do tomorrow night has had to be brought forward to tonight.'

David shrugged. `That's all right, I'll go. What time is her plane due?'

`Nine o'clock. Scandinavian Airlines. Terminal 3.'

`I'll be there.'

`Thanks, David. You're a terrific friend ... and I mean that.'

Fifty

London
July 1994

_____/

At ten minutes to eight, the doorbell rang.

'We'll have to make it brief,' Duncan said, his voice rough with agitation as Phil let him in. 'I'm almost out of my mind wondering who they are. Which publisher? Names, that's what I want. *Names*. Christ, you can't trust anyone these days.'

'Come and sit down,' Phil said with solicitude, leading the way into the study. 'Then I'll tell you all about it.'

As soon as he entered the study Duncan's eyes were immediately drawn to the drinks cabinet in the corner. 'Can I have a drink? I need one.'

'A drink?' Phil's eyes were less friendly than his voice as he indicated a chair by the desk. 'What drink would you like?'

'Scotch. I shouldn't really drink when I'm driving. But as it's just the one – make it a large one.'

Phil poured a scotch, not too large, and handed it to Duncan.

Duncan nodded gratefully, took a slug, smacked his lips. 'I needed that! Listen, Gaines, I can't tell you what this means to me – and I've been thinking – and you're right! We independent publishers should watch out for each other. No mergers, mind, but no point falling out.' He reached into his inner pocket. 'Can I smoke a cigar?'

'Certainly.' Phil found him an ashtray.

Duncan lit up and puffed a cloud of smoke. 'Now, let's get down to business. Show me this evidence.'

'Very well.'

Phil remained standing as he opened a drawer in the desk and lifted out some large manila envelopes. From the first he removed a number of photographs of Joanne, in the company of various young men, and laid them one by one on the desk.

'Your wife, I believe.'

Duncan stared in puzzlement at the photographs, from one to the other. Then he slowly looked up at Phil in realisation.

'It was all a trick ... just to get me here. And the publisher – the one doing all the dirty business behind my back – it's you, Gaines, it's bloody *you!*'

Phil smiled. 'As Muhammad Ali used to say – you ain't as dumb as you look.'

'You would go this far? For a merger?'

Duncan stared again at the pictures of Joanne. Then with a sudden lunge grabbed them into his hands and ripped them to pieces, flung the pieces across the desk, and jumped to his feet.

'There, Gaines. That's what I think of your dirty blackmail – *nothing!* Not shocked. And *not* impressed.'

He turned and stormed out of the room.

But out of the house he could not get. The front door was locked.

Puzzled, he turned the handle and pulled and pulled.

Then he realised it was Chub-locked. And Gaines had the key. He had been so distracted on arrival, he had not even noticed Gaines locking the door behind him. He felt even more distracted now.

He turned and stared towards the open door of the study as if suddenly sensing something direful. He was locked in.

He swallowed. Felt pain. He needed his nitrolingual spray. Needed a nifedipine tablet. But they were in the car. Outside. And he was locked in.

Slowly, he walked back into the study. Phil was still standing behind the desk, very calm, waiting.

James Duncan regarded him with a wary look of fear. 'This is not just about business, is it Gaines? This is madness. What is it you want?'

'I want to show you these.' From a second envelope Phil removed another set of photographs and laid them one by one on the desk.

`Come and take a closer look, Duncan. They're good shots. Very clear. Especially of you.'

Duncan walked unsteadily towards the pictures. He stared, and stared, from one to the other.

`Oh my God! Oh my God—'

`Now this particular girl,' Phil tapped a photograph, `is what the police refer to as "a known common prostitute." Known, that is, to the police. In fact they all are. All of these girls have convictions for street soliciting.'

Phil looked at James Duncan. `Not very fair, is it? The man is allowed off with a warning while the girl is convicted. I mean, you *did* receive a warning, didn't you, Duncan? A few years ago? Before you went on this latest binge.'

Duncan was speechless, all his aggression gone. His face was like ceiling plaster. He reached for the glass of whisky on the desk, emptied the glass in a gulp, his voice coming out in a hiss.

`How did you get these? How did you get them?'

Phil shrugged, as if the answer was obvious. `Money. Private Investigators. All ex-police. I bought the best.'

`You—' Duncan shook his head in disbelief. `You vicious bastard.'

`Me? A vicious bastard?' Phil's tone was neutral. `I don't spend my nights beating up young prostitutes.'

`What is it you want, Gaines? A merger?'

`A merger?' Phil smiled contemptuously. `I had no intention of merging with you, Duncan. I intended to take you over, lock and stock, and then kick you out with the rest of the garbage. And I still intend to do that. But first, there's a lot of damage to be done with these photographs, isn't there?'

Duncan's eyes enlarged on the photographs. He flopped onto the chair he had vacated earlier, his face convulsed.

`You handed me the knife, Duncan.' Phil grabbed up a photograph. `This is your dirty work – not mine. If you hadn't gone whoring these pictures could not have been taken. If you had not set yourself up on a pedestal as Mr *Gentleman* Publisher, these pictures could not do the damage they inevitably will. *You* handed me a knife of your own making, Duncan. And now I'm going to use it to make you bleed.'

`What—' Duncan looked as if he was in some kind of unfathomable nightmare. `*What-is-it-you-want?* How can I even consider your blackmail, when you won't tell me what you *want!*'

`Blackmail?' Phil looked affronted. `This is not blackmail, Duncan. These photographs are not up for discussion, or subject to negotiation. These photographs are going to be used. Have no illusions about that. Because first thing tomorrow morning, copies of these photographs – all showing your car and registration number – are going to be delivered by courier to the Vice Squad at Paddington Green Police Station.'

Duncan was staring at Phil in a way he had never stared at anyone before, horrified and disbelieving.

`And also first thing tomorrow morning,' Phil continued, `copies of these photographs are going to be delivered by courier to all your business associates. And to the wives of all your friends in Berkshire. Especially to the *wives* of all your old buddies at the Golf Club—' He smiled a little. `And so by tomorrow night, Duncan, you are going to be nothing more than a big buzz of bad news.'

James Duncan could not move, could not speak.

`You see, Duncan, what I actually *want*, is this. I want to see you ruined. Publicly humiliated. Drowned in your own degradation. I want people to see you for the bastard that you are. The fake that you are. The whorefucker that you are. Oh, make no mistake, Duncan, this is *vengeance* I'm wreaking, and I've been a long time waiting.'

James Duncan looked as if he was impaled to the seat, his gaze fixed in rigid horror on his tormentor's dark eyes.

`Why?' he asked in terrified bewilderment. `What do you have against me? You hated me that first time I met you. You refused to shake my hand. I didn't even know you. You were a stranger! Why? For Christ's sake – *why?*'

'You killed my mother.'

'Your mother?' Duncan looked even more bewildered. 'I've never even met your mother! So how could I kill her?'

He stood up. 'Listen, Gaines – all I know is that I'm locked in a house with a mad man. You've obviously mistaken me for somebody else. I've no idea what you're talking about. And I have a *heart* condition. I need one of my nifedipine tablets. I'm supposed to take two a day. But they're outside in my car.'

'I don't give a damn about your tablets! I don't care if you drop dead at my feet!' Phil's fist smashed down on the desk. '*Sit down!*'

Duncan was not even aware that he had stood up. He sat back down, faint with panic as his eyes fell once more on the photographs of the prostitutes. He reached out to touch one and saw that his hands were trembling violently. He had no doubt that Gaines intended to use the photographs, but if he did, it would be the end of him, the end of everything. Even the Golf Club would be barred to him.

'You still don't remember her, do you? Fourteen years is a long time, Duncan. But there are some things that some people *never* forget.'

'Fourteen years ... ' Duncan said slowly. 'That was ... 1980...' And finally he realised what Gaines was talking about. 'The woman...'

'The woman,' Phil echoed. 'In court, they described her as a waitress. But she was much more than that. Shall I tell you something more about her, Duncan?'

Duncan swallowed.

'She was lovely and caring and one of the hardest working women in the world. She looked in her mid-twenties but was actually thirty-five. It was late and it was dark and she was on her way home after completing a four-to-eleven shift at the restaurant. She was feeling happy, because the night before she had finished the final pages of her first book. She was delighted with herself. She had finally done it. And now, for the first time in her life, something might work out for her. Something to look forward to. Something good and something to come.

`But as eager as she must have been to get home, she waited at the crossing for the traffic lights to turn red. But her waiting didn't save her, did it? Not from the drunken maniac who came speeding through the red lights and broke nearly every bone in her body.'

The room was deathly quiet. Duncan tried to speak, tried to swallow again, but there was no spit in his mouth.

`You were stinking drunk, and you killed her. But due to the perversity of the law you could not be charged with murder or even manslaughter – you could only be charged under the Road Traffic Act with being above the alcohol limit while in control of a motor vehicle. Your sentence nothing more than a three-year driving ban and a fine of £150. Is that justice? And is that why you forgot it so easily? Because you got off so lightly?'

`It was an accident,' Duncan insisted feebly. `An unfortunate accident.'

`It was a bloody *crime!* You were stinking drunk, driving like a maniac at seventy-five miles an hour in a thirty-mile zone. Straight through a red light! Smashing into her as she walked on the crossing. She didn't even get a chance to turn her head and see you coming. And that's why you still don't know what she looks like, because the only time you ever saw her, her face was covered in blood!'

`Yes, yes, she died – but *my* only crime was having too much to drink. I never intended to kill her ... If only you knew the grief it has caused me since. The years of silent suffering. The angina. And no – I didn't forget! I could *never* forget. The death of that woman haunts me every day—'

`You dirty, snivelling, lying fake! Don't you *dare* insult me with your lies and false grief. *You can't even remember her name!*'

Phil was staring at Duncan with hatred and revulsion, asking him the same question he had asked himself a hundred times in the past three years.

'Christ! — how many people does a man kill in his lifetime? None, usually. So when a terrible event like that happens, surely the person responsible would at least remember his victim's *name*.'

'I *do* remember her name,' Duncan insisted. 'Yes, yes, I do!'

'What is it?'

Duncan swallowed. 'Gaines ... Mrs Gaines ... But I never knew she was connected to you...'

'*Fuck you*, Duncan!' Phil pointed to a framed poster on the study wall. Look behind you! Her name is there – big enough for a bat to see. And here—' He snatched up a copy of Marian Barnard's book from the desk and held it square in front of Duncan.

'Look at it, Duncan, the name of the woman you killed, *Marian Barnard*. The same name that fourteen years ago you heard read out in court at least *six* times – the name of your unfortunate victim. The same name that was printed in the newspaper report. Yet not *once* – not since that first night I met you when Martin Pellmann mentioned her book – have you shown even a hint of recognition or the slightest memory of her name. You killed her and then you promptly forgot her ... my thirty-five-year old mother ... Marian Barnard.'

Duncan was stunned. 'Marian Barnard ... the dead author ... she was your *mother?*'

'Yes, and unlucky for you she had a son. But you didn't know that, did you? Because in court they kept referring to her as *Miss* Marian Barnard. But I've been on your tail ever since, Duncan, and now I've got you, I'm going to make you *pay* in *full* – not only for what you did to her – but for *laughing* about it afterwards.'

Oh God, Oh Christ – now Duncan knew there was no hope of a reprieve.

Suddenly Phil raised the hardback book in his hand and

swung it across the desk — smashing it across Duncan's face. 'You unfeeling pile of pigshit! You took away my mother's *life*! Smashed and battered her and took away her *life!* Then you didn't even have the decency to remember her name.'

Duncan was in shock, the smash from the book had brought blood pouring from his nose onto his shirt, his hand was over his chest, his voice shrill and shaking. 'Gaines, Christ, Gaines, call an ambulance! I think I'm dying!'

'Then die,' Phil said coldly. 'Do yourself and me one great big favour. Because whether you are well or ill, I'm determined to destroy you, finish you, take away your every hope, every ambition, every triumph. On her death I swore it.'

He threw down the book and began to gather up the photographs. 'And I'm going to start with copies of these. Tomorrow morning. You can bet your house on it.'

'Gaines, please ... an ambulance.'

Phil glanced at him, implacable and unpitying, and continued filing the photographs back inside the envelope.

'Did you ring for an ambulance that night, Duncan? Or did you just stand there watching her bleed to death on the road. Yes, that's what the witness in court said you did. Just stood there watching her bleed to death, while smoking a cigar.'

He put the photographs back in the drawer and turned the key.

'But what I will do, is open the front door for you. Now you know what's going to happen, and why.' He raised an eyebrow. 'Now you may leave.'

Duncan was slowly rising from the chair, clutching the arms as he pushed himself up, swaying dizzily. Through a haze of pain he saw Gaines come around the desk and walk past him indifferently.

'You bastard ... You vicious *bastard!*' A sudden upsurge of rage propelled him into a furious charge after Gaines, his huge fists raised to attack.

Phil turned swiftly as Duncan gasped and flopped against

him; instinctively Phil caught him in his arms, staggered with him, regained his balance, then stood firmly holding the collapsed man against his chest.

After a silence ... after a very long silence ... when Phil could hear nothing but the sound of his own breathing, he slowly laid Duncan back onto the floor.

James Duncan's silver-grey eyes stared up at him, enlarged and sightless. The eyes of a dead man.

Phil stood gazing down at him, furious. `You swine,' he finally murmured. `You got off lightly again.'

Fifty-One

London
July 1994
_____/

Rena almost screamed when she saw the white ambulance parked outside the house, its red lights flashing in the dark.

`Phil!'

David rammed the brakes and brought the car to a stop a few yards behind the ambulance. Both jumped out and ran towards the house. The paramedics were wheeling a stretcher down the drive. The body and face were covered in a red blanket.

`Phil!' Rena gasped again, and clutched at David. They stood holding each other and staring as the body came closer.

`Who?' David asked the paramedics, then moved forward himself and lifted the blanket back from the face.

`Duncan!'

Rena stared, first in relief, then in bewilderment.

`How?' David asked one of the paramedics.

`Heart attack. Seems he just collapsed in the middle of a business meeting. The coroner's police found his nitrolingual spray and nifedipines in his car. Stupid fool had been suffering from angina for years, yet *still* smoked cigars heavily. He was smoking one not long before he collapsed.' The paramedic shook his head. `Why won't these people *listen?*'

David was feeling a strange sense of unease. `Are you *sure* it was a heart attack?'

`Yeh, positive, all the signs.'

`Why has he got blood on his face?'

`Seems he was standing, then suddenly crashed down, hitting his face hard against the edge of the desk. The one I feel sorry for is the poor guy inside. Imagine having something like that happening to you? A business acquaintance dropping dead at your feet. The coroner's police are still in there talking to him.'

The two police officers were leaving the house as Rena and David approached the front door.

'Who are you?' the policewoman asked.

'I'm his wife—' Rena pointed, 'the man inside – I'm his wife.'

'Oh, I see. Well I'm glad you've come. Your husband seems perfectly all right at the moment, but later he may show symptoms of delayed shock. It's quite a natural reaction after something like this. At first it doesn't really sink in, all actions become instinctive, calling the police and so on. It's only on realising that someone is actually dead that shock takes over. I think you had better go inside.'

'Have you finished here?' David asked.

The policewoman nodded, calm and efficient. 'Yes, we've finished here. The autopsy will probably be tomorrow.'

Her radio crackled into life, a voice spoke calmly with nightmarish automatism, informing her of another death somewhere else in London.

David and Rena went inside.

Phil was in the drawing-room. He turned as they entered, and calmly met the questioning look in Rena's eyes.

Rena still could not fully comprehend what had happened, but she also was feeling a strange sense of unease. 'Phil ... James Duncan ... Who is he?'

'The drunk driver who killed my mother.'

'What?' And it was then Rena knew, with a sudden certainty, why James Duncan had been invited to the party. The merger had been a charade. A trap Phil had baited to draw James Duncan closer.

'Your mother?' Now it was David Gallagher who did not fully comprehend.

Phil looked at David. 'My mother, Marian Barnard.'

'*Marian Barnard!*' David could only stare at Phil in

disbelieving astonishment. 'But you told me that Marian Barnard—'

'I know I did, David, but I lied.'

'Why?'

'Because the truth was nobody's business, but mine.'

Rena had to know the truth. 'Phil ... James Duncan ... Did you kill him?'

'No.'

'The blood on his face?'

'I hit him with her book – the book of her *life* – I smashed it across his face.'

'But did you kill him?'

'No. He had angina. A rotten heart. A mean soul. And he drank heavily and continually smoked cigars – all culminating in a heart attack.'

'You did nothing else ... except hit him with a book?'

Phil hesitated. 'Yes, I did do something else,' he admitted, 'but don't worry, it was nothing that could be termed illegal.'

'What did you do?'

'I scared the life out of him.'

Fifty-Two

London
August 1994

_____/

Two weeks later, James Duncan's two sisters, Helen and Felicity, paid a visit to Gaines Publishing.

The two women sat on chairs opposite Phil's desk and he listened to what they had to say.

`You see, Mr Gaines,' Helen said primly, `although James's share in the firm now pass on in two equal parts to both myself and Felicity – Daddy did *insist* upon that in his own will, didn't he Felicity?'

`Daddy did, Helen.'

Helen nodded, and turned back. `But James also had a huge life insurance policy. And James always said that his will would provide a substantial bequest to each of us. But now we discover that Joanne is the *only* beneficiary of his will. James, in his meanness and duplicity, has left everything to the slut.'

`Everything to the slut,' Felicity echoed.

`And nothing to us.'

`Nothing to us.'

`So, what we wish to know, Mr Gaines, is whether you are still intent upon taking over Garland Press. At the figure formerly mentioned?'

Phil had no interest in Garland's, but he had used these two women when he thought he might need them, and now he would have to pay for it.

`Yes,' Phil said. `But there will be no seats on the board. It will be a complete take-over.'

`Absolutely *no* seats on the board?' Helen asked. `Not even for James's widow?'

`No,' Phil said. `Not even for his widow.'

Helen smiled triumphantly. `Then we have no objections to the terms. Do we Felicity?'

`No objections, Helen.'

`No, by God!' Helen exclaimed. `She won't get a penny out of us! And that insurance money will only last her for a year at the most. The way *she* spends. And *then* what will she do?'

Phil had the absurd feeling that he was expected to give an opinion. He stood up quickly to signal the end of the meeting.

`I shall discuss it with my solicitor this afternoon.

Later that afternoon, Phil's solicitor was sitting on the opposite side of the desk, various deeds in his hands as he clarified the situation.

`Now, when you formed this company, you had no need of loans from banks. Every penny was supplied by you. At that time, David Gallagher, who was to be your Editorial Director, had no capital. But the board had to have two shareholding directors. So we agreed that you should own ninety-nine per cent of the shares, and David would own one per cent.'

Phil nodded, trying to conceal his impatience while the lawyer continued, `After that, a number of other department heads became co-opted directors, well remunerated with good salaries and bonuses, but no shares. That left—'

`All I want to know,' Phil interrupted, `is can I do this? Legally – can I do it?'

`Most certainly. This firm is yours, Mr Gaines. You can do whatever you like. But remember, whatever you do, you still must have at least *two* shareholding directors.'

In his office, David Gallagher was staring at the brown parcel his secretary handed to him. It obviously contained a script, but it was what was written in huge black letters across the front of the parcel that made him stare – *DAVID GALLAGHER – PERSONAL*

`I don't believe it,' said David, glancing up at his secretary. `I know that handwriting. It's from John Houlihan! When did this come?'

`It was delivered to reception a few minutes ago, by John Houlihan himself. He told Carol that it must be delivered directly to you and nobody else.'

`Well, well,' David grinned. `The mountain finally came to Mohammed ... But is it a cut-down revamped version of his awful *magnum opus*, I wonder?'

An hour later, as everyone was leaving their offices and going home, Phil appeared at David's desk.

`Can I have a word with you, David?'

David didn't even glance up, too engrossed in his reading. `Not now, Phil. Later, later...'

Phil raised an eyebrow, and quietly left.

It was the office cleaner that made David eventually realise that everyone had gone home except himself.

`You not going 'ome, Mr Gallagher?' she asked him curiously as she lifted up his waste-paper bin. `You know what they say about all work and no play— '

`Yes, yes, I'm going now,' David said, as he gathered up Houlihan's script to finish it at home.

As soon as he got home, David made a sandwich and a cup of coffee then sat down at his desk and returned with excitement to Houlihan's new thriller – typed at such a cracking pace that almost all the commas and stops were missing.

Nevertheless, it was brilliant, David finally concluded with a smile. The old pain-in-the-ass had done it again – written a uniquely original page-turning thriller that was almost impossible to put down.

Instinctively, David reached for his pencil and started editing.

At last he looked up, the final page completed. He glanced at his watch and saw it was nearly five o'clock in the morning.

He gathered up the pages, stacked them neatly, and was about to put them back in their folder when his eye was caught by Houlihan's accompanying letter – in particular, the P.S. scrawled at the end:

P.S. DG – I'd be obliged if you would contact me immediately after you have read it – JH.

David sat thoughtful for a moment, then a wicked grin moved on his face as he reached for the telephone.

Why not? Houlihan did request *immediately*. And Houlihan was a man who didn't like to be kept waiting.

In blackness, the telephone on the bedside table rang.

A grunt, a groan, then a hand finally switched on the bedside light, illuminating the face of John Houlihan – looking like he'd just survived a bomb-blast.

He was still blinking as he picked up the phone. `Yeah ... Yeah, this is me. Who are you? ... Listen, what time is it? Oh wait – the room is spinning ... Where am I? ... No, I've no idea.' Houlihan looked around him blearily. `I don't recognise this place at all.'

He looked over his other shoulder and saw Nancy fast asleep in the bed, oblivious to lights and the ringing of the telephone.

Houlihan turned back and nodded as he spoke into the phone.

`It's okay, I'm all right, I'm at home. Well I must be, because my wife's here in the bed and she's not a woman for sleeping with other men ... Look, will you wait a second while I go and get a mouthwash?'

He returned a minute later carrying a glass of Jamesons and sat on the side of the bed in his pyjamas. He gulped a slug of whiskey, and lifted the phone again.

`I'm back, but tell me, who did you say you were again? ... Oh, David Gallagher?' Houlihan's face lit up with delight. `You got the script?'

He took another slug of Jamesons. 'Yeah, I'm back on the bottle and writing great. Total sobriety doesn't agree with me. Makes me too serious ... What? No, of course I'm not drinking too much. I promised Nancy I wouldn't. But she allowed me to have a few over the odds tonight because I'm celebrating the completion of my new script. I only finished it last night, you know? After *slaving* night and day for months on end ... What? You've read it already? So? Well? What do you think of it?'

Houlihan's face lit up in blissful radiance. 'Brilliant? You're not jessing me now? You mean that?'

At the other end of the line, David smiled wryly. Houlihan was hoping for more compliments about his book, but 'Brilliant' was enough.

'I loved writing it,' Houlihan said excitedly. 'Enjoyed every back-breaking and head-scratching minute of it!'

David grinned. 'Yes, I knew you were back on form and writing up a storm. You left out most of the punctuation.'

'Ah, punctuation me arse! Who gives a damn about full stops and semi-colons when the typewriter is pounding a rhapsody! Listen –did I ever tell you what Christy Brown said about those writers who fiddle away with their full stops and commas? He said –"You don't stop to depict each raindrop when you're painting a thunderstorm."'

David rotated his eyes upwards. Houlihan was simply incorrigible. No other editor would put up with him.

'So you'll put them in for me, will you? The full stops and commas. Same as you always do.'

David smiled and rubbed his chin but did not reply.

'And you think the book is brilliant?'

'Even better than your first.'

'Honestly?'

'Honestly.'

Houlihan's shout of glee almost burst David's eardrum.

'I knew I could do it!' Houlihan roared down the phone. 'Those other cross-eyed bastards think I'm finished. Shows you how wrong they were! I'll *never* be finished. Not till I'm dead. Listen – just as long as I can hold a pen or bash a typewriter I'll always have a whip to crack. Betcher balls I will!'

`I'll let you go back to sleep now,' David said with sly grin, knowing he had ruined Houlihan's sleep for the rest of the night. The man's excitement was almost palpable – even from the other end of a phone line.

Houlihan was speaking again but the words were obscured by a gurgling sound. `Sorry?' David said. `I didn't hear that.'

`Because...' Houlihan went on more clearly, `I was seriously considering – and I mean *very seriously* considering – giving the whole thing up.'

`One more thing,' David said, his expression straightening. `Before I decide whether we should make you an offer for this script, and before I will agree to edit you, there is something I feel must be resolved between us, once and for all.'

In his bedroom John Houlihan frowned as he listened. He took a sip of his whiskey, and sighed sadly.

`Yeah, sorry ... sorry about that, David, I was just a bit, you know ... out of line.' He heaved another sigh, full of remorse, and answered the next question.

`Why? You want to know *why* I sent the script direct to you this time? Well now, I'll tell you just *why*. Because I was thinking – and I mean *very seriously* thinking – about everything. And what I came up with is this – you're a man that's always treated me right, David Gallagher. Yes, you are. And I don't know why I never appreciated it before. But there you go. Success can blind a man.'

`Is that an apology, by an chance?' David asked.

Houlihan drained back his glass, then put it down with a thud of emphasis. `Even my sarcastic little digs – you always responded to my digs and jibes with the dignity of a gentlemen. Never lowered yourself to argue back. A gentleman now. That's what you are, David Gallagher. And my fist in the face of anyone who says anything different from now on. And Nancy

agrees with me – all the way. You're a true *gentleman*, David.
And boyo, that's something rare!'

David was smiling.

At the other end of the line, Houlihan was frowning
furiously. `Not like that Phil Gaines. That basket case! And a
bloody *rude* basket case he is too!'

Phil laughed the following morning when David recounted the
conversation.

`So it's me he hates now, not you?'

`Yes, I'm a gentleman and you're a basket case.'

`So? Is Houlihan back with us? Are we taking his new
script?'

`If we don't, another publisher will snap it up in a week. It's a
sure-fire winner. But apart from that, Houlihan says that from
now on, he won't allow anyone to handle his scripts but David
Gallagher – a *gentleman* of the first order!'

`So, how much?'

David shrugged. `Based on his last sales, I thought, perhaps,
£125,000 for world rights. He's still got no agent, so he'll give us
the lot.'

Phil stood thoughtful. `This business of Duncan's,' he said,
changing the subject. `The take-over. I think the name should
be changed.'

`Yes, so you said the other day. Wipe out Garland's name
altogether.'

`No, I don't mean that. I mean the name of our place. I think
it should be changed to Gaines and Gallagher.'

David stared at him. `Bloody hell ... Phil, what are you
talking about?'

`This publishing house. Gaines and Gallagher. My money
and your management. A straight split.'

`You mean ... joint ownership?'

`Why not?'

`Why not?' David suddenly stood up, looking confused. `I'll

tell you why not ... because although I may have made a lot of money in the past few years, I have nothing near the amount to buy a half share in the firm, not even a fifth. Do you *know* how much Gaines Publishing is worth?'

'David, all I want from you is your agreement, and your signature on the relevant deeds.' Phil shrugged tiredly. 'You've run beside me all the way. Every step since Cambridge. So why not Gaines and Gallagher. Money doesn't come into it.'

David felt weak. He sat down. His brain was still in shock. It was like a dream. Long ago. His own publishing house. A foolish dream. A cruel joke. Phil may be a millionaire, but he was nobody's fool. He had more than doubled the personal fortune he had received from his grandmother. And although he was capable of being extremely generous, he was never *stupid* with money.

He looked at Phil. 'This *is* a joke, isn't it?'

'No, David, no joke.'

'So, what you're saying - now correct me if I'm wrong – you want to just hand over half the firm to me - as a *gift*.'

'Why not?'

'More appropriately – *why*? There's no reason to it.'

'There's a lot of reason to it. Sound business reasons. What's the matter? Don't you want it?'

After a silence, David said dazedly, 'Just like that? Straight down the middle?'

'Straight down the middle. Fifty-four per cent to me, forty-one to you.'

'Bloody hell!'

Now David knew Phil really *was* serious. Phil never made a deal which took away his control. And this was no exception. Nevertheless, forty-one per cent of a firm with a book value of £25 million – in return for the scratch of a pen.

'Hang on,' David said. 'Fifty-four and forty-one is only ninety-five. Who gets the other five per cent?'

'Miranda Alvin. She too has run with us all the way, every

467

step since Cambridge. I think she should be given a stake in the firm. Do you agree?'

'God, you really *are* serious.' David still couldn't believe it. And still couldn't *understand* it.

'I'm not going to pressure you, David, but why don't you and I go out to an early lunch and I'll explain to you some of those reasons of mine. Then we can discuss it with Miranda. Then you both can think about it, and let me know your decision in three weeks.'

'Why three weeks?'

'It will take that long to have the deeds drawn up. Apart from that, I won't be around for the next three weeks. I'm going away for a while.'

'Going where?'

Phil smiled. 'Paradise.'

Epilogue

The Balinese believed the sea was full of demons, but Phil couldn't see any. He swam deeper, coasting through the shifting patches of light and dark beneath the waters surface. He felt as light as a shadow gliding over the aquamarine depths dappled in sapphire and purple.

Surfacing, he pulled down his snorkel mask and looked up at the heat-hazed sky for a moment. He turned and floated on his back, savouring the sea's gentle caress. It was not a good day for surfers; the sea was very calm, almost as calm as he was. Over the past fourteen days the tight coil of tension inside him had slowly unwound. Now he felt regenerated, as ready to begin a new life as a newborn.

He had left Rena back in the hotel, fiddling with the humidity-control before indulging in a late afternoon sleep. She was tired, she said. Too tired to swim again. They had spent a week on the island of Moyo, enjoying a second honeymoon, but now they were on Bali itself, at Nusa Dua.

He looked towards the red haze of the sun, wondering how long he had been amusing himself in the sea. He turned and began to swim back to the beach.

On the beach, he dried his hair then threw down his towel and sat for a while, his arms resting on his knees as he watched the sea for a time.

Tonight. He would have to tell Rena tonight. He had thought of telling her a number of times over the past fourteen days, but somehow the right moment had not come.

So it had to be tonight.

•

Bali's Grand Hyatt was an exquisite hotel, built in the design of a Balinese water palace, surrounded by acres of tropical gardens, and linked by a series of lily ponds and blue lagoons, all leading down to a stretch of soft white beach. As dusk fell and the Chinese lanterns blazed into light, the view out to sea was stunning.

Hand in hand, Phil and Rena strolled under the silvery lights of the gardens, breathing in the balmy fragrance of the lush flowers. It was truly like Paradise – well, some place between heaven and earth, with one sunlit day following another.

They dined on Chinese cuisine in the hotel's air-conditioned restaurant. Phil waited until they had finished eating – deferring further until after the waiter had poured more wine. Then he took a deep breath and, hesitantly, began to tell Rena of his plans for the future.

She listened silently and without interruption, only the occasional expression flitting across her face gave him some hint of her reaction.

Finally, he looked at her questioningly. `Well, what do you think?'

`America? ... I know that's what you have always wanted, Phil. To live there. But—' she smiled excitedly, `I didn't think it would be so soon.'

He smiled with her, feeling relief. `You've always loved New York, haven't you?'

`*Ja*, since the first time you took me there.'

`And you always knew, didn't you, Rena, that we would be going to live there eventually?'

Rena nodded. She had known it from the day she married him. Phil was the son and grandson of an American and that was a part of his identity he did not want to lose. And as for her – the only place she wanted to live was the place where he was.

`But...' she repeated, `I didn't think it would be so soon.' The more they talked about it, the more excited she became.

He had worked it all out. Talked it all out with his friends in New York. Had been planning it for months. Working out all the legalities with Tom Kennett. He was going to start over – open another publishing house, in America. David Gallagher would manage the London house, and Phil the one in New York. It could be done, his friends had agreed. All he needed was the money and the guts. And he had plenty of both.

`Two of my publishing friends over there have already agreed to come in with me straight away, Phil said. `And Tom Kennett has already got a realtor in search for suitable premises. He'll be there to meet us when we arrive.'

`Tom Kennett?'

`Yes.'

`When we arrive?'

`Ah, didn't I tell you? We're not going back to England tomorrow. We're going from here to New York. Just for a few days.'

Rena was dumbstruck! `You have booked the tickets. Before we left London?'

`Well, yes, I did. Whatever your overall response, I knew you wouldn't object to a few days in NYC.'

She laughed. `Why did you not tell me?'

`Well, you were so excited about Bali, I thought, one excitement at a time.'

Rena's nerves were sizzling, she tried to calm down. `You are wise, Phil, I am so excited and I should not have too much excitement. I was going to wait until we went back to England, but as we are not going back to England, I may as well tell you now ... I am pregnant.'

Now it was Phil's turn to be stunned. `Pregnant? Are you sure? I thought you were on the pill? I thought you wanted to wait?'

She smiled at him. `You said it was up to me to choose when I would get pregnant, so I chose. I knew I didn't want to wait any longer. I threw away the pills.'

'Why didn't you discuss it with me?'

'Why didn't you discuss America with me?'

'Because I knew you wanted to live in America as much as I did. It was supposed to be a wonderful surprise for you.'

'And I knew you wanted me to have a baby even *more* than I did,' Rena rejoined. 'And is it not a wonderful surprise for you?'

Phil was silent, closed his eyes, and Rena felt moisture behind her own lids. They were going to be family now ... a family ... it was what he had always wanted.

Phil lifted her hand to his lips and kissed her fingertips. 'Are you sure, Rena?'

'Sure about what?'

'Sure that you're pregnant?'

Rena nodded. 'I had a test in Malmö. *Ja*, pregnant. Then I had another test before we left England. Yes, pregnant. Then this afternoon I went to the Hotel pharmacy and bought a tester and did another test. Yes, pregnant. That makes three positives. So, *ja*, I am sure.'

They left the restaurant and took the path along the beach, breathing in the warm air and ignoring the soft murmur of the sea as they discussed the future. With a baby on the way, Phil decided, the sooner they got settled in America the better. So, an apartment overlooking Central Park, and the occasional weekends at the country house in Massachusetts.

The beautiful big house on the outskirts of Harvard, Massachusetts was still there, still his, still owned by a Gaines.

Phil sighed. 'Alexander, at least, would be happy about that.'

'And Jimmy will be able to visit us in New York.' Rena had loved Jimmy from the first day they had met.

'The thing about New York and New Yorkers,' Phil said suddenly, 'is they all have a "Get it done yesterday," attitude to everything. Which, normally, I like. Even the way they speak is done with economy – the fewer the syllables, the faster they can say it.'

Rena giggled. `I love the way Americans talk, like Tom Kennett, all those wisecracks.'

`No, no, you're missing the point. What I'm saying is that it's okay for New Yorkers to rush, rush, rush – but you must not. You hear me, Rena? You must maintain that Swedish calm of yours, and take life very easy from now on.'

The sound of a plane roaring away from Denpasar Airport made Phil look up at the sky. He watched the plane climb higher and higher, its lights blinking, and then as it disappeared into the distance, he noticed the silvery slice of a new moon high above them.

A new moon? New beginnings? It was a good omen.

He pointed to the new moon. `Make a wish, Rena.'

Rena closed her eyes and made a wish.

Phil looked up at the moon and made his own wish, with his eyes open.

New York
April 1995

The birth was much quicker and easier than Rena had expected. She gave one last push and there was a triumphant cry from the midwife. A few seconds later the midwife held up a baby girl and smiled. `Welcome to the world, honey!'

It had all happened so quickly, the baby was already born when Phil arrived at the hospital.

But as young as she was, the likeness was unmistakable. Phil's daughter was the image of Marian.

Her hair was black and her eyes were a dark sapphire blue – even the shape of the face – somehow all the cells and genes of his mother had passed down through him to his child. And as soon as he saw her, Phil knew. He knew that all the love and care and comfort that had been denied his mother would be given now to this child, his little girl, Marian and Marc's grandchild.

`She doesn't look anything like me,' Rena said, but didn't seem to mind, smiling adoringly at the baby in her arms.

`She's stunning ... gorgeous ... beautiful—' Phil dragged his eyes away from his little girl and smiled at Rena. `Or maybe I should just borrow that old phrase from Jack Kerouac, because, really, to describe her – "the only word is wow."'

Later that evening they named their daughter – Marian Marcella Gaines.

Ghosts in Sunlight

Coming soon from Payges Publishing

Following the critically acclaimed *Tread Softly On My Dreams* and *Fire Hill On The Hill* — after a long wait for her thousands of fans all over the world — the third and final book in Gretta Curran Browne's historical trilogy —

By Eastern Windows

A young redcoat returning from the American War of Independence arrives home in Scotland's island of Mull, only to leave again for service in India where he meets Jane Jarvis, a lovely young white girl from the Caribbean, who becomes the greatest love, and the greatest tragedy, of his life.

Set in the beauty of Scotland, the magic of India and the turbulence of early Australia, *By Eastern Windows* is based on a true story and the private letters of the people involved.

ISBN 978-0-9558208-2-3

September 2008

www.paygespublishing.com